The Secret
of the
Lady's Maid

Darcie Wilde is the author of:

The Secret of the Lady's Maid
The Secret of the Lost Pearls
A Counterfeit Suitor
A Lady Compromised
And Dangerous to Know
A Purely Private Matter
A Useful Woman

The Secret of the Lady's Maid

DARCIE WILDE

KENSINGTON
PUBLISHING CORP.

www.kensingtonbooks.com

KENSINGTON BOOKS are published by

Kensington Publishing Corp.
119 West 40th Street
New York, NY 10018

All Kensington titles, imprints, and distributed lines are available at special quantity discounts for bulk purchases for sales promotion, premiums, fund-raising, educational, or institutional use. Special book excerpts or customized printings can also be created to fit specific needs. For details, write or phone the office of the Kensington Special Sales Manager: Attn. Special Sales Department. Kensington Publishing Corp, 119 West 40th Street, New York, NY 10018. Phone: 1-800-221-2647.

Library of Congress Control Number: 2023944254

The K with book logo Reg. U.S. Pat. & TM. Off.

ISBN: 978-1-4967-3803-5
First Kensington Hardcover Edition: January 2024

ISBN: 978-1-4967-3804-2 (e-book)

10 9 8 7 6 5 4 3 2 1

Printed in the United States of America

The Secret
of the
Lady's Maid

PROLOGUE

A Bad Business

*". . . then it must be treason; and see it I must, by
all that's good or by all that's bad—"*

Edgeworth, Maria, *Belinda*

London
February 1820

Adam Harkness stood in the shadow of a slouching, half-timbered house. The tiny alley around him—which went by the name of Cato Street—was dark and quiet. The noise from the nearby pubs and gin shops oozed between its close-packed buildings, but no sound rose from the alley itself. Its few soot-smudged houses had all been tightly shuttered against the raw February night. It was easy to imagine the folk inside tucked up in their quilts and sound asleep.

He'd had some luck for his vigil. The moon was near full, and the sky unusually clear, which meant he had a fair bit of light to see by. But it also meant it was unusually cold and the needle-sharp February air pressed hard against his skin. Adam shifted his weight slightly to try to keep his feet from going numb, but kept his attention on the stable across the way.

A flickering lantern showed through the hayloft's crooked shutters. Every few seconds, a passing shadow blotted out the faint light. That told Adam that unlike the rest of the alley, somebody remained awake in that loft. In fact, if he'd counted correctly, roughly twenty somebodys were busy as bees in there.

But busy with what? There's the question.

They'd each arrived singly. They were all men, but other than that, they'd been a ragged, varied bunch. One wore a cobbler's leather apron. One was a Black gentleman dressed in a frock coat who could have been a clergyman or a schoolmaster. One wore a coat so tattered it hardly deserved the name.

They'd scuttled down the street with their collars turned up and their hats pulled low. When they stepped up to the stable door, they looked about carefully before slipping inside.

Left to himself, Adam might have decided they were a group of petty thieves and pickpockets. But according to his superiors at Bow Street—the cobbler, the schoolmaster, the tattered man, and all the rest in that shuttered loft—were bent on nothing less than high treason.

Just this morning, Adam had been called into John Townsend's opulent private office, along with Stephen Lavender, Sam Tauton, and Sampson Goutier. Goutier was the only patrol captain present. He was an expert navigator of the tangled world that was London after dark, and the only reason he had not yet been made a principal officer was that Parliament only authorized eight such men to serve at a time.

John Townsend's agitation was made plain by the way he had paced for a full moment behind his broad desk before speaking a single a word.

These men intend to murder the entire Privy Council when they sit down to dinner in Grosvenor Street, he'd said. *His Grace, the Earl of Harrowby, Lord President of the Privy*

Council, was stopped in Hyde Park by a man calling himself Hiden. This Hiden gave His Grace a full outline of their plot.

And His Grace believed this fantasy? Goutier had asked incredulously.

His Grace had good reason to believe it, snapped Townsend. *It is now for us to act on the matter.*

How could these men even know about a ministerial dinner? asked Lavender. He was a narrow man with a long face and strict ideas about law and order. He and Adam had butted heads more than once.

It's published in the papers, said Townsend. *One of their number saw the notice.*

Surely, said Adam, *the first thing to do is make sure that this Hiden is telling the truth. Where can we find him?*

But apparently, His Grace had neglected to ask that. Hiden had delivered his warning, and disappeared. He thought, however, that Hiden could be one of the cowmen who pastured their animals on the green.

The argument over how to proceed lasted half an hour. Goutier and Sam Tauton agreed with Adam that they needed to find Hiden and make sure this report was accurate. Lavender, on the other hand, argued that they couldn't waste the time.

If we hesitate, we could wake up to a revolution in the streets. We need to arrest these men at once. It'll be safer all around.

Townsend had agreed with Lavender, but Adam stood his ground.

If it turns out this report is a mistake, or madness, Bow Street will look like fools, he said. *And when the newspapers get hold of it, they will mock His Grace, and us, for jumping at shadows.*

The argument worked, at least in part. Townsend saw it as his duty to protect Bow Street's reputation as well as the king's peace. So, he reluctantly agreed to allow Adam to find out what he could. However, he also declared no men would be spared for the mission. Adam was entirely on his own.

Now, standing in the cold and the dark, Adam had to admit *something* was happening in that hayloft. But if it was some dread and murderous conspiracy, the participants were remarkably sloppy. The man he'd sent to the stable door to test the waters had walked right in, and that was over two hours ago. Adam had heard no sounds of a struggle, or other commotion.

In fact, all he heard now was the rhythmic call of the watch. "Two of the clock and all's well! Two of the clock and all's well!"

Christ, I hope it is. Adam let his breath out slowly. The vapor rose in front of his eyes, shining silver in the moonlight.

The plan was not anywhere near as strong as he'd have liked, but they had no time to come up with anything better. The ministerial dinner was in two days. At least, it would have been if it had not already been canceled. This particular turn of events, however, had not been reported to the newspapers.

The watchman's call faded away. Adam waited, measuring time by the beating of his heart, the shadows passing this way and that in the hayloft and the slow deadening of all sensation in his toes and fingertips.

At last, the stable door dragged itself open. Adam willed himself to stillness. His eyes had adapted well enough to the dark that he could make out the shadow of a tall, lean man as he slipped from the darkness. The man glanced at the sky to gauge the weather. Then, he hunched his back against the knife-edged wind that sliced through the alley and scurried away.

Adam gave himself a count of thirty to see if anyone else would emerge to follow this man, but the stable door remained closed. Upstairs, the erratic shadows moved back and forth, just as before. No shout rose.

Adam pulled his hat brim lower, stuffed his hands into his pockets, and set off after the tall man. Out on the main street, he passed the doorway where Goutier kept watch, and turned his collar up. That was the signal they'd agreed to. All was indeed well. He would meet them back at Bow Street.

Townsend had not authorized any men to assist Adam in his vigil. Goutier and Townsend had insisted on coming along anyway. At least, if they were asked, they could truthfully say they had never gone into the alley.

The further the tall man walked from Cato Street, the easier he moved. By the time he'd gone a quarter of a mile, his conspirator's scuttle had changed to the easy, swinging gait of a man without a care in the world.

When the man reached the Dappled Mare carriage house, he rapped on the door. After a long moment, that door opened and a boy emerged carrying a lantern. The man handed the boy a few coins and sent him running toward the stables. Some moments later, an enclosed carriage drawn by a pair of matched chestnuts was driven up to the door. The tall man climbed inside, but left the carriage door open.

Adam took a last look about himself. Satisfied that he was not followed, he crossed the cobbles, climbed into the carriage, and latched the door. The warmth from the foot stove enfolded him like a blessing. The tall man pounded on the roof. As soon as the carriage lumbered forward, he drew off his slouching hat and cast it aside.

"Well, Mr. Harkness." Sanderson Faulks combed his fingers through his fair hair. "I believe I must thank you for a most entertaining evening. When I write my memoirs—which I hasten to assure you will not be published until long after I have ceased to breathe—this will take a prominent place."

Adam grinned. He'd made Faulks's acquaintance several years ago. Since then, the man had given him some good help during more than one investigation. Faulks was a confirmed

member of the dandy set, and made his living buying and
selling art for London's upper crust. He also dabbled in money
lending and was a merciless card sharp, and was the first person Adam had thought of for this errand.

Why me? Faulks had asked.

*Because I trust you. Because you are deeply observant, but
nobody in the neighborhood is likely to know you.* He remembered how Faulks's smile had altered ever so slightly, as
if to warn him not to make assumptions.

*If this lot are habitual criminals, they might spot a Bow
Street man,* Adam told him. *And last, but not least, I am asking you because if anyone finds out you went into that stable
tonight, Townsend can't sack you for it.*

"So, what did you see?" Adam asked.

Faulks returned a thin smile. "If the most honorable magistrates at Bow Street believe that hayloft houses a dangerous
nest of radicals, they are entirely mistaken. What I saw was a
half-deluded, half-desperate congregation of lost men. I
walked in without challenge. I kept myself to a corner of the
room for several fatiguing hours, and not one of 'em so much
as asked my business. I had one confide to me that he only
came to these 'meetings' because there was always something
to eat."

Relief filled Adam, but it was not enough to entirely ease
his suspicions. Why had the Earl of Harrowby been willing
to believe that this gathering represented a real danger? Had
they missed something?

"Were they armed?" Adam asked.

"After a fashion. There were a handful of pikes, cutlasses,
and other such dangerous antiques. I had a look at one of
their guns and would wager it would be as likely to blow up
in the owner's hands as it would to fire. Still, if not opposed
too firmly, they might pose some sort of danger to the resi-
dents of the alley."

"Did they talk at all about their plans?"

"One fellow, Thistlewood, did. He was what passed as their ringleader. He assured the rest that they could easily storm Grosvenor Street and murder the cabinet. At the same time, parties of their men would also steal cannon from various armories and militia posts, and throw up a series of barricades around the town. After this, they would form a provisional government, burn all the paper money, and distribute the gold in the Bank of London to the poor."

"With twenty men?" said Adam.

"Well, that point was somewhat in dispute. Thistlewood insisted that this gathering was only one small part of the larger rebellion. He said that another man, by the name of Edwards, had assured him there were tens of thousands ready to rise up all across London."

"Was Edwards in the hayloft?"

"No," said Faulks. "Nor did anyone seem to expect him. I don't know that it signifies, but it struck me as an additional oddity."

Adam nodded. "Thank you, Mr. Faulks. I am in your debt."

"What will you do now?"

"I'll report back to Mr. Birnie and Mr. Townsend. With any luck, what you've observed will be enough to soothe the fears of His Grace and the Privy Council. Then, we can round these men up quietly, charge them with being a public nuisance on a cold night, and be done with it."

"And if you can't?" Mr. Faulks inquired.

"Then God help those half-desperate, half-deluded men," said Adam. "Because the charge on their heads will be high treason, and every last one of them will finish up dead."

CHAPTER 1

Market Day

"I . . . have nothing worse than folly to conceal:
that's bad enough—"
Edgeworth, Maria, *Belinda*

London
April, 1820

"Oh, not again," muttered Alice Littlefield as the fresh round of raindrops pattered down onto the market cobbles. "I was sure we were done for the day!"

"Wishful thinking, I'm afraid," sighed Rosalind. All around them, the market's patrons put up their hoods or scuttled for shelter. Barrowkeepers and stall merchants hurried to pull canvas and oil cloths over their goods.

Thankfully, Rosalind and Alice stood under the book-seller's awning. Alice had spent the past several minutes en-gaged in a spirited attempt to convince Mr. Fraiser to reduce the price on his somewhat battered copy of *History of a Six Weeks Tour* by sixpence.

Rosalind's decision to accompany Alice and Amelia on the morning's errands had been largely impulse. London's glitter-ing social season would begin in another fortnight, and

Rosalind was finding herself increasingly wrapped up in her role as what Alice termed a "discreet social consultant" for London's *haut ton*.

As a young woman, Rosalind had expected adulthood to bring her a good marriage. This would naturally be followed by a pleasing domestic existence as wife, hostess, and mother. But when her father abandoned their family, all those expectations shattered. With the help of her godmother, Rosalind had cobbled together a kind of existence as what society termed "a useful woman"—one who helped out her more fortunate friends by arranging their social lives, dealing with their correspondence and helping run their households.

Most such ladies endured a depressed and dependent life. But Rosalind discovered she possessed a particular talent for assisting ladies in serious trouble, even when that trouble involved theft, blackmail, or murder. What had begun as a haphazard means for an unmarried woman to eke out an existence had turned into a living.

Now, that living had showed distinct signs of becoming a success. In addition to a gratifying number of social invitations, Rosalind found herself with a thick stack of letters from ladies who wished to consult her about matters that ranged from promoting charitable entertainments to finding missing relatives. More such letters had arrived by this morning's post. It was all very promising, but it also meant a great many decisions needed to be made, detailed plans drawn up, and extra help enlisted. It was dizzying. Rosalind found herself in need of a moment's pause. A morning out of doors perusing stalls, barrels, and barrows in the market had seemed like the perfect solution.

It also brought the possibility of seeing Adam Harkness. She'd sent a note to his mother's house letting him know that she and Alice planned to be at Drummond's tea rooms at eleven o'clock, should Mrs. Harkness and any member of her household care to join them. She had received an answer saying that Mrs. Harkness was engaged, but that Adam Harkness might well be found in Drummond's at that time.

"There. That's done." Alice tucked the book into her basket. She saw Rosalind's furrowed brow. "Don't worry," she said. "We'll be in plenty of time."

"Yes, yes, I know," said Rosalind hurridly. "It's just . . . well, I haven't been able to see Mr. Harkness very often since—"

"Since Cato Street," Alice finished for her, softly.

Rosalind nodded.

"Do you think he's still involved with the investigations?"

"He hasn't been able to say much, but I'm certain he is." All the more certain because he had said so little.

Alice nodded. "Well, whatever his part is, it can't last much longer. George says everyone agrees the trial must be soon, and it's sure to be a Bedlam," she added.

"Well, that's only to be expected. They did plot to murder the entire Privy Council at dinner."

Saying it out loud, the business sounded mad. In fact, Adam believed it was exactly that—pure madness. However, the Privy Council, the magistrates at Bow Street, and even the Crown, took the matter in deadly earnest. Therefore, the trial was going forward, and the charge would be high treason.

Adam had been involved in many difficult cases, and dealt with dangerous men. But this one felt different. As the time dragged on, Adam's humor had faded and his silences had grown. So had his his absences.

"I don't see Amelia anywhere," Alice interrupted Rosalind's brooding. Amelia McGowan was their housemaid. She was a stout, cheerful, ginger-haired young woman who had proved to be an able assistant to Rosalind in several of her more unusual consultations.

"Amelia knows to meet us at the tea rooms," Rosalind said. In answer, Alice wrinkled her nose at the rain, but Rosalind saw real worry in her eyes.

"Is something the matter?"

Alice shrugged. "Amelia's been . . . off the past fortnight or so. I'm sure you've noticed."

Rosalind hadn't. That realization startled, and shamed her. The household she managed was not a large one. Amelia was their only maid who lived in. If there was a problem, she should have noticed, no matter how busy she had been.

But then, the relationship between Amelia and Alice had recently developed into something much more than that of employer and servant, and even more than that of friends.

"I've tried to get her to tell me what's wrong," Alice said. "But she just smiles and says she had a fight with the green-grocer's wife, or her friend couldn't go to the play, or something like that."

"Well, perhaps we'll see her along the way," said Rosalind reassuringly. "We can look in at Lorimer's. I believe Mrs. Singh—" Mrs. Singh was their new cook "—sent her there for some blackberry cordial."

But they found no sign of Amelia at Lormier's Apothecary, so they continued on toward the tea rooms. The rain strengthened, causing them to duck their heads and gather up their skirts in a vain attempt to keep their hems dry.

Between the market noise and the drumming of the rain, Rosalind almost missed the shout.

"Miss Alice!"

Alice froze. Rosalind put her head up.

"Miss Alice! Miss Thorne! Help!"

It was Amelia.

Rosalind looked about wildly, but her bonnet's wide brim hampered her view. Alice grabbed her arm and wrenched her around. Now, Rosalind faced a narrow lane that opened onto a rain-soaked courtyard. A crowd had begun to gather in the yard, but between the onlookers, Rosalind saw Amelia crouched in a puddle. Beside her, a dark-haired woman sprawled on the muddy stones.

Alice moved first. Ignoring the ruts and puddles, she charged down the tiny lane and dropped to her knees beside Amelia. Rosalind yanked her wits together. She spied a young man slouching in the threshold of a shuttered shop, hands in his pockets, watching the excitement.

"Porter!" she cried. The young man started, and straightened, reflexively tugging at his hat brim. "We need a cab! At once!" She held up her reticule to signal she had the money to pay.

"Aye, miss!" He pelted away across the marketplace.

That done, Rosalind pushed her way through the swelling crowd that clogged the lane and ringed about Amelia, Alice, and the prostrate young woman. Voices rose and fell around her.

"Poor dear!"

"Get some brandy in 'er. Who's got a flask?"

". . . no better than she should be . . ."

Either Amelia or Alice must have turned the young woman over because she now lay on her side. Her coat was unbuttoned and her muslin dress was soaked by rain. Everything about her from bonnet to boots was good quality, although now completely spoiled by rain. Cold turned her white face and bare hands blue.

As Rosalind bent down, the young woman shuddered, and wretched painfully, but nothing came up.

"Amy . . ." she croaked.

"Hush, Cate," breathed Amelia. "It's all right. We're going home."

"I can't," breathed the young woman. "I can't."

"Never you mind now. Trust Amy and lie quiet."

"Oh, the poor child!" A woman dressed all in widow's black from boots to bonnet darted forward and knelt beside the girl—Cate, Amelia called her. "Come, help me get her up."

The woman reached out with black-gloved hands and grasped Cate's wrists. A dozen well-meaning people surged forward to assist, but a new voice held them back.

"Bow Street! Bow Street. Shift, now! Let me through!"

It was Adam. *Oh, thank Heaven*, thought Rosalind as he shoved his way unceremoniously through the milling crowd.

"Lie still, lie still, my dear. All will be well." The widow kept hold of Cate's wrists. "Will you help me with her, sir?" she asked as Adam reached them. "My carriage is nearby."

"Amy," croaked Cate. "Amy, please."

Amelia looked to Rosalind, mute and pleading. Rosalind understood at once, not everything, but enough.

"There's no need," said Rosalind to the widow. "We are her friends. We'll see she's gotten safely home."

"Oh but surely . . ." the woman began.

Gently, but firmly, Rosalind drew Cate's hands out of the widow's grasp. "We must hurry before she takes a turn for the worse. Mr. Harkness, if you please."

"If you'll forgive me." Adam bent down between them and scooped the young woman into his arms. Rosalind thought she saw a flash of anger in the other woman's eyes, and wondered about it. But she could not delay any further.

"I'm having a cab brought," she told Adam. "He should be out in the square."

Adam nodded and turned, cradling the girl carefully. The crowd parted reluctantly to let him through. Alice grabbed Amelia's arm and dragged her after him. Rosalind followed them all.

"It's all right, it's all right," Alice was saying, as much to the onlookers as to Amelia. "She's with friends now. We'll take good care of her."

"God bless the poor soul," someone murmured.

"Heaven help her."

"Bound to be some man . . ."

As soon as they reached the main square, Rosalind spotted the porter waving his arm and pointing to the four-wheeled cab making its cautious way between the stalls.

Rosalind beckoned to Adam. The cab's driver jumped

down to open the door. Amelia and Alice climbed in, and turned to help Adam bundle Cate inside. Rosalind paused just long enough to drop a pair of coins into the porter's hands.

As Rosalind climbed up into the cab, Adam stripped off his great coat and passed it to her. She opened her mouth to protest, but he just closed her hands with his. "She needs the warmth. I'll ride up with the driver," he said.

Rosalind nodded and got up onto the bench across from the other three women. Amelia had wrapped her arms around Cate's shoulders. The look on the maid's face was both fierce and frightened. Rosalind felt sure Amelia was willing her own warmth into the body of the insensible young woman. Alice perched on the seat beside her.

The cab jostled as Adam and the driver clambered up onto the box. The driver touched up his horses and they lurched forward.

Moving carefully, Rosalind laid Adam's coat over Cate, and tucked it around her. She stirred, and her eyes fluttered open, but only for a heartbeat before she sagged back into Amelia's arms.

"Who is she, Amelia?" asked Alice as she began to chafe Cate's hands between her own.

Amelia swallowed. "Catherine Levitton. She . . . I worked for her family two years back."

Miss Levitton's breath came in a rattling wheeze. The sound sent a shiver crawling up Rosalind's spine.

"She'll need a doctor," said Alice.

Rosalind nodded. "There's a man up the street from us. We'll try there first. Amelia, have you any idea what brought her to this state?"

Amelia shook her head, but caution flickered behind her eyes. Alice caught it too, and frowned.

The cab rattled on. Rosalind found herself counting Miss Levitton's breaths. It seemed to her that they were coming more slowly, even as the cab picked up its speed. All the while, Amelia held onto her, stroking her shoulders, murmuring encouragement.

Alice's face was stony, but she kept hold of Miss Levitton's hands, offering what warmth and comfort she had to her and Amelia both.

At long last, the cab pulled into Portman Square, and turned onto Orchard Street. Miss Levitton, who had been lying quiet, shuddered violently, and began to wretch yet again.

Adam pulled the door open. Rosalind climbed down at once.

"Adam, will you go to number 12 and bring Dr. Kempshead? This young woman is very bad."

"At once." He pressed Rosalind's hand briefly, and then called up to the driver. "You stay and help the ladies, Johnson!"

Johnson touched the brim of his hat in answer. He was a burly, weathered man, and had no difficulty carrying Miss Levitton inside and up the stairs. While Rosalind let him into the guest room, Alice ran to the linen cupboard. Amelia disappeared below stairs, hopefully, to get a hot brick for the young woman's feet and perhaps some brandy.

If she can be made to swallow it.

As soon as Cate Levitton was laid on the clean bed, Rosalind dismissed Mr. Johnson, telling him that if he went to the kitchen, he could get his fee from Mrs. Singh. As soon as the man was gone, she set to work on getting Cate out of her sopping clothes.

Cate shuddered. She struggled, and coughed. Rosalind rolled her onto her side. She coughed violently and wretched yet again. Rosalind's skin crawled in sympathy.

Alice shouldered open the door, her arms heaped with blankets and nightclothes. In a matter of minutes, they had gotten Miss Levitton into a clean nightdress with dry stockings on her feet and a flannel cap over her wet hair. The guest room had no fireplace, so Rosalind laid all three quilts Alice had brought over her.

Amelia appeared with hot water and towels and a basin. Her eyes were bright red from crying, and her face was almost as pale as her friend's.

Miss Levitton rolled onto her back. Her eyes flickered open for a moment. Her mouth moved. Rosalind thought she meant to speak, but her face contorted and her body spasmed. Alice grabbed the basin out of Amelia's hands and Rosalind rolled the poor girl toward it. But again, nothing came out. The shudders slowed, and stilled. Miss Levitton's eyes drifted shut. Her entire body slumped.

"Oh, no," breathed Alice.

Rosalind saw it too. She turned the girl onto her back and leaned close, trying to feel for breath or pulse. As she did, she heard heavy feet pounding up the stairs.

A lean, grizzled man with prodigious sideburns burst into the room. He dropped his worn valise onto the bed.

"You! Back! Out!" The doctor barked at Rosalind. He dropped his bag and began rolling up his sleeves. "You!" He pointed at Alice. "Get her head up, put that bolster under her! She can't breathe lolling about like that! You!" This was to Amelia. "Open those curtains! We need light in here!"

Alice and Amelia moved at once to obey. So did Rosalind. She backed out of the room and closed the door. She stood there for a moment, her hand pressed against her stomach as she tried to collect her whirling thoughts.

She heard movement downstairs.

Adam.

Rosalind hurried down to meet him.

CHAPTER 2

Sordid Companions

"It was quite indifferent to me how they got money, provided they did get it."

Edgeworth, Maria, *Belinda*

Francesca Finch sailed into the dingy flat. She looked around her with disgust. The place seemed worse than ever, with its whitewashed walls that were more gray than white and all the stiff, uncomfortable furnishings. Drab curtains hung where there ought to have been doors. The fire smoked and the lone window was cracked, so that no matter how many rags they stuffed into the sill, a knife-edged draft still sliced through.

"What happened, Fran?" Jack turned down one corner of the paper he was reading to look at her. He sat in front of their tiny hearth, with his feet propped up on the hob. A teapot and a plate of sandwiches waited on the table at his elbow. Apparently impervious to the cold, he was in just his waistcoat, shirtsleeves, and stocking feet. "Did you find the girl?"

"Yes, I found her." Francesca jerked at the fingers of her

black gloves. "For all the good it does us." She tossed the gloves onto the horsehair sofa and sent her black bonnet sailing after them.

"Can't say I like the sound of that," said Jack.

Jack Beachamp was a handsome man, in a raw, unpolished way. He still kept the burly frame he'd earned as a prizefighter before he had given up the sporting life to become a thief-taker. His naturally pale skin was permanently bronzed by sun and wind, his hands were scarred and calloused, and his long nose was crooked. His curling, dark hair hung about his ears, as long as any poet's. The combination gave him a roguish, dangerous look, like a highwayman from the old days.

In contrast to broad, dark Jack, Francesca herself was a golden willow wand. She'd the luck to be born with bright blond hair and lively blue eyes. Her mother said her face would be her fortune, but Francesca quickly learned that beauty—and the men it attracted—were not to be depended on. So, she'd set about acquiring a set of skills to add onto her pretty looks. She gained her polish from a lady's maid who had fallen on hard times and was happy to give lessons in exchange for gin money. Now, Fran could pass as anyone, from an upstairs maid to the daughter of a baronet.

Well, maybe sister of a baronet, these days, she thought irritably.

"It turns out the plaguey little creature managed to run to a friend—some serving girl—and collapsed just as she got there." Francesca dropped gracelessly onto the shabby settee, letting her arms and legs sprawl wide. "Before I could get proper hold of her, the girl's mistress showed up and whisked her away."

Which was what truly infuriated her. She'd stood there and let the little chit be snatched, quite literally, out of her grasp. *I should have said I was her aunt or sister or any blasted thing. I never should have let them bundle her off so easily.*

"But you followed them?" Jack prompted.

"I didn't need to," Fran said, more to the ceiling than to him. "I know where they went."

"Then what's the trouble?"

"The mistress of this serving girl is the ever so troublesome Miss Rosalind Thorne."

"Who?" Jack cocked a curious brow at her.

Fran pushed herself upright. "Rosalind Thorne is the guard dog of London's *ton*. She specializes in getting our grand ladies out of whatever troubles they may have gotten themselves into."

"Oh! *That* Miss Thorne!" said Jack. "Rumor has it she's the reason Russell Fullerton decided to head for foreign parts."

"That's her," said Fran. "And do you remember the dead man found in Almack's ballroom? Or the dead woman found in the courtyard of Marlborough House?"

Jack shook his head.

"That's because Miss Thorne was there to cover them over." Fran reached for the chipped teapot and poured a cup of dark brew. "The woman is a veritable female sextant. She's made a career of burying the worst secrets of the great and not so good. They all run to her when there's some ugly business that might sully their snow-white reputations, and she makes it go away." Francesca snorted. "Clever game. I should have thought of it."

"And now this Miss Thorne has our little Cate?"

"So it would seem." Francesca slurped the bitter tea. "Give me a sandwich." She and Jack were in the habit of managing for themselves. Even when times were good, the two of them kept few servants. Servants watched, and they talked, and that would never do for such a household as theirs.

Jack passed the plate, which was as chipped as the pot.

"Do you think Miss Thorne knows what she's got in Cate Levitton?" asked Jack.

"If she doesn't yet, she will soon. It's my understanding she's on speaking terms with half the servants in London as well as their mistresses." Francesca bit the sandwich, then pulled back and stared at it. "Fish paste?"

Jack shrugged. "The best I could do today."

Why is there never any money? They'd brought it in by the fistful over the years, but it always seemed to vanish like a dream.

"Could it be that Cate's aunt has hired this Miss Thorne?" Jack asked.

"It could be." Francesca munched angrily. "Sick or not, the old woman is still sharp."

Jack leaned forward and rested his elbows on his knees. "Well, I agree this is an unwelcome turn of events. But all is not necessarily lost. How did the girl look when you left her?"

"Bad. Serves her right for trying to run out on me," Fran added. "From the look of her, she could peg out before she has a chance to say anything."

Jack spread his hands. "So, we will watch the house, and hope for the best."

"That's not going to be enough."

"All right. Say it's not. What do you want to do?"

Now, that is the question, isn't it? "If the girl lives, we've got to winkle her out of there," Fran said slowly. "She still owes us."

Jack nodded. "And while you're at it, you can remind her that your silence isn't going to come cheap."

As he spoke, Fran felt the first stirrings of hope. Maybe they could turn this disaster to good account. Blackmail was much more Jack's trade than her own, but perhaps Cate could be turned into a steady source of income. One they could draw on to get themselves a proper house, all turned out in comfort and style.

And proper food, she thought as she finished the limp sandwich.

Jack was getting to his feet.

"Where are you off to?" she asked.

He touched the side of his nose. "Government job. Stafford wants that radical MP watched."

"Make sure he pays you this time," she said.

"No fear, my love. I'll be getting more than enough to satisfy that pirate downstairs." Jack shrugged into his overcoat. "In the meantime, you can start working on how to bring Cate safely back into our little fold."

"Without Miss Thorne queering the pitch," Fran muttered. "That will be fun."

Jack leaned down and kissed her.

"Cheer up, my dear. We've been in far worse spots. After all"—he grinned—"how much trouble could one genteel spinster lady make for the likes of you and me?"

CHAPTER 3

Unfortunate Possibilities

". . . cases of obstinacy are always dangerous in proportion to the weakness of the patient."

Edgeworth, Maria, *Belinda*

Rosalind entered her spacious front parlor. She and Alice had only taken the Orchard Street house a few months ago, and sometimes, its room and comfort still surprised her. Just now, however, her whole focus was on Adam.

He crouched in front of the hearth. The fire had been badly banked and he was struggling to get it lit. His rain-soaked hat and coat had been slung over the slat-backed chair and he had rolled back his shirtsleeves to expose his tanned and muscled forearms.

Rosalind watched his careful, patient strikes at the tinder-box, and how, when its sparks failed to catch, he paused and adjusted the kindling, and tried again.

He looked tired. There were times, Rosalind knew, when he did not sleep at night. Instead, he paced the streets, following the routes of the watchmen on duty, lost in thought. If she was out late for some engagement—at the opera, or theater, or a party she had helped organize—they might even cross paths. She never asked him if it was deliberate on his part, and he never asked if she looked for him.

But when she did see him, she would always watch him for as long as she dared. And no matter how brief the moment, or how much of a crowd stood between them, Adam always knew when she was there. He would turn, and meet her gaze, and smile the small, crooked smile that had always been her undoing.

At last, the tinder and kindling caught and Adam was able to straighten up and turn toward her. As soon as he did, Rosalind moved forward, and took both his hands. They said nothing, just stood with each other for a long moment. She wanted to kiss him, to hold him close and be held until the tightness in her chest eased. But there were strangers in the house, and she could not risk being seen.

"How is she?" Adam asked.

"Very bad," said Rosalind. "However, we've got her warm and dry. If she's strong, she might still rally."

Adam looked toward the door, and the hallway beyond. Rosalind could tell some grim idea had worked its way into his careful mind.

"Do you know who she is?" he asked.

"Her name is Catherine Levitton. Amelia worked for her family before she came to us."

"Ah." Adam knew the story behind Amelia's previous dismissal, or as much of it as Rosalind did. "And how is Alice? This cannot be . . . easy for her."

"One of the things that has always amazed me about Alice is her generosity of spirit. While Amelia needs her support, she'll have it. Besides, it wouldn't be fair otherwise."

Adam quirked a brow. "Fair?"

Rosalind felt herself smile, in spite of everything. "If Alice is going to quarrel, she's going to wait until her opposite is at their best. Otherwise it's taking advantage. I remember once, she nursed George through an influenza for two weeks without a cross word." George was Alice's brother. Before his marriage, they had both lived together and worked for the newspaper the *Morning Chronicle*. "Then, she made sure he ate a good breakfast before she spent an hour upbraiding him for running to report on a fire without a coat, which was the source of the infection in the first place."

"That sounds like Alice," Adam agreed. Some of the weariness faded from his eyes.

It was then that Mrs. Singh arrived, bearing a tray with the tea things and a quantity of ham and butter sandwiches. Mrs. Singh was a tiny, widowed Sikh woman. She had come to London from Bombay more than a decade before with her sister, and her sister's children. While Mrs. Singh hired out as a cook and housekeeper, her sister worked as an illustrator for the ladies' periodicals.

"Thank you, Mrs. Singh," said Rosalind. "And will you please go upstairs and find out if the doctor needs anything? At the very least we'll want hot drinks for Alice and Amelia—"

"It's already in hand, miss," she replied. "I'll be taking tea up to them next."

When Mrs. Singh left, Rosalind sat down on the Holland blue sofa and began the ritual of pouring out the tea. She handed Adam a cup and a sandwich.

"Thank you." He sat in the round-backed chair beside her and devoured the sandwich in four huge bites. If Rosalind had been less well acquainted with his mother, she might have wondered if he had been eating properly.

"What happened with this young woman . . . Miss Levitton?" Adam asked. "How did Amelia come to find her?"

Before Rosalind could make any answer, the parlor door opened and Dr. Kempshead entered. His sleeves were still rolled up and his sideburns positively bristled when he saw Rosalind and Adam seated quietly at the tea tray.

"How is she, Doctor?" asked Rosalind at once.

"Alive," he snapped. "For now. What she'll be in an hour,

heaven only knows. Miss . . . Thorne, is it?" He squinted at her. "Now, I flatter myself I am a modern thinker and a charitable man. I understand that not all ladies are so fortunate as to find themselves careful husbands, or are lucky enough to know the shelter of a loving family. But if you allow a young girl in your charge to wander about without chaperonage until—"

"You are mistaken, Dr. Kempshead," said Adam firmly. "The young woman is a stranger here."

Dr. Kempshead's mouth shut abruptly.

"She was discovered insensible in the marketplace," said Rosalind. "We brought her here and sent for you to see if anything could be done."

The doctor bowed his head and took a deep breath. "Then I am mistaken in my assumptions. I apologize." He bowed briefly.

"There is no need," replied Rosalind. "Will you sit and have some tea?"

"Thank you." Rosalind had fixed his cup (plenty of sugar and no milk) and handed it to him. She offered him a sandwich as well.

Dr. Kempshead ate like a man who didn't know if he'd ever have time to finish and found it best to get the business done with.

"She's suffering badly from the cold and the damp," he said between bites. "But there's some other underlying condition there. She has a will to vomit, but nothing left in her, and no fever. In fact, she's taking far longer than I'd hoped to get warm. I've given her laudanum, and we will see what a good sleep may accomplish."

Rosalind was relieved to note Dr. Kempshead said nothing about bleeding or cupping, or, worse, that the young woman was obviously hysterical and not to be indulged in her bad behaviors.

"Can you say at all what may have happened?" asked Adam.

The doctor crammed the last of the sandwich in his mouth and washed it down with a swallow of tea. "I'd say she was healthy enough, until recently. And of good family, too, to judge by her hair and hands. What can have possessed her people to let her out of the house in such weather, and such a condition?"

"I wish I could tell you," said Rosalind. "But we know nothing of her."

"It's possible she snuck away on her own," said Adam.

The doctor pulled a face. He also drained his cup. "Well, if she makes it through the night, I recommend continued quiet, warmth, and a light diet. Your cook seems a good, sensible woman, and she says she has experience in the sickroom. Broth, tea, and barley water are what's needed until the patient can tolerate anything more. Then it should be calf's foot jelly and gruel. Make sure the windows are kept open during the warmth of the day and . . ." He paused. "You have something to say, Miss Thorne?"

Rosalind realized she was staring.

"I apologize, Dr. Kempshead," she said. "I am used to more . . . intervention and prescribing from a doctor."

"Hmph. Yes, well, I'm not surprised. Most of our medical men are thinking of their pockets rather than their patients. No. Nature will heal that girl, or not. In either case, you must contact her people as soon as possible. And when they come for her, I will give them the speech I meant for you." He set his cup down. "I'll be back tomorrow. Call me if she worsens." He stood, but when Rosalind and Adam moved to do the same, he just waved them off. "Don't bother, I'll show myself out. Good day."

The doctor bowed to Rosalind and then to Adam and strode out the door.

The door shut. Rosalind raised her brows. So did Adam.

"I like him," he said.

"He seems refreshingly sensible," Rosalind agreed. "I think our patient is in good hands."

"She is in your hands," said Adam. "There are none better."

Rosalind raised her chin to demonstrate her imperviousness to such blatant flattery. Adam smiled and leaned close.

A soft scratching sounded at the door. It opened almost immediately, and Amelia stepped inside. Her hands were correctly folded in front of her, and her eyes were downcast. She looked the model of the proper parlor maid, if a bedraggled one, and entirely unlike her usual self.

"Miss Alice . . ." Amelia croaked, and then stopped, and tried again. "Miss Alice said you'd want to know how . . . things are. She said she'd sit with Cate—with Miss Levitton—while I came down."

"Yes, of course," said Rosalind at once. "Now you sit by the fire."

Amelia sank stiffly onto the stool near the coal scuttle. She hadn't changed her clothes, and even from a distance Rosalind could see her hands were white with cold. Nor was the rest of her much better. Amelia's face was sickly gray, and her eyes were bright red from crying. Rosalind poured another cup of tea and added a heaping spoonful of sugar and a large dollop of milk. Adam carried the cup to Amelia and put it into her hands.

Amelia sipped her tea, then gulped it.

"Was Miss Levitton able to speak to you?" asked Rosalind.

Amelia shook her head. "No, miss. She didn't wake up at all, not even when that doctor poured the laudanum down her."

Rosalind fell silent for a moment, considering the young woman in front of her, and the one who lay upstairs. "Is this

Miss Levitton by any chance related to Mrs. Wilhelmena Levitton? Or Mrs. Marianna Levitton?" she asked.

"Some of your ladies?" Adam asked Rosalind.

"Not directly. Mrs. Wilhelmena has a husband who is on the rise in the business world and she's an active hostess. Louisa is acquainted with her. As for Mrs. Marianna Levitton, I've only heard rumors of her," Rosalind answered. "She was active in the bluestocking set some years back, and she still has a great deal of influence in certain circles. I believe she has a hand in radical politics, or at least she used to." Rosalind saw Adam tense, ever so slightly, at the word *radical*. "She moved to Bath some years ago, I believe."

"Those Levittons are Cate's family," said Amelia. "Wilhelmena is married to her older brother. And she—after I was—the family sent Cate to Bath to be Mrs. Marianna Levitton's companion."

"I had no notion Marianna Levitton had returned to London," Rosalind went on. She turned back to Amelia. "How did you discover Cate?" It was shockingly casual to call a young lady she did not know by her first name, but all the female Levittions in this discussion were otherwise becoming difficult to distinguish.

Amelia swallowed, and swallowed again. Adam pulled a handkerchief from his coat pocket and handed it to her. Amelia murmured her thanks and applied it to her eyes and nose.

"I'm sorry. I—" She took a deep breath. "I'm better. I am." Rosalind let this obvious falsehood pass. "I first saw her again a week ago."

Rosalind drew back in surprise. Alice had sensed something was wrong, and here it was.

Amelia cringed. "I'm sorry. I should have told you. I know I should. You've always—you've always treated me decently, and I should not have kept this hid."

"So why did you?" Rosalind asked.

"It was private," she said.

Rosalind nodded, and waited.

"Cate . . . she was waiting for me on the square when I came back from the market, last Wednesday," said Amelia. "I brought her to the house. She was very upset."

"About what?" asked Adam.

"She wouldn't say. All she told me was that she needed to leave Mrs. Levitton's house. She asked . . . she asked if I could help her, for the sake of our old friendship." Amelia flushed crimson. Her hands shook. "I said she should talk to you, miss. That you helped women like her with their difficulties. But she wouldn't listen. She left." Amelia shuddered again. "And I let her go. I never should have. I should have dragged her back."

"This is not your fault," said Rosalind firmly. "Whatever happened, I know you did everything you could."

It was clear Amelia did not believe her, but she did not protest any further.

"After that, I didn't see her again, not till today. She was outside the apothecary. I think she was waiting for me. She knew this was my market day. I think . . . I think maybe she'd even been out all the night. She was so sick. I tried to get her to come with me, but she . . . she collapsed and . . ." She could go no further.

"Amelia?" said Adam softly. She looked at him, startled. "Amelia, did she have spasms at all when she collapsed? Or vomit?"

"She tried, but there was nothing. Like you saw. She shook so badly, I thought she'd do herself an injury. I thought it was the cold, or maybe some sort of fit." Amelia choked off a sob and pressed the back of her hand against her mouth. Adam nodded, his face solemn. Rosalind felt again that he was holding something back. Now, however, was not the time to press him.

Rosalind turned back to Amelia. "Do you know where Marianna Levitton lives? She should be told what's happened."

Amelia bit her lip. "No, I, that is, I heard she has a house in Brook Street for when she's in town, but she never was before this, so now I don't know. It was after . . . that is . . ."

"No matter." Rosalind went to the bookshelf beside her writing desk and brought down her copy of *Boyle's Court and Country Guide*. She looked up the listings for Brook Street. "Yes, here she is. Mrs. Levitton, 24 Upper Brook Street. We can try there, and if she is not at home, one of the staff will know where she can be found."

"No, you mustn't," cried Amelia. "Please. Something's happened to C . . . Miss Levitton. I can't send her away until we know she'll be all right."

Rosalind expected this protest, and understood it. She had her counterarguments ready. If, as Amelia suspected, Miss Levitton had been out all night, her family was surely frightened and searching for her. They might have some information about Miss Levitton's condition that would help the doctor.

But the look on Adam's face, and the tiny shake of his head, stopped Rosalind from saying any of this.

"Very well," she told Amelia. "We will wait until Cate is able to talk."

"Thank you, miss," said Amelia. "I'll go upstairs and sit with her. If that's all right?" she added.

"Of course it is. But you must change first. You will be no good to your friend if you take a chill."

Amelia bobbed her curtsy and left them. Rosalind turned at once to Adam.

"You suspect something," she said. "When you asked Amelia about Cate's condition when she was discovered. You had something in mind."

Adam was silent for a moment. "I only saw her for a few

minutes," he said finally. "But her condition reminded me sharply of a bad night back when I was still a patrol officer. A hue and cry had been raised to bring us into the house of a baker. The man was in convulsions, and retching, and unnaturally pale, very much like how we found Miss Levitton."

"What was the matter with him?"

"He had been poisoned," said Adam. "With arsenic."

CHAPTER 4

This Troubling Work

"What a treasure to meet with anything like a new heart!—all hearts, nowadays, are second-hand, at best."

Edgeworth, Maria, *Belinda*

It was a long moment before Rosalind felt she could speak. Arsenic was easy enough to come by. It was possible they even had some in the house, to help control rats and mice.

"If it is arsenic . . . what can be done?" Rosalind asked.

Adam shook his head and Rosalind felt her heart sink. "If it is poison, she's been removed from the source, and that's the most important thing. Otherwise, it's as the doctor said. If Miss Levitton makes it through the night, then there's at least a chance she'll recover." He paused, and Rosalind read the uncertainty in his eyes.

"Unless she harmed herself," she said so he would not have to. "In which case, she may try again."

He nodded soberly. "But if she wanted to die, why would she seek Amelia out?"

Neither one of them had any answer to that. Uncomfortable, and unusually restless, Rosalind set about reordering the tea things. Adam turned away, allowing her a moment to collect herself. Instead, he looked over the tidy line of invitation cards arrayed on the mantel.

"You'll be busy soon," he remarked.

"Yes. It's rather surprising," said Rosalind. It was easier to speak of ordinary things, just for this moment. "I worried that I would be cut entirely once I started formalizing arrangements with my ladies." Gently bred women did not work for pay, or at least, they did not let it be seen that they did. Rosalind's compensation from the women she assisted had previously been in the form of gifts, loans, and practical assistance. But earlier in the year she had hired a man of business to help regularize her income.

For Rosalind, it was a step over a very broad line.

"Well, it looks instead as if you are now very much in demand," Adam remarked. "What do you suppose happened?"

She gave a small shrug. "Some is the support of friends. The rest . . . I expect it is what usually happens in society. Someone talked. Then, someone else enlarged on the theme, and I became a novelty. Novelties are always popular at a dinner party."

"I hope you don't think of yourself just as a novelty."

"I don't know what to think of myself sometimes. Especially as it seems I cannot stop from dragging you into my troubles." Rosalind paused, and met his gaze. "I promise you, Adam, when I sent my note to invite you to drink tea this morning, I only meant for us to keep a moment's company."

Adam's blue eyes glowed with affection, and humor. "Rosalind, I have the greatest respect for your powers of organization. But even you could not rise to this height. Besides," he added, "the reason I wanted to meet you was so I could drag you into *my* troubles."

"What's happened?"

"It's not—"

She cut him off. "You will not insult my understanding by saying it's not important."

"I wouldn't dare," he replied soberly. "But the truth is, I don't know whether it's important or not." Adam's eyes went distant, remembering and considering something far beyond her pleasant parlor. "I've been asked . . ." He stopped, and started again. "I've been invited to a meeting with some men I do not know if I can trust."

Rosalind waited.

"It concerns the Cato Street . . . business." The last word sounded thick with bitterness. "And the man who issued the invitation has not been entirely forthcoming about why he wants to speak with me."

"I'd tell you to take care, but I know you will."

His expression turned rueful. "If I was taking care, I think I would not go at all."

"What is it you're afraid of?" Rosalind paused. "Or perhaps I should ask what is it you believe you should be afraid of?"

Adam looked out the window and did not answer for a long moment. "I believe that the men taken in the raid at Cato Street are being made an example of. I believe that example will be dramatic, and brutal, and that it is very likely most of them do not truly deserve it."

"Despite the fact that they did cause the death of one of your fellow officers?"

The newspapers had been full of accounts of what happened when the men at Cato Street were taken. The Coldstream Guards had even been turned out to support the contingent of Bow Street constables. It had been universally described as a heroic action against a gang of determined and armed radicals.

Adam described it as an unholy mess with no one taking proper charge, resulting in the death of one of the runners.

Worse, Adam himself had been actively prevented from joining the raid. Even before it began, his superiors sent Adam
running about the city on a series of errands to other policing
stations, and to several great houses that were being guarded
by squadrons of constables in case riots should break out.
Supposedly, this had been to make sure good communication
and order were maintained among the guards.

"If our mad revolutionaries had simply been watched and
followed, they could easily have been arrested one by one,
and Smithers would still be alive," said Adam grimly. "But
Townsend and Magistrate Birnie wanted to make a grand
show of snaring the whole flock of them."

Rosalind nodded. The most senior of Bow Street's principal officers, John Townsend, had come to prominence by discovering a gang of dangerous Irish radicals in the heart of
London. Through Adam, she knew he longed to recreate that
success.

"Do you really think Townsend would send eleven men to
the gallows to burnish his reputation?"

Adam did not answer that, at least, not directly.

"There is something underneath this that will not let me
rest, Rosalind," he said. "I should set it aside. I am *ordered*
to set it aside, but it nags at me."

"Intuition comes from experience. What is your experience with such matters?"

"In high treason? Very little," Adam admitted. "But these
men—they're mad, and they're hungry. The leader, Thistlewood, has some history of troublemaking, but he's not very
good at it. The same with the rest. I don't think one of them
could plan a successful raid on a game preserve, let alone the
destruction of public order."

"Is there any way I can help?" she asked.

Rosalind watched Adam consider telling her there was
nothing. She frowned at him. He raised his brows in answer.
She shook her head, and he closed his eyes in surrender.

This small absurdity sent a slow warmth spreading through Rosalind, but that vanished as soon as Adam brought out a letter, folded and sealed with wax and string.

"This contains the name of the man I am to meet, along with a copy of the letter he wrote to me." He handed it to her. "If you do not hear from me or Captain Goutier tomorrow . . . make sure this gets to Sam Tauton."

It took all the careful training of Rosalind's lifetime to keep her face still as she set the letter carefully beside the tea tray. He'd never asked such a thing of her before. London's coroner might ask Rosalind to assist in a matter that touched an aristocratic family, but Adam tried to make sure Bow Street's business stayed at arm's length from her.

Until now, it seemed.

"What is the supposed purpose of this meeting?" she asked.

"I am told there is a committee for the defense of the Cato Street men, and that it, or they, hope for my assistance."

"That will not make Mr. Townsend any happier with you."

"No, it won't, especially if it's genuine." Bow Street officers could be put at the service of any gentleman who requested them, providing that gentleman was willing to pay the fees. However, due to the small number of officers, it was up to the magistrates to choose which requests got answered. The magistrates, and Mr. Townsend.

While Rosalind considered this, another, unbidden thought slipped into her mind. She frowned.

"What's troubling you?" asked Adam.

"I've had an idea, but I don't like it."

"Tell me."

"Amelia says our Miss Levitton has been living with her aunt, Mrs. Marianna Levitton. I have been wracking my brains for some excuse I can use to call on Mrs. Levitton without letting her know we're sheltering Cate here. However, she's involved in radical politics, and here"—she held up the letter—"are a group of radicals working for the defense of the Cato Street men. . . ."

"And you wonder if you could represent yourself as raising funds, or awareness, or some such, for that defense," Adam finished for her.

"Which would mean I was using your work for my own ends."

"Which would be a problem," agreed Adam. "If I had not had a thought of my own."

Rosalind smiled. "Tell me."

"Since I first heard the story of the Cato Street plot, there's been one thing that made no sense to me. Why on earth would the head of His Majesty's Privy Council be willing to believe a random stranger he met in the park about a murder plot?" He paused, and Rosalind waited. "One possibility is that he was expecting this news."

"Do you actually suspect the whole business was orchestrated somehow?" It sounded nearly as mad as the Cato Street plot itself, but Adam's face remained serious.

"Again, I don't know. But as the matter has been described—His Grace was alerted to the plot when a man came up to him in Hyde Park, and gave him a note. Now, why would His Grace instantly believe some stranger?"

"Were you thinking that there might be some gossip among our political hostesses that would help explain His Grace's actions?"

"Yes."

"Then we may help each other in this."

"As we always have."

Rosalind met Adam's gaze. He said nothing. But he came to sit beside her, and he kissed her. The gesture was slow, gentle, and deeply reassuring. When it was over, they stayed close, hands clasped, enjoying this moment together when there was nothing to do, and nothing to hide.

This moment when she could be simply, fully in love, no matter what might happen next.

And what happened next might be dangerous indeed.

Because Adam had made it perfectly clear that he could be walking into a trap.

CHAPTER 5

Causes and Consequences

"Love quarrels are easily made up, but of money quarrels there is no end."

Edgeworth, Maria, *Belinda*

After Adam left, Rosalind took her time. She had another cup of tea. She ate another sandwich. She listened to the crackle of the fire Adam had lit, and the silence of the house beyond it.

Finally, she rang for Mrs. Singh to come clear the tea things. She also considered that, one way or another, they needed to afford at least one more housemaid.

Then, as composed as she could be, Rosalind climbed the stairs.

No sound came from the spare bedroom, but the door was slightly ajar. Rosalind pushed it back.

Cate Levitton lay under her quilts, her pale face turned to the side. Whether she was asleep or unconscious, Rosalind could not tell.

Alice and Amelia, on the other hand, were sound asleep. Both slumped in slat-backed chairs, leaning head and shoulders together, their hands clasped. Alice snored, a sound

Rosalind remembered very well from their time together at boarding school. Amelia shifted a little closer.

Rosalind let out a long, slow breath.

Rosalind had no name for her relationship with Adam Harkness. She loved him, and did not doubt this. That he loved her in return was an unshakeable fact. But there the matter rested. Whatever the wishes of their hearts might be, they remained ensnared by the labyrinth of law and custom that governed the personal relationship of two individuals.

Rosalind could not marry a man from the working classes and keep her own closely guarded gentility. Her place in society would inevitably and irrevocably follow his. As for Adam—he already supported his mother and his younger siblings. His erratic pay as a Bow Street officer did not permit him to add a wife to this list, never mind the child, or children, that would follow.

But as frustrated as she might become with her curtailed choices, Rosalind did realize that for her and Adam at least there existed some precedent. Society acknowledged that such love as theirs did happen, whether it was a good idea or not.

Alice, and Amelia, and poor Cate Levitton did not have even this much.

Just as Rosalind moved to close the door, Alice's snore cut off, and her eyes opened. Alice had always possessed an uncanny talent for becoming fully and instantly awake. Her gaze met Rosalind's without any confusion, or embarrassment. She just eased her way out from under Amelia, setting the maid back so she was propped up by the wall and the bedside table. Her hand lingered on Amelia's shoulder for just a moment before she moved to join Rosalind in the corridor.

"What did the doctor say?" Alice pulled the door shut.

"He said Miss Levitton has every chance, if she survives the night."

"But?"

Rosalind drew Alice further away from the door. "Adam thinks she may have been poisoned."

Alice swayed slightly, but betrayed no other hint of her shock.

"How?" she asked.

"Arsenic."

Fear took Alice, but only for a moment. Her instincts as a newspaper writer were too strong. "Odd that the doctor should miss something like that."

"He may never have seen such a case."

"I suppose. Well. Should we tell Amelia?"

"What do you think?" asked Rosalind.

Alice wrapped her arms around herself as if she felt a sudden chill. "Obviously, we need to talk with her about Cate. But she's in a state, Rose. She's trying not to show it, but she's halfway between fear and fury and she doesn't know what—"

Before she could get any further, a muffled thump sounded from the bedroom. Alice, one step ahead of Rosalind, ran back to the room and threw open the door.

Amelia was at Cate's beside. The chair had fallen over onto the hearth rug. Cate's eyes were open, and she looked wildly about her as she struggled to rise.

"Where am I?" she croaked.

"You're in Miss Thorne's house, Cate," said Amelia. "It's all right. Look, here she is to see how you do."

"Rest yourself, Miss Levitton." Rosalind stepped up to the bed where she could more easily be seen. "You're among friends."

Cate's gaze swept the room again. "What happened to me?"

"You collapsed in the market," Amelia told her.

"I don't remember."

"Do not task yourself," said Rosalind. "It does not matter."

Cate clearly did not agree. She struggled to lift herself out of the bed. "I need . . . I have to go. . . ."

This was too much for Alice. "Fiddlesticks." She strode forward and firmly pressed Cate back onto the bolsters. "You're in no state to go anywhere."

"How long have I been here?"

"Less than a day," said Rosalind. "How long have you been away from your home?"

Cate turned her face away. Amelia shook her shoulder, gently. "Come on, Cate. It's all right."

"I left last night," Cate told them.

Rosalind nodded, unsurprised. "Amelia says you live with your aunt. She is sure to be worried. She should be told where you are."

"No!" rasped Cate. "No, please."

"Why not, Cate?" asked Amelia. "What's happened?"

Cate closed her eyes.

"We're not going anywhere," said Alice. "So you might as well look at us."

"Alice," murmured Rosalind. But Alice's words had the desired effect. Cate opened her eyes.

"If you're in any trouble," said Rosalind, "we will do our best to help you."

Cate's gaze fastened on Amelia. Something intense and unspoken passed between the two women. Cate had met Amelia a week ago, Rosalind remembered. What had they talked about then? What were they holding back now?

"I can't," said Cate at last. "I just can't. Please. I just need to rest a little. Then I'll be on my way."

"Nonsense," snapped Alice. "You can't even stand up."

"Just tell Miss Thorne what happened," Amelia urged. "Did you quarrel with Mrs. Levitton?" asked Amelia.

"No, no." Cate's voice was harsh but emphatic. "She's never been . . . she's always been kind to me."

"Then what?" demanded Amelia, plainly exasperated.

Cate closed her eyes again. But the way she sagged back

onto the pillows told Rosalind that this wasn't just stubborn-ness. What little strength she'd recovered was ebbing quickly away.

"Miss Levitton," Rosalind said. "You are welcome to stay until you are better. If you want to leave after that, we cannot stop you. But you say your aunt has always been kind to you. Surely, she's worried that you haven't come home. Let me at least tell her you're alive and safe with friends."

"Tomorrow," Cate said weakly. "If I'm still here. To-morrow."

"Very well," Rosalind told her. "We'll let you rest."

"I'll stay until you're asleep." Amelia looked anxiously to Alice and Rosalind. "If that's all right?"

"Of course it is," said Alice. "Come along, Rosalind." She pulled Rosalind out of the room, shut the door, and moved them both out of earshot.

"Well, what do you think?" asked Alice softly.

"I think that girl is frightened," Rosalind answered. "And I think we should probably lock her door tonight."

"You think somebody might try to get in?"

"More likely that she'll try to get out."

Alice wrinkled her nose. "She wouldn't get far."

"No. But she also might tumble down the stairs while trying."

"Hmm. Yes, I hadn't thought of that."

"Alice—" Rosalind hesitated. "Has Amelia told you any-thing about . . ."

"About the Levittons?" said Alice. "Very little. It's a deli-cate subject, as you can imagine."

"Yes, I can see that it would be."

"She did say they were not a happy family, and that there were a lot of quarrels. Usually about money."

Rosalind found this to be entirely unsurprising.

"Rosalind." Alice stopped and started again. "You've never . . . questioned my particular friendships, and I have always been profoundly grateful for that. Please believe, I never meant to bring trouble to our house. I never thought . . . I didn't ask to . . ."

"Alice." Rosalind touched her friend's hand. "Do you love Amelia?"

"I think I might," Alice whispered.

"Does she love you?"

"Yes." She spoke the word without hesitation, but her eyes betrayed a greater uncertainty. "But now, I don't know if she loves me enough."

Rosalind nodded. She understood that particular dilemma all too well.

"Perhaps I should break things off before this"—Alice's gaze strayed back toward the door of the spare room—"whatever it is, gets any worse."

"We do not have anywhere near enough information to determine if such a drastic step is required," said Rosalind.

Alice sniffed and pulled a handkerchief out of her sleeve. "Of course you'd say that. It is entirely like you."

"Would you rather I said something else?"

"No. You are perfect."

Hardly. But Rosalind smiled at her friend. "Will you do me a very great favor and try to get some sleep?"

Alice's expression turned rueful. "I don't think I can. But that's all right. I'm still working on those page proofs Mr. Colburn sent. If that doesn't put me to sleep, I am past salvation."

"I'll leave you to it then, and see you in the morning." Rosalind started toward her own room, but Alice stopped her.

"Rosalind?"

"Yes?" Rosalind turned to meet her gaze.

"Thank you."

Rosalind embraced her friend and said good night. It wasn't until she was safe behind her own door that she allowed her calm expression to melt under the weight of the worry inside her.

Poisoned, Adam had said about Cate Levitton. *With arsenic.*

A shudder crept up Rosalind's spine. Under other circumstances, she might have wondered if the girl had attempted to end her own life. But Adam was right. She was not likely to have taken poison, and then spent the night waiting for a friend to find her. Especially such a friend as Amelia. Whatever this business was, it was not some lover's impassioned drama. She felt sure of that.

Someone else had decided Cate Levitton should not live.

CHAPTER 6

A Private Meeting

"I cannot depend on any of these 'honorable men.'"

Edgeworth, Maria, *Belinda*

It was one of the world's many contradictions, but the best place for a man to hide was in the midst of a crowd. This being true, the Cocoa Tree coffeehouse was one of London's best possible sites for a clandestine meeting. The Cocoa Tree was an immensely popular place to drink coffee, hear the news, conduct business, and argue politics. It carried all the London papers, and the walls were plastered with notices of auctions, sales, and laborers needed.

One notice in particular caught Adam's eye. It had been partly torn, and other more recent bills crowded up against and partway over it. Nonetheless, it remained legible.

LONDON GAZETTE EXTRAORDINARY
Thursday, February 24, 1820
Whereas Arthur Thistlewood stands charged
with high treason, and also with the willful murder
of Richard Smithers, a reward of *One Thousand*

Pounds is hereby offered to any persons or person who shall discover and apprehend . . .

The rest of the bill had been plastered over with an announcement of an auction taking place in three days.

One thousand pounds. An entire family could live out their days on that much money, and still have something to leave to their children. Such a sum would tempt any man.

But even as he thought about that, Adam noted the date on the handbill. The Cato Street raid had happened in the small hours of the morning that same day. This notice must have been published at breakneck speed.

Adam tucked this thought in the back of his mind, and turned to find the person he was there to meet. His letter informed him the man would be at the table in the back, furthest from the fire.

The coffeehouse was perhaps half-full, but the noise was twice as loud as it should have been. Each patron seemed to be determined to outshout his neighbor as they argued business, politics, horses, stocks, schemes, and rumors.

As Adam shouldered his way over to the battered table, he glimpsed Sampson Goutier lounging in the chimney corner listening with amused interest to two men arguing beside him.

Goutier did not so much as glance up as Adam passed.

As Adam reached the rear of the coffeehouse, a man rose to his feet. "Mr. Harkness?"

Adam greeted the man with a slight bow. "Sir Richard?"

Sir Richard Phillips returned his bow. He was a short, neat man with a keen eye. He wore the buff breeches and blue coat that had been the preferred uniform of radicals since the days of the American war. Adam had the sense that this was a man used to trusting his own judgment, and that judgment might be very sharp indeed.

Sir Richard gestured to a chair. Adam sat, and when Sir

Richard held up the coffeepot, he nodded and accepted the cup that the man filled for him.

"Do you have my letter with you?"

Adam took the letter from his coat pocket and handed it across. Sir Richard perused it briefly and then tucked it away in his own pocket.

"Forgive me if I seem overly suspicious. It's important to be sure of whom we're dealing with in this business."

"And exactly what is this business, Sir Richard?" asked Adam.

"It is as I indicated in the letter," he said. "The men of Cato Street are unjustly accused. I represent a committee formed for their defense."

Adam was careful to keep his face still. "They were found with a cache of weaponry. Their leader, Thistlewood, has already admitted that he planned to take an army into the streets. When the Coldstream Guards and Bow Street came to arrest them, they fought back with deadly result."

"All of what you say is true. But there's another fact to be considered."

"What is that?"

"Have you heard of a man named George Edwards associated with this business?"

"I have. His name was included on the warrant, and mentioned in the prisoner statements." Sanderson Faulks had also mentioned it, but Adam did not feel the need to say so at this time.

"Do you know who Edwards is?" Sir Richard asked him.

"Do you?" returned Adam.

Sir Richard smiled, an expression without warmth or humor. "He's a spy, Mr. Harkness."

Adam arched his brows, and waited.

Sir Richard leaned forward. "Surely you know he attempted to claim a reward for informing on the Cato Street men."

Adam did know it. Several of the men, including Arthur Thistlewood, had named Edwards as the chief instigator of the plot.

Instigator, and financier. Thistlewood claimed this Edwards had given him money to buy the arms stored in the hayloft.

But then, if he was found guilty, hanging was the least of the punishments Thistlewood and his fellows could face. Such a bleak future might easily tempt a man to try to shift the blame.

"Edwards never got that reward," Sir Richard was saying. "He vanished the next day. No one knows where he is now." His face grew thoughtful. "Unless you've heard something?"

Adam did not bother to answer that. "Sir Richard, forgive me, but what is your interest in this business?"

Sir Richard drank his coffee. "Well, I could say it's to see justice done, and uphold the rights of man and subjects of the Crown, but I dare say you wouldn't believe that."

"It's a fine sentiment," said Adam.

The corner of Sir Richard's mouth twitched. "These are not savory characters, Mr. Harkness. I've spoken with Thistlewood. Once, he may have been a great orator and agitator. Now, I'm afraid he's quite mad. Are he and his colleagues a threat to public order? Probably. But"—Sir Richard raised one finger—"if they are telling the truth, they did not come together on their own. They were egged on, lied to, and *paid*"—now that finger stabbed the table—"by a man who is not on trial. This man might have orchestrated the whole business out of simple greed. Or"—Sir Richard leaned forward—"he might have been put up to the business by men in power in order to suppress a public demonstration of public will. *That* is our interest." Sir Richard sat back and raised his cup. "It is not to say these men are innocents, but it is likely that the one who really created this public danger did it because he was promised payment. That man should be in the dock with the rest of them. They deserve to have the fact of this external involvement—whatever its origin—taken into consideration when they are tried."

Adam sipped at his coffee and found it strong and harsh, but flavorful. He considered the man in front of him.

Public rewards and private fees were used daily to discover information about all sorts of crimes. As a system, it was ripe for abuse. Bow Street's officers and runners alike were barely paid enough to survive. They depended on the fees from private individuals to make up their meager salaries. Adam had seen arrests made simply to collect the payment. The practice was even worse among London's small army of thief-takers, some of whom worked hand in glove with the thieves they were supposed to help capture.

Knowing all this, it was easy to imagine someone egging on a set of madmen and then turning them over to the Crown, all for the sake of the reward.

Especially if that reward was a thousand pounds.

Sir Richard eyed him shrewdly. "You're wondering whether you can trust me."

"No offense," replied Adam.

"None taken. You should be wondering. For all you know, I could be another Edwards, intent on luring you into a trap."

There was no need for Adam to answer that. "What do you want from me?" he asked instead.

"Simply put, we want you to find Edwards and let us know his whereabouts," said Sir Richard. "That's all. It will be our job as the committee for the defense to make sure he's brought to court."

It sounded perfectly reasonable, and simple—assuming that locating a man who did not want to be found was ever a simple task.

Adam took another swallow of coffee. "Why me?"

"Your reputation precedes you, Mr. Harkness. Your recent

actions in Manchester and elsewhere have gained you a great deal of credit among those of us who are reform minded."

Sir Richard spoke sincerely, and it might have been the truth. Adam wondered if the man understood what a double-edged sword such regard might be.

"I very much doubt the magistrate will agree to assign me to assist your efforts," said Adam.

"Yes, I'm aware of Mr. Birnie's leanings, and Mr. Townsend's. We were hoping you might agree to do what you could in an individual capacity. The committee's backers have agreed to put up a reward for bringing Edwards to us."

Adam arched a brow.

"We're matching the amount for Thistlewood. One thousand pounds."

Adam felt himself go very still. *So*. That same incentive that might have driven this Edwards to send eleven men to the gallows was being used to induce Adam to help save them.

Before, he'd thought how it was an amount that might tempt any man. Now that it was presented to him, Adam felt keenly aware how much temptation it really was.

He stood up. "You'll have my answer tomorrow."

"That's all I ask." Sir Richard did not stand, but he stretched out his hand. Adam clasped it, reclaimed his hat, and elbowed his way through the crowd that spilled out the door and into the street.

He walked to the corner and stopped as if to stretch his shoulders. Something itched at the back of his neck, and he did not like it. He looked up at the low clouds, and made a fuss of turning up his collar. All the time, he listened, trying to tease out each stray sound from the clamor of the midnight street.

A man's silhouette detached itself from the shadows. Captain Goutier. They didn't bother to acknowledge each other. Adam began to walk, and Goutier simply fell into step beside him. The big man walked with a steady, measured stride that was an artifact of his years with the foot patrols.

"Well?" Goutier asked. "What was it all about? Sal gave me an earful for being out late. Reminds me I promised to give up nights."

"My apologies to Sal," said Adam. "As to what it's about, I've been asked to find this Edwards character."

"By that toff?"

Adam nodded. His shoulders would not relax. Something was still wrong. "That toff used to be the sheriff of London," he said. His hands remained loose at his sides, every inch of him on the alert. "He's gone into politics since, and stands with the radicals. Seems he and his friends are keen on proving this Edwards is, or was, a government spy, and that the Cato men would not have gone so far in on their plot if he hadn't urged them all into it."

Goutier considered this. He also rolled his shoulders. That was enough to tell Adam that Goutier felt it, too—the sense of something out of step in the cold, crowded dark.

"Seems to me I heard you say something like that yourself," Goutier remarked.

"Seems to me I heard that, too." Adam walked on in silence for a few steps, his ears still straining and his nerves still on the alert. Then, he caught it. "Seems to me that's not all I heard," he said softly, conversationally.

Goutier glanced toward the heavens, as if they were discussing the weather. "Me either."

They walked on. The way in front of them bent and narrowed. The windows in the buildings on either side were shuttered and the doors locked. There was nowhere to hide, or to get away. They walked on.

An alley opened on Goutier's left. It was as black as pitch and barely wide enough to let a man through.

"Well, here's me," said Goutier. "Good night, Harkness."

They clasped hands. Goutier turned down the alley and

vanished into the dark. Adam continued up the street. Now that he was on his own, there was no mistaking the sounds behind him—a rustle of cloth, the scrape of a boot sole against the cobbles. He picked up a footpad.

Adam kept his stride even and slow. The way in front of him curved toward the high street. He stepped out onto the cobbles, and immediately had to dodge a couple hardy souls who were (amazingly) still awake, and sober enough to stand. Up ahead, at his right hand was a shop with shutters covering its bowed windows.

There was his chance.

He walked past the window bay, and then leapt backward, flattening himself against the shop's wall.

A man's lean and slouching silhouette trotted right past him.

Adam lunged.

His fingers closed on the stranger's coat collar. Adam whirled around, swinging them both about, and tossing his footpad straight into Sampson Goutier's waiting arms.

Goutier grabbed the footpad in a bear hug and lifted him off the ground. But the man had managed to keep one arm free. He grabbed Goutier's ear and twisted hard. Goutier cursed and held, but his grip must have loosened just enough. The footpad slithered to the ground. Adam grabbed for his coat again, but the man dodged. He landed a hard kick at Adam's ankle, and then planted a fist in his stomach hard enough to double him over.

Goutier grabbed at the man, and shouted. Adam jerked upright. Goutier was scowling in pain, and their footpad was haring off down the street.

"Had a knife," grunted Goutier. His left hand clutched his right. There was just enough light for Adam to see the sheen of blood between his fingers.

"Damn," Adam cursed. He also pulled his kerchief out of his pocket. "Here, let me see that."

"A scratch," said Goutier, but he held his hand out any-way. "I'll get far worse from Sal when I get home. Did you get a look at him?"

"Not a good one." Adam tied off the knot. "He was muf-fled up to his eyes."

"I don't like this, Harkness." Goutier eyed the street un-easily. "Not after that little meeting you just had."

"Nor do I," said Adam softly. "Nor do I."

CHAPTER 7

Family Matters

"He would have started with horror at the idea of disturbing the peace of a family; but in her family, he said, here was no peace to disturb . . ."

Edgeworth, Maria, *Belinda*

Morning brought with it two pieces of good news. First, Cate was visibly improved, and sleeping peacefully. Second, there was a note from Adam beside Rosalind's breakfast plate.

All is well. I will call as soon as I can.

Rosalind read the words and told herself she had never doubted it would be so. At the same time, she was conscious of breathing easier, and finding that she had more appetite for Mrs. Singh's delicious milk and oat porridge than she had initially believed.

She was also aware, however, that her day still contained significant challenges. Usually, when Rosalind had to pay a call on a lady she had not previously met, there was a great deal of preparation. She would write or call on mutual acquaintances to learn about the lady. She would review accounts in the newspapers of dinner parties or other entertainments to see where the lady's name appeared on guest lists.

But there had been no time for her usual researches, and Rosalind arrived at the door of 24 Upper Brook Street feeling unusually nervous.

The church bells had just finished tolling the noon hour when Rosalind paid off her cab driver. The time for paying social calls began at eleven, but to present oneself exactly as the social hour began could smack of desperation.

Marianna Levitton's neighborhood was not the height of popularity, but the house facades, as well as the uniforms and liveries on the servants who came and went signaled wealth and fashion. The street itself was quiet. Only a few vans made their way down its well-maintained cobblestones. A manservant scrubbed the stairs at another house. A nurse pushed her pram sedately down the walk on the far side of the street.

Two carriages waited in front of number 24 as Rosalind approached. The first was driving off, and a stout woman bundled in a blue coat and bonnet was hurrying down the steps toward the other.

Mrs. Levitton was having a busy morning.

The house itself was not the largest in the street, but it was still substantial. Built of pale stone, it had the graceful colonnaded entrance and curved brick steps that had been the fashion a generation ago. The brass on the knocker and lamp had been well polished. Mrs. Levitton might hold radical notions, but she nonetheless employed a staff that was diligent about the traditional housekeeping details.

A footman in a neat slate-blue uniform answered the door. Rosalind presented her card, and asked whether Mrs. Levitton was at home.

"I'm sorry"—the footman glanced discretely at her card—"Miss Thorne. Neither Mrs. Marianna Levitton nor Mrs. Beatrice Levitton is at home to visitors." This was, of course, merely a polite code for denying a person admittance.

Mrs. Beatrice Levitton? This was not a name Rosalind had heard. She was again conscious of arriving at a disadvantage.

"My business is with Mrs. Marianna Levitton," said Rosalind. "And I am afraid it is of a somewhat urgent nature."

The footman remained unmoved. "I am sorry, miss."

"I apologize for the inconvenience," said Rosalind. "But perhaps I could leave my name in the visiting book?" Many ladies kept a visiting book in their hallway. This practice allowed visitors to leave a note, as well as their card.

The footman bowed and stepped back, allowing Rosalind to enter the house. When she did, Rosalind was hard-pressed not to stare.

The tiled and paneled foyer was filled with flowers. The house might have been celebrating a wedding, or a funeral. Baskets of hothouse fruits waited among the flowers. The salver on the mahogany table beside the visiting book overflowed with cards and letters. Rosalind felt her brows inch upward.

She had just picked up the pen provided when a woman descended the polished oak stairs.

"Kinnesly—" the woman began, but stopped when she saw Rosalind.

"Miss Rosalind Thorne to call on Mrs. Marianna Levitton," said the footman, Kinnesly, at once.

Rosalind curtsied. "I must apologize for intruding. I understand Mrs. Levitton is not at home, but I had hoped to leave a note."

The woman stepped closer. She was older than Rosalind. Gray streaked her dark hair. Her fine-boned face looked wan and tired. Her black dress accentuated her naturally pale complexion. *A widow?* Rosalind realized there was something in the shape of the woman's jaw and the set of her eyes that reminded Rosalind sharply of Cate.

"Miss Thorne?" the woman said. "The Miss Thorne who is Lady Jersey's friend?"

"I have the honor of the acquaintance," replied Rosalind. Lady Jersey was the leader of the Board of Patronesses for Almack's Assembly Rooms, and one of the ruling powers among the *haut ton.*

The woman hesitated, clearly torn, but only for a moment. "I am Mrs. Beatrice Levitton. I don't wish to presume, but if you have a moment to spare, I would like to speak with you."

"Certainly," said Rosalind.

"Thank you." Beatrice Levitton turned to her footman. "Kinnesly, have some tea brought to the morning room."

Kinnesly bowed. Beatrice showed Rosalind through to a sunny room with curved walls painted green and decorated with plaster rosettes and wreathes. The bowed windows looked out onto a muddy, walled garden. Tentative shoots had just begun to poke through the sodden earth.

It was a scene of fragile hope. A similar hope seemed to flicker behind Beatrice's dark eyes.

"You will forgive me if I seem importunate, Miss Thorne. I recognize we are not acquainted. However, I have heard something of your"—she hesitated, searching for the correct word—"talent for assisting women with certain private difficulties."

"I hope I have been able to help my friends," Rosalind murmured. Having strangers recognize her name was still new to Rosalind, and not at all comfortable.

"Yes. Your friends," echoed Beatrice. "Which I am not. I am not even the one you meant to call on. But the truth is, I was just this morning planning on writing you, and now you've arrived—it is as if I've been handed a gift."

Despite her curiosity, Rosalind made sure to keep her expression calm. "Is there something you wished to consult with me about?"

"Very much. I . . ." Her words seemed to choke her. Her hand strayed to her throat. "My daughter is missing."

Her words jolted Rosalind. Was this exhausted widow Cate's mother?

"I am very sorry to hear this," said Rosalind evenly. "When was she last seen?"

"Tuesday. We thought—I thought—she was attending a private concert with friends." She spoke in a rush, voice and fluttering hands betraying her agitation. "But she did not return for dinner, or indeed, at all."

"What steps have been taken?" asked Rosalind. "What do her friends say?"

"Her friends say there was no concert, and they did not see her at all yesterday." Beatrice choked again, and Rosalind realized she was fighting to keep back a sob.

"Catherine *must* be found, Miss Thorne," said Beatrice. "I must know that—"

She got no further. The door opened. Rosalind turned, expecting the tea, but instead two gentlemen entered. A single glance told Rosalind the first of them was related to both Cate and Beatrice. He looked to be perhaps thirty years of age and shared the family's dark hair and eyes, as well as their delicate features. But for him, that fine boned face had a slightly dangerous cast, suggesting a cutting wit, and unyielding opinion.

In contrast, the second man had a round face and a ready smile. Combined with his wide-set blue eyes, it gave him an open, cheerful appearance. His dress was precise, but not the edge of fashion. The entire impression was one of a simple, plain-dealing sort.

Rosalind rose to her feet. She felt the slender man's eyes drinking in her dress, her features and movement, and judging each thing he saw.

"Marcus, Harold," said Beatrice. "What are you doing here?"

"I came to hear how Aunt Marianna does." Marcus, the first of the men, kept his attention on Rosalind as he spoke. "Has the doctor been?"

"Not yet," replied Beatrice. "However, the nurse says she is rather better this morning. This is Miss Rosalind Thorne," she added, gesturing toward Rosalind. Rosalind made a curtsy. Both men returned polite, but brief, bows. "Miss Thorne, my eldest son, Marcus Levitton, and Mr. Harold Davenport. Miss Thorne came to call on Marianna," she told them.

Mr. Levitton narrowed his eyes, ever so slightly. "We have not met, I think," he said. "And I don't believe I've heard your name from my aunt."

Meaning she was intruding, and not to be trusted, at least, not by him.

"I am sorry to inform you my aunt is not at home to visitors," Mr. Levitton went on. "I trust you will be able to call again at another time?"

It was a complete dismissal. The only correct response was for Rosalind to take her leave.

But the door opened again. This time, it was the footman, Kinnesly, with the tea tray, which he set down on the table.

"If you please, ma'am," he said to Beatrice. "Mrs. Levitton is awake. She heard that Miss Thorne came to call, and asks will she come up."

"She's awake?" said Mr. Davenport, a trifle too brightly. "But this is excellent news. I felt certain she would rally for us. I was just saying as much to Marcus."

Mr. Levitton did not seem to share this sunny assessment. "You may tell my aunt that Miss Thorne has already left," he said to Kinnesly. "You will excuse us," he added to Rosalind. "But my aunt has been ill these past weeks. It is extremely inadvisable for her to tax her strength with visitors."

"I am sure Miss Thorne will stay no more than a moment," said Beatrice crisply.

"Nonetheless," said Mr. Levitton, "I cannot allow—"

Beatrice, however, was not prepared to hear him out. "I should not like to have to tell Aunt Marianna that *you* sent her caller away. The resulting agitation would not be good for her."

Mr. Levitton's face tightened. Rosalind suspected that if she had not been here, he would have shouted.

"What's the harm, Levitton?" inquired Mr. Davenport. "If it will give your aunt a bit of a distraction? Good for her, surely. And as your mother says, it will only be for a moment."

"Ever the diplomat, Davenport," said Mr. Levitton, and Rosalind suspected it was not meant as a compliment. "If I am to be overridden, I suppose I can only beg that Miss Thorne will keep in mind what I have said."

"I assure you, Mr. Levitton," said Rosalind, "I will stay no longer than necessary, and if Mrs. Levitton appears at all fatigued, I will leave at once."

With that, Mr. Levitton stood back. But there was no concession in his dark gaze as he watched Rosalind and his mother pass. As they left the room, he fell into step behind them, almost as if he felt they might break and run if he were not there to watch.

Kinnesly led the three of them back through the flower-filled hall. A woman in a feathered bonnet and silk cloak looked up from the visiting book.

"Beatrice!" she cried, and surged forward to grasp the widow's hands. "Marcus! How does dear, dear Marianna? I thought she was not receiving today!" She eyed Kinnesly and Rosalind with equal suspicion.

Marcus bowed stiffly. "She is still very ill, Mrs. Shrieveport. Miss Thorne is here on a matter of urgent business."

"Well." The lady had dark, birdlike, and intensely curious

eyes. "Then I must not detain you. You will tell her I asked after her?"

"Of course," replied Marcus coldly.

Mrs. Shrieveport took the hint and withdrew, allowing the little procession to continue up the stairs and into a dim boudoir. The fire had been built up high, and Mrs. Levitton huddled close beside it in a deep, comfortable chair. Layers of embroidered shawls wrapped her shoulders, and more had been piled over her lap. Netted fingerless gloves covered her hands.

Despite the fact that Marianna Levitton was seated, and hunched, Rosalind thought she must be a tall woman. A gray flannel cap covered her snow-white hair. Her complexion was very pale and clear. She was also bone thin—not merely slender, but emaciated. Her eyes were sunken back into her head, but they still shone bright and fierce with her determination. An odor of sickness hovered around her, as thick and unyeilding as the London fog, and Rosalind felt certain that nothing but force of will kept her upright in her chair.

Rosalind remembered the grim tone of Adam's voice as he pronounced the word *poison* and felt a deep, slow chill creep up her spine.

A woman in a nurse's gray day dress and white apron stood beside Mrs. Levitton's chair. Rosalind recognized her, but she had no chance to say hello.

"You are Miss Rosalind Thorne?" inquired Mrs. Levitton. Her voice was harsh and raw. Rosalind's skin prickled in sympathy to hear it.

"I thought you were acquainted," said Marcus.

"I apologize if there was any misunderstanding, Mr. Levitton," said Rosalind.

Mr. Levitton was not placated. "This is ridiculous! You must . . ."

Beatrice moved to protest, but it was Mrs. Levitton who spoke first.

"Marcus," she rasped. "Be quiet or leave. I don't care which."

"Aunt, you are not well," Mr. Levitton declared. "You cannot—"

Mrs. Levitton ignored this. "Beatrice, if you cannot make your son keep still, take him out of here. My head is aching beyond endurance. And no," she added, as the nurse stirred, "I do not want a powder. I want to talk to Miss Thorne while I am still able to do so."

"But—" began Marcus.

"Get out!" she shrilled.

Marcus wavered, but evidently decided that the fight was not worth it, yet. He returned a bow of extreme dignity and held open the door so his mother could exit first.

"No," she said. "I'll stay. If I may?" she asked Mrs. Levitton.

The old woman made a gesture of assent.

Marcus's glance was equal parts measuring and a warning, to his mother, and to Rosalind.

The door closed. Rosalind felt it like the closing of a prison cell. She called on her years of training to keep her face composed and placid.

It must have been sufficient.

"You do not appear shocked by us, Miss Thorne." Mrs. Levitton sagged back in her chair. "I can only assume that in your—perambulations among the great and good—you've seen worse."

"Illness and worry can strain the most patient families," replied Rosalind, and was amazed at how calm her voice sounded. She knew there were a hundred reasons Cate, and her aunt, might be ill. But the grim possibility of poison had settled deep into her mind, and she was having difficulty seeing past it.

She took refuge in everyday courtesy.

"Mrs. Hepplewhite," said Rosalind to the nurse. "How very good to see you here."

"Miss Thorne." Mrs. Hepplewhite curtsied.

"Mrs. Hepplewhite nursed a friend of mine," Rosalind told the Levittons. "You are in excellent hands."

"I'm in God's hands," snapped Marianna.

"As are we all," replied Rosalind.

"Mmph." A shudder ran through the older woman. She began to cough. Mrs. Hepplewhite moved instantly, leaning her back in the chair, putting a glass of water in her hand and helping her drink. Beatrice twisted her hands, but made no move to help, or to interfere.

Rosalind did not let herself move, or speak. She could barely breathe.

When Mrs. Levitton recovered, she leaned back in her chair, her breath rattling and her throat straining.

"Sit down, Beatrice," she gasped harshly. "You'll make yourself ill."

"I am already ill!" Beatrice snapped. "My daughter is missing, and nothing is being done! She was in *your* care. You *promised* you would watch over her! You *promised* . . ."

"Sit, sit." Mrs. Levitton's hand flapped impatiently.

Beatrice sat. Another gesture from Mrs. Levitton indicated Rosalind should do the same. Rosalind obeyed, choosing the chair as far from the roaring fire as she could.

"Did my sister-in-law tell you of our missing girl?" wheezed Mrs. Levitton.

"She told me her daughter has not been home since Tuesday," replied Rosalind softly.

"And I assume Marcus still won't approve any kind of search?" Mrs. Levitton directed this question to Beatrice.

Tears shone in Beatrice's dark, tired eyes. "He says Cate's made her bed and can lie in it."

"He would. The man has raised disapproval to a high art."

Beatrice pulled a crumpled handkerchief from her sleeve and held it to her nose. Anger colored her pale cheeks and the tears that had been building silently now began to fall.

"I am glad Beatrice contrived to send for you, Miss Thorne," said Mrs. Levitton. Rosalind did not correct her. "Cate is reckless, but she is not a bad girl. We need her found. Without fuss, if that can be managed. May we count on your assistance? You may apply to me to cover any expense."

Beatrice turned her distraught face to Rosalind. "If there's anything you can do, please . . ."

Rosalind found she had to swallow a large portion of guilt. She reminded herself firmly that Cate was also in distress, that she had run from this house, and her life could well be in danger.

So could Mrs. Levitton's.

Rosalind took a deep breath. "It is my experience that young ladies who run away seldom go far," she said. "Usually, it is a gesture resulting from some intense but temporary discontent and they are found safely lodged with friends, that is if they have not eloped—"

Rosalind was unprepared for the effect the word would have on Beatrice. The woman blanched dead white and gripped her chair arm as if she might topple over.

"Cate did not elope," said Mrs. Levitton firmly.

"Have her rooms been searched for letters or other clues as to where she might have gone? Has she friends to whom she could apply for help?"

"We did look," said Beatrice. "But we found nothing. As for friends—" Beatrice twisted her handkerchief.

"Cate has been living with me in Bath," said Mrs. Levitton. "She has no acquaintance in London."

In this, Mrs. Levitton was mistaken, but Rosalind could hardly say so. Mrs. Levitton's breath had begun to rattle in her throat. Mrs. Hepplewhite moved forward, and Mrs. Levitton clutched at her arm, her whole body shuddering.

Rosalind got to her feet at once. "Perhaps I could be shown

Cate's rooms? I may be able to find something useful that was missed."

"I'll take you," said Beatrice.

Beatrice took her out into the corridor and closed the door. Both of them pretended to ignore the sounds of distress that followed them as they walked on.

CHAPTER 8

A Question of Responsibility

. . . we joined forces and nothing could stand against us.

Edgeworth, Maria, *Belinda*

The sun had barely touched the rooftops when Adam descended the stairs of his family home. He was, however, far from the first one awake. The whole Harkness household rose early and got straight about the day's business. Adam's mother and his sister, Meg, were invariably up well before the sun. Adam was generally woken up by the sounds of the two of them throwing open the shutters, feeding the hens and geese, gathering in the eggs, and calling out to the neighbors as they came into the common yard for water from the pump. Then, the kitchen fire must be lit, the porridge pounded and set to boil. Meg must take her basket to market, or, if some of the birds had been sold, meet the carter who would deliver them to the purchaser.

Then, of course, Adam's two younger brothers must be roused from their beds. This was his task when he was home. The pair of sturdy boys were fast growing into gangly, sharp, loud youths with bottomless appetites. Once awake, both of them would be downstairs in an eyeblink to polish off por-ridge, bread, cheese, and butter before running out to their apprenticeships. The boys lived at home to save the cost of bed and board that would otherwise have to be paid to their masters.

Adam's third brother, the only one of them who proved to have any patience for books or writing, was a warehouse clerk now and had his own rooms. Three months of the household egg money had gone to purchase Davey's black coat.

Meg's two children were now old enough to dress each other. They came tumbling down the stairs along with the rest of the Harkness pack and climbed up on the benches at the long table. They joined in the talk, and the teasing, while his mother ladled scoop after scoop of her hot porridge into their wooden bowls.

Eventually, his other sister, Jenny, would come across the yard to join them all, probably with her newest baby in her arms. Jenny and her husband had the house on the other side of the poultry yard. Tom was home from sea just now, but was as busy as if he was away. Like a number of ex-sailors, he'd found work in the Drury Lane theater—shifting scenery, doing carpentry work, rigging the ropes to fly the big flats in and out. This was the height of his theater season and he might be away twelve or more hours at a stretch.

It was loud and chaotic. It was home. His family's cheerful madness never failed to lift Adam's spirits. For much of his life, he'd assumed he'd find a wife from one of the nearby streets, and they'd take another of the nearby houses and set about adding to the Harkness flock.

Then he'd met Rosalind Thorne, and everything had changed in an instant. Now he did not know what his future would hold, except that it must somehow hold her. With the memory of Sir Richard and his thousand-pound reward lurk-ing in the back of his mind, Adam sat down to bread and

porridge, and to listen to his mother and Meg cheerfully be-
rating all and sundry for their manners, their dress, and their
failure to chew their food.

The one thing Adam's father had handed down to his family was this house. It had belonged to Harknesses for genera-
tions and it gave them the sort of safe haven too many of
their neighbors lacked. But despite the house, money was always precarious. Even when his father was alive, there had
been times when they'd gone hungry, and they might have to
scrabble to find something to burn in the hearth. His sisters
had gone into service for a time, and he'd been sent to relatives in the country. He'd been told it was for his health, but
even as a boy he'd known it was also to save the cost of his
board.

A thousand pounds could give his entire family a security
they had never known before.

It could also destroy the man he tried to be.

A knock sounded and the door to the street pushed open a
moment later. Sampson Goutier ducked under the low lintel,
taking off his hat as he did so.

"Good morning, Captain Goutier!" called Mother genially. "Sit yourself down and have some breakfast."

"Thank you, but I've already had mine." Goutier did take
a seat at the end of the bench and accepted the mug of tea
Mother deposited in front of him. Since Goutier and Adam
often worked together, Goutier would frequently stop by of a
morning, so the two of them could walk to the station together. Meg asked after Goutier's wife and infant son.
Goutier settled comfortably into the noisy banter as Adam
finished his breakfast, claimed his own hat, and kissed his
mother.

Outside, the two men wove their way through the crowded
streets and alleyways that defined Adam's neighborhood.
Here, houses were small and families were large, so much of
life was lived out in the open. The streets were filled with

women at work, children at play, and men passing to and fro, on their way to their own jobs, or to drink away what they'd already brought home.

Adam noticed Goutier rubbing a spot behind his right ear. His wounded hand had been expertly wrapped in clean gauze.

"You all right?" Adam asked.

"Pfft," Goutier snorted dismissively. "I've taken worse. I was surprised, that's all. Getting soft." He chuckled, but his eyes were serious. "If I catch that fellow again, we'll have words, him and me."

"I pity the fellow then," said Adam easily.

"Decided what you're going to do yet?"

"No," Adam admitted. "Not really. I'm going to look at the statements again, see if I can pick up any hint that what Sir Richard says is true—that this Edwards engineered the business at Cato Street."

"And if it turns out he did?"

"Then I'll find him."

"You, one of Bow Street's most respected officers, are going to expose a government spy?" said Goutier. "Mind if I ask why you'd do such a fool thing?"

"Because I don't like the smell of this," said Adam.

"Siding with radicals now, Harkness?"

"I don't know."

Goutier shook his head. "I don't understand you, Harkness. You've been tapped by Townsend as his favorite. The prince . . . the *king* knows your name, and asks for you personally when he's got a job that needs doing. And you're getting ready to dance with their enemies."

"I know," said Adam.

"It makes no sense, man!"

"I know."

"You going to keep saying that?"

"I don't know."

2Darcie Wilde

Goutier barked out a laugh. "Well, if I was you I'd figure it out in a hurry. Straddling the fence is not safe. A man stays like that too long, he gets his balls caught." He paused. "I hope you know at least you're being used. This Sir Richard and his friends, whoever they turn out to be, came to you because you can get into Bow Street's records, and they can't."

"It's worse than that," said Adam. "I'm being used, and bribed."

Goutier pursed his lips. "How much?"

"They're matching the reward for Thistlewood. A thousand pounds."

Goutier swore. "That's a sum to make a man think twice."

"Yes," breathed Adam. "Yes it is."

"So that's what this waffling is about then," said Goutier. "You're trying to talk yourself round. Make sure you're not doing it just for the money."

Adam said nothing. Goutier nodded.

"It's a hell of a question."

"It is." Adam sighed in frustration. "It's down to this. Sir Richard and his lot, they look at Peterloo, at Cato Street, and they say, "Something's wrong here. We should try to fix it." His Honor Mr. Birnie, and Townsend, and their supporters all take a look at the same events and say we should punish those men until they're too broken to do any such thing again. Which side would you rather put your hands to?"

Goutier shook his head. "This is your Miss Thorne's doing."

"What do you mean by that?" said Adam, more sharply than he'd meant to.

But Goutier just arched a knowing brow. "Don't get me wrong, I have nothing but respect for Miss Thorne. She's an amazing woman. But she has protections and privileges, that you and I don't. There's those who will look out for her because she's one of them, born to their class. That's not something we can say."

It rankled Adam to hear Goutier say as much so openly, but he couldn't argue. He knew full well that Rosalind belonged to a different class from him, and had been raised to far different standards and expectations than he had been.

She knew it, too. He remembered one day she had come to visit his house. She had met all his madcap family and fit in among them cheerfully and easily. His sisters liked her. His mother did as well. The children adored her, and not just because she brought presents and sweets. She would laugh with them and run about the yard in games of chase, and tell them stories and patiently answer their thousand questions.

At the same time, he'd caught her surreptitiously watching his mother, and all her work, especially her constant doings in the kitchen. He'd seen the dismay in her eyes then. Not that a woman should have to do so much, but in understanding that she had no idea how to manage a house, a family, without servants. And although she knew it was merely a matter of how she was raised, rather than a demonstration of worth, it had still stung her and left her with a strong feeling of being an outsider.

He'd felt the same way the times he'd donned a black coat and white breeches and stepped out among the *haut ton*. There had been a thousand tiny rituals and silent understandings that he was not a part of. He'd also felt keenly how he was an object of curiosity, and not a little disdain. He was also aware that Rosalind's own position was suspect just because she was too near to him.

"Oi," said Goutier. "You still with us?"

"Sorry. Woolgathering."

"Gathering something, that's for sure." Goutier chuckled. "Let me tell you what I know, Adam Harkness. Those in power plan to stay there. They're not going to tolerate tuppeny-hapenny revolutionaries. And you may have stood before the king, he may have praised your name, but if the men in charge decide you've betrayed them when they've been so very condescending to you, no Member of Parliement is going to be able to save your righteous ass."

"If you'd rather not be seen with me . . ."

Goutier regarded him soberly. "What, and miss my chance to find the fellow that knifed me? Not a chance." He smiled, but the expression quickly faded. "But just be careful, all right? I don't want to be explaining to Sal that we're going to be up and moving down to Botany Bay."

"You have my word."

"Well, there's a comfort," said Goutier blandly. "What will you do in the meantime?"

"I want a talk with this man Hiden," he said. "He's the one who turned up in the park with a note about a mad conspiracy, and was instantly believed. There's something going on there, and I want to know what it is."

"And then?"

"And then we'll just have to see," said Adam. "Because whatever is there it's got someone worried enough to murder some men, hide some others, and pay out a lot of money to make sure all goes their way."

CHAPTER 9

The Contents of a Single Room

*". . . now he suspected her of artifice in every
word, look, and motion . . ."*

Edgeworth, Maria, *Belinda*

Cate Levitton had plainly been allowed to decorate her
own rooms. Rosalind could not imagine that Mrs. Levitton would have chosen so much rose pink, nor such a quantity of ruffles.

Beatrice drifted to the vanity table and rested her fingertips on its surface, as if it could offer a touchstone to her daughter. Rosalind's guilt swelled. She abhorred secrets. She had watched them destroy her family. But Cate had asked for Rosalind's confidence, and Rosalind had given it. She was not ready to break that promise. Not even while she watched Cate's mother struggle to control her grief, and anger.

"Mrs. Levitton, why was Cate sent to live with her aunt?" she asked. She knew the answer, of course, but she wanted to know what Beatrice would say.

"There was some trouble, with a servant," Beatrice told her. She did not look at Rosalind. Instead, she straightened the mirror, and the hairbrush on the table. "It was thought better that Cate not be in town for a while. Mrs. Levitton seemed quite settled in Bath, so we thought—" But she did not finish her thought.

"Do Cate and Mrs. Levitton get along?"

Beatrice glanced toward the door. "I did not have much contact with her after she went to stay with Marianna. I believed her to be happy enough. Marianna can be a hard woman, but she is not cruel. She was very willing to take Cate into her care. At the time, I thought it would be better than keeping her at home." She looked to the door again. "Her father, my husband, he was . . . very angry at her conduct."

"As was Marcus?" prompted Rosalind.

"Yes. Marcus was already married, at the time, and had his own establishment. I only went to live with him and his family after my husband died." She smoothed down the skirt of her mourning dress. "But, well, he takes great care of his reputation."

"I understand."

"Do you?" Beatrice's voice sharpened. "You have no children, Miss Thorne. Do you understand what a blow it is to find you were entirely mistaken in their nature? And to discover that what you've tried to do for them has only made matters worse?"

This last word hung in the air. Beatrice drew back, biting her lip. "I'm sorry. You will forget that, if you please. It is only that it has been so difficult—"

"Think no more of it," said Rosalind.

"I had better go make sure of Marcus," Beatrice said. "Will you be all right?" She stopped. "How ridiculous of me, I . . ."

"I shall be perfectly all right," Rosalind assured her. "But, may I ask a favor?"

"If it will help, anything."

"Can you ask Mrs. Hepplewhite to come speak with me?"

Beatrice frowned. "The nurse? But why?"

"It is possible Mrs. Hepplewhite saw or heard something that could help us. And as she knows me, she may be more willing to speak in confidence than—"

"Than one of the other servants," Beatrice finished for her. "Yes, of course. I'll see to it."

Rosalind closed the door behind Beatrice. She stood there for a moment, willing herself to breathe calmly. It was not easy. Her hands trembled, and the unwelcome sensation of tears prickled behind her eyes. She swallowed to clear her throat, and swallowed again.

Sitting and speaking calmly with Marianna Levitton may have been the most difficult thing she had ever done. A lifetime's training had given her the ability to set aside her feelings, no matter how violent, and maintain that polite and disinterested facade required of a gentlewoman in a social setting. But this was different. Marianna was obviously ill to the point of death. And the cause of it might well be a slow and deliberate act of murder.

And she might already have spoken with the perpetrator.

Rosalind was not a cynic. She had seen for herself the good inside most people. Still, she knew that resentments within families could grow intensely bitter, and that there was no easy way to escape them.

Rosalind closed her eyes, and drew in another breath.

I must be calm. I must think.

Rationally, she knew she could be putting too much weight on Adam's words. It was possible that he had been wrong, and there was no poison. Cate, reckless and distracted by—something—had succumbed to a girlish impulse, left the house, and wandered the streets until she'd found Amelia in the market. Her illness could simply be the result of exposure and exhaustion. Mrs. Levitton's poor health could be the unfortunate consequence of age and infection.

She wanted it to be true. But she needed to be certain. Rosalind turned to face the pretty boudoir.

Where does a girl hide what's important? Her gaze swept the room. Not under the bolsters or mattresses. The maids would find anything there when they turned and aired the beds.

So, where?

Rosalind sat down at the writing desk. It was a delicate, spindle-legged affair. The writing area was covered in leather. An inkwell, pens, and a letter opener were all laid out, ready for use. The body of the table had three drawers. The central drawer held paper, quills, penknife, and shell-pink sealing wax. The left-hand drawer held a quantity of stationery printed with an elaborate, curling *C*.

Cate might have been sent here in disgrace, but Mrs. Levitton had not hesitated to spend money on her niece.

The right-hand drawer held correspondence, bundled in ribbons of various colors. A quick glance suggested they were missives from various friends. Rosalind was not yet ready to read Cate's letters, although it might still come to that. She had not, however, really expected to find anything there. If Cate was so cavalier with her secrets, they would have already been discovered.

Like the writing desk, the jewel cabinet was unlocked. Rosalind pulled out the drawers. There were some very nice pieces, but nothing of enormous value. She closed these as well, and turned to face the room, a frown furrowing her brow.

Then, she spotted the workbasket by the chair at the window. Rosalind opened the lid and rummaged through it. She found reels of thread, a half-completed bit of fancy work, a glove with loose beading, and a silk reticule with a torn seam.

Rosalind plucked the reticule out of the basket, and paused. It crinkled stiffly in her hand, like there was something inside. Impatiently, Rosalind picked at the knotted drawstring until it gave.

Two paper slips slithered out onto the floor.

Rosalind picked them up, and was instantly assailed by memory. She had been a girl, searching through her father's desk. Father had abandoned the family. Mother was in her room insisting that nothing was wrong, and she cried herself into a collapse if anyone suggested otherwise. Rosalind, with the help of the family's housekeeper, was looking for any clue as to where her father gone, or, failing that, any money or notes he might have left behind. What Rosalind had found instead was an entire drawer of receipts very similar to these two.

They were pledges from a pawnbroker. From several pawn-brokers, in her father's case. The ones in Rosalind's hand now both came from a single shop—Temple & Trigg. According to the tidy handwriting, the first slip was a pledge against a gold and topaz necklace. The second was against a matching bracelet.

Well. Rosalind slid the receipts back into the bag and re-knotted the cord.

The fact of the pledges made sense. If Cate had been planning to run away she would need money. Still, it seemed odd that Cate would seek a loan against her jewelry, rather than try to sell it outright.

But, if she had been planning to leave, and thought far enough ahead to get herself some money, then it made no sense that she would be found alone, ill and destitute in the market. The most naive schoolgirl could not expect to get very far on foot without luggage and traveling clothes. And why, of all things, would she decide to just wander about on the chance of meeting Amelia?

Rosalind's thoughts halted in their tracks.

Amelia had told Rosalind and Alice that Cate had come to her a week ago. What had she said? Rosalind frowned, trying to remember.

I brought her to the house, she'd said . . . *she needed to leave Mrs. Levitton's house. She asked . . . she asked if I could help her . . . I said she should talk to you . . . But she wouldn't listen. She left.*

What Amelia did not say was whether or not she had helped Cate. Rosalind's frown deepened.

Was it possible Cate had left something behind at the house, such as a box, or even a trunk? Could Cate have arranged to meet Amelia in the market to retrieve it?

Had this plan been complicated by the fact of Rosalind and Alice impulsively deciding to accompany Amelia that day? Amelia had certainly not been in the best mood that morning, oddly snappish and distant. Alice had remarked that Amelia had been "off" lately. Rosalind, preoccupied with her own business, had set this aside to be dealt with later.

That was beginning to seem like a mistake.

A knock sounded on the door. Rosalind, on a moment's impulse, tucked the pawnshop receipts into her sleeve.

"Come in," she said.

The door opened, and Mrs. Hepplewhite walked in.

"I was told you wished to talk to me?"

"Yes, thank you."

Mrs. Hepplewhite carefully closed the door. When she turned again, she stood ramrod straight, her hands folded in front of her. "I never had a chance to say so, Miss Thorne, but I always appreciated the care you took over Julia Oslander. It wasn't fair, what happened to her, and you tried to do right."

Julia Oslander had also been a nurse. She had died of violence, and Rosalind had a role in discovering the perpetrator. A number of Mrs. Oslander's fellow nurses had attended her funeral. Mrs. Hepplewhite had been among them.

"Thank you, Mrs. Hepplewhite. That means a great deal

to me." Rosalind knew a moment's indecision. But she pushed it aside. The consequences of inaction were too dire. She could risk a bit of embarrassment. "I have something to tell you, but I confess, I have no idea how to begin." Rosalind paused. "This is, for the moment, in confidence."

Mrs. Hepplewhite raised her brows.

"To begin with, I know where Cate Levitton is."

Mrs. Hepplewhite's face betrayed not the least surprise. "You'll pardon me for saying so, Miss Thorne, but her aunt and her mother would like very much to know that."

"Yes. I haven't said anything because there is a very real possibility that the young woman has been poisoned."

Mrs. Hepplewhite's face remained impassive. Rosalind supposed that as a nurse, she'd heard a great deal of speculation and suspicion in the sickroom.

"Has she had a doctor?" Mrs. Hepplewhite asked.

"Indeed she has."

"Does the doctor agree with this . . . possibility?"

"He has not yet rendered an opinion," said Rosalind. "I would not have spoken at all, if it were not for the possibility that the same poison is being administered to Mrs. Levitton."

That, finally, caused Mrs. Hepplewhite to draw back, startled into an expression of affront, and anger.

"What manner of poison is this supposed to be?"

"Arsenic."

She waited for Mrs. Hepplewhite to protest, and was prepared for her shock, and her rejection of this possibility. But the nurse was silent. Her eyes flickered back and forth, searching her own memory and experience.

"I've never seen a case myself," she said at last. "But I have heard of it. It . . . it could be. But it also could be any of a hundred other things. And no one else in the house is ill."

"Except Cate," said Rosalind. "She was near to death when my maid found her."

Mrs. Hepplewhite's face hardened. "This is a very ugly thing you're saying, Miss Thorne. I hope you've no intention of telling my patient."

"I would certainly like to avoid it." Mrs. Hepplewhite did not seem at all reassured by this, and Rosalind could not blame her. "And I am aware I am prying, but, could you tell me if there is anything Mrs. Levitton eats or drinks that is not shared by the rest of the house?"

Mrs. Hepplewhite was quiet again. Rosalind held her breath. The nurse could refuse to answer. She could declare that Rosalind had no business making such accusations.

"No," said Mrs. Hepplewhite at last. "The barley water, perhaps. But I prepare that myself, so there can be no question it is wholesome. The rest is prepared by the cook, and that means the servants might share in what's left at any time, and any broth or stock might be made into other dishes for the house . . ." She paused then. Something had occurred to her. Rosalind's heart thumped once.

"There's the tea." Mrs. Hepplewhite spoke slowly, as if making some reluctant confession.

Rosalind waited.

"Mrs. Levitton is particular about her tea," the nurse said. "She has a special order standing with Mr. Twining, and she keeps it in a locked caddy—you know how some ladies are." Rosalind shared a look with Mrs. Hepplewhite. They both did indeed know this. "Most days, she's had me make her a cup . . ." Mrs. Hepplewhite clamped her mouth shut to keep the next words from escaping. "No. I wouldn't credit it. That would mean someone in the *house*—"

"Which is why I don't like to say where Cate is just yet," said Rosalind.

"I won't believe it. This is a *respectable* house." She spoke firmly, waiting for Rosalind to contradict her.

"I could very well be wrong," Rosalind admitted. "But it

is also true that since she has been with us, Cate has improved. And you say that no other member of the house has become ill." Which would argue against an infectious complaint. Rosalind knew she did not need to say this. She could already tell that Mrs. Hepplewhite had thought it.

Mrs. Hepplewhite drew herself up. "I won't believe it. With all due respect, Miss Thorne, you're wrong this time."

"I sincerely hope so." Rosalind put every bit of feeling she had into the words. "All I ask is that you help me eliminate the possibility."

Mrs. Hepplewhite said nothing, but at least she was not refusing out of hand.

"Will you stop giving her that particular tea? For a week only, to see if she grows stronger? If she does not improve, then I am indeed wrong, and I will not importune you with my suspicions again. If she should improve, however . . ."

"That would not necessarily mean you were correct."

"No," agreed Rosalind. "But isn't it worth the attempt?"

Mrs. Hepplewhite was silent for a long time. Rosalind put all her energies into remaining calm and quiet. If she pressed too hard, the nurse would simply turn away from her.

The knock sounded like a thunderclap. Both women jumped.

The door opened and a man leaned in. Harold Davenport.

"Hullo!" Mr. Davenport smiled tentatively. "Miss Thorne, was hoping I might have a word?"

"You'll excuse me." Mrs. Hepplewhite made a brief curtsy and was gone.

Rosalind struggled to keep her hands from curling into fists. "Do please come in, Mr. Davenport," she said.

"Thank you." Mr. Davenport did come in. He also left the door wide open, as propriety demanded. Rosalind again noted his round, open face and cheerful blue eyes. His hair and clothing were very neat. It was clear he took care over his appearance. She was particularly struck by his hands, which were scrupulously clean with carefully trimmed and polished fingernails.

"I was wondering had you found anything? Family's all in a twist, and nothing I say seems to calm them down. Not good for anybody, especially not Mrs. Marianna."

"Pardon me for asking, Mr. Davenport, but what is your relation to the family?"

Mr. Davenport chuckled.

"No one's thought to mention it to you, have they?" His expression shifted to one of self-deprecation. "You see, Cate and I were—are, I hope—engaged to be married."

CHAPTER 10

The Boundaries of Friendship

*"No, secrecy is my first object. Nay, do not reason
with me; it is a subject on which I cannot, will
not, reason."*

Edgeworth, Maria, *Belinda*

"How does our patient?" asked Mrs. Singh as Amelia
entered the kitchen.

Amelia blinked heavily at her. Mrs. Singh *tsked* and
pushed a cup of tea to her. Amelia drank gratefully. She was
used to long nights and longer days, but just now she felt like
she'd been put through a mangle. All those hours just watching Cate breathe. Finding herself full of all her old feelings
one minute, but filled with nothing but fury the next, and not
knowing what to do.

Miss Alice knew she'd been lying. She was sure of it. And
what Miss Alice knew, Miss Thorne knew.

"She's awake," said Amelia, belatedly. "I was hoping there
might be something I could take her."

"Certainly there is. I've been keeping it warm for her."
Mrs. Singh turned to the pot on the stove and ladled out a

bowl of her special porridge. Mrs. Singh had opinions about gruel, and English cooking in general. They tended to range from inedible to unspeakable.

"Thank you," said Amelia, extra politely. Now was not the time to risk one of the cook's lectures. "I'll take the tray. You've enough to do."

"Thank you." Mrs. Singh set the bowl of porridge in place. "Make sure she eats it all. She needs her strength, poor thing."

"I will," Amelia promised.

Mrs. Singh added the teapot and cup to the tray. Then, she paused and looked Amelia directly in the eye. "Our misses are very kind," she said. "I would be very sorry to see their good hearts leading this house into trouble."

Amelia wanted to scream, or at least snap back. But it wouldn't make anything better. Mrs. Singh had eyes and ears of her own. What's more, the cook had become protective of this job, and this house where she was fully respected for her skills and experience. Mrs. Singh would fight to protect what she had, and there were plenty of ways she could make Amelia's life miserable if she chose.

"I'd be sorry, too, Mrs. Singh, believe me."

"I do believe you," said the cook. "But we may believe and still be sorry."

Amelia tried to muster her temper. She'd been looking out for Miss Rosalind and Miss Alice far longer than Mrs. Singh. Who was this woman to suggest Amelia didn't care for them, or for this house?

But making trouble was the last thing she could afford. So, Amelia swallowed all her feeling and took the tray.

Upstairs, she shouldered the door to Cate's room open without knocking. She turned around, and froze.

Cate, shaky as a newborn lamb, stood beside her bed.

Amelia gaped. "You bloody idiot, what are you doing!"

Cate gasped, lost her balance, and collapsed back onto the bed. Amelia dropped the tray onto the table and rushed to her.

"Do you want to break your silly neck?" She rolled, shoved, and generally manhandled Cate back under the bed-clothes.

"I'm sorry," Cate gasped. "I'm so sorry."

"So you keep saying," fumed Amelia. "If you was as sorry as all that, you might try doing as you're told."

"Will you help me?" Cate whispered.

"What have I been doing?" Amelia demanded. "You're here, aren't you? Instead of dead in the gutter, which I'm starting to believe you deserve!"

Cate turned her face away. "Maybe I do."

"Oh, stop it. Here." Amelia grabbed up the tray and set it over Cate's lap. "Eat your porridge, and get some of that tea in you as well." Amelia dropped into the bedside chair and folded her arms. "And I'm staying right here until you finish."

"All of it?" Cate eyed the bowl uncertainly.

Amelia nodded. "If you don't, I'll have Mrs. Singh after me. So you may as well get started."

Remembering Cate's sweet tooth, Amelia had included a bowl of sugar lumps on the tray. Cate stirred three into her porridge. She ate slowly at first, and then with more appetite. Amelia felt her anger soften, at least a little. It felt a bit like old times. Back then, Amelia would bring Cate her breakfast in bed, and then they'd sit giggling about whatever party Cate had been to, and how ridiculous everybody there was. Eventually, those giggles would turn to whispers—of their dreams, their feelings, and what they'd do as soon as they were able to run away.

A slow warmth stole over Amelia, followed fast by anger at herself. How could she let her mind linger over those times? She already knew how that story ended.

Didn't she?

Cate poured herself a cup of tea, added two more sugar lumps, and drank.

"Amelia?" she said softly.

"Yes?"

"What . . . what did you tell them, about me?"

The treacherous warmth faded away, smothered by other, colder memories. "You mean about us?"

"Well, yes, and about my coming here."

"You know what I told them," said Amelia warily. "That you asked for my help to run away. They want to know why you came to me." *I want to know why.*

"But you didn't tell them?" asked Cate. "I mean, you've still got my bag and everything?"

Amelia sighed. "Yes, I've still got your bag. But if you think I'm going to help you leave this house before you can even stand up . . ."

"No, no, I just, I just wanted to know it was safe. I'll behave. I will. Look." She took another big spoonful of porridge. "Mmmmm . . . I feel better already."

She smiled so sweetly that for a moment Amelia forgot to be annoyed with her, but only for a moment.

"What's going on, Cate? Why'd you come . . . ?" *Why'd you come bother me? When I'd gotten over you? When I'd found a situation I'd never imagined, when I'd found someone real . . . ?*

Cate's face fell. "I thought you'd be pleased to see me."

Amelia made herself ignore that woebegone look. *I've seen it before.* "Why would I? After what you did?"

"You said you loved me."

"And *you* said I seduced and threatened you."

"I didn't! That was my brother!" cried Cate, but Amelia glared at her and she stopped. "I had to go along, Amelia. You know I did! Papa threatened to put me out on the street with just what I stood up in if I didn't swear what Everett said was true!"

"Did you even once think what they'd do to me?" *Did you even look out the window to see me in the street, in the* street, *turned out without a character, or my wages?*

"It's easy for someone like you," said Cate.

Amelia felt her jaw drop. "*Easy?*" she sputtered. "Is that what you think!"

"Of course it is!" Cate snapped. "You can always get another situation. I was the one who was stuck with them!" She jerked her chin toward the door, as if her family waited on the other side.

"Just what do you think you know about it?" Amelia demanded. "You've never had to face a night without a roof over your head! Never had to wake up in the morning with no idea how you were going to live! I spent a month not knowing where my next meal was coming from, and none of the registry offices would touch me because I had no reference! If Miss Thorne hadn't come along, I'd've had to . . ." She stopped. She wasn't going to say it. She didn't want to remember that she'd been hungry enough to think of going on the game. But she had.

Cate was staring.

"I thought I was giving you your freedom," she whispered. "More freedom than I'd ever have."

"Well, you were wrong." Amelia slumped backward in her chair, suddenly exhausted.

Cate stirred her spoon through her porridge. Finally, she asked, "Do you love her? That Alice Littlefield?" Amelia looked away. "I saw the way you looked at her."

"That is none of your business," muttered Amelia.

Cate set her spoon down. "I still love you, Amelia," she whispered. "I never stopped. I tried to find you. The second I got back to London, I went to every registry office I could, trying to find where you'd gone."

"You're just saying that because you need me."

"I'm saying it because it's true." Cate leaned across the

tray. Amelia made the mistake of looking into her earnest, pleading eyes. "Listen, things have changed. I've got money now. When I leave here, you could come with me."

Amelia felt her heart clench hard. "What are you talking about?"

Cate clasped her hand, and Amelia felt a rush of treasonous warmth. "Come with me, Amelia," she said eagerly. "We can go to Paris, like we talked about. Or Italy. Geneva. New York. *Anywhere.*"

"You're serious."

"Yes. I love you, Amelia. Please." Cate squeezed her fingers hard. "Come with me."

Amelia stared at their hands. Every inch of her remembered Cate's touch. How warm it made her, how strong and daring she'd felt when they were alone together. "I . . . I'll think about it."

"Will you? Will you really?"

"Yes. I promise." *Because I can't help it now, can I?*

Cate smiled the sunshine smile that Amelia remembered so well. "All right, then." She took her last spoonful of porridge. "There!" she said triumphantly. "You can tell Mrs. Singh you saw me eat every bite."

"Good girl." Amelia stood and picked up the tray. "I'll leave you the tea. You get some rest now."

"Yes, ma'am." Mischief sparkled in Cate's eyes. "You'll come back soon?"

Amelia promised, and tried not to look like she was hurrying out the door.

Amelia took the tray back down to the kitchen and reported to Mrs. Singh that Amelia had indeed eaten it all. In return, Mrs. Singh reported that Miss Alice had asked to see her.

Amelia swallowed and said she'd go at once. She turned away before she had to watch Mrs. Singh's eyes narrow.

Miss Alice had claimed the back parlor as her own. Amelia knocked on the door and went in.

The parlor was a riot. Occasionally, Amelia made an attempt at tidying, but there was no keeping up with it. Books and papers covered every surface. No fewer than three stacks of newspapers teetered on chairs and footstools.

Miss Alice sat at her worktable, bent so low over the typeset sheets she called "page proofs" that her nose all but touched the paper.

"Did you need something, miss?" asked Amelia.

"I need Mr. Colburn's typesetter to get a new pair of spectacles," Alice muttered. "How can one man make so many mistakes?" She drew her pencil through a line and wrote a note in the margin. Then she tossed her pencil down and sat back with a sigh.

"How's Miss Levitton doing?" she asked.

"She's much better," said Amelia. "I think the doctor will be pleased."

"Well, that's good. Did she tell you anything about why she's run away?"

Amelia shook her head. "I tried to get her to talk, but she's stubborn." The second part was true. The first, a bit less so. The truth was, she'd been so wrapped up in the fact of Cate asking her to run away, too, that she'd forgotten to ask why she was running at all.

Or maybe it was because Cate had been wanting to run as long as Amelia had known her.

"Well, we'll have to trust to Rosalind's wits then." Alice got up and poured herself a cup of coffee from the pot that waited on the hearth.

"Miss Thorne?" Amelia felt a cold knot of fear forming in her stomach. "What's she—"

Alice drank the coffee and made a face. Probably she

found it too strong. How long had it been sitting there? Knowing Miss Alice, it might well have been from yesterday.

"Don't say anything to Cate just yet," Miss Alice told Amelia. "But Rosalind's gone to see her aunt."

The knot of fear tightened sharply. "But Ca . . . Miss Levitton, she doesn't want any of that lot to know where she is."

"It's all right." Alice waved her cup. "Rosalind won't give the game away. She's got a plan. She always does."

That was true, and usually it was a good plan. But the fear remained.

Miss Alice, of course, saw something was wrong. "Amelia?" she said, and the gentleness in her voice cut straight through to Amelia's battered heart. "It's just you and me, here. If you have something . . . anything . . . you want to tell me, you know I won't say a word if you don't want me to. Not even to Rosalind."

Those eyes. Those beautiful brown eyes. She could just drown in them. Every time Amelia saw even a little bit of disappointment in Alice's eyes, she wanted to cry, or to fight the whole world, just to make Miss Alice smile again.

Everything was so *different* with her. Miss Alice listened when Amelia talked, and she understood what she heard. She'd been knocked around a bit, Miss Alice had, and she knew how much it meant to have something real to hold on to. Someone real. She didn't spin daydreams about Paris and Geneva. She talked about a little house, maybe in Cheapside. A bit of garden. Books for her, and a job outside service for Amelia.

They'd already spent so much time together. All those hours just the two of them, as Alice patiently taught Amelia to read out of the newspapers and novels from Mr. Clements's circulating library. Amelia had tried to repay the favor by teaching Alice to sew, which only led to the pair of them laughing in despair at her attempt to alter her own frocks. They'd even gone out walking in the park together, and to the theater, and fireworks display, and the panorama in Hyde Park. Just two friends, having a day out. Not hiding a thing.

Well, maybe hiding something. Amelia bit her lip.

Alice set the coffee cup on the mantel and instead took Amelia's hand. "It'll be all right, Amelia. Whatever it is. We'll work it out together."

"I know." Amelia closed her fingers around Alice's. Such a tiny hand, but so different from Cate's. Miss Alice's hands were rougher, ink stained, and stronger. Clever. Capable.

Amelia wanted to believe. She didn't want to be bothered by old feelings and old dreams. But they were inside her, and she couldn't let them go.

She made herself smile, and made herself mean it.

Alice leaned in and swiftly kissed her cheek. "I'll let you go. We've both got work."

Amelia smiled, and blushed, and hurried away.

And tried not to see the flicker of doubt in Miss Alice's eyes as she closed the door.

CHAPTER 11

The Best Laid Plans

"He is not *a man, whose whole consequence, if he were married, would depend on his wife—"*

Edgeworth, Maria, *Belinda*

"I'm sorry," said Rosalind to Mr. Davenport, whose smile had not shifted one iota. "I had no idea Cate was engaged."

"Well, the thing hasn't been formally announced yet," Mr. Davenport told her. "But I proposed, and she accepted, and we have Mrs. Levitton's approval, which is the important thing." He rolled his cheerful eyes toward the door.

"We thought to wed quickly, you know," he went on, "so that Marianna could be there. At least, I'd thought that was the plan." He rubbed his hands together uneasily. "Cate, it seems, had other ideas."

Despite his polished nails, Mr. Davenport's hands were rough around the edges, Rosalind noted. This was a man who had done hard work in his life.

"Forgive me, Mr. Davenport." Rosalind found herself struggling to catch up with the new ideas, and fears, that this sudden announcement raised in her mind. "But . . ."

"I don't seem very upset about losing my bride?" Mr. Davenport suggested.

"Just so," agreed Rosalind. She appreciated his plain speaking, but at the same time she wondered at it.

"Well, I know Cate, you see."

Rosalind prepared herself to hear that Cate was headstrong and reckless and needed to be taken in hand. Again, she was surprised.

"Cate's smart," Mr. Davenport went on. "Like her aunt. Sharp as a new pin, if truth be told." He paused, and then smiled genially. "I've surprised you, have I? I'm not like other men, Miss Thorne. They may want a pretty, docile little thing to decorate their dining table and dither over choosing a dress, but I prefer spirit, and intellect."

Rosalind permitted her brows to rise.

"I've tried to tell Marcus that Cate's too smart to be bullied about, but the man will simply not listen." Mr. Davenport shook his head. "Miss Thorne, I know everyone is worried. I'm worried, but I'm not frightened, yet, and I won't be. Not without reason. It's my opinion that if Cate's left us, it's because that's what she wanted. And if . . ." He stopped and took a deep breath. "If you do find her, will you tell her that if she ran away because of me, there's no need? If she wants to cry off the engagement, I'll take the blame, and there won't be any trouble."

This was quite generous and, frankly, as surprising as anything he'd said yet. Not many freshly jilted men would be prepared to consider a nervous fiancée's feelings, let alone be willing to take the blame. Rosalind found herself impressed, or she would have, except for the memory of Cate lying so very ill in her bed, possibly poisoned, and that of Mrs. Levitton upstairs, probably dying. These facts cast a cloud over the whole of the house and all its occupants.

"If I may ask, Mr. Davenport," said Rosalind. "How did you come to know the family?"

"I worked for old Mr. Levitton, Mrs. Marianna's husband. He took me into the business when I was a boy." Mr. Davenport chuckled. "Practically raised me, if the truth be known. I spent some years as a mining engineer, and then became a foreman. I'm head of the business now. We've got twelve shafts open and—" He stopped, suddenly aware he was running down a tangent. "But that's not what you want to hear. I used to visit Mrs. Levitton in Bath and give her reports on how the mines were doing."

"Do you mean to say Mr. Levitton left his business in his wife's hands?" This was past unusual. It was shocking.

"Oh, yes. Lock, stock, and barrel. Only fair, you know. She ran the whole concern almost from the day she married him."

Rosalind felt herself staring. Mr. Davenport nodded.

"From what I've heard, old Levitton was running things straight into the ground when he married. Don't get me wrong, Miss Thorne. He was a good man, and an excellent engineer. But he had no head for business. Talk of money just made him impatient.

"Anyway, as I heard the story, just when all looked lost, Mrs. Levitton took the reins. She sacked all the fellows who were skimming off the cream, hired new crews under new terms, and kept the books herself. When there was finally some profit from the mines, she took that money and poured it into London property, and other businesses. There's two breweries, if I recall, and a carting business, and a stagecoach line, and I don't know what else. When she's in health, she runs it all herself. I just look out for the mines."

"And what does Marcus Levitton do?"

"Runs through his income and fumes that his aunt ought to have handed him all businesses when her husband died. Wears it like the proverbial crown of thorns." He smiled, indicating he knew that might be taken as a pun on her name. She smiled in return, to let him know she had heard all the possible puns and was more than ready to ignore them, thank you.

"May I ask why Marcus doesn't approve of you marrying Cate?"

Mr. Davenport arched his brows. "Should have thought it obvious, Miss Thorne. Especially to a woman of your experience. I'm not of their class, am I?" He held up his rough hands. "Orphan boy, parents are God-knows-who, marrying a gently reared lady like Cate Levitton? Not to be thought of!" He chuckled again. Rosalind returned a polite smile and hoped he hadn't seen her wince. "Then there was the money, of course. Mrs. Marianna planned to gift us with the mines when I married Cate, and a good share of the profits from her other businesses to go with them."

"She surely knew that would make her family angry."

"She didn't care. They'd never welcomed her, she said, no matter how hard she tried. Hectored and hounded her after Levitton died. Saw that for myself," he added, and some of his habitual levity dimmed. "At any rate, after years of that sort of thing, she does not now see it as her particular responsibility to look after them."

"Then, Mrs. Marianna Levitton . . ." began Rosalind.

"Is old Mr. Levitton's second wife," said Mr. Davenport.

"I see," said Rosalind.

"Yes, I rather expect you do," said Davenport gravely.

"Were you aware of Miss Levitton's, and Mrs. Levitton's quarrels with the rest of the family?"

"Oh, yes. Cate made sure I was. Yelled at me, actually." He rubbed his hands together again. "I'd scared her a bit, you see, with my proposal. She couldn't believe I meant what I said, and tried to frighten me off. But I'm not like other men, Miss Thorne. A girl has as much a right to her past as I have to mine. Marriage is a fresh start for all concerned."

That was the second time Mr. Davenport had declared

himself unlike other men, Rosalind noted. He clearly valued his own unique qualities. She had to admit, however, that his was a refreshingly candid attitude.

"Did Mrs. Levitton urge Cate to accept you?"

"She told me confidentially that she hoped Cate would. She wasn't going to insist on it, or threaten to cut her off, or any of that sort of nonsense. But she did hope. She has always taken an interest in me, you see. Maybe"—he glanced toward the door—"because she's never had a son of her own."

"And how did Everett feel about the match?" She had not yet met Cate's second brother, and she wondered which side of the family divide he stood on.

"It's hard to know what Everett feels about anything," said Mr. Davenport. "His goal in life is to smooth things over and make everybody happy. Unfortunately"—Mr. Davenport sighed—"he's not very good at it. Always seems to think a big, dramatic gesture will do the trick. Like the dinner the night before Cate ran off."

"Dinner?" echoed Rosalind.

"Oh, yes. Everett got Marianna's permission to borrow her dining room for a supper party—me, Cate, and 'a few friends.' But what he didn't tell anybody was that those few friends were Marcus and Wilhelmena. The idea was if we'd all sit down together—with Marianna, if she was strong enough—we could all talk through our differences."

"And it did not work?"

Mr. Davenport looked toward the ceiling for patience. "Utter disaster. Marcus refused to speak at all. Poor Wilhelmena tried to keep up the conversation, as did Everett. Cate seemed determined to give everyone a piece of her mind. When it was time for us fellows to settle down with the port, Marcus spent a good quarter of an hour abusing his brother for a fool. I thought it was going to come to blows."

"And Cate's mother?"

"Beatrice retreated early, pleaded a headache, I think."

Rosalind remembered Beatrice's despairing words about her children's natures, and found she could well understand that she might prefer solitude to watching yet another quarrel between them.

"But did Beatrice approve of your proposed marriage?"

"Oh, yes, she was all for it. Thought it would settle Cate down." He chuckled. "Usually what they say about the man, isn't it?"

It was. Mr. Davenport did not seem to need settling. But neither did he seem to have much depth to him. The way he talked, the smile on his face and in his eyes, they all left Rosalind feeling that she was missing something. Or that he was.

"Anyway," Mr. Davenport continued. "I've said more than I should, and not a lot of it to the point. What I meant to tell you was, if there's anything I can do to help, you've only to say the word. Beatrice knows where I can be found." He hesitated. "Unless there's anything I can do now, of course?"

Rosalind considered. "Can you tell me anything about the time before Cate left? Whether there was any change in her or in the family's attitude toward her? Or if she seemed preoccupied or anything of the kind?"

"Well, she was worried about old Mrs. Levitton, of course. We all were. And moving back to London wasn't the easiest thing for her either, I think. Having her mother in the house was worse."

Rosalind felt her brows arch. "Beatrice is living here?"

"Oh, yes. Came to help out, as they say. Came to get away from Marcus, I should imagine." His mouth puckered. "Beatrice had been staying with Marcus and his family since her husband died. That would be a bit over a year now. I'd imagine that would be plenty, and then some. Anyway, she's been trying to mend things between Mrs. Levitton and Cate, but it was slow going, even when Everett could resist shoving his oar in." This time, Rosalind felt there was a real bite in Mr. Davenport's words.

"And this was before Mrs. Levitton became ill?"

Mr. Davenport scratched his chin. "Happened about the same time, I think. Mrs. Levitton blamed some bad oysters initially, but the thing never seemed to clear up."

"Cate was ill, too, I believe?"

"Oh, no. Slightly bilious here and there, but never really sick. Not as long as I've known her."

Which argued for a strong constitution, and not one that could be destroyed by a single night out in the rain. But neither did it fit with the speculation about Marianna being slowly poisoned. If there was a poisoner, why would they disguise one attempt as lingering illness, but not the other?

"If I can ask one other thing, Mr. Davenport."

"Anything you like."

"Did you ever hear Cate complain about money?" Her hand wanted to stray to her sleeve, and the pawnbroker's receipts she had hidden there. She kept it still.

"Money?" echoed Mr. Davenport. "Good lord, no. Mrs. Marianna kept her well supplied. Instructed the tradespeople to send the bills to her, and all such. Said she couldn't bear it when a woman's companion was kept looking like a drudge and living like a nun, especially when they were family." He paused, taking in Rosalind's expression. "Again surprised?"

Rosalind found she was not, at least not about the money. The room around her said that Mrs. Levitton had decided to be generous with her niece. Cate may have been sent to her aunt in disgrace, but Mrs. Marianna had made sure she was comfortable and relatively free.

But if Mrs. Marianna was so generous, why was Cate visiting a pawnbroker?

And was that jewelry even hers to pawn?

CHAPTER 12

Leading Questions

"If some people had distinguished themselves a little less in the world . . . it would have been as well."

Edgeworth, Maria, *Belinda*

When Adam and Goutier reached the Bow Street Police Station, they parted ways. Goutier went immediately to the patrol room to meet with his men and the other captains. There, he would hear both the news and the business of the day. Adam made his way around the edges of the crowded, noisy lobby.

Most of the actual peacekeeping in the city was done by the militia units, as directed by the magistrates and Parliament. Murder and violent loss of life was the business of the coroner. Smuggling was the province of the customs offices and the river police. While Bow Street and its sister stations might bolster these other powers, they existed primarily to break up brawls, recover lost property, and find missing persons.

But this was London, and that meant there was more than

enough of all of these things to keep the lobby full and the officers and runners busy from dawn until dusk, and beyond. The clerk's job was to record any complaints and concerns brought to them, to direct people to the courts (or out the doors), and generally try to keep some order among the steady stream of human beings that came and went from the most famous station of London's fragmented fraternity of police offices.

Today, as on most mornings, Mr. Stafford, Bow Street's chief clerk, sat on his high stool helping bring order to the crowds that inevitably gathered in the lobby of the police station. But this was only a small part of his duties. He also recorded statements from witnesses and prisoners, managed the station's vast library of files and papers, and oversaw the transcription of records for the trials in the magistrate's court.

Stafford fit the ideal most people carried of a senior clerk— a pale, lean man with stooped shoulders and a crooked neck from years of leaning over books and papers. His cuffs were always clean, but his fingers were permanently stained with ink and dust. He ruled his junior clerks with a firm hand, insisting on sobriety, reliability, and discretion. At the same time, he did not make any demands of those under his supervision that he did not adhere to himself. In the days immediately following the Cato Street arrests, Stafford never seemed to leave the station. He was constantly busy taking statements from witnesses and prisoners, and making sure all the officers involved were carefully deposed. Adam had seen Mrs. Stafford more during those few days than he normally did in a year, as she kept coming by with hot meals for her husband.

When Stafford saw Adam standing at the edge of the milling crowd, he nodded, and signaled to one of his junior men to come take over his station.

"Mr. Harkness," said Stafford as he reached Adam, his

voice calm, but there was a certain tightness around the edges. "How can I help you?"

"I was hoping to see the witness statements from the Cato Street arrests."

Adam was unsurprised to see a hint of irritation in the man's eyes. Stafford guarded his papers like a dragon guarded his gold. But there was something else there, too—an unusual wariness. "To what end, if I may ask?"

"Several men escaped arrest that night," Adam replied. "They need to be found. Before the trial, if it can be done."

Stafford blinked. "Has Mr. Townsend approved this?"

This was a question that required a very careful answer. "Mr. Townsend has agreed that the men are a danger and should be found." Which was true. "I want to go through the statements again, get a list of whom we should still be on the lookout for, and see if there're any hints as to where they've gotten themselves to."

Adam expected Stafford to refer him to one of the junior clerks and be on his way. But the man in front of him shifted uneasily.

"In the ordinary way, I'd say of course," Stafford told him. "But as the trial is sure to be soon, many of the papers are with the magistrate. I couldn't possibly retrieve them without Mr. Birnie's permission."

"Well, I'll have a word with His Honor, then," said Adam. "But you do still have some?"

"Ye . . . es, a few officer statements and so on."

"Good. I'll have those."

Stafford plainly wanted to refuse. Adam felt an unfamiliar disquiet growing inside him.

"Mr. Harkness," Stafford said. "You have my deepest respect, you always have, but you seem to be under the misapprehension that this is some ordinary inquiry. It is not. These men committed treason. Extraordinary precaution must be taken for all aspects of this matter."

"These men are accused of attempting to commit trea-son," Adam corrected him. "And if that is proved true, it is vital that the facts of their attempt are fully understood, and that all the men involved are located and brought to heel."

Adam waited.

It was known that Stafford had other men under his con-trol beyond the clerks. There were only eight principal offi-cers to cover the whole of England. In order to do even a fragment of the work it was charged with, Bow Street made use of its own network of informants. Even thief-takers could be co-opted. Those persons had to be interviewed when they had information to give, and they had to be paid. That job also fell to Stafford.

Indeed, if George Edwards really was the spy that Sir Richard claimed, Stafford might well have been the one he contacted about the budding conspiracy at Cato Street.

Adam could simply ask Stafford if he knew Edwards, but he held his tongue. That wariness and tension in the clerk's expression told him he needed to know more before he asked direct questions. He did not like his access to information being determined by Stafford's judgment.

Normally, he would have gone to the prison and spoken to the accused men himself. In this case there was an additional impediment to that. As accused traitors, the Cato Street men were being held in the Tower of London. For all Adam could get to them, they might as well have been on the moon.

At last, Stafford sighed. "Very well, Mr. Harkness." The words, and the bow, were more exasperated than polite.

"Thank you, Mr. Stafford." Adam returned Stafford's bow and left him there to go join his fellow officers in the ward-room, at least the ones who were in town. A principal officer might be sent anywhere in England at any time. Just now, John Sayer was off in Penzance, and Daniel Bishop was up in Colchester.

The remaining six of them sat around the long table with strong mugs of tea. Mornings such as this were a relaxed and informal time. The men exchanged ideas and information, much of it sprinkled with rough humor and highly spiced observations.

Adam was finishing off his second mug of tea, and listening to Stephen Lavender talk about a housebreaking ring that was giving him particular trouble, when John Townsend swept into the room.

"A word, Mr. Harkness," Townsend said as he breezed past them all and headed straight for his private office.

Sam Tauton rolled his eyes. Adam took another quick swallow of tea and followed Townsend into his sanctuary.

Technically, John Townsend was simply another principal officer, which put him and Adam at the same level. But in truth, Townsend ran Bow Street. This office was full proof of that. It was the only private room in the station, and it was filled with Townsend's collections—clocks and snuff boxes, paintings and figurines, all from grateful patrons, many of them connected with the royal family. Townsend had personally overseen the security for the Prince of Wales before he ascended the throne, and even in winter, he constantly wore the broad-brimmed white hat the prince had given him.

Townsend settled behind his desk and laid a stack of folders and papers in front of him.

Adam closed the office door, and waited. Townsend leaned back in his chair and folded his hands over his considerable paunch.

"I just met Mr. Stafford in the hallway," said Townsend. "He represented to me that you had been asking for some of the records from the Cato Street arrests." He nodded at the stack of papers in front of him.

Adam said nothing. It was better to let Townsend talk.

Townsend cocked his head. "Mr. Harkness, would it surprise you if I admitted this Cato Street raid is a bad business?"

It would, truth be told, but Adam still said nothing.

"Oh, yes," Townsend went on. "A bad, uncomfortable business. These men . . . they're not provocateurs. Not serious ones at any rate," he added. "Ah, now we have that famous inscrutable face of yours. Yes. I admit it. I had hoped that at Cato Street we would be breaking the back of a dangerous and hardened gang of criminals. I was anticipating being able to report to His Majesty that we had swept away a great and terrible threat to the king's peace. Instead, what do we have?" He waved his hand over the papers in disgust and dismissal. "A botched arrest, and around a dozen ill-assorted vagabonds with a handful of pathetic weapons, and a dead officer. But!" He held up his index finger. "Just because they were not formidable, does not mean these men were not and are not dangerous. If they are allowed to roam free, then who is to say they won't try again? And what then? Another raid, another debacle, another dead officer? Or worse, they make use of those weapons, and we have dead innocents?"

"And if they were deluded into action by a provocateur?" asked Adam quietly.

"They permitted themselves to be deluded," said Townsend. "They could have walked away at any moment. They did not. They were not merely ripe to be used, Harkness, they were ready and eager to be used. And that is what the magistrates, and we ourselves, must consider."

"So, if there was a provocateur, he bears no blame in leading eleven men to their deaths?"

Townsend raised his brows in surprise. "Why should he?"

"Because they might not have acted but for him."

"*Might* not." Townsend leaned heavily on that word. "We do not deal in mights or maybes. We deal in plain facts. They did act. They have confessed."

"Not all of them."

"Enough of them. Harkness, if the law is harsh, it is still the law, and it is not our business to question it." He laid his hand over the files. "We are subjects of the Crown, Mr. Harkness. Our loyalty is proved by our obedience, and our firm faith that those whom the Almighty has placed over us know better than we ourselves can."

"Then it is our duty to find all the men responsible for the plot," said Adam. "If some are still out there, they could continue to prove useful to those who wish to cause more mischief. Surely it is our duty to eliminate what remains of the threat to the king's peace?"

Townsend looked him directly in the eye. "And that is what you intend?"

Adam met his gaze. "That is precisely what I intend."

"Then I wish you good hunting." Townsend lifted his hand off the papers. "Keep me informed what you find."

Adam picked up the files, and made very sure to remember to bow.

CHAPTER 13

A Private Consultation

*"—that may be a useful secret in my profession;
pray impart it to me."*

Edgeworth, Maria, *Belinda*

Mr. Stafford did not like clandestine meetings. Secrecy invited suspicion, and inspection. It was far better to do things out in the open, and keep to form and routine in all aspects of business.

Therefore, he had made it his habit to leave the station at precisely noon every day. After that, his routine varied. He might seek a luncheon at the Brown Bear public house. Or, he might run an errand for Mrs. Stafford. Or, if the weather was fine, he might take a brisk walk, possibly stopping at the post office or booksellers.

Every day, he would be back at his post by half past one. His junior clerks claimed they could set a clock by him.

Today, after a stretch of cold and rain, the weather had broken. Mr. Stafford left the station as the bells tolled noon and set out toward the booksellers. Mrs. Stafford had asked him to pick up the latest volume by Mrs. Gore, and he was happy to oblige.

On the way, he decided, as he often did, to pause for a drink at the Black Crow. The public house was a haunt of the city's army of government and bank clerks. Every profession needed a gathering place, and theirs was no exception.

"Now, then, Mr. Stafford," the landlord greeted him as he entered.

"Hullo, Mr. Phelps," Stafford returned. "A pint of the lager, if you would."

"Of course, sir."

Stafford took a seat in a back corner. The chatter and complaints flowed around him. The landlord arrived with his beer, and left with coins in his hand. Stafford drank, and waited.

A few minutes later, a man wearing the black coat that was the uniform of all those who made their living with a ledger and a pen walked in. The new man surveyed the room casually. Just as casually, he stopped at the bar to collect a mug of beer, and came over to Stafford's table.

If anyone cared to look, they might see that the man's face was unusually sun-bronzed and his shoulders were broader than was normal for a clerk. They might also note he wore his dark hair tied back in a sailor's queue. Perhaps they'd think he clerked in the naval office, if they thought of him at all, which they would not. There was nothing unusual in his presence here, any more than there was in Stafford's.

"Mr. Stafford," said the man. When he called himself anything, he was Jack Beachamp. This was probably not the name he had been born under, but he had never given Stafford a reason to care about that. "I trust you've no objection to my joining you?"

"None at all." Stafford gestured with his tankard to the other chair. Beachamp sat, taking off his round-crowned hat and hanging it on the peg on the wall at Stafford's back. He raised his tankard. "Your health, sir."

Stafford's lips twitched into a thin smile. They both drank.

"What have you learned?" Stafford asked quietly.

"This and that." Beachamp smiled brightly. Stafford was careful to keep his face expressionless, as he fished the wallet out of his breast pocket and laid it on the table between them. In the next eyeblink, it was gone. Even though he sat right in front of the man, Stafford had barely seen his hands move.

"Now then," said Mr. Stafford over the rim of his tankard. "What have you learned?"

The man smiled, dramatically sly and conspiratorial. Stafford suppressed a grimace.

"Your Sir Richard is a busy man," he said. "And he does keep some interesting company. Once he left Parliament yesterday, he made himself a tour of no less than four coffeehouses and chophouses up and down the city."

"Name them," said Stafford, pulling a small notebook and pencil out of his coat pocket. "Who did he meet with?"

Beachamp reeled off his list of names. Stafford jotted them down in his particular script—half shorthand, half personal code. He was aware that Beachamp watched him the entire time he talked.

". . . and then he finished up at the Cocoa Tree," Beachamp was saying. "Met with one more fellow. Seems that this committee for the defense of the Cato Street coves is getting up a reward."

"For what purpose?"

"For finding some fellow named Edwards. They think if they can lay hands on him, their friends sitting in the Tower will slip the noose."

Stafford snorted impatiently. "There's nothing Edwards can do for them."

"I don't know. Sir Richard seemed very intent on finding him."

"Sir Richard and his cronies are fools," Stafford snapped. "If they weren't, they wouldn't be wasting his time on a covey of dead men. Who did he meet at the Cocoa Tree? If you can't name them, describe them."

Beachamp eyed him for a long time. "Hatchet-faced fellow, yellow hair. Quiet bloke. Listened more than he talked."

"Beachamp, I advise you to think very carefully. Are you sure about this man?"

"Sure as I'm standing here," he proclaimed.

"And that's all?" Stafford prompted.

"That's all." Beachamp nodded.

Beachamp was lying. That was not the problem. The problem was that Sir Richard and his committee of radicals were serious about unearthing Edwards. That did not sit well with Stafford. Especially coming as it did on the heels of Adam Harkness requesting the records and statements from the prisoners and witnesses.

Stafford pictured Harkness's calm face as he talked. *Several men escaped arrest that night. They need to be found. Before the trial, if it can be done.*

Several men. They need to be found. The words repeated themselves in Stafford's mind.

Could he have meant they needed to be found in order to help kick holes in the government's case?

Because the man Beachamp just described as meeting with Sir Richard could easily have been Adam Harkness.

Stafford had watched Harkness since he had come to Bow Street from the highway patrol. He was scrupulously honest and had a first-rate mind. His association with the unusual Miss Rosalind Thorne caused a bit of a stir, but Stafford was no moralist. What did concern him was that Harkness also made no secret of his sensibilities. He had in fact come within a hair's breadth of being sacked because he would not, or could not, understand that order and stability should be Bow Street's primary considerations, over and above the letter of the law.

Harkness had an expensive lady love. Harkness had radical sympathies. Harkness had arrived at the station this morning, looking like a man who had stayed out too late.

Beachamp was lying to him about Sir Richard's last meeting. He knew who this "hatchet-faced" man was.

Perhaps I am jumping to conclusions. Perhaps all these things were entirely unrelated.

But then again, perhaps not.

Stafford tucked his book away, finished his beer, and got to his feet. He tossed an extra coin to the landlord to cover the cost of the other man's beer, and turned his steps back toward Bow Street.

Mrs. Stafford would have to wait for her book. He had work to do.

CHAPTER 14

An Introduction to the Peacemaker

"He could be all things to all men—and all women."

Edgeworth, Maria, *Belinda*

Rosalind finished her search of Cate's room without turning up anything else remarkable. After some consideration, she removed the pawnbroker's receipts from her sleeve and tucked them into her reticule. She might show them to Cate and ask her about them, or, if the girl proved uncommunicative, she could send Sanderson Faulks to make inquiries after the pledged items.

Hopefully, however, Amelia and Alice would help Cate trust that she was among friends, and the young woman would be willing to tell her story.

Rosalind found herself feeling unusually awkward. It was seldom she was left alone in a house where her position was so ambiguous. She rang the bell and inquired of the maid where she might find Mrs. Beatrice Levitton. Beatrice, it seemed, was in the first-floor drawing room and had let it be known that she hoped Miss Thorne would come speak with her there.

However, when Rosalind entered the airy and pleasant room, Beatrice was not alone. A brown-haired man sat with her, holding her hand. The man rose as Rosalind stepped forward.

"Miss Thorne," said Beatrice. "Everett, this is Miss Rosalind Thorne. Miss Thorne, my youngest son, Everett."

After everything Mr. Davenport had told her, Rosalind found herself observing Everett Levitton with a great deal of curiosity. Everett took after his mother in looks. They had the same open face and wide-set eyes. His hair was a middling brown, worn just long enough to brush his shirt collar. He cultivated a healthy pair of sideburns. Like his mother, he had an anxious air. But where she was worn to the bone, he was full of energy, all of it tightly but imperfectly reined in.

He bowed politely to Rosalind, who made her curtsy in answer.

"Miss Thorne is here at your aunt's request." Beatrice motioned Rosalind to a tapestry-backed chair. "She may be able to help find Cate."

"Really?" Everett looked again at Rosalind, as if he could not believe such a statement. "Well, that would be a relief, I must say. I've been out scouring the streets and racking my brains as to where she could have gone, but I've come up a complete blank."

"Have you seen your sister since she returned to town?"

"Well, not until recently." Everett resumed his place at his mother's side. "I did see her once or twice after Mama came to look after Aunt Marianna, and I was there when she let us know Davenport had declared his intentions. That's what's all so surprising about this!" he burst out. "It seemed like things were all coming back together."

"Mr. Davenport seems to be a great friend of the family," Rosalind remarked.

"Oh, yes," began Everett, but then he seemed to think the better of it. "Well, he's a friend of mine. Marcus is hard to make friends with," he added with an uneasy laugh. "He's a good man, don't mistake me, but he's very private, very reserved. People sometimes mistake that for pride. It can take a good deal of time to get to know him."

"But you tried to make a bridge between them, did you not? I understand you arranged a dinner for Cate, Harold, and Marcus and his wife."

"Yes, well." Everett's eyes cut sideways to his mother. Beatrice's shoulders sagged, as if she could not bear the weight of any more failure. "It seemed like a good idea. Get everyone to the table and talk, you know? Unfortunately, Marcus and Cate are both very stubborn people. Harold did his best. Wilhelmena too, but . . ." He just shook his head. "Over the port, Marcus made it very plain he did not appreciate my efforts."

Which was a much milder description than Harold had given her. *I thought it was going to come to blows.*

While the men were at their port, Wilhelmena and Cate would have been drinking tea in the sitting room. Rosalind itched to know how that conversation had gone.

"I should have stayed," said Beatrice. "I should not have left. I knew Cate was upset. I *knew* she would not talk sensibly with Marcus. I should not—"

Everett cut his mother off. "How do you plan to go about tracing Cate? She hasn't exactly left a note. Or has she? We looked everywhere we could think of."

"From the description I've had of Miss Levitton's last few days at home, I think she decided to run away for reasons of her own." Rosalind spoke calmly, hoping her words would, in some measure, give Beatrice some reassurance. "I do not believe she eloped, or was otherwise pressured or persuaded, as girls can sometimes be. If she is not with London friends, she has most likely returned to Bath."

Everett's eyes lit up. "I hadn't thought of it that way, but yes, you're sure to be right. Don't you think, Mama?"

"I certainly hope so," murmured Beatrice.

"You'll surely want to be off at once," said Everett. "What can I do to help? Can I drive you somewhere?"

"Not at present," said Rosalind. "I had hoped for a few more minutes . . ."

He smiled, and did not wait for her to finish. "And I'm in the way, am I? Story of my life. Ask anyone. Especially Marcus." He winked. "Is Davenport about?" he asked his mother. "I'll just go have a word. See if I can shake loose anything he might remember. And hear how Aunt Marianna does, of course. Poor old thing. Strong as an ox usually." He shook his head, his clear eyes clouding over in sympathy, but only for a moment. Then, he kissed his mother's cheek and bowed toward Rosalind and strode for the door.

Beatrice smiled fondly after him before turning back to Rosalind.

"I must apologize for Everett," she said. "Gravity does not come naturally to him. Much to his brother's despair," she added.

"It must be difficult to have two sons with such naturally different dispositions."

Beatrice winced. "Marcus could never learn to appreciate Everett's temperament. Neither could his father." Her gaze was distant, remembering something, and her fingers knotted in the black skirt of her mourning dress. "My husband was a stern man, Miss Thorne. Marcus took his example very much to heart. When it was determined that Cate must be sent away, he took his father's side."

"And Everett?" asked Rosalind.

"He urged Catherine to apologize, and to explain that she had been coerced. When she would not, he went to Marcus and my husband himself and told them what had really happened."

"What really happened?" echoed Rosalind.

"Amelia McGowan corrupted my daughter, Miss Thorne,"

said Beatrice bitterly. "She found the weakness in Cate's nature and took shameless advantage."

Rosalind bit her tongue. "And Everett told her father and Marcus this?"

"He urged them to talk to Catherine, and to remember she was only a girl, really." She paused. "He was always like that, ever since he was a boy. Always trying to make peace, to get everyone to get along and not fight."

Rosalind wondered if Beatrice realized how much this revealed about her uneasy family life. "Did Catherine also say she was coerced?"

"She did, in the end, at least. And I am glad she did, because it was only that that kept my husband from ordering her from the house immediately."

Beatrice spoke these last words in a whisper. Rosalind got the impression that she could not have lifted her voice then, even if she had tried.

"I am sure my husband's heart would have softened, but he was not granted the time," Beatrice went on. Rosalind could not tell whether she believed this, or whether it was simply pious hope. "After the funeral, I thought Marcus would be ready to make some gesture of reconciliation, but he seems to have taken Cate's exile as a deathbed wish from their father." Beatrice glanced away, her face strained.

"If I may ask, how did you view her engagement to Mr. Davenport?"

Beatrice looked surprised. "I was delighted for her, of course. It is true his origins are not all that might be wished, but Mr. Davenport is a solid man. He is sensible but not grim, and he is also a man of the world without too many . . . romantic notions about women, if you understand what I mean."

Rosalind thought that she did. Beatrice meant that Mr. Davenport did not expect a pure and perfect wife without a past, ideas, or opinions of her own.

"And that he has Marianna's trust, is, of course priceless,"

Beatrice went on. "Indeed, I have wondered if there might have been some matchmaking going on there, but of course I could not ask."

"Of course not," agreed Rosalind. A question occurred to her. Guilt wrestled briefly with curiosity, and it was curiosity that won. "Mrs. Levitton, may I ask—where do you think Cate has gone?"

Beatrice sighed, and for a moment, Rosalind thought she would begin to weep. "I don't know. I haven't really been near her for nearly three years. She'd grown so independent. . . . When I came to stay, when Marianna became ill, she was very quiet and kept her distance. She was polite to me, but I could not convince her I was genuinely interested in reconciliation. I tried to be patient. After all, she had reason to be disappointed in me." Beatrice paused, obviously debating whether to say what was truly in her thoughts. "What I'm most afraid of is that the girl's returned."

"The girl?"

"Amelia McGowan. She may have returned and kidnapped her, or convinced poor Cate to run away with her."

Rosalind concentrated on keeping her mouth firmly shut.

"This is why we need you, you see." Beatrice clasped her hands on her lap. "We could never raise such a possibility with a Bow Street man. I cannot even convince Marcus to consider it. That's what's behind his anger, Miss Thorne. He wants to find Cate, but he's afraid that the search might bring her shame to public notice. Everyone knows that those Bow Street men take bribes from newspaper writers to gossip about respectable families."

"I certainly know that is widely rumored," said Rosalind. "Like most rumors, I believe, it contains some truth and a great deal of exaggeration."

"I daresay," murmured Beatrice. "But it is not a risk I can take. Not with . . ." She paused. "Mr. Davenport does not know why Catherine was really sent to her aunt. If he finds out, he may cry off."

Rosalind did not reply. Mr. Davenport did know, at least, he thought he did. He'd never actually given her any details about what exactly Cate had told him, and it had become painfully clear that Cate was not above lying to save herself.

"If Cate can be persuaded to return," Beatrice was saying. "If she, if *we*, can say the whole incident was nothing more than a girl's nerves, or even a delicacy of feeling since she was still not fully reconciled with her brother—" Beatrice let her sentence trail off hopefully. She also glanced at the door. Then, she tucked two fingers into her sleeve and brought out a paper.

"I have this." Beatrice handed the paper to Rosalind. "It's the name of the agency through which we hired McGowan. They may have heard from her."

"Yes, of course. Thank you," murmured Rosalind. She opened the note, and read, and then tucked it inside her own sleeve. "I shall certainly add it to my inquiries. In the meantime, I found a number of letters in Cate's room. This seems to show that Cate does have some acquaintance of her own in town. It might help if you were to write and ask after her."

Beatrice looked at her blankly for a moment. "Oh. No. I couldn't. There might be talk. Marcus . . ."

Rosalind looked at her, quietly and steadily. Beatrice's words died away. She rubbed her brow. "You must think me very stupid."

"I think you are very distressed, and that you have been estranged from your daughter for a long time." Rosalind also thought that Beatrice was a very conventional woman who found herself dropped into a situation that she was unprepared to deal with. Most women were not encouraged to consider their own private lives, let alone those of their children.

Indeed, Beatrice was already blushing, and clearly wishing to hide it. "Yes. Well. If it will help us find her, I will do as you suggest."

"I believe it will help," said Rosalind. It would ease the helplessness that so clearly threatened to overwhelm Beatrice. And it might produce some detail or confidence that would help her understand what had led Cate to run away.

Or whether she might have tried to poison her benefactress. Or herself.

"Well." Beatrice was attempting to sound brisk, but the truth was, her tone seemed more than a little desperate. "I must not keep you any longer. How did you come?"

"By cab," answered Rosalind.

"I know my mother-in-law will not object to your using her carriage to return." She reached for the bell.

"Thank you," said Rosalind. "But that will not be necessary. I have several calls to make in the neighborhood."

"Oh." Beatrice plainly wanted to ask where and what for, but etiquette forbid. A fact that Rosalind had been counting on. "Very well. Thank you very much for your time and—" She hesitated again. "If . . . if you do speak with Catherine before I do, please tell her that I miss her. That I am sorry . . . that I love her and I ask only to know that she is safe and well."

Rosalind touched Beatrice's hand. "I will. I promise you that. I will call again soon if I may?"

"Thank you," said Beatrice. "That would be greatly appreciated."

A few minutes later, Rosalind stepped out into the afternoon sunshine. The street was beginning to fill with evening traffic, carriages returning home in time for their occupants to change before emerging again to go to dinner, or the theater. A nurse in neat gray pushed her pram on the far side of the street.

The day remained fine, if slightly cool. Rosalind found herself sighing with relief. Despite what she'd told Beatrice, she did not really have any calls nearby. She simply wanted some time out of doors, to walk and to think about all that she had learned. Including about the pawnbroker's receipts that she'd found hidden in Cate's room.

What was clear was that the Levitton family's resentments did not begin or end with Cate's relationship with a member of the household staff. If what Mr. Davenport had told her was true, questions of money, and of pride, haunted the family.

In truth, Rosalind found herself wondering if the chance to strike back at Marcus was what spurred Cate into accepting Mr. Davenport. With the marriage, Cate would gain the fortune Marcus felt was rightfully his. If that was the case, she might have come to regret a decision made in haste, and anger.

Under normal circumstances, that would have been reason enough for a young woman to run away. These, however, were not normal circumstances. Mrs. Levitton might be being slowly poisoned. That cold and dangerous fact changed everything.

But Rosalind could not know if it was fact. Not yet. Not unless Mrs. Hepplewhite agreed to help her. And there was no way of knowing if she would, at least, not yet.

And if she does refuse? Rosalind asked herself. *Then I will simply have to find another way. If there's time,* she added, and that thought put a hitch in her breathing.

And even if Mrs. Hepplewhite did agree, it would not explain what happened to Cate. Not why she'd decided to run away, nor why she had become so suddenly and violently ill the night she did leave. Was she also poisoned? If so, when and how? It could not be by the same means as Mrs. Levitton. She was dying slowly. Cate had gone from being healthy enough to argue with her family at dinner to collapsing in the street in a matter of hours.

This whole matter left Rosalind uneasy in a way that her

work seldom did. She did not like the feeling that she did not know whom she had taken into her house, or what trouble the girl had brought with her. She might have been tempted to simply let Beatrice take Cate home.

But she was not alone in this. Amelia, and Alice, needed answers, for their own peace of mind, and for peace between them.

Rosalind was not prepared to let them down.

Mrs. Hepplewhite was adjusting the curtains in the sick-room when she saw Miss Thorne leave the house, turn her face toward the high street, and set off at a brisk pace.

She turned and contemplated her patient. Mrs. Levitton lay in a nest of quilts and pillows, as pale and still as if she had already died. It was only the faint, ragged wheeze of her breath that gave her away.

Mrs. Hepplewhite did not approve of drama. It was the first thing she banished from any sickroom where she was given charge. Cleanliness. Fresh air. Plain food. Plain speaking. That was what a patient required. It was harmful to indulge a patient's imaginings. It was doubly harmful to indulge the fancies of nervous relatives.

Mrs. Hepplewhite did not deny Miss Thorne was an extraordinary person. She could see through a brick wall, as the saying went. The last time Mrs. Hepplewhite had met her, she'd been looking into some letters that had gone missing from Mrs. Cantwell, who happened to be in Mrs. Hepplewhite's charge. The woman had been fretting so about them that she could not rest. For two days, Miss Thorne had been a quiet, orderly presence in the house. By the third day, she found the source of the problem. Mrs. Hepplewhite never knew exactly what it was, but the change in Mrs. Cantwell was undeniable. The source of the drama was thus removed, and with it went the last of the contagion.

But now? With this talk of poison? It was outrageous that Miss Thorne should even suggest such a thing. It was not to be taken seriously. Such matters were not what one found in a respectable house, among respectable people.

And yet . . . Mrs. Hepplewhite frowned at her patient, wishing her skin was less translucent, and that she had been able to keep more food down today. She wished for any number of things that were simply not the case.

Mrs. Hepplewhite strode out into the private sitting room and sat at the table that had been put aside for her use. She wrote a brief note, folded and sealed it. Then, after checking to make certain her patient was still asleep, she descended the backstairs to find the kitchen boy, exactly where he usually was—asleep on an overturned bucket in the scullery.

"On your feet, Jimmy," she said. The boy, to his young credit, jumped up, rubbing his eyes with the back of one hand.

"Yes, ma'am?" He yawned.

"I need you to take this around to Mr. Twining, quick as you can. Bring what he gives you straight up to me." She gave the boy a coin, and then she added another. "If anyone asks, you are to say I sent you to the apothecary."

"But why—"

Mrs. Hepplewhite pressed her index finger against the boy's lips. "Ask me no questions, I'll tell you no lies. Off with you."

Jimmy looked at the shillings in his fist, tugged his forelock, and ran out the back door, quick as a scalded cat. Mrs. Hepplewhite watched him go.

Drama was antithetical to healing. However, sometimes, when a case reached a crisis, extraordinary measures became necessary.

Mrs. Hepplewhite smoothed her apron and returned to her duties.

CHAPTER 15

Doubtful Companions

*"I think her friendship more to be dreaded than
her enmity."*

Edgeworth, Maria, *Belinda*

Well, that's torn it.

Fran Finch watched as Miss Thorne exited the Levitton house and walked briskly from the square. She found she needed to resist a childish urge to stick her tongue out at the woman's retreating back. Instead, she jiggled the pram that held the porcelain baby doll all tucked up under its blanket. She'd been walking back and forth in her nurse's getup for three solid hours. She hadn't dared do anything else while Rosalind Thorne remained in the house. Thankfully, her contact inside had felt the same.

But now, as Fran watched, a parlor maid in a gray cloak and ruffled bonnet hurried up the Levittons' area stairs and scuttled toward the tiny green space at the center of the square.

Idiot, thought Fran as she calmly wheeled her pram about. *Going to draw attention to herself running out like a scared rabbit.*

The little park was provided with an ornamental fountain with a broad ledge. The parlor maid sat down, apparently getting ready to enjoy the rare bit of sunshine. Fran pushed the pram up to her.

"Hullo," said Fran cheerfully. "Do you mind if we share your spot?" She jiggled the pram gently as if soothing a baby.

"Not a bit." The maid slid sideways, just a little.

Fran sat down. She also checked on the doll, in case anyone was watching from any of the houses. The square around them remained quiet. No one was working on the stoops, and no one was lingering about on the cobbles.

"What can you tell me?" she murmured to the maid, whose name was Talmidge.

"About what?" asked Talmidge.

Fran resisted the urge to sigh, or pinch the little idiot. "That Miss Thorne for starters."

The girl shrugged. "Not much. Came in asking for the old lady. Was almost turned away at the door. Mrs. Beatrice stopped her, though. Seems to think she can help find where Miss Cate's got herself to. Seems the old lady agrees."

"Miss Thorne saw the old lady?" Fran struggled to keep the worry out of her voice.

"Old lady insisted on it," said Talmidge. "Let her look through the girl's rooms and all. Mr. Davenport talked with her, too, and Mr. Everett, an' Mrs. Beatrice was with her for nearly half an hour afterward."

Considering that Miss Thorne knew exactly where Cate Levitton was, that was all very strange. *Or maybe not.* Miss Thorne might well be looking to see just how much money she could wrestle out of the family.

That she'd got into Cate's rooms was a worry. No telling what that fool girl left lying about.

"How's the old lady doing?" asked Fran.

Talmidge shrugged. "Who knows? It don't look good, you ask me, but that nurse they've got up with her, she's a tight-lipped thing. Says it's in God's hands. Which don't sound all that hopeful, does it?"

"No, it does not," agreed Fran. She reached into her buttoned apron pocket, pulled out a coin, and laid it on the fountain ledge for Talmidge to pick up. "Thanks, Tally."

"Ta, Fran." And just like that, the coin was gone and Talmidge was on her feet and on her way.

Fran stayed where she was until Tally was safe back in the house. Then she got up herself and started walking, pushing her pram and thinking furiously all the while.

It certainly looked as if Miss Thorne had considered all the angles when she snatched little Cate off the street. The question was, how much had she convinced Cate to tell her about Fran and their business?

Is Cate stupid enough to spill her guts?

Yes, Fran decided, she was. Especially if she was given tea and sympathy by a plausible, genteel lady with a reputation for helping little, rich things in trouble. Cate had always made a habit of crying on other people's shoulders.

This thought left Fran disquieted, and more than a little angry. She needed to get herself home. She had to think, and to plan, before Cate and her new friends were able to make any real trouble.

London was a patchwork place. Fine neighborhoods existed cheek-by-jowl with sprawling marketplaces and the anonymous mazes of slums and rookeries. Fran made it her business to know all the alleys and mews that ran alongside any house she picked as her target, including old lady Levitton's.

Within minutes, Fran had left behind the quiet square and entered the bustle, noise, and stink of the open market. Along the way, she'd tossed her apron and cap into the pram and covered them, and the doll, with the blanket. Now she just looked like a harassed mother hurrying home. No different from the hundred others shouldering their way between the stalls. On impulse, and because being suspicious and annoyed tended to make her hungry, she stopped at the cookshop and bought a couple of pies. She had no idea when Jack would be home tonight. If he was late, she'd leave his out for him. She could get a jug of cider as well and . . .

"Hullo, Franny," drawled a familiar voice in her ear.

Don't look frightened, Fran told herself as she turned.

"Hullo, Jenny." Fran pasted a friendly smile on her face. "How's things?"

Jenny Cranston was a slim girl with dull yellow hair and blue eyes as sharp as bottle shards. Her plain dress had grimy hems and threadbare sleeves. Anyone who saw her would look right past her, unless perhaps they happened to notice her slender hands with their long, slim fingers. They were an arresting feature on an otherwise entirely unremarkable girl.

They also were stunningly good with window latches. Jenny Cee, as she was known around the alleys, could scale a wall like a spider and get into windows on the second and third stories that the family would swear had been locked up tighter than the Bank of England.

"Saw you was coming from the squares." Jenny folded her arms and lounged against the wall. "Any good pickings there?"

Fran cursed herself several times over. Nobody should have been able to follow her, especially not Jenny Cee. But she'd been too busy with her own thoughts and not paying proper attention.

She kept all this out of her face, and just shrugged. "Maybe. Had a word with a girl I know. There's a house belongs to a sick old lady. Might be there's a few bits and bobs there that no one'd miss."

The idea of those "bits and bobs" caused a greedy leer to

spread across Jenny's grubby face. "And of course, you wouldn't think of making a try without your friends, now would you?"

Fran looked Jenny straight in the eyes. "Never in life."

"That's good. Only some of the girls was wondering, seeing as you still owe us all from the last job."

And there it was. The real trouble Cate caused with her little midnight flit. Fran felt her teeth begin to grind.

"Listen, Jenny," she said. "It's been a long day. I was just heading over to Madam Geneva's. What would you say to a quick nip o' gin, just to cheer the heart, eh?"

Jenny's eyes lit up at the mention of gin, as Fran knew they would. "All right then." She pushed herself away from the wall. "No harm in a little nip."

Madam Geneva's wasn't even a proper shop—just a window in the back of a house that looked onto a courtyard surrounded by three- and four-story tenement buildings. Fran dropped a few pennies in "Madam" G's greasy fist and in return got a jug of gin, another of water, and two crockery mugs that might have been clean once upon a time.

Jenny'd kicked a couple of urchins off a bench made from two barrels and a board. Fran put down the bottle and jug between them. Fran filled Jenny's mug first, so the girl was drinking, and not paying attention to see that Fran poured only a drop of the stuff into her own cup before topping it off with plenty of water.

"Ah! That's better." Jenny slapped her empty mug down. "Will say this for you, Franny, you always had an open hand."

"Well, where would any of us be without our friends?" Fran poured Jenny out another healthy measure of gin.

Jenny downed this, too. When she finished, her cheeks were flushed red. "That's what we don't understand, me and the girls. Why would you hold out on us? Now me"—she tapped her chest—"I stood up for you. We can trust Franny, I said. Depend on it. Something's gone wrong, but Franny will put it to rights. You just watch."

"And what did the girls say to that?"

"They wanted to know when." She leaned forward. "No offense, Fran, eh? You know how it is. Times is hard for everybody. And the girls ain't asking for nothin' they ain't earned."

"I know it." Which was the worst part. "And if you'd just tell me who it is talking that way, I'd explain it to them myself. No need for you to get in the middle."

But Jenny wasn't falling for this line. "Ah, now, no need for you to bother yourself." She grinned, showing all her crooked teeth. "You just tell me when the girls can expect their share, and I'll let 'em all know, an' that'll be that."

Which meant the girls didn't want her to know which of them had been grumbling. They still feared her, and still felt like they needed her. That was a good sign.

But if they'd sent Jenny to start making threats, it meant their patience wasn't going to stretch much farther.

"Well, there's the problem, Jenny," Fran said. "I can't say for sure when I'll get the cash. The runners have been sniffing around the shop. We've had to lay low for a bit."

"That is a problem." Jenny pushed her mug forward for Fran to refill. "But what say you put up a little something, eh? On account, like? I can take that back to the girls and let 'em know what you told me." Her eyes turned dark, and dangerously clear despite the amount of gin she'd just drunk. "I'd hate to have to tell 'em you were holding out, or maybe that you and that fancy man of yours were thinking about getting yourselves out of town before you pays what you owes." She grinned again. This time the look reminded Fran of one of the stray dogs that wandered the rookeries—the ones that had gotten hungry enough to be dangerous.

"As if I'd ever do a runner on me girls," said Fran. "You

know you can trust me." She held up the jug. "We can drink to it."

Not two hours later, Jenny had keeled right over onto the cobbles. Fran collected the empty crockery and took it all back to the window. She tossed Madame G an extra penny. "Let her sleep, will you?" The old lady grunted and Fran grabbed her pram and dragged it out of the yard behind her.

What a bloody mess!

If Cate Levitton wasn't dead already, Fran might just finish the girl off. But she couldn't admit to Jenny she'd been robbed. Certainly not by milk-faced, high-toned Cate. There wasn't one of the girls would ever go along with her on a job again if they learned she'd been played for a prat by a schoolgirl.

But it had happened, and now that schoolgirl was in the hands of Rosalind Thorne, who looked all set to try to make off with the money that rightly belonged to Fran, and the girls. But mostly to Fran.

Well, let her try. Fran would see that everything wound up exactly where it belonged.

CHAPTER 16

A Family Portrait

"[She] was a great dabbler in politics; for she was almost as fond of power as of money . . ."

Edgeworth, Maria, *Belinda*

The temptation to return home immediately was strong. Rosalind wanted to sit with Cate, to speak to her plainly and hear what replies she had to make. The pawnshop receipts in her reticule invited a dozen different questions.

But so did the Levittons themselves. Rosalind had not had time to learn anything about them before she entered into this business. She must make up for it now. Fortunately, she knew where to begin. She would call on Honoria Aimesworth.

Strictly speaking, it was too late in the afternoon for paying calls. Thankfully Rosalind and Honoria were on such terms as to make it easy to set such formality aside. They were not precisely friends, but they were also more than simple acquaintances. Honoria's brother had died under unfortunate circumstances, and Rosalind had helped discover the person responsible. Honoria, in turn, became one of Rosalind's most reliable conduits for news and gossip among the *haut ton* because she did not care whom she might offend by speaking the truth.

When Honoria's footman answered the door, he recognized Rosalind, greeted her by name, and asked her to step up into a rather imposing sitting room hung with burgundy silk. Honoria herself arrived a few minutes later.

"Well, Rosalind," she said. "And here I was thinking we were to have a dull evening. Tea, if you would, Robinson," she added to the footman.

"How are you, Honoria?" Rosalind asked as they settled themselves. "How is your father?"

"Burrowing away with his blueprints," said Honoria with an air of weary patience. "He wants to build an observatory."

Honoria's father was a keen amateur architect. Unfortunately, he possessed far more ambition than skill. Since the loss of his son, his plans had become grander, but his abilities had decreased, partly due to the fact that he sought solace for his grief in a bottle of brandy.

"And how is Alice?" Honoria asked Rosalind. "I hear she's written a novel. Should I be concerned?"

Rosalind smiled. "Alice admires you. There's nothing in the book that will cause you an instant's worry."

Honoria's smile indicated she intended to withhold judgment. "Well, you may tell her that I shall reserve my copy at the bookseller immediately, and inform my acquaintance they should do the same."

The tea arrived, and they both busied themselves with the minutia of cups being fixed and slices of cheese-and-onion tart being cut.

At last, Honoria leaned back and regarded Rosalind. "It seems that Alice is not the only one making a name for herself. Frankly, I would not have expected it of you."

"It was not my decision."

"I'd dispute that, but I'm tired. I spent the entire morning closeted with father's solicitors. So, tell me, to what do I owe the honor of this visit?"

Rosalind set her own cup down. "Honoria, do you know Mrs. Marianna Levitton?"

Honoria's brows arched. "Marianna? You've crossed her path, have you? Whatever for?"

"I can't say. But you do know her?"

"We've found ourselves in the same circles on occasion," Honoria admitted.

"Political circles?"

"Here and there, but other interests as well. She's a business-woman, you know, and I find I aspire to be."

"I had heard something of that." It was in fact part of the reason Rosalind had chosen Honoria to speak with.

"Yes. Despite all attempts on the part of the men of the United Kingdom, there are a number of ways that a woman with a competence can expand her fortune, quite beyond marriage or the stock exchange. Mrs. Levitton, for example, owns interests in a brewery, a bakery, and a carting concern, not to mention several livery stables."

"There's a mining concern as well, I believe," said Rosalind.

"When she finds the time to sleep, I have no idea." There was the warmth of admiration under Honoria's words. "But there are more women like her about than one might think. Certainly more than we were allowed to know about when we were girls."

"And you're following her example?"

"Which is also yours, although I think you won't care for my mentioning it."

It was a mild rebuke, but it still stung. "I was never as comfortable with defiance as you, Honoria."

"Very true," she agreed easily. "And yet here we both are."

"So it would seem."

"And while I've no notion of your plans, I do not see myself marrying, and father's money won't last forever, especially if I want to maintain this house and keep my mother at bay. So, something must be done. I'm looking at investing in a print shop," she said. "London will always need its broadsheets and handbills, and a woman may purchase an interest in a business with much less trouble than she may purchase a piece of land."

Rosalind nodded. The rules of land purchase were much more formalized than the process of investment. Those rules frequently turned into barriers where a woman was concerned.

"I understand Marianna is, or was, the late Mr. Levitton's second wife," said Rosalind.

"Yes. She captivated him when he was on holiday in Bath, or so the story goes. He was there to take the waters and bury his grief, or escape his creditors, depending on whom you listen to. She was a bright star that beckoned to him, or some such nonsense. Of course, it may have simply been her money that beckoned."

"She had her own money?"

Honoria nodded. "A family inheritance, and she'd already been dabbling in business."

"I hadn't realized. I thought she'd just taken over her husband's mines after the marriage."

"She did that, too. I've heard, in fact, that it was the mines she married him for. She wanted scope for her talents, and he provided her the opportunity."

"How did her husband die?" asked Rosalind.

Honoria's brows arched. "A very interesting question, coming from you. However, it was entirely unexceptional. A pair of drunken idiots driving hell-for-leather down a narrow road caused his carriage to overturn. His neck was broken, and he died on the spot."

Rosalind was silent for a moment, acknowledging the tragedy. "He seems to have left her much of the estate."

"He left her the whole of the estate. There was no non-sense of entails or any of that, so he could do with it as he pleased. Froze the rest of the family out entirely. It is my understanding the eldest nephew was a bare inch from taking the matter to court, on the grounds that he was the nearest male relative and as such he should be allowed to oversee the family affairs."

Marcus, thought Rosalind. "What stopped him?"

"The younger nephew, as it turns out. Everett Levitton pointed out that it would make the entire clan look ridiculous, especially as there was not a leg to stand on, other than Marcus Levitton's masculinity. Even in these times, it seems that was not an entirely reliable argument. Especially as Marianna could afford a whole host of very clever attorneys."

"What about their mother, Beatrice?"

Honoria shook her head. "Unflaggingly conventional. Marianna's brother was a stern and upright man, and he sought a pretty woman who could be counted on to make no stir at all. He died just a bit over a year ago, and is survived by Marcus and Everett and that daughter no one wants to talk about. I've never met any of them," she added. "It is very safe to say we do not move in the same circles."

"Is Marianna still involved with the radicals?"

"One of their most popular hostesses," said Honoria. "She pushes them to try to secure the vote for female small holders as well as male."

"Goodness," Rosalind murmured. The broadening of male suffrage was a subject of arguments in Commons, and the motive behind the popular uprising at Peterloo. But hardly anyone was so radical as to call openly for the franchise to extend to women.

"Yes. Goodness," said Honoria dryly. "So many of us say we should be running things, but so few of us actually go out and do something about it. But Marianna has a great deal of nerve."

"What else has she?"

Honoria considered. "She's very stubborn, as you may imagine. She's very sure she's correct in nearly all circumstances, and also that those who do not agree with her must be shown that they are wrong."

Rosalind thought of Marcus and his stern demeanor and personal certainty. No wonder he and his aunt did not get along.

"What of the rest of the family?"

Honoria sighed. "I do hope you're planning to tell me what this is about one day."

"As soon as I can, I promise."

"I'll hold you to it. Also, you owe me a dinner. I have a couple of bankers I need to impress, and their wives were all a-twitter when they found out I knew you."

"Oh, dear."

Honoria smiled. "The price of your success," she said airily. Then, she paused, started. "Good gracious, Rosalind. Are you *blushing*?"

Rosalind's hand flew to her cheek. It felt distinctly warm.

Honoria laughed. "Heavens! What is the world coming to when I can draw a blush from Rosalind Thorne?"

Honoria's words only deepened the warmth on Rosalind's cheeks. "I do apologize."

Honoria sobered. "No, I do. You know how I am, Rosalind, all sharp corners and disdain. But what's the matter? Surely you want to be a success?"

"Yes, yes. I'm simply being ridiculous."

"In what way?"

Rosalind frowned. She rarely spoke of her uneasiness with the changes she had initiated in her life, and yet she would still lie awake at night.

"There's a much larger world beyond the ball rooms and the drawing rooms that I was raised to," she said slowly.

"And the more I see of it, the more I want to run back inside that other world, shut the door, and draw the curtains."

Honoria waved this away. "You'd stifle inside of a week."

"I'm not so certain."

"You would. Besides, it's too late. You can't go back any more than I can. Or Alice can. Surely she's pointed this out."

"On more than one occasion," Rosalind admitted. "And she's right. So are you." She frowned at the tea things. "I don't even know why I'd want to go back to the girl I used to be, but the feelings won't leave me."

"You can miss a life that never came to pass, you know. And it always looks simpler."

"I believed myself to be more practical than that."

"You are. The proof is that against all temptations and expectations, you did *not* stay in the drawing room with the drapes closed."

"I suppose." Rosalind took a swallow of her cooling tea, and set the cup back down.

"In any case," said Honoria, "I do hope this unexpected timidity will not keep you from my dinner party. You're in fashion this year, and as I said, I need these bankers in good humor toward me."

"For your print shop?"

"And one or two other things I've in mind."

"I wish you luck."

"Wish me a good enough cook to impress these men."

"I may know of someone who could help there."

Honoria's eyes lit up. "If you can find me a French chef, all is forgiven and I will tell you anything you wish to know from now until eternity."

Rosalind smiled. "I'll write to my friend immediately."

"And once again, you show me how you manage so well." Her eyes lit with humor, but she quickly turned serious. "Rosalind, if you're involved with Marianna, I'd advise you to be careful. She's shrewd. She puts on the genteel mask as well as any of us, but she's tough as nails and she does not like to be disappointed."

"I will be on my guard," Rosalind said.

"You should be. Because she also knows how much other people value their reputations. And if she thought she had reason, she would not be above destroying yours."

CHAPTER 17

The Other Side of the Story

"It is too late for me to think of being a heroine."
Edgeworth, Maria, *Belinda*

When Rosalind returned home from her call on Honoria, Amelia was there to help her off with her things. She looked better, Rosalind noted. She was still pale, but her eyes were no longer swollen and her manner had regained some of its usual energy.

"How is Cate?" Rosalind asked her.

"Much better," answered Amelia. "The doctor has been, and he said she was out of danger. He left a list of instructions and says he will be back tomorrow."

"Is she strong enough to talk with me, do you think?"

Amelia bit her lip, and Rosalind watched the unfamiliar wariness flicker behind her eyes. "The doctor said she shouldn't be tired."

"I will be as quick as I can," Rosalind promised. "Where is Alice?"

"Gone to visit her brother's family." George's wife, Hannah, was expecting their first child soon, and Alice went to see them both on an almost daily basis. She was, she confided to Rosalind, helping George with his writing assignments because as an expectant father, he was having a great deal of trouble concentrating. She was also, she said, taking him out on walks so that Hannah could have a moment without him hovering over her.

"Tell her I'm home and would like to speak with her."

"Yes, miss."

"Is there anything else I should know?" asked Rosalind.

Amelia met her gaze easily. "No, miss."

Rosalind nodded and took herself upstairs.

She received a soft reply in response to her knock on Cate's door. When she entered, it was to see Cate sitting up in her bed with a book in her hands. She laid it aside as soon as Rosalind entered. Cate was still pale and the dark circles under her eyes looked like bruises, but her gaze was clear and alert, if not entirely easy.

"Hello, Miss Levitton." Rosalind closed the door behind herself.

"Miss Thorne." Cate pushed herself up straighter, or at least she tried to. "I cannot thank you enough for all you have done for me."

"I'm only glad we were able to help. Amelia tells me you are doing better."

Uncertainty flickered behind Cate's bruised eyes at the mention of Amelia's name. "Yes. I am much better. I hope I will not have to trouble you much longer."

"We'll discuss that later," said Rosalind. "May I sit down?"

"Yes, of course."

Rosalind drew up the bedside chair. "I was hoping to talk with you about how you came to be here."

"My own foolishness," Cate said. "I wanted to see Amelia. After, well, everything, I wanted to be sure she was all right." She swallowed. "My family dismissed her, and it was my fault. I expect you know about that?"

"Amelia's told me," said Rosalind.

Cate smoothed her hands over the bedclothes. Rosalind would have given a great deal to know what she was thinking in that moment.

"I didn't want anyone to know where I was going," Cate said. "I was afraid there would be a row if my brother found out I wanted to see Amelia. So, I left the house early in the morning. I didn't realize I already had a fever, and I think that must have affected my judgment."

"And that is all there was to it?" asked Rosalind.

"Yes," Cate said. "It was simple foolishness, you see. Foolishness and lack of proper boots." She smiled a little, and even managed to raise a faint blush.

Rosalind watched this display of girlish innocence and had to squash a surge of anger. "Miss Levitton, I have said I wish to help you, and I do." Rosalind spoke carefully, keeping her voice even and measured. "Obviously, this is for Amelia's sake, and for Alice's, as well as for your own. But in order for me to be able to help, you must trust me."

"I am trusting you," Cate protested. "I . . ."

"You are lying to me," said Rosalind.

Cate's mouth shut like a trap.

"I went to see your aunt today."

"You . . . but . . . you promised . . . you . . ."

"I needed to know whom I had in my house, and what sort of person my friends, and my staff, were dealing with." She paused to let that sink in.

"I did not tell your aunt where you are, yet," Rosalind went on. "Or your mother. Or your fiancée."

"Oh," said Cate. "You met Harold."

"Yes. And he and your aunt, and your mother, all asked if I could help find you."

"*You?*" The incredulity in her voice stung Rosalind's pride.

I am becoming not only notorious, but vain, she admonished herself.

"As I believe you have been informed, I occasionally help society's ladies with their difficult problems."

"I know Amelia said something about it, but I did not realize"—Cate swallowed—"I did not realize I had become one of those problems."

Rosalind felt her patience begin to fray. "I suspect you know you have, and that you knew before you came here."

"Because I'm engaged?" said Cate, and Rosalind heard the bitterness in her voice. "Or because . . ." She looked at the door again.

Rosalind did not bother to answer. "Why did you run away from your aunt's house?"

Cate was watching her, and judging her. Rosalind could see the calculations flickering behind the girl's eyes. Cate might believe herself to be canny and closed off, but Rosalind had a great deal of experience in judging the quality of people's silence. Cate was trying to decide what Rosalind would believe, and how much she could safely hold back.

Anger sparked again. The possibility that this duplicitous young woman held some sway over Amelia—and through her over Alice—was enough to make Rosalind forget herself entirely. She clamped down hard on the surge of emotion, and forced herself to listen, and to watch.

Cate must have felt the change in her, because her cheeks paled.

"I left because I couldn't stand the idea of marrying Harold." The words came in a rush. "I thought I could. He's not bad, not really. I just . . . I couldn't stand the idea of spending the rest of my life lying to maintain appearances and keep my family happy. I had to do something."

This certainly had the ring of truth, and it fit well with what she'd learned. Setting aside the matter of her personal preferences, Cate would hardly be the first young woman who saw the approach of her wedding and realized that the bargain she'd made was not one she could live with.

But there was something else. Possibly a great deal else. Rosalind thought about the pawnshop tickets so carefully hidden in Cate's room. She thought about how very ill Mrs. Levitton had been, and the chance of poison. And about Cate's attempt to lie to her.

Rosalind reminded herself that she did not have the facts yet. She had suspicions, but there were many of them, and they were dangerous.

"How long had you been planning your escape?" she asked.

"Not long," she said. "A month, perhaps. I might not even have gone through with it, but Harold was insisting. He wanted to be sure Marianna could be at the wedding, and she was so ill. We all thought she was going to die soon." She stopped. "How was she when you saw her?"

"Not well, but I am told she is very strong."

Cate's smile was faint, but genuine. "Oh, yes. Stronger than anyone would credit." There was a world of meaning behind those words, and Rosalind wondered at it.

"Anyway," Cate went on, "I realized that I wouldn't be able to put Harold off much longer, so I knew my only option was to leave."

"Did you finally realize this at your brother's dinner party?"

"Oh, you heard about that as well." Cate sighed. "No, it was before that. But it was the dinner that convinced me I couldn't wait any longer. Everett meant well. He always does, but like most of his plans, it was a disaster from beginning to end. Marcus wanted me to grovel, Mother wanted me to be a good girl. Everett wanted me to keep on blaming Amelia for . . . everything."

"What did Mr. Davenport want?"

"A second helping of fish, as near as I can recall."

"He did not try to support you?" *Or the match?*

"He listened to Marcus rant for a few minutes and then

turned to me and said, 'Doesn't matter a bit, so long as Mrs. Levitton approves of us. More wine, my dear?' "

Rosalind actually found herself impressed at this display of *sangfroid*. And he was not wrong. If Cate was of age, her brother could not stop her marriage, and if it was Mrs. Levitton who was going to set the couple up in life, Marcus had no leverage beyond his anger.

"What about Marcus's wife, Wilhelmena? What did she have to say?"

"Did you meet Wilhelmena?"

"Not yet."

"Well, when you do, you will see she has very little to say when Marcus is in the room. My brother is a jealous man, and Wilhelmena has learned to tread very carefully around him."

"What about when he was not in the room? When you two went out to take tea after dinner?"

Cate shook her head. "I can't even remember what was said. All I could think was I had to get out of there as quickly as possible. That's why I was in the market," she said. "I was two days earlier than Amelia and I had agreed upon."

"Do you remember when you began to feel ill?"

"Not really. I was fine at dinner. I was uncomfortable as I was getting ready to go. At first I thought it was nerves and then—" She shook her head. "I don't remember much after that. I must have fallen into a delirium."

Rosalind agreed this was quite likely. "Where did you plan to go, ultimately?"

"Edinburgh," she said. "I have some friends there."

"Are they expecting you?"

"No," admitted Cate. "Not entirely. But they won't turn me away."

"A journey like that takes money."

"Yes. I've been saving my pin money, and I sold some of my jewelry."

"Sold?"

Cate blinked. "Yes. There are jewelers who will buy such things, you know."

Rosalind considered. If she told Cate about the pawn-broker's receipts, she might shock her into saying more than she intended. On the other hand, she might also anger her into running away again. Rosalind had met very few people who could react calmly to news that their personal things had been riffled by a stranger.

"Do you still plan to go to Edinburgh?"

"Yes," said Cate. "I have enough to last for a bit. I don't know what I'll do, but at least I'll have some time to think."

"Your mother is very worried about you."

Cate looked away.

"Will you write to her? You do not need to tell her where you are, just that you are well."

"Do you know she did not write to me once after my father packed me off to Aunt Marianna? Not once."

There was a genuine bitterness in Cate's words. Rosalind remembered Beatrice in her black dress describing her late husband. *My husband was a stern man, Miss Thorne. Marcus took his example very much to heart.*

"It may have been she was prevented from writing," suggested Rosalind.

"Yes, well, she has friends she could have trusted a letter to, if she'd wanted, and it wasn't as if she didn't know where Aunt Marianna lived." Cate stopped, remembering herself suddenly. "I'm sorry. I know I should forgive her, but I can't do it. Not yet." She took a deep breath. "But yes, I will write."

"Good," said Rosalind. "Now, if you are to stay, we will need to get you some things."

Cate smiled. "But I have some things."

"You do?"

"Oh, yes," she said, obviously pleased that she had managed to surprise Rosalind. "You know I came here to Amelia? I don't suppose she told you I left a bag with her?"

"No," said Rosalind. "She did not tell us that."

"It's not her fault. I asked her not to. I know I've put her in a very bad spot," she added. "I just didn't want to leave a packed valise about the house in case anyone found it and started to ask questions. So, I brought it here and asked her to hide it for me."

"Well, that is convenient," said Rosalind. "I'll make sure Amelia brings it to you."

"Thank you. For everything. I really did not mean to impose on you this way."

"Rest." Rosalind got to her feet. "We will talk again later."

Rosalind closed Cate's door behind her and went quickly to her own rooms. She did not want Alice, or Amelia, to happen on her before she regained control of her features and her faculties.

She now knew that Cate Levitton was a liar, but what sort of liar? Did she simply not trust Rosalind, who was, after all, a stranger to her?

Or was she holding on to deeper secrets?

CHAPTER 18

Plans Discussed over Dinner

*"She begins by saying she is determined to think
for herself, and she is determined to act for
herself—and then it is all over with her."*

Edgeworth, Maria, *Belinda*

By the time Fran got back to the flat, she was tired and in
a fine temper. After leaving Jenny snoring in Madame
Geneva's yard, she'd set about making the rounds of all the
girls' usual haunts. She found Polly and Nan easy enough in
old Mrs. Prescott's boardinghouse. She'd given them a jug of
cider, and a few pounds, "on account," just as Jenny had suggested. They'd toasted and talked readily enough, but neither
one of them gave any hint as to who sent Jenny to talk to her.

Pinky was a bit harder to track down, but Fran eventually
found her down in Drury Lane, taking her chances dipping
into pockets to see what she might come up with. She was a
fair dip, was little Pinky, but she was a better housebreaker.
Fran treated her to a pie and a dram of pale ale, but got exactly nothing for her trouble.

Which meant either the girls were united in their suspicions,
or Jenny had spun a line of talk, and was acting on her own.

Uncertainty and an empty purse always put Fran in a foul mood, so when Jack came breezing in all smiles, she just eyed him from the table where she sat with the remains of her pie and a mug of strong tea.

He had been bending to kiss her, but he saw the sour look on her face and stopped. "What's the matter?"

"I've had a little visit from Jenny Cee. She *followed* me."

"Oh." Jack tossed aside his hat and coat and drew up a chair. "Wanted money, I'll wager?"

"And wanted to let me know the other girls did, too. I spent the rest of the day, and the rest of our coin"—she gestured to the deflated drawstring purse that slumped beside the teapot—"keeping them all quiet." She glared again. "So you'd better have some good news for me, Jack Beachamp."

"Well, you can cheer up then, my love." He kicked his long legs out and poured himself a measure of the thick, black tea. "Because we are not going to have to worry about money for a fine long time."

"Since when did old Stafford become so generous?"

Jack took a long swallow of tea and smacked his lips in apparent relish. "Not Stafford. Oh, no. You and me, my girl, are about to be in the pay of the high sheriff of London himself!"

"Have you been drinking?" Fran demanded.

"Not a drop." He held up his right hand in promise. "But listen here, you know that MP I told you Stafford wanted watched?"

"Yeah?" said Fran warily.

"Well, it turns out he's Sir Richard Phillips, ex-sheriff and now noted radical. He's put up a reward for finding the man he says is the government spy responsible for all that mess round in Cato Street."

The word *reward* had a warm and lovely sound, but Fran wasn't about to let herself get too excited. "How much?"

"A thousand pounds, my love!" Jack leaned back, grinning and waiting for her exclamations and praise.

"A thousand pounds your love?" she sneered. "But didn't you say this MP met up with a runner? What's to keep him from nabbing the little spy first?"

"Won't be a problem. I'm already two steps ahead of him."

Fran stabbed her knife into the remains of her pie. "How could you have gotten ahead of a Bow Street Runner?"

Jack laid his hand over his breast. "I'm wounded, Franny. Haven't I been keeping ahead of those clodpoles all my life? Isn't that how we got together, you and me?" He smiled fondly at her. "Now, I'll admit this particular fellow's got a reputation. I did some asking around about him. He's got a fancy nickname in the papers and all. Watchdog Harkness they call him. Friendly with the king, and all sorts. But that just makes my job easier."

"How's that then?"

"Because he's got something to lose," Jack said. "I'm going to find Mr. Edwards, but I won't nab him straightaway. Oh, no. I'll keep watch on him, until Mr. Harkness shows up. Then, I'll make it clear to Harkness that if he does not turn Edwards over to me, I'll tell his boss that he took money to try to muck up the government's own case against the Cato Street men."

Fran didn't answer immediately. She looked at Jack's lovely, grinning face, and made herself think through everything he'd said, not once, but twice, looking for the flaws.

"Why would you wait for him? Why not just take Edwards to the MP?"

"Because once Harkness is in my net, I can not only sell Edwards off to the MP, I can sell Mr. Stafford the fact that it was Mr. Harkness who handed Edwards to the radicals and their defense committee." He raised his mug in salute to his own cleverness.

"Even if it wasn't?"

"Even if it wasn't," he agreed. "Unless, of course, it happens that Mr. Harkness can afford to pay better than Stafford."

"Very nice," said Fran. "If it happens."

"Of course it will happen." Jack waved his mug. "We're covered coming and going. So, cheer up, my girl!" He leaned forward and chucked her under the chin. "And give us a kiss. We're about to be very rich!"

He gave her a peck on the cheek, and tried to shift to kiss her on the mouth, but Fran turned away, not harsh though.

"When's this blessed event set to occur?"

"Shouldn't be more than a day or two. Harkness is sure to be in a hurry. He's got to round up Edwards before the trial."

"What do we do until then?" she asked. "I handed out everything I had to keep the girls quiet, and it wasn't enough. Soon as Jenny's through with her hangover, they'll all be back, looking for more."

Jack pulled a wallet out of his coat and tossed it down. "That'll hold us for a couple of days. And you can put the girls off for that long, I'm sure."

Fran sighed. He was not in a mood to listen to her worries. Sometimes she wondered why she stayed with him. Especially times like this. But then, he was so good at the game, and so pretty to look at, and if he was right—oh, then they could be in clover.

And this could work, just like he said. Maybe. A thousand pounds was certainly worth a bit of a gamble.

In for a penny, thought Fran as she took up the wallet and leafed through its contents. *In for a pound.*

"All right, we'll play it your way." She closed the wallet up again. "But in that case, I'm going to have a little word with our Cate."

She watched Jack roll this around in his head for a moment. "Are you sure? From what you've said, this Miss Thorne is a clever one."

"All the more reason to make sure Cate's keeping her mouth shut," said Fran. "If she takes it into her head to start telling tales, we could both end up in the nick before you have a chance to put this fine plan of yours into action."

"Mmm. I hadn't thought of that."

No, you never do, do you? Fran sighed again. "I'll just go make sure she knows to keep quiet, and while I'm at it, I'll get what's ours. That way, I'll be able to settle accounts with Jenny and the girls." She raised her mug. "And then you and me, we keep all the rest."

CHAPTER 19

A Proposal

"Then why persist in the same kind of life? you say. Why, my dear, because I could not stop . . ."

Edgeworth, Maria, *Belinda*

There were many advantages to sharing a house with Alice. The spirited company, the pooled resources, and of course, Alice's acquaintance were of added assistance when Rosalind needed to reach into the various levels of London society.

But the greatest advantage—although Rosalind might blush to admit it—was the fact that with Alice sharing her residence, Rosalind could receive calls from an unescorted gentleman without risk of serious censure.

Rosalind descended the stairs to find Adam in her front parlor. He smiled to see her, and her heart thumped. She closed the door, and let herself be pulled into his arms. His warmth surrounded her and she allowed herself to luxuriate in the sensation.

"I'm sorry I could not come earlier," he said when they separated. "The day was more complicated than I hoped for."

"Even if you did come, you would not have found me at

home," Rosalind told him. "My day also became complicated. Have you eaten?"

"Mother will have something for me at home."

"But do you actually intend to go home from here?" Rosalind inquired.

Adam held up his hands in defeat. Rosalind rang the bell for Amelia. "Please tell Mrs. Singh that Mr. Harkness will be joining us for supper." Rosalind and Alice both preferred an early meal, especially during the season when either of them might be spending their nights at routs or balls.

"How does your guest?" Adam asked. "I am guessing she's better?"

"Much," said Rosalind. "The doctor believes her to be out of danger."

"I'm glad to hear it."

"Yes. It raises a host of questions as to what's to be done next, but I would rather have to answer them than not."

Adam nodded his agreement.

"Has she told you anything of her circumstances?"

"She's told me a great deal. I'm just not certain all of it is the truth."

Rosalind told Adam about her visit to the Levittons, and then with Honoria. He listened with patient attention and made no interruption. Rosalind went on to describe what Cate had told her about her reasons for leaving. She also showed him the pawnshop receipts.

"What will you do?" asked Adam.

"What I can." She shook her head. "I've never been in such circumstances. I do not like feeling so uncertain."

"I sympathize," said Adam. "Deeply."

"What happened with your defense committee men?" she asked, grateful for a chance to change the subject from the unsettling events surrounding so many Levittons.

"The man I met was Sir Richard Phillips."

"The member of Parliament?"

Adam nodded. "And radical, and former sheriff of London. He and his friends are the ones attempting a defense of the Cato Street men. They've even engaged a barrister, from what I hear."

"Is that allowed?" Recently, Rosalind had been forced to become more closely acquainted with the proceedings of the criminal courts. According to law and custom, defendants could seek legal advice, but they were not always permitted to have an attorney in court with them.

"In cases of treason, it is allowed," said Adam. "But what they want me for is to track down a missing man, one George Edwards. They think he's the real instigator of the plot, and that he is in the pay of the government."

"What do you think?"

"I've spent the morning going through the witness statements, at least some of them, and I think it's possible." He paused. "But I might not be thinking straight."

"Why not?" Rosalind arched her brows in genuine surprise.

Adam met her gaze, his blue eyes serious. "Sir Richard offered me a reward for finding Edwards. A thousand pounds."

Rosalind sucked in a quick breath.

"Three hundred of that would take care of my mother until the youngest were grown, even if my brothers were not able to help her with the housekeeping. The rest—that's an income. For life, if it's managed carefully. And I imagine you know someone who could help with that."

"Yes," murmured Rosalind. "Louisa's husband would be glad to help, I'm sure."

"So you see," said Adam quietly, "if I find this George Edwards, and I bring him to Sir Richard, I could afford to marry, if the lady was willing."

Rosalind felt her throat constrict. A strange energy spread through her. She'd resigned herself to the impossibility of marriage to Adam. She had accustomed herself to waiting and managing.

Now, he told her, marriage might be possible.

Her faith in Adam's skills as an officer ran deep. If this man, Edwards, could be found, Adam would find him. He could claim that reward. And then . . . and then . . .

If the lady was willing.

Rosalind found herself filled with hope, but lying just beneath it was another feeling that was nothing short of terror. And that terror was quickly, horribly dissolving into shame.

She had no idea what Adam saw in her face, but he quickly took her hand. "I'm sorry, Rosalind. I shouldn't have said it like that. We haven't had a chance to really talk. I never asked you what you wanted."

She pressed his hand. The shame deepened, leaving her sick. Her stomach, her heart, her whole body was suddenly clenched tight.

"I love you," she said plainly. "I loved you from the moment I first saw you on the stairs."

He smiled. "And I you."

"That's not what frightens me."

"What then?" he asked.

Rosalind meant to speak, but the words would not come to order. There was only a fragmented jumble in her mind. She did not understand herself in this moment. She did not understand why she could not speak sensibly, or quiet the emotions that roiled inside her. In the blink of an eye, she had become a stranger to herself—a weak, incomprehensible stranger. She did not want Adam to see her this way, not when he was offering her what she should want most.

"Marriage," she blurted the word out. "There's so much loss in it, for a woman."

"For you," said Adam.

"For me," she agreed. "And . . . and then when the children come . . ." She bowed her head. "This isn't something I've said," she whispered. "Not even to Alice."

"Tell me."

She wanted to, but the words choked her. She'd never spoken this way. She did not know for sure that she could. Even to Adam. Especially to Adam, who saw a future for them and had moved to make it happen while she dithered uselessly. "Adam . . . I'm not certain that I want children. To go through labor, to risk my life, for that possibility. I know my time is limited, I know I am unnatural—"

"Rosalind."

She looked up at him. Looked into the deep eyes that had never failed to see the truth of her.

"I love you, Rosalind," he said. "*You*. Not some theory, or possibility, or ideal. I love the unique, astonishing fact of you, and that is what I will always love."

He kissed her. She clung to him, returning the kisses with all the force she had. Driven past words, past her own understanding, it was all she could do.

A soft knock sounded on the door. Adam and Rosalind sprang apart like guilty children. Rosalind put a hand to her blushing cheek. Adam smiled and smoothed a stray lock of her hair behind her ear. His touch burned. It was astonishing. It was deeply unsettling. She did not know what to do.

He was still smiling, his expression gentle and full of understanding. He stepped back and bowed, ever so slightly. Rosalind found herself able to straighten up, her mind quiet, at least on the surface.

"Come in," she said.

It was Alice. She strode into the room, the hems of the old, blue wrapper she habitually wore over her plain day dress flapping behind her.

"Rosalind, this came for you by hand." She held out a lumpy package wrapped in brown paper.

"Thank you." Rosalind took the package. She met Alice's gaze. Her friend kept her face admirably straight. Neither of them remarked on why it might be Alice who brought the package into the room, rather than Amelia or Mrs. Singh.

"The boy said he was told not to wait for a reply," Alice told her. "Oh, and Mrs. Singh says supper will be ready in ten minutes."

Alice sailed out and closed the door.

Adam looked at Rosalind, and she looked back. He raised his brows, and she raised hers. In the next heartbeat, they both burst out laughing.

"Oh, dear." Rosalind dropped onto the sofa, short of breath from laughter and feeling infinitely lighter. "I can't think what's so funny." She wiped at the corners of her eyes.

Adam pulled a clean handkerchief out of his pocket and handed it to her. "Does it matter?"

"I suppose not." She wiped her eyes, and her nose.

"Were you expecting this?" He nodded at the package. It was soft, and had been tied at its mouth, like a pudding ready for steaming.

"If it's what I think, I've been praying for it," Rosalind told him.

"Allow me." Adam pulled out his pocketknife, slit the string on the package, and opened the paper. Inside was a pile of loose tea leaves.

Rosalind sucked in a careful breath. She also closed the paper again, twisting the mouth tight. She met Adam's gaze. He said nothing, waiting for her to open the note that accompanied the package.

> *Dear Miss Thorne,*
> *Somewhat against my better instincts, I have enclosed what you requested. It has now been two days since my patient has partaken of the aforementioned.*

Her doctor believes her heart has steadied some, but that it is too soon to tell if this is a genuine improvement.

I shall consider all that you have said, and remain vigilant.

Yours,

Constance Hepplewhite

"What is it?" asked Adam.

Rosalind closed the paper carefully. "When I visited Mrs. Levitton, I was able to speak with her nurse. I know her slightly, and I raised the possibility of poison. It seems that Mrs. Levitton keeps a private stock of tea for her own use, and that the whole household knew about it." She held up the package. The skin on her hand seemed to shrivel from touching the paper. She told herself to stop being ridiculous. This was not entirely efficacious. "I asked her to freshen the tea, and send me what there was in the caddy. Until this moment, I was not sure that she would. It was after all a rather outrageous suggestion, and I have no proof." She frowned at the package, as if willing it to give up its secrets. "Is there any way to make certain? If it is poisoned?"

"Can you leave it with me?" Adam asked. "I have some ideas. And Sir David might as well." Sir David Royce was the coroner for London and Westminster. He and Adam had worked closely together on more than one occasion. "And if Mrs. Levitton and Miss Levitton both continue to improve, that will certainly be a sign that our fears were correct."

Rosalind could not fully suppress her shudder.

"Yes," said Adam solemnly. "I agree."

He pocketed the package, took her hand and kissed it. Despite her uncertainties, Rosalind felt herself smile. But only for a moment.

"Adam, you said, before, that you were not sure you were

thinking straight when it came to this Mr. Edwards. Was that because of the money?"

Adam nodded. "Do I see that a paid spy led eleven vulnerable men to disaster because that is what the facts reveal? Or do I see this because I am offered a reward I very much want?" He pressed her hand gently. "And right now I don't know."

"Then you will do what you always have done," she said. "Find out. Find this Mr. Edwards, hear what he has to say. In the meantime, I might be able to learn something about Sir Richard and his defense committee that will help clarify matters."

He touched her cheek. "And the rest?"

Her answer was cut off by a knock at the door. "Rosalind?" called Alice. "Supper's ready, and I'm starved. Mrs. Singh is already put out and if you don't both come and eat a good meal, we'll all be in serious trouble."

Rosalind looked at Adam and he rolled his eyes, and she nodded, and they both laughed again. Rosalind rose and brushed down her skirt. Adam stood, and bowed elaborately, and let her precede him out the door.

Rosalind tried not to think too much about the fact that he had proposed marriage to her, and that she had not yet answered him.

CHAPTER 20

Unwelcome Revelations

"What a simpleton, to know so little of the nature of curiosity!"

Edgeworth, Maria, *Belinda*

"There you go." Amelia laid the supper tray across Cate's lap. "Best eat it while it's hot."

"It smells delicious," said Cate. Amelia had to agree. It was one of Mrs. Singh's special stews, full of vegetables and spices that Amelia had never even heard of before the cook came. Amelia had to admit it had all taken some getting used to, but now she couldn't get enough. Mrs. Singh asserted that the proper food could heal better than anything in the apothecary's shop. Looking at Cate now, Amelia wondered if there wasn't something to it after all.

"I wasn't sure I'd ever really be hungry again." Cate took up a healthy spoonful of the rich broth. "Heavens, that's good."

"I'll leave you to it then."

"Amelia?"

"Yes?"

"Can you bring me my bag?" she asked, and smiled. "I'll

be ready to get up soon, maybe even tomorrow, and I've got to have something to wear."

"All right," agreed Amelia. "I've been keeping it upstairs."

"It seems it's just as well I left it with you, doesn't it? The way things have turned out?" Cate's smile turned just a little bit cheeky. "Now we don't have to make shift to get me clean things."

"Right," said Amelia. "You eat that up, I'll go get it."

"Thank you."

Amelia smiled and bobbed a quick curtsy, more as a joke than anything else, and tried not to feel too much warmth as Cate winked at her. Just like she tried not to see the flicker of . . . *something* in her eyes when she pointed out she had a very good reason for wanting her bag.

Amelia McGowan, you have a nasty, suspicious mind.

Cate had already explained about why she'd run away, and how she'd decided to go to the market to meet Amelia, instead of coming straight to the door.

I didn't want to be seen, she said. I know your Miss Thorne knows absolutely everybody, and I wasn't sure if she knew my mother, and might say something to her if she found out. . . .

Of course, neither one of them had been able to predict that Miss Thorne would choose that day to come to the market.

It was all perfectly reasonable. There was only one problem. Cate was a liar. She knew nothing about Miss Thorne except what Amelia had told her.

And this lie was hardly the first, or the worst. Still, it made Amelia's heart, and her head, ache. She wished that she could just tidy away all those old feelings for Cate and get on with her life. How could she even think about running off with someone she didn't trust?

How could she even want to?

Amelia's stomach grumbled, bringing her back to more everyday concerns. Supper would be waiting for her below-stairs. Good and hot. Then, she had the kitchen to clean and the beds to turn down and a dozen other tasks before she'd even get a chance to sit down again. And the misses and Mr. Harkness would probably want tea, and heaven knew what Cate might want next. She should just hurry and get the bag, and then take her chance to get off her feet for a few minutes while she had it.

Amelia uttered a few words she never would have said out loud if anyone was near, and climbed the narrow backstairs to her room.

One of the best things about working for Miss Thorne and Miss Alice was the room. True, there was no hearth, but there was a chimney to give off enough heat to keep things snug. She had a good rug on the floor, and if the chair was worn, it was comfortable. There was a footstool to go with it, and a stout table and thick curtains on a window that looked out over the square, not to mention a lock on her door. Not that there was anyone in this house that she needed to keep out, in the general way, but it was nice to have the possibility, if she ever needed it.

Probably she should not be picturing Miss Alice standing beside the bed while Amelia turned the key, just to make sure no one came in to find them. Certainly thoughts of Miss Alice had nothing to do with the reason she turned the lock now.

Amelia had kept Cate's valise in the back of her little closet, underneath the winter quilts and the extra pillow. She hadn't looked in it. Not once. She'd told herself she must trust Cate. No, that wasn't even true. She'd told herself that if there was anything out of the ordinary about that valise, she was better off not knowing.

Ask me no questions, I'll tell you no lies, her mother had always said. Well, the questions were being asked, and Amelia had already lied. But Cate had lied more. And there had been something in her eyes. Something in the way she watched Amelia that Amelia had recognized, even if she hadn't wanted to. It was the look Cate got when she was trying to judge if she was likely to get her way.

Amelia took a deep breath and opened the valise.

What confronted her was nothing more suspicious than a jumble of clothing—a couple of badly crumpled gowns and petticoats. A nightdress. A pair of half boots. Some handkerchiefs. All of it had been tossed higgledy-piggledy into the bag, along with a beaded reticule that proved to contain a few bank notes and some coins—all amounting to the princely sum of twenty pounds, six shillings, and ninepence.

Amelia lifted up one badly wrinkled day dress, looking it up and down in disgust.

And who's going to be left wasting an entire day trying to salvage that, I should like to know? Amelia McGowan, who else? Her jaw clenched. *Well, I'll be blowed if I will. Not without orders. I'm not her maid anymore.*

She made herself shove the dresses back into the valise and snap the latches shut. She grabbed the handle, with every intention of walking back to Cate's room, dropping it by her bed, and walking out.

But as she hefted the bag, she stopped.

Something was wrong. She hefted it again.

It's too heavy, she thought.

Amelia set the valise back down on her bed. She stared at it, her heart in her mouth.

Don't be ridiculous, she sneered at herself. She threw the valise open, and in a single motion dumped all of Cate's belongings onto her faded quilt. She hefted the bag again.

She was right. It was far too heavy.

Amelia shoved both hands into the empty valise up to the elbow, and felt carefully about the black, silk-lined inside. It took a minute, but her experienced fingertips caught on the bulk of a clumsily stitched seam that ran all along the bag's bottom.

Someone had cut out the bottom lining and then resewed it. And judging by how uneven that seam felt, it wasn't anybody who had any kind of skill with a needle.

Cate had always hated fancy work and mending.

Amelia went to her workbasket and yanked out her sharpest scissors. She paused for a minute, listening for footsteps or rustling cloth that might mean someone was listening at the door. But there was no sound. She gritted her teeth, reached back into the bag, and carefully slit those clumsy seams. She folded the flap of black silk away to reveal a layer of thin board.

Amelia took a deep breath and lifted the board out to reveal the space underneath, and a pile of old rags.

Amelia stared at them, her heart pounding hard in her throat and an odd mix of disappointment and relief surging in her blood.

Well, that's that, she tried to tell herself. *Nothing to see. Best put it all back and go get your supper.*

But she didn't move. She swallowed and gathered her nerve, and reached back into the bag.

The rags proved to be an untidy nest. Inside waited six brown paper packages, tucked up like eggs in straw.

Amelia hefted one of the packages, squeezing it as if it was a piece of fruit she needed to check for ripeness. She felt sharp edges shift inside the paper and her breath caught.

Quickly, Amelia sliced through the string and unrolled the paper. As it opened, the fading daylight caught sparks in a riot of dark blue and ice white.

Glass? she thought.

But it wasn't glass. It was a heap of gemstones. Diamonds and sapphires set in brilliant gold.

Amelia lifted the necklace and stared.

Oh, Cate, she thought. *You bleeding idiot!*

CHAPTER 21

A Guest at the Breakfast Table

"I . . . have nothing worse than folly to conceal:
that's bad enough—"

Edgeworth, Maria, *Belinda*

Rosalind, as usual, was the first down to breakfast. The dining room had a lovely nook formed by the bowed windows and was furnished with a small table and chairs. It was an ideal place for a light breakfast.

This morning, the world outside was shrouded in fog. Gray droplets speckled the windowpanes. It was so dim that the lamps were all lit, lending the room a cozy glow as Rosalind came in to find the table already laid out with a pot of tea for her, and one of coffee for Alice. The morning post waited on a salver on the sideboard, alongside a stack of the day's early papers. At the very top of this stack waited a hand-delivered note addressed to her in Adam's hand.

Her heart in her mouth, Rosalind opened the note. It was brief, and very much to the point.

*Took that package to a rat catcher I know. He says
it's arsenic for certain, and that there's three fewer rats
in the cellars at the Brown Bear.*
    A.H.

"What's the matter, Rosalind?" Alice came into the dining
room. "You've gone quite pale."

Rosalind passed her Adam's note. Alice read it in silence
and then handed it back.

"Part of me had hoped this was all going to prove to be a
suspicious fancy." Rosalind folded the paper tightly, as if she
could prevent its news from escaping.

"What will you do now?" asked Alice.

"I must go to Mrs. Levitton at once."

"At least give yourself time to eat something," said Alice.
"Waste your morning egg, and Mrs. Singh won't speak to either of us for a week."

"Yes, all right," agreed Rosalind reluctantly. She sat,
poured out the strong tea, and sipped, or she tried to. Her
stomach felt curdled.

Alice was looking at her own coffee. "Hearing about poison first thing in the morning does rather spoil the taste,
doesn't it?"

Rosalind nodded absently. Mrs. Singh arrived then with a
lightly boiled egg for each of them, along with a rack of
toast. While Rosalind carefully sawed off the top of hers,
Alice knocked hers open with a single expert stroke of her
spoon and immediately set about dipping bits of toast into
the yolk.

"Will you tell Cate?" Alice asked around a mouthful of
toast. "About Adam's note?"

"I don't know." Rosalind spooned some egg onto her toast
and made herself eat. She told herself she would do no one
any good if she was fainting with hunger throughout the day.
"I confess, I'm still not entirely sure what to make of Cate.

Would it be too much to ask you to keep an eye on her today?"

"You still think she might try to run away from us?"

"Yes. She's stronger now, and she's very obviously been lying about what drove her out of Mrs. Levitton's house." Last night, over Mrs. Singh's chicken and root vegetable ragu, Rosalind had relayed the details of her conversation with Cate.

Alice spooned some extra sugar into her coffee. "I won't pretend to be the most disinterested observer in this case," she said. "But I'm certain this business about running away to avoid marriage is far from the whole story." She paused. "Do you think Cate had anything to do with this . . . attempt on Mrs. Levitton's life? I mean, I know it's possible she was poisoned, too, but—"

"No," said Rosalind, and it was a relief to be certain about one aspect of this unsavory business. "If she was poisoning Mrs. Levitton, why would she plan to run away before she knew she would succeed? And what would she gain by it? She had a promise of a large settlement when she married Mr. Davenport. Why not marry him, take the money, and run away afterward? No one is hanged for simple desertion."

"Well, you leave her to me," said Alice. "I'll soon have our answers. Now, what about you?"

Rosalind paused in the act of spooning out some more egg. "What do you mean?"

"What of you and Adam? Something's happened between you. If I'd had to watch one more caring glance or faint blush last night at dinner, I would have screamed. You may now praise my discretion and restraint," she added primly.

"Your discretion is always appreciated." Rosalind scraped her spoon delicately around the inside of her shell and heaped the last bit of egg onto her toast.

"But you're not going to tell me what's going on?"

Rosalind ate her toast and egg. She swallowed. She added some more tea to her cup, and sipped. Alice narrowed her eyes.

Rosalind set her cup down.

"Adam proposed to me," she said.

"Oh," said Alice. "Did you answer him?"

"No."

"Why on earth not? You love him. You turned down a *duke* for the man. A duke you'd been pining after for years."

She might be simplifying the exact circumstances, but Alice was not entirely wrong. Rosalind had turned down an invitation to be courted and married, from Devon Winterbourne, who was the Duke of Castlemaine, and her feelings for Adam had been a major consideration in that decision.

"I don't know if I want to be married," said Rosalind. "Not even to Adam," she added in a forlorn whisper.

"Oh, Rosalind." Alice took her hand. "I'm sorry."

Rosalind pressed her friend's sturdy fingers, and then drew back. "It's my own fault. I cannot separate what I've lived through from—" She realized she had no idea how to finish that sentence.

"You will find your way, Rosalind," said Alice.

"I wish I could be so confident."

"You will," Alice told her firmly. "When has there been a problem set in front of you that you've failed to solve? You'll be through it quicker than . . . than a three-minute egg." She crunched her toast. "And please don't tell Mr. Colburn about that particular metaphor. I'll come up with something better after breakfast."

Rosalind could not help but laugh. "Oh, Alice, what would I do without you?"

"Well, how convenient you will never have to find out."

"Won't I?"

"No," replied Alice promptly. "I'm a confirmed spinster, after all. I shall write my books and my gossip and make so little money that no one will bother to pay any attention to me, and live exactly as I please. That includes being your very best friend in the whole world."

"And Amelia?"

For a moment, Alice's confident cheer faltered. "Amelia is making up her mind. We still have a few things to say to each other, but I expect that—"

The door to the dining room swung open. Alice and Rosalind turned their heads to see Cate Levitton walk gingerly into the room. She wore a rather wrinkled dress of blue-sprigged muslin, trimmed with ribbons and three tiers of ruffles. She looked pale, but seemed steady on her feet.

"Good morning," said Cate. "I'm sorry if I'm intruding, but I really could not stay in bed another minute. I'm afraid I snuck out while Amelia was busy." She smiled, and Rosalind had the feeling she was trying the expression on to see how it was received.

"Well, it's good to see you on your feet," said Alice before Rosalind was able to speak. "However, you'd better sit now." Alice got up and brought another chair to the breakfast table. "We don't want any dramatic slumping to the floor and so on."

"Thank you." Cate sat and Rosalind rang the bell. Amelia appeared a moment later. She stared at Cate, very surprised, and more than a little accusing.

Cate tried to cover her blush by helping herself to the last slice of toast.

"Can you tell Mrs. Singh we'll need another egg, please?" said Rosalind. "And some more toast."

"Yes, miss," murmured Amelia. She retreated quickly, and let the door slam behind her.

Cate winced.

"I'm delighted to see you so much better," said Rosalind. "Do you prefer coffee or tea?"

"Tea, if you please," answered Cate. "With sugar, if there is any?"

Rosalind poured her a cup, and Alice pushed the sugar bowl toward her. "We're a bit informal here in the mornings."

"So is my aunt," said Cate. "I'm very used to it." She helped herself to three large lumps of sugar. Rosalind felt her teeth begin to ache in sympathy. As she stirred, Cate asked, "I was wondering if I might borrow paper and pen? I need to write to my mother."

"Excellent," said Alice. "You can use the table in my book room."

"Thank you," said Cate, with only the slightest hesitation. "There might be some other letters, too. To my friends in Edinburgh, to let them know I've been delayed."

"Is that still your plan?" inquired Alice. "To go to Edinburgh?"

"It's either that or go home," said Cate. "And . . . I'm not ready to go home."

Rosalind watched Cate in silence for a moment. She could tell Cate felt her scrutiny and was trying not to squirm, or blush.

"Will you leave without speaking to Mr. Davenport?" Rosalind asked her.

"I'll enclose a note for him when I write my mother." Cate spoke quickly, as if she'd expected the question and had her answer all ready.

"And your aunt?"

Cate swallowed. "I don't know what I would tell her." It was, Rosalind thought, the first unguarded thing she'd said since she'd come to the table. "But I'll write her as well. To thank her for all she's done."

"Well, that seems to be settled," said Alice.

If Cate heard the undercurrent in Alice's words, she ignored it. "Yes. I hope to be on my way within a few days. A week at the most."

"Edinburgh is quite a distance," said Rosalind. "And you will be alone."

"I've made the trip before," Cate assured her. "I'm familiar with all the stages. And I made sure I'd have enough money before I left. So." She took a deep breath. "I know it's not the done thing, but there's really nothing to worry about. I'm only sorry to have imposed upon you for so long."

"Amelia's friends are more than welcome here," said Rosalind.

At this, Cate's cheeks turned bright pink. Of course Alice noticed as quickly as Rosalind did.

"Have you let her know your plans?"

"We have not had much of a chance to speak," murmured Cate, clearly disconcerted to be in the company of people who would refer openly of her association with a parlor maid.

"Well, as long as you are tidying things up, I think you'd better," said Alice frankly. "That is, unless you plan to take her with you?"

Cate started, badly. Tea sloshed from her cup.

"Oh, dear." Alice passed her a napkin.

"My own fault," murmured Cate.

Rosalind rose from the table. "You will excuse me? I also have some correspondence I must attend to. Miss Levitton, once you have written those letters to your family, Miss Littlefield will see that they are delivered."

"Oh, I wouldn't want to—" began Cate, but Alice was already waving her words away.

"You also don't want to be found, yet. I can make sure it gets there without anyone being able to ask questions." She beamed.

Rosalind looked pointedly at Alice, but Alice was pouring more coffee and offering Cate the toast, and paying no attention to her. Rosalind had no choice but to leave them there and go to her parlor.

But she was certain Cate had understood Alice's veiled message. Cate might wish them to believe she was no cause for concern, and that they should not pay too much attention to her. But Alice, at least, did not believe that for an instant. She would be keeping a steady eye on Cate.

The question now became, what would Cate do about that?

CHAPTER 22

A Quiet Walk in the Park

*"My inquiries after him were indefatigable, but
for some time unsuccessful . . ."*

Edgeworth, Maria, *Belinda*

A thick, dank fog shrouded Hyde Park. Adam made his
way cautiously across the slick grass. He carried a lantern, but the feeble light did nothing to drive back the gray
and yellow vapors that blotted out the sunlight.

Normally, Adam would have waited until the fog lifted,
but time was short. There was no knowing when the Cato
Street trial would come up on the docket. Trials were held in
the order in which the cases came in. Even on such an important matter, the court might only have a few hours' notice before the case was brought. If this wild goose chase he had set
himself was to do any good at all, Adam could not afford to
waste the morning.

Hyde Park was a huge, green expanse in the middle of the
city. Herds of deer wandered among the trees. Pleasure seekers sailed on the Serpentine and drove along Rotten Row.
Cowherds pastured their animals on the grass, and sold the
milk to those same pleasure seekers.

According to the records Stafford had reluctantly given him, the man, Hiden, who had passed word of the Cato Street conspiracy to the president of the Privy Council, was a member of this fraternity of London cowherds.

Adam raised his lantern in a vain attempt to see more than an arm's length in front of him and blessed his country boyhood. He was able to move with confidence across the uneven ground and make something resembling a straight track across the green. The fog muffled all sound, but gradually, he was able to make out the soft lowing of cattle. Adam angled his path up a gentle hill toward a cluster of shapes that could have been anything from a line of shrubs to a group of standing stones. Slowly, though, the shadows resolved themselves into a small herd of brown cows, munching contentedly on the sodden grass. A wrinkled man on a three-legged stool, leaned up against one of the cows, milking steadily.

As Adam emerged from the fog, a stout girl, probably the milkman's daughter, caught up a covered pail and lugged it toward Adam.

"A drink of fresh milk for you, sir?"

"Gladly." Adam gave her his pennies and accepted the ladle. He drank it off and handed it back. "I'm looking for a cowman named Hiden. Do you know him?"

The girl hesitated but the old man answered. "What'cher want with him?" he asked, without looking up from the cow or stopping his task.

"Aye," said a voice from the fog. "What'cher want with me?"

A slight, slouching figure stepped out of the mist. Patched clothes hung loose on a lean frame. Damp and dirt left his hair stringy. He carried a cow prod as tall as he was. Even in the dim lantern light, Adam could see Hiden wore the wary, hardened look of a man who always expected trouble.

The old milkman seemed to expect trouble as well. He patted the side of his cow. "Suzy, go fetch me Strawberry. Buttercup here's finished."

The girl, as quick on the uptake as any of the men, scurried away, leaving her bucket and ladle behind.

"My name's Harkness," said Adam to Hiden and the milkman. "I'm here from Bow Street. I've some questions about the doings in Cato Street."

"I've nowt to say," declared Hiden.

"You were willing enough to talk before," Adam pointed out. "And you brought that warning note to His Grace, the Earl of Harrowby."

"And what have I got for my troubles?" demanded Hiden. "Some lot of officious fellows saying 'Go there, come here, keep yourself where we can see you, or we'll come after you.'" He scowled. "'And never mind we said there'd be money for you, you just do what you're told, or you'll be in the Tower with the rest of 'em—'"

"Who told you that?" Adam asked.

Hiden spat. "I'm done with the lot of yez, hear me? You can all go to the devil!" He brandished his prod and then wheeled around. Adam moved forward, but Hiden had already disappeared into the fog, leaving Adam standing there with his lantern and his questions, and feeling nothing short of foolish.

A rusty laugh cut through his self-recrimination. "Well, that didn't go so well for you, m'boy, did it?" wheezed the milkman.

"No." Adam sighed. "That it did not."

The milkman reached under his arm and gave himself a good scratch. "All you mighty Robin Redbreasts, with nothing better to do than scare a poor man out of his wits." He also spat into the grass, echoing Hiden's sentiments. "For the lot a' yez."

Adam considered the milkman. The set of his shoulders and the glint in his eye said he wanted an argument. And any man who wanted an argument wanted to talk.

"Has someone been out giving Hiden a hard time?" Adam asked him.

"You should know, shouldn't you? He was one a' yours."

"Did he give his name?"

The milkman eyed him warily. "I warned Hiden," he said finally. "Told him keep hisself to hisself. Don't go mucking about with troublemakers, I sez. World is what it is, and it ain't bein' changed by a bunch of dafties yelling and bargin' about. But he wouldn't listen. And where's it got him, eh?" He poked a finger toward Adam. "We got one lot's promising to free the poor. Then that doesn't work out, an' we got the other lot promising to pay a fortune if Hiden makes his mark on their paper and swears this thing he can't even read is all right and true. And does that money they promised show up? It does not, and I coulda told him that, too. Can't trust any of 'em, I sez."

Adam nodded. "What you're saying is true," he acknowledged. "Now I'll tell you another truth. If someone's out and about making additional trouble and using Bow Street's name to do it, I want a word with him."

The man spat again. "Why should the likes of me believe the likes of you?"

"Cuz you're a smart one," said Adam. "You can tell the measure of a man. And that's why I'm going to believe what you tell me now." To prove his good intent, Adam fished in his pocket and brought out a pair of shillings.

The milkman looked at the coins, and then at Adam. His old eyes were searching, and sly, but he didn't reach for the coins right away. Instead, he scratched under his arm again, and then rubbed his stubbled chin, as if struggling to reach some conclusion of his own. Then, in a great, mocking display, he swept his slouching hat off his head and held it out to Adam. Adam dropped the coins in. The man claimed them. In another show of insolence, he bit the edge of one to make sure it was good.

Evidently deciding the shillings passed muster, the milk-man tucked them into his waistcoat pocket.

"It were a tall fella. Dark hair. Soft hands. Good clothes. Had him a scarlet waistcoat and black cravat. All the trim-mings. Came round, just yesterday. Just about scared the wits outta old Hiden." He gave out another rusty laugh, remem-bering. "Telling him that he's bound for the gallows with all the rest of 'em if he don't answer true."

"Did he give a name, this fellow?"

"Beacher, Beauchamp, something of the kind. Started with a *B* anyway."

Silently, Adam ran down the list of officers and runners he knew, but there was no one who matched the description the milkman gave.

"What did this Mr. B. want to know about?"

The corner of the cowman's mouth curled up in a smile.

"Mr. B, as you calls him, he wanted to know what Hiden knew about the ones that got away. Accused him of helping them slip the net. Especially this fella Edwards."

"Did he bother to ask you about this missing Edwards?"

The man grinned, displaying all his crooked, broken teeth. "He did not."

"What could you have told him if he had?" Adam brought out two more coins.

The sly smile returned. This time there was no nonsense with the hat. He just held out his hand. Adam dropped the coins onto his palm.

"I'd'a told him to go see Celia Ings," said the milkman. "Billy Ings himself used to come down here of a morning, grousing about this and that, and boasting all about this Thistlewood and his mighty friends." The milkman tapped his nose. "A man that goes quiet about his work can hear a good deal."

Adam nodded. Ings was one of the men waiting to go on trial. Celia must be a relative. Possibly his wife.

"Was Edwards one of those friends Ings talked about?"

"Happens he was," said the milkman. "A mighty rich and clever friend at that. Promised them all the money in the Bank of England once the revolution came."

"Do you know where I'd find Celia Ings?"

The milkman gave him directions, at least as far as he could, but told him he could "ask anyone." Celia was well known, it seemed, as was her man. Adam thanked him for his time.

The milkman shrugged. "Doin' nowt but looking after me own," he said, and raised his voice. "Suzy! Where you at, you fool girl!"

Adam left the man to his business, and started back down the hill. Overhead, he could just make out the feeble disk of the sun, already high in the sky. The fog hadn't lifted at all. The world still felt slowed and thickened. What sounds there were seemed sluggish—the cows on their hill, the horses' hooves, and the cautious rattle of carriages, the honk of discontented geese.

The footsteps moving carefully across the grass behind him.

Instinct tensed Adam's shoulders. He raised his feeble lantern and struck off at an angle, heading back for the carriage road, and what crowds would be out on such a morning.

The footsteps followed.

Adam cursed silently. He should have brought someone with him. It was not his habit to run away, but if the man behind him now was the same footpad who'd followed him and Goutier out of the Cocoa Tree the other night, he was dangerous. Turning to face him alone was a pointless risk. If this new footpad didn't want a fight, he could just melt away into this blasted fog.

But there was more than one way to skin a cat of this kind. Adam considered. The neighborhoods around the park were mostly occupied by the *haut ton* and their families. He did not know many persons in that rarified circle.

But there was someone.

The ground underneath Adam's boots changed from wet grass to hard-packed dirt as he reached the carriage road. Adam raised his lantern again to get what few bearings the fog was willing to give up. Then, he turned abruptly to the left, and headed for the park gates.

The footsteps followed.

CHAPTER 23

An Uncomfortable Conversation

". . . her ideas were in too great and painful confusion."

Edgeworth, Maria, *Belinda*

How did one tell a woman she had been poisoned? That question occupied Rosalind for the entire cab ride to Mrs. Levitton's house. After supper last night, she had written a note to Mrs. Levitton asking permission to call early. By the time she'd been ready to retire, a footman arrived, carrying a reply stating that Mrs. Levitton would be ready to see her at any time she might choose.

The footman received her at the door. The maid took her up to Mrs. Levitton's rooms. Mrs. Hepplewhite curtsied when Rosalind entered. The nurse's face betrayed nothing—neither of what she'd done, nor any curiosity to know what Rosalind had discovered.

"Miss Thorne." Mrs. Levitton lay in bed, propped up with bolsters and pillows with several layers of cashmere shawls wrapped around her shoulders. Her color was somewhat better than the last time Rosalind had seen her, and her voice a little stronger. "What have you to tell me?"

How do you tell someone . . . ? The question ran through Rosalind's mind for the hundredth time.

It was imperative that they not be overheard. But there was the maid standing by the door, and the footman in the hall. Of the family, Beatrice, at least, was somewhere in the house. She might not want to wait to find out if Rosalind had brought fresh news about Cate. Any of the other Levittons might arrive at any moment, and come to the room uninvited. On another morning, she might suggest they go into the garden, but that was impossible. No reputable nurse would allow a patient in Mrs. Levitton's supposed condition to be taken outside in this fog.

Mrs. Levitton seemed to understand her hesitation. "You may go, Talmidge," she said to the maid. "And tell Kinnesly I am not to be disturbed, by anyone. That includes any of my relations."

"Yes, ma'am." Talmidge curtsied, and left the room, closing the door behind her.

"Marcus will fume," said Mrs. Levitton to Rosalind. "But we shall have to risk it. Now, sit down, Miss Thorne, and tell me what brings you here so early."

Mrs. Hepplewhite moved a tapestry chair to the bedside. Rosalind sat, smoothing her skirts needlessly.

How . . . Rosalind shook the question away. There was no good method. She could only be direct. "Mrs. Levitton, there has been an attempt on your life."

Mrs. Levitton paused for a single heartbeat. "If this is a joke, it is in very poor taste, Miss Thorne."

"I am not joking, Mrs. Levitton. Your private stock of tea has been tainted with arsenic."

"Nonsense. I drank some of that tea just this morning, and I have not felt so well in almost a week."

"It is not the same tea. The original has been replaced, and has been subjected to an analysis. It is poisoned, and that poison is arsenic."

After this declaration, Mrs. Levitton remained rigid and still, at least for a moment. Then, slowly, she crumpled in on herself, pressing her hand hard against her breast. Mrs. Hepplewhite hurried around the far side of the bed to grasp her shoulders.

"Let go!" snapped Mrs. Levitton, and the nurse, affronted, pulled her hands away.

Mrs. Levitton stayed as she was, bowed over her hand, her breathing rapid and harsh. For a moment, Rosalind thought the other woman might be sick. But slowly, Mrs. Levitton regained control of herself and straightened up to fix Rosalind with her piercing gaze.

"This is a hard, distasteful thing you've told me, Miss Thorne." The words rasped in Mrs. Levitton's throat. "Do you know who is responsible for this . . . this outrage?"

"No. I only know that it happened. I received confirmation this morning from a trusted individual." She paused. "Where is the tea caddy kept?"

"There." She nodded to a lovely cabinet of burled maple with a marble top. "And yes, it is still there."

"Is the cabinet itself locked?"

"No, but the caddy is."

"And who keeps that key?"

"I do," Mrs. Levitton said grimly. "But the whole house knows where it is." She waved toward the mantel, and Rosalind saw a carved box sitting there.

"Is there any servant you have dismissed recently? Perhaps with whom you have had trouble or a falling out?"

Mrs. Levitton snorted. "I recognize it is a common failing of the upper classes to blame their servants for everything, but it is not a weakness I share. No working person would be fool enough to risk their necks in such a ridiculous manner."

"I am inclined to agree," said Rosalind. "But the question had to be asked."

"I suppose," muttered Mrs. Levitton. "Well, Miss Thorne, how do we proceed? Do I barricade my door? Hire a food taster? Hepplewhite here is most dedicated, but I think she will not agree to take on that particular duty."

"Certainly not," said Mrs. Hepplewhite.

"I wish I had a good answer for you," said Rosalind. "But this is beyond my experience."

"And mine, I do assure you." Mrs. Levitton plucked restlessly at her bedcoverings. "Do we assume it is one of my relatives?"

"I do not assume anything," said Rosalind. "I have been wrong too many times."

"Very wise. But I require some plan of action, Miss Thorne."

Rosalind resisted the urge to bite her lip, or to pluck at her skirts in imitation of Mrs. Levitton's uneasy movements. "It would seem that the poisoner's plan was to send you into a slow decline. Therefore, it might be prudent to keep up the appearance of illness."

"Or else they might be inclined to try to hasten things along?" Mrs. Levitton shuddered, the tremor giving the lie to her calm, waspish tone. "There's sense in that, but I do not like the idea of lying in my bed, waiting. My nerves are strong, but even I have my limits."

"I understand. If you will allow, I will continue to speak to your family, with the excuse that I am still helping search for Cate. Hopefully, we will be able to uncover more information."

Mrs. Levitton was silent for a long moment. Her sharp eyes darted back and forth, following the pattern of her private thoughts. Rosalind felt her own nerves tighten.

"And what can you tell me of Cate?" Mrs. Levitton asked finally. "May I take it you do know where she is?"

Rosalind was startled, but not entirely so. She knew Mrs. Levitton had a very quick mind. "Yes."

"And you have for a while, I imagine?"

"Yes. She was very ill when she was discovered, and it was by observing her that the possibility of poison was raised."

Mrs. Levitton's expression hardened. "And that was why you pretended not to know anything about her?"

"Yes," said Rosalind. "I thought to protect her from whoever might have done this thing."

Mrs. Levitton nodded, reluctantly. "But she is well now?"

"She is out of danger and rapidly regaining her strength."

"Does she say why she left?"

"She says it was because she decided she did not want to marry Harold Davenport."

"Stupid girl," snapped Mrs. Levitton. "It was all arranged. She would have had everything she could want, including her freedom. Harold would make no fuss about how she chose to live."

"It can be hard to face the prospect of a lifetime filled with deception."

"Every woman, Miss Thorne, must commit some deception. It is the only way we survive in this world."

Rosalind said nothing. She did not want to agree, but the point was a difficult one to argue.

"Where did she think she was going? And how? I was generous with her, but I didn't give her anything like enough pin money to set herself up independently."

"It seems she has been pawning some jewelry. I found two receipts from a broker in her room." She paused. "I am sorry to have to ask this, but has any of your jewelry gone missing?"

"What you mean to ask is has Cate robbed me as well as poisoned me?"

"For what it may be worth, I do not believe Cate is the one who has poisoned you."

"Heaven spare me." Mrs. Levitton sighed. "However, to answer your question, no, I am not aware that anything has gone missing, but I will have my maid make sure of it. In the meantime, Miss Thorne, you may proceed as you think best, and I will wait here. You may continue to apply to me for any expenses. I will allow you a week."

"Mrs. Levitton . . ."

"A week," she repeated. "I have work to do, Miss Thorne. A life to lead. I will not spend what is left of my days locked in my rooms. Neither will I permit myself to be harangued by Beatrice every day for failing to find her daughter. Now, I may not think much of her. She always was a dull person and she permitted herself to be worn down by her late husband. But she doted on Catherine and does not deserve to suffer because the girl has taken flight."

"Miss Levitton has promised to write to her mother today and say she is safe and well."

"That, I'm afraid, will only change the nature of Beatrice's harangues. A week, Miss Thorne."

"Very well," said Rosalind. "A week. But I have another question." Mrs. Levitton gestured for her to continue. "Why did you decide to return to London just now?"

Mrs. Levitton was silent for a moment, considering her words.

Or her available answers? Rosalind suppressed the thought, but it did not go easily.

"It was time," she said at last. "The old king was failing, the Prince Regent was believed to be a man of the world, with reformist leanings. The uprising at Peterloo showed that the people are not only ready for change, they are demanding it, and the radicals in Parliament were rallying for a fight. They may withhold the vote from us, Miss Thorne, but there is plenty a woman can do to influence events if she tries, and especially if she has money." Her eyes gleamed. "And then came this Cato Street business. You've read the papers?"

"A few, yes," said Rosalind. In fact, when the papers were not talking of the old king's death or the new king's rage against the queen, they were talking about Cato Street. George

Littlefield had even been roped into providing grist for that particular mill. All this was in addition to what Adam had been able to tell her.

"A committee for their defense has been organized," said Mrs. Levitton. "Several radical members of Parliament have joined. I am able to lend them some financial backing, and—" She waved her hand, indicating all that had followed. "You frown, Miss Thorne."

The fact was, Rosalind had frowned to keep from blushing. "I am thinking that sometimes we come very close to making a mistake, and are only saved by luck."

Marianna looked at her very hard. "I will ask you about that at another time."

"Was it known that you were once again involving yourself in politics?"

"I make no secret of it." She lowered her heavy brows. "You cannot think that has something to do with this attempt on my life?"

"I don't know," said Rosalind. "Political intrigue is far beyond my realm of expertise. However, it is my understanding that even while there is fresh movement toward reform, there is also a very strong movement to stop reform, and possibly at any cost."

"As we may see from the fact that eleven impoverished men are being held in the Tower for something they did not do." Mrs. Levitton stopped. "What is your view of the matter, Miss Thorne?"

"I do not yet have all the facts," said Rosalind. "Therefore, I do not care to venture an opinion."

"You are a diplomat. That is to be expected." A pained expression crossed her face, and her cheeks grew pale. Mrs. Hepplewhite moved forward.

"I'm all right," said Mrs. Levitton. "You may withdraw."

"I will not," Mrs. Hepplewhite replied. "Because you are

not. I must insist that this interview end. You still need to rest. Miss Thorne will excuse us."

Rosalind recognized the tone in Mrs. Hepplewhite's voice and knew that argument was impossible. She got to her feet. "I will call again tomorrow if I may?"

"If you do not, I will send for you." Mrs. Levitton sank back onto her bolsters.

Mrs. Hepplewhite adjusted her patient's shawls and laid a hand on her forehead. Mrs. Levitton mumbled something angrily, but Mrs. Hepplewhite did not take her hand away.

"Since you seem to be intent on perpetuating this ruse," Mrs. Hepplewhite said, "may I suggest Miss Thorne go to the breakfast room and say that you suffered a sudden collapse?"

"Why, Hepplewhite," said Mrs. Levitton approvingly. "What an excellent idea." Some light returned to her tired eyes. Then she said to Rosalind, "I am trusting you, Miss Thorne. I require answers."

Rosalind made her curtsy and took her leave. As she descended the stairs, her thoughts returned to what Honoria had told her. *I'd advise you to be careful. . . . She puts on the genteel mask as well as any of us, but she's tough as nails—*

And she does not like to be disappointed.

CHAPTER 24

Turning the Tables

*"... it is not every man who has the clearness of
head sufficient to know his duty to his neighbor."*

Edgeworth, Maria, *Belinda*

"Mr. Harkness." Sanderson Faulks emerged from his
dressing room. The dandy wore a long, scarlet, velvet dressing gown trimmed with black satin over his immaculate fawn linen shirt. "You will excuse my dishabille. I'm
afraid I was not entirely prepared for company at this hour."

It occurred to Adam that Faulks was a perfect fit for his
environment. The sitting room of his new, expensive flat was
filled with paintings, books, and statuary. The furniture was
overstuffed, the rugs thick. The thick, green, velvet curtains
had been closed against the damp outside and a cheery fire
blazed in the marble hearth.

Adam's experience had led him to distrust men with a strong
taste for luxury. They tended to think themselves innately superior to others, and that could be destructive, especially when
combined with money or power. Faulks, however, seemed to
love art and luxury for their own sake, and without passing
judgment on others who did not share his tastes, or have the
means to pursue them.

"I apologize," Adam told him. "I wouldn't have disturbed you if I had any choice."

"I am intrigued." Faulks dropped carelessly onto his sofa. "Pray, do tell me what brings you here!"

"I picked up a footpad in the park this morning," said Adam. "I think he's the same man who followed me from a meeting several nights ago. I expect that he's watching your door now, waiting for me to come back out."

"How rude," remarked Faulks. "Should I send my man to chase him away?"

Adam smiled briefly. "I'd rather you sent your man round to Bow Street with a message from me. With luck, my colleagues and I can catch the man and find out what he's after."

"Aside from your good self." Faulks smiled. "My desk is there"—he waved his hand—"all writing implements and anything else you may need are entirely at your disposal."

Adam thanked him and took up pen and ink. Tauton should be in the station by now. Goutier might take longer to track down, as he would be out with his patrol. Hopefully, the footpad was prepared to wait.

When Adam finished his note, Faulks rang the bell, and a man—presumably the valet—appeared. He was older, square built, and stoic. His coat was plain to the point of being drab, but perfectly cut and immaculately clean.

Faulks gave the man his instructions and the man received them, and the note, without a word.

This done, Sanderson rang his bell again, this time for breakfast. While he gave his orders, Adam moved to the front windows. Taking care to keep to one side, he shifted the green curtain and peered down into the street.

The fog had just begun to lift, allowing Adam a fair view of the street. Faulks lived in a lively and fashionable neighborhood. There was a fair amount of traffic in the road, and a healthy number of loungers at the corners, and in the alleys between the houses. Any one of them could be Adam's footpad. His personal bet was on either the man watching a cluster of porters settle down to their card game, or the fellow coming out of the tavern with a pot of drink in his hand. He'd have to rely on Goutier and Tauton to sort out who was who.

"Come sit down, Mr. Harkness."

A table had been set beside the sofa, and laid with coffee, rolls, jam, and butter. Sanderson poured a cup of coffee for Harkness, and indicated he should help himself to the food. He poured his own cup and added healthy amounts of cream and sugar.

Adam drank the excellent coffee gratefully. The morning's chill still clung to his skin. Faulks split a roll and spread it thickly with jam and butter. At last, he leaned back and watched Adam buttering his own bread.

"Do you know, Mr. Harkness, it occurs to me I know nothing of your background."

"My background?" echoed Adam, startled.

"Yes." Sanderson took a healthy bite of a roll and immediately blotted his lips with his napkin. "I know you, obviously, and your profession. I know you have the good fortune of having secured the interest of the most admirable Miss Thorne, but you yourself remain something of a conundrum."

"That's not a word that's ever been applied to me."

"I'm surprised. Because your speech does not match your station."

Adam let his brows arch.

"Indeed, if you were a character in one of Miss Littlefield's adventures, I'd suspect you of being an errant earl or something of the kind."

Adam chuckled. "If that's the case, my mother's been keeping secrets. May I ask why you're bringing this up now?"

For one of the few times since he'd met the man, Adam saw Faulks look disconcerted.

"We've touched on the subject before, but I admit, as time

has gone on, I have felt a certain . . . urgency growing around the matter of you and Miss Thorne. I find I wish to know more about you, for her sake."

Adam said nothing.

"Yes, I do know that if Miss Thorne realized I was attempting to intervene in any way regarding a man upon whom she chose to bestow her admiration, she would flay me alive." Adam cocked his head. Sanderson laughed. "No, you are correct. Miss Littlefield would flay me alive. Miss Thorne would simply stop speaking to me, which would be worse. And yet here I am, risking what I consider the most precious friendship I possess." The words were light, but Faulks's expression was perfectly serious. "Who are you, Mr. Harkness?"

Adam considered this question, and decided to take it at face value.

"I am the eldest son of Adam Horatio Harkness," he said. "My father was a builder, and he married Johanna Hutchison, a poulterer who kept a stall in Covent Garden. He died when I was still a boy," he said. "Shortly after that, I fell ill to a dampness in my lungs. At least, that's what the apothecary said it was. He said that I must be sent away from London. My mother found a distant cousin who worked as a gamekeeper on an estate in Suffolk, and I was sent there.

"I spent the first month in bed, barely able to breathe." Adam set his cup down so that the involuntary tremor in his hand would not make it slosh, or rattle. "My cousin's wife, Addy Hutchison, was childless, but with me she had a chance to be the mother she'd always longed to be. She was determined that I would live. She spent hours at my bedside. Quite literally spoon fed me. And when I could sit up, she called in the vicar to see to my moral education, since I was not yet strong enough to go to church. The vicar, Mr. Beckenridge, decided to make a sort of experiment of me. He taught me to read, and to write, and spent as much time training me to say my aitches as Mrs. Hutchison did brewing me teas and feeding me broth. Later he wrote a pamphlet calling for universal public education of the working class, using me as a prime example of what could be done."

Faulks made a noise that might have been approval, or astonishment.

"Things were going hard at home, so my mother was glad to let my cousins keep me," Adam went on. "When I was strong enough, my cousin started taking me out with him on his rounds. He taught me to ride, and to shoot, with the idea to train me up as an under-gamekeeper. I might not have minded the work, except for the poachers."

"A dangerous lot, we are told," remarked Faulks.

"A starving, desperate lot, more like," said Adam. "And often they're just tenant farmers trying to keep the rabbits and the pheasants from destroying the gardens they're depending on to get their family through the winter."

Faulks nodded once.

"My cousin was a good man," Adam went on. "He tried to be fair. He knew that many men poached because their families were hungry, but he had his own job to consider and . . . it was hard. There was a lot of bad feeling, and from what I saw, the game laws were too harsh, and the enforcement could be simply unjust.

"So, when I heard they were recruiting for the highway patrol, I decided to try my luck there instead. I'd felt I'd do better chasing after highwaymen rather than old men and boys. It would also let me come back home to London, and my family. I barely knew my older sisters at that point, never mind my youngest brothers. But they welcomed me back, as if I'd never left." He took another swallow of coffee. "That, Mr. Faulks, is my background."

"Unexpected," murmured Faulks.

"How so?"

"I find that I envy you." He poured himself more coffee. "Not your bucolic interlude. I myself would have probably perished from boredom, but you have had the luck of a family that is not only affectionate, but practical and competent. It is an enviable combination."

Adam bowed his head in acknowledgment.

"What is your next move?" asked Faulks, and if he changed the subject a bit too quickly, Adam did not feel the need to remark on it.

"As soon as my colleagues arrive, I'm going to find who's been following me," said Adam. "And then I'm going to find out why."

"You know that if I can be of any assistance . . ."

"Thank you." Adam cut him off. "But not this time. If this is my man, he's already wounded a patrol captain." *Not to mention given me a few bruises of my own.* "This needs to stay in official hands."

Faulks ceded the point without argument, and turned the conversation to platitudes and news of the day. In this way, he gave Adam a chance to simply sit and listen and gather himself, which Adam appreciated.

They had just emptied the coffeepot when the manservant reentered the room, followed by Sampson Goutier.

Adam introduced Captain Goutier to Faulks. Faulks rose and bowed.

"You must both forgive me," he said. "I have business to attend to. Vaughn, you are to follow any instructions the gentlemen may have." With this, Faulks sauntered out of the room.

Goutier raised his brows.

"I'll explain our host later," said Adam. "What can you tell me?"

"You were right," he said. "Our man is waiting outside."

"Show me?"

Moving carefully, Goutier stepped to the side of the window, just as Adam had earlier.

"There." Goutier lifted the curtain and nodded to the

street below. "Beside the barber's. The round-crowned hat and blue coat, standing by the porters playing cards."

So, he'd been right. Adam kept himself back from the window so he wouldn't be seen if anyone happened to glance up. He scanned the street until he picked out the ragged knot of men. From this angle, he mainly saw battered hats and stooped shoulders under brown coats. They all hunkered around a packing crate while the crowds flowed around them. One man stood beside them, arms folded, one foot braced against the shop wall. It seemed he was watching the game, but Adam could tell by the angle of his head that his attention was trained on the front door of Faulks's building.

"Did he see you come in?"

"Not me," said Goutier. "Split off from Tauton, took a wide turn, and came up the backstairs."

"Where's Tauton now?"

"In the cookshop." Goutier nodded toward the establishment next to the barber's. Apparently, business was brisk. Waiters ran out with baskets while people jostled each other to crowd inside. Now Adam made out Tauton's thick-set form standing outside with his hat pulled low and the remains of a chicken leg in his hand.

"All right," said Adam, and Goutier let the curtain fall back into place. "I'm in no mood to muck about with this fellow."

"Me neither." Goutier rubbed his bandaged hand. "Figured you and I could steer him toward Tauton. I'll go out the same way I came in, skirt the crowd, so I'm on his left."

"Good. When I see you're in place, I'll go out the front, and get him to follow me. Then we'll see if he's willing to come along for a quiet word."

Goutier's smile was grim. "What do you think the odds of that are?"

"We're about to find out," replied Adam. "Let's go."

CHAPTER 25

The Results of a Sudden Shock

"I determined to try the poison of jealousy, by way of an alternative."

Edgeworth, Maria, *Belinda*

Alice sat at her desk, surrounded by her heaps of books and papers. She had her page proofs spread out across her desk in front of her. A cup of coffee carried in from breakfast waited close to hand. But rather than attending to her pages, she was surreptitiously watching Cate Levitton writing letters.

Cate sat at the smaller table by the window. Alice had moved the stacks of magazines and newspapers to the second chair to clear a working space for her, and found an inkwell that had not gone dry, and a pen that had a good tip.

From where Alice sat she could see the girl's sharp profile as she bent over the paper. Cate was objectively pretty, Alice decided. Thin and wan, with large, deep eyes. She had the kind of delicacy that made people protective. And kept them from asking questions. She wrote diligently, and without any little habits—like chewing on the end of her pen or twiddling the corners of her pages.

Alice took her pen out of her mouth and laid it down.

She knew that the easiest way to discover anything about Cate would be to ask Amelia straight out what she knew about the young woman, and about what Cate had been telling her. And Alice would have done exactly that, had it not been for one thing.

It was very clear Amelia still had feelings for Cate.

Alice dropped her gaze back to her pages, and tried very hard to ignore the pinch of jealousy in her heart. Jealousy was useless. Worse, it was petty. Alice could not abide pettiness.

But even as she reminded herself of this, jealousy pinched harder. She could practically feel the bruise forming.

Alice did not want to put Amelia in the position of having to tell tales on a friend. That meant Alice had to ferret out Miss Cate Levitton's secrets for herself.

Which led to yet another problem. The fact that she had no idea how to begin. Which simply annoyed her.

Cate straightened up and laid her pen down.

"Finished?" asked Alice brightly.

"Finally." Cate blotted the letter methodically. "I'm afraid I'm not much of a correspondent."

"Not everyone enjoys writing," said Alice. "If you give that to me, I'll see it gets to where it needs to go."

Cate sealed the letter and handed it over to Alice. Then, she hesitated. "Amelia says you taught her to read," she said suddenly.

"We traded lessons," said Alice. "I taught her her letters and she taught me sewing. Or I should say, she tried to. I'm afraid I was a pathetically poor study." Alice pulled a face. At the same time, a warmth spread through her as she remembered the nights when the two of them sat so close together, laughing over Alice's attempts to pin and hem and darn in such a way that did not produce catastrophic lumps in her stockings. She remembered Amelia's hand on hers, trying to help her thread a needle.

"Amelia, however, has a marvelously quick mind," said Alice, before she could start to blush. "I helped her begin, but she mostly taught herself from the papers and magazines. I think she spent every free minute reading, half days included."

"I was . . . surprised to hear it," said Cate. "I didn't think . . . I never . . ." She twisted her hands. "I knew she couldn't read. But I never thought she might want to."

Several tart replies occurred to Alice. She swallowed all of them and tried not to wince at the taste.

"My father didn't like his servants to read, especially the maids," Cate went on. "He said reading would just give them ideas above their station."

"It's a popular belief," Alice acknowledged.

"Yes, but I shouldn't have accepted it. I should . . ." Cate stopped again. "She's a friend. I should have known she wanted to read. I should have helped her."

"When you're looking over your shoulder, you can always see something you should have done," said Alice. "Sometimes it's real, sometimes it isn't. All you can do is your best."

Cate's mouth twitched, but Alice couldn't tell whether she was trying to suppress a smile or a frown. "I didn't even manage that much. If I had, I wouldn't be in this mess." She dropped her gaze. "And I would have written her, if I'd known. I would have explained everything so much sooner."

Which meant Amelia hadn't written to her, either. Alice wondered how Cate felt about that. Then she wondered if Amelia had even thought to send Cate a letter.

The pinch was back.

"Cate, tell me about your friends in Edinburgh," said Alice, partly because she genuinely wanted to know, and partly because it was a distraction from thoughts of Amelia.

She watched Cate considering her next words. Cate Levitton, it seemed, was in the habit of weighing up the people around her and adjusting her answers, and her demeanor, accordingly.

Alice wondered if Rosalind had noticed how often that happened.

"Their name is Wallace," said Cate. "They're sisters—Dorothea and Margaret. I met them in Bath. Their father is a jeweler."

"A jeweler?" said Alice. "That's unusual." Normally, a girl of Cate's class would not be encouraged to attend any gathering where she might accidentally mingle with artisans and their families.

Cate understood what she meant. "Well, things are much more relaxed in Bath than in London. All sorts of people mix together." Which was, of course, one of the reason Bath, and similar watering places, were sneered at by many members of the *haut ton*.

"What brought the family to Bath?" Alice asked.

"Their father, Mr. Gregory Wallace, was there on business," said Cate. "He brought Dora and Peg with him so they could have a holiday."

"Was their mother with them as well?"

"No, she died when they were both young. They were raised by their grandmother for a time. They are both accomplished musicians," she went on. "Dora plays pianoforte and Margaret the flute. We played together a few times."

"You're musical?" Alice was genuinely surprised. "I didn't realize."

"I play viola," said Cate. "Dora and Margaret tell me I'm good. I don't think I'm as good as I should be, but when I practiced with them, I could feel myself getting better, if you understand what I mean."

"I do." Alice also had the feeling that for once, Cate was telling the truth.

"We've been corresponding regularly, well, as regularly as I can, and they've invited me to stay several times. So, when I needed somewhere to go, I thought of them."

"Well, I would love to hear you play," said Alice. "It's not often we have music in the house. It's one talent Rosalind does not possess. And I'm simply hopeless."

"I'd be glad to, but I, well, obviously, I had to leave my instrument behind." Cate looked down at her empty hands. "I was hoping I could send for it once I get settled."

"I don't mean to pry," said Alice. Cate raised her brows, and Alice could not help but laugh. "All right, I do mean to pry. But what exactly are your plans? Surely a jeweler's family cannot take on a permanent guest, and even in Edinburgh one is expected to pay for board and lodging."

"I was hoping . . . Well, Dora and Peg get invited to play parties and routs and so on. Professionally, I mean. I thought I might join them." She paused. "They've even talked about going on the stage."

It was not much of a plan, but it was something. And who knew? If Cate and her friends possessed the art of pleasing as well as a talent for music, they might manage to make a living. People did. Women did.

Is Amelia planning to go with you? The question surfaced before Alice could stop it.

Alice got to her feet. "I was thinking we might take a stroll. The weather's fine this morning, and I'm sure the fresh air would do you good."

"Fine?" Cate frowned at her. "There's a fog out there."

"Best thing in the world for the skin," said Alice briskly. "And amazingly refreshing."

"I'm not sure the doctor would approve."

"We won't tell him."

"What about Miss Thorne? I'm supposed to be in hiding, aren't I?"

"Do we think any of your family is lurking about out-side?"

Alice would not have believed it possible, but Cate's pale cheeks actually lost yet more color. "I hope not."

"Well, then." Alice rang the bell.

Amelia appeared so quickly, she must have been waiting by the door.

"I'm sure you've got a thousand things to do, but I was going to take Cate for a walk. Perhaps down to the market. I was hoping you'd come along."

Amelia's gaze flickered from Alice to Cate.

Alice was a veteran of London's ballrooms, first as a debutante, and then as a gossip writer. She had learned to accurately read the varied language of the meaningful glance.

Amelia's to Cate said *Don't make me do this.*

Cate's silent reply was *We have to.*

The fierce little pinch was back in the depths of Alice's heart. But this time it wasn't jealousy.

It was fear.

By the time coats, bonnets, baskets, and bags were all claimed, the fog had begun to lift.

Alice picked her way down the slick front steps to the flag-stone walk. She turned her face toward the hazy sky and in-haled deeply. The air in London was seldom what one would call truly fresh, but to Alice, just being out of doors was a restorative. It was a trait she shared with Rosalind. A brisk walk could always be counted on to shake her thoughts into proper, or at least useful order.

Perhaps today it would shake loose the correct questions to ask Cate Levitton. Something was not right about the girl. Alice could feel it, and that feeling went beyond jealousy, and beyond the creeping, unfamiliar doubts that had plagued her for so much of the morning.

She was certain Cate Levitton was lying, but for all her skills as a gossip and a writer, she couldn't seem to tease out what the young woman was lying *about*.

"Oh, Amelia, help me with this," said Cate behind her. "I'm useless."

Amelia and Cate stood together on the top stair. Amelia slung her market basket on her arm and reached up to repin Cate's bonnet, which had slipped to an awkward angle. Actually, the bonnet belonged to Alice. Cate's had been ruined by the rain, and Alice had loaned her this one. It was not one of her favorites. Pink did not particularly suit her.

Of course, it suited Cate admirably.

"Don't fuss," muttered Amelia, as she pulled and replaced the long pins. "Now." She stood back, admiring her handiwork.

Admiring Cate.

Alice bit her lower lip hard.

When Amelia turned, her gaze met Alice's.

I'm sorry, her look said. *Truly.*

I know, replied Alice in her heart. *I do.*

Now, Cate turned as well. She smiled, at Alice, at the brightening day, at the passersby on the pleasant street.

Then, she froze. Her pale face turned dead white.

Alice whirled around. Her gaze swept the street. She saw women walking in pairs, she saw maids and tradesmen, nurses with their prams and charges, a gentleman in a tall hat, a cab waiting for a fare.

"Cate!" screamed Amelia.

Alice spun again, just in time to see Cate's eyes roll back in her head. She lurched sideways. And fell.

CHAPTER 26

The Beauty

"A young lady's chief business is to please in society."

Edgeworth, Maria, *Belinda*

"Oh, Miss Thorne!" cried Beatrice as Rosalind entered the breakfast room. "Kinnesly said you had arrived. Have you any news about Cate?"

Like the rest of the house, the breakfast room was bright and airy. It was furnished in the simple, modern style with pale blue walls, comfortable furnishings, and thick rugs. Everett sat at the table with Beatrice, and rose to bow as Rosalind came in. Another woman, whom Rosalind did not know, was there as well. A toast-crumbed plate and half-drunk cup of tea sat in front of her.

"I have made several new inquiries," said Rosalind. "And I hope we may hear something shortly. Perhaps as soon as today."

"There!" cried Everett. "How's that for news?"

"Oh, I hope . . . I pray. . . ." Beatrice clutched her son's arm. The other woman stared into her teacup.

"There, there, Mother," said Everett. "You must calm yourself. Now, Miss Thorne, I was just thinking I should go up to see Aunt Marianna after breakfast. How is she?"

"I'm afraid she is not as well as she appeared at first," Rosalind said. "While we were talking, she seemed to collapse, and her nurse urged me to leave."

"Should we send for the doctor?" asked Everett anxiously.

"Mrs. Hepplewhite has all in hand for the moment, I believe."

"That woman has been invaluable." Beatrice rallied herself to speak coolly. "And the doctor said he would call later today." She paused. "But I'm neglectful. Miss Thorne, I don't believe you have met my daughter-in-law, Mrs. Marcus Levitton. Wilhelmena, this is Miss Rosalind Thorne."

Rosalind had spent her life in and among the *haut ton*. In that society, the cultivation of personal beauty was regarded as one of a woman's foremost duties. But Wilhelmena Levitton was surely one of the most striking women Rosalind had ever seen. She was, Rosalind judged, in her late twenties, but her face was still unlined and her complexion a clear rose and white. She possessed rich, raven-black hair and brilliant, summer-green eyes. Her body was slim, as current fashion demanded, and her cream and yellow day dress was cut exactly to the current mode, with a high waist and fitted sleeves. She held herself in the light, easy manner that Rosalind's deportment masters had tried, and failed, to teach her.

"I am very glad to meet you, Miss Thorne." Wilhelmena's voice was low and clear.

"Have you eaten?" inquired Beatrice. "Will you join us?"

"Thank you." Rosalind took a place at the table and allowed Everett to fetch her a cup of coffee from the urn on the sideboard.

Accepting a cup of coffee in the same house where she knew a poisoning had occurred proved singularly unnerving. Rosalind told herself not to be ridiculous. She reminded herself that whoever had done this thing had a definite purpose in mind. That purpose could hardly include contaminating an entire coffee urn.

Despite these silent admonishments, Rosalind found she could only manage a delicate sip.

"Now, what of these inquiries about Cate?" asked Beatrice. "To whom have you applied? What have they said?"

"Miss Thorne believes Cate may have taken shelter with friends," Everett told Wilhelmena. "You were in her confidence more than the rest of us, Mena. Perhaps you can think of someone she might have turned to?"

"I would not say we were confidantes," Wilhelmena protested. "And I'm sure I didn't have a chance to meet anyone you do not already know about."

"Oh, come, Mena," said Everett. "You can tell us." He nodded meaningfully toward the closed door. "Your lord and master needn't know."

Wilhelmena blushed.

"Everett, don't tease," said Beatrice.

"I'm sorry," said Everett immediately. "I spoke out of turn. You mustn't mind me, Miss Thorne," he went on. "We've all been so worried about Aunt, and Cate. The truth is that my brother's simply a very careful husband. He treasures his reputation, and that of his wife, so he's sometimes strict about whom she associates with." Another man might have said this with a twist of irony or disapproval, but Everett stated this as simple fact.

"Marcus has a great deal to worry about," put in Wilhelmena. "I'm sure Aunt hasn't made it any easier. As for my relationship with Cate—When Marcus and I were in Bath, she and I attended a few private concerts while Marcus was out on business. But it was no more than that. And I will thank you not to say anything to my husband on the subject of whom I may or may not keep company with," she added.

"You know I would never do anything to cause trouble between—" began Everett.

Wilhelmena cut him off. "Certainly you would never mean to."

Rosalind felt certain there was a quarrel underneath those words and that it was old and deep.

"Did you and Mr. Levitton travel to Bath frequently?" Rosalind asked Wilhelmena.

"We generally divide summers between Bath and Brighton," she replied. "My husband always says business is done at the dinner table, and so he prefers to be where society is."

"He's quite correct," said Rosalind. "I've observed something similar many times."

"And are you anticipating a busy season for yourself?"

It was a neat and polite change of subject. "I have received several invitations," Rosalind replied. "I expect it will be a tolerably busy time."

"You are fortunate," said Wilhelmena. "I know it is the done thing to complain about how frantic one is during the season, but I would far rather feel too busy than neglected and dull."

"No one could think of neglecting you," said Everett. "You hold sway over us all."

He seemed to mean this as flattery, but Wilhelmena's smile was tight, and obviously forced.

Beatrice clearly noticed as well. "Everett, please," she said wearily. "No one has the patience now."

"I'm so sorry," said Everett at once. "I only meant—"

"It doesn't matter," said Beatrice.

"Oh, no," said Wilhelmena. "I did not take it as a tease. Just—we're all on edge, you see, Miss Thorne. Between Cate's disappearance and Marianna's illness, we are none of us at our best. I only wish—"

Before Wilhelmena could finish, the door opened and Kinnesly entered with a letter on the silver salver.

"Mrs. Levitton, this came for you." Kinnesly bowed and presented the salver to Beatrice. "The messenger said it was a matter of some urgency."

Beatrice took the note, and her cheeks flushed bright red.

"This is Cate's writing!" she cried. "Kinnesly! Who brought this? Are they still here? Bring them here immediately!"

Kinnesly bowed briefly and retreated. Forgetting everyone around her, Beatrice broke the seal and opened the letter. She read silently, urgently. Rosalind dropped her gaze, making a show of giving her hostess some privacy. From under her lowered lids, she glanced surreptitiously at Wilhelmena, and Everett. Everett was pale. His hand on the tablecloth moved toward Wilhelmena, just a little. But then he seemed to catch himself, and took his hand quickly off the table.

If Wilhelmena noticed this furtive gesture, she gave no sign. Her attention remained fixed on Beatrice. Rosalind could not help but notice that her cheeks had gone as pale as Everett's.

She wondered about this. She also remembered that it was Everett who organized the disastrous dinner before Cate had run away. And before she had fallen so deathly ill.

The door opened again, and once again Kinnesly entered. He bowed to Beatrice. "I'm so sorry, ma'am. The messenger has gone, and left no name, nor any indication where the letter was given to him."

Beatrice lowered the letter and took several deep breaths. "Thank you, Kinnesly."

The footman withdrew and Beatrice turned to her family, and to Rosalind. "She writes—" Her hands trembled and she had to begin again. "Cate writes that she is safe and well and she apologizes for her conduct."

"Does she say where she is?" asked Everett.

Beatrice shook her head. "No. That she does not tell me. But it is her hand, and it is very clear."

"Well, that's good. No, it's marvelous!" Everett got to his feet. "I'll go track down Davenport. He'll want to hear at once. You'll excuse me, Mother? Wilhelmena? Miss Thorne?" He bowed to Wilhelmena and Rosalind and pressed a quick kiss on his mother's hand before taking himself out of the room.

"She encloses a letter for Marianna." Beatrice held up the second letter. "I should go to her. Miss Thorne, you will excuse me?"

"Of course. Forgive me, but do you wish me to continue my inquiries?"

Beatrice was already on her feet. She hesitated.

"Yes," she said quietly. "Please. If, no, *when* you locate her, do not let her know she's found. I would not have her agitated any further, but I must know where she is and whom she is with."

Rosalind nodded, and Beatrice hurried from the room, leaving Rosalind alone with Wilhelmena.

The two women regarded each other.

"I feel I must apologize for these awkward circumstances," said Wilhelmena.

"There is no need at all." Rosalind rose. "I am delighted to know that Cate is safe and well. You must excuse my hurry, but it may be the messenger can be traced."

The truth was Rosalind wanted to leave before Beatrice could return with more awkward questions about her investigations.

"I should go as well," Wilhelmena said. "My husband will want to know what's happened, and it may be some time before Everett remembers to tell him. He means well, but he can be quite careless." She rang the bell, and when Kinnesly appeared, she said, "Miss Thorne is leaving; have her coat and bonnet brought."

Kinnesly bowed and went to retrieve Rosalind's things. The two women faced each other. Wilhelmena smoothed her skirts, clearly hesitating.

"Was there something you wished to say to me, Mrs. Levitton?" asked Rosalind.

Again, there was an awkward pause, and the loss of color in Wilhelmena's smooth, pink cheeks.

"No," she said. "Or rather, there may be." She lifted her gaze. "Perhaps you could call? I will be at home tomorrow."

"Of course." Rosalind made her curtsy. "Thank you. I would be delighted."

Wilhelmena nodded and Rosalind took her leave. Kinnesly met her by the front door, trailed by a parlor maid who helped her on with coat and bonnet. Rosalind turned to allow the young woman to help her on with her coat, and to allow herself a moment to look over the visiting book and cards sitting out on the foyer table, along with new baskets of fruit and flowers. On top of the heap of visiting cards, she saw several belonging to members of Parliament and their wives. The banking trades were not neglected, according to the bold handwriting in the book.

The maid settled Rosalind's bonnet on her head and Rosalind's time was up. She tied her ribbons and headed out the front door, refusing the footman's offer to send a boy to fetch a cab. It seemed she could not visit this house without feeling the need to walk for a time to restore some kind of order to her urgent thoughts.

Rosalind had navigated matters of life and death before. That they had become such a part of her life still astonished her. But this was different from her previous entanglements in so many ways—not the least of which was the sense of urgency. Mrs. Levitton was not dead, and not likely to die soon. This fact would soon be noticed by the poisoner—whoever they might be.

Perhaps they would decide that they had shot their bolt, leave well enough alone, and allow Mrs. Levitton to live out the rest of her natural days.

That, however, could hardly be counted on.

Part of Rosalind's mind cried out there was no way to solve this riddle. There was no way to spool back time to find out who might have stolen the key to Mrs. Levitton's tea caddy. It could have been any family member, or servant, or even one of Mrs. Levitton's many visitors. Rosalind knew there were ample opportunities to cause mischief in a house like this, if the perpetrator was clever, and, more importantly, patient.

But Rosalind also knew that secrets were difficult to keep. The larger and more dangerous they were, the harder it became to hold them in check, especially once an outsider became aware of their existence.

Whether they realized it or not, the Levittons had already begun to put some of their secrets on display. There was clearly some undercurrent between Wilhelmena and Everett, although she did not yet understand its contours. And why had Everett hurried to tell Harold Davenport the news about Cate, but could not be counted on to tell that same news to his brother?

Perhaps he assumed that one of the women would tell Marcus. Still, Rosalind found herself wondering what lay behind this apparent carelessness.

What had been Everett's true purpose in arranging for that dinner, and deceiving his family into attending? She had been told he was a very poor diplomat. That would seem to confirm this assessment. Or was there something else?

She shook her head. A single person could not be poisoned at a family dinner. Not only would there be no time to contaminate the food, there would be nothing that would be eaten by one particular person.

And what possible reason could Everett Levitton have to poison Cate? Or Marianna?

Rosalind squared her shoulders. She would definitely take Wilhelmena up on her invitation to call tomorrow. Perhaps she would find some answers then. In the meantime, she had a very different appointment to keep. This one with Messrs. Temple and Trigg, who had proved willing to take the jewels offered to them by a young woman in pawn.

Jewels that might very well properly belong to Mrs. Levitton.

CHAPTER 27

A Strange Confluence of Events

"... it was my pride to lose with as much gaiety
as anybody else could win ..."
Edgeworth, Maria, *Belinda*

Goutier was the first to leave Faulks's flat. He retreated quickly down the same backstairs he'd used to arrive unseen from the street. Adam took up his post at the window again, and waited.

After a long moment, Goutier stepped out of the alley that snaked alongside Faulks's building. Adam's attention shifted to their man, the footpad. There was no mistaking when he noticed Goutier, who was, after all, not hard to miss, being a burly Black man nearly six feet tall in a crowd of much shorter, paler persons.

Goutier adjusted his hat and walked deliberately down the street, away from the cookshop where Tauton was still loitering.

As soon as Adam was certain the footpad's attention had been caught, he bolted out of the flat and down the front stairs.

When he reached the street though, Adam changed his pace. Now, he was moving quickly, but with deliberation. He set off in the opposite direction from Goutier, striding along the sidewalks as if he'd never noticed the footpad lounging with the other men. While Goutier turned the corner past the wine shop, Adam headed for the cookshop, and Tauton lounging against the wall, gnawing his chicken leg.

Come on, he thought toward the footpad. *You're not just going to stand there, are you?*

He was not. From the corner of his eye, Adam saw the footpad tug on his hat brim. Perhaps he said something to the card players, because they all laughed. Then, the footpad tucked his hands in his pockets and strolled away, moving easily and without concern in the same direction as Adam.

Adam passed Tauton, and the doorway of the cookshop. As he did, Tauton pushed himself away from the wall where he was lounging, and stepped right into the other man's path.

"Now then, friend," Tauton said. "I want a word with you."

The footpad pulled up short, and tried to duck around Tauton, but Adam had already pivoted, and now stood between the footpad and the street. The man turned on his heel, and found himself face to face, or rather nose to shoulder, with Sampson Goutier.

"You're nicked." Goutier laid his heavy, bandaged hand on the footpad's shoulder. "So no fuss this time, eh?"

"Who are you?" the man demanded. "What right—"

"We're Bow Street," said Tauton cheerily. "And you, my fine fellow, are Jack Beachamp, thief-taker. At least you used to be. You may have found it useful to change your name a time or two."

"Who the devil . . . ?" the man demanded.

"Sam Tauton." Tauton touched his battered hat brim with the chicken bone. "We've had dealings, you and me." Tauton's memory for faces was legendary around Bow Street. He could recall any person he'd met, no matter how many years might have passed.

Beachamp blinked in a surprise Adam felt sure was feigned.

"By God, so it is!" Beachamp cried, as if suddenly meeting an old friend. "I didn't recognize you. These two some of yours?" He jerked his chin toward Adam and Goutier. "You need to teach them better manners, Tauton! They just about scared the life out of me the other night."

"Now then, Jackie, you keep a civil tongue," Tauton warned him. "Maybe we should get off the street for our talk?" Tauton looked to Adam, who nodded in agreement. They were already getting plenty of curious glances, and some of the passersby had slowed down to have a look. Then, there was the possibility that Beachamp might still try to cut and run. Adam didn't want to have to dodge traffic and crowds trying to catch him, especially if some in the crowd took it into their heads to help a fleeing man on general principles.

A few minutes later, the four of them were all safely stowed in the little yard behind the wine shop, surrounded by stacks of empty barrels and heaps of ash and refuse. The proprietor was a Frenchman, and professed himself only too glad to be of any assistance, however small, to the officers of Bow Street.

Goutier planted himself beside the yard's iron gate. Adam took up his station between the shop's back door and the area stairs that led down to the cellar.

"Now then, Jackie." Tauton heaved a barrel off the nearest pile and sat down on it. The wooden slats creaked dangerously. "Would you like to explain why you were hanging about the Cocoa Tree and following honest officers out on their night's work?"

"You really think I was *following*—" Beachamp's face was a study of shocked innocence. He spread his hands. "I had no idea who you were when I left the Cocoa Tree. As for why I was there, I was on business, and I thought *you* were following *me*."

"So, of course, that wasn't you following me from the park this morning?" Adam asked him.

"The park?" Beachamp blinked again, the picture of confusion. "What would I be doing in the park, especially on such a morning as we had today? Look, Tauton, you want to know what I'm doing, all you have to do is ask, and I'll tell you."

"All right. Tell us." Tauton leaned back and folded his arms. The barrel creaked again. Adam found himself hoping this interview wouldn't finish with Tauton on the ground.

Beachamp looked around him, making sure he met each of the officers' eyes in turn. *Just what are you looking for?* Adam wondered. He also got the distinct feeling the man was sorting through his mental inventory, trying to come up with exactly the right story to distract his little audience.

Adam prepared himself to be entertained.

At last, Beachamp said, "I'm on a job myself. A girl's gone missing. The family's scared to death and they want her found. This street here's pretty much Bachelor's Row, now, isn't it? And I've had word the girl was seen in the neighborhood. I was keeping an eye out for her. That's all."

"Pull the other one, Jackie," drawled Tauton. "It's got bells on."

"I swear it's the truth!" cried Beachamp. "That's why I was at the Cocoa Tree last night. I was asking after the girl. I was on my way home, minding my own business, when these two"—he waved at Adam and Goutier—"jump out at me. Well, what am I supposed to think but that they're after my purse?"

"What's this girl's name?" asked Adam.

"Cate Levitton."

Adam felt himself go very still. Goutier, who knew him well, noticed, and covered over the sudden silence.

"And why would a girl's family be talking with you?"

"Well, that's my business, isn't it?" said Beachamp. "Finding what's lost. Ask Tauton, here."

"Oh, aye, he does find all sorts of things." Tauton grinned. "Sometimes even before they've been lost."

Beachamp's cheeky grin stiffened. "Now you're the one needs to keep a civil tongue. All I'm guilty of is doing a job when your lot can't."

"Tell us about this missing girl," said Adam. "What's her name again?"

Beachamp frowned, and for a moment Adam thought he was going to refuse to talk.

"Like I just told you, her name's Levitton. Catherine Levitton. The family calls her Cate. She acts, or acted, as companion to her widowed aunt. By all accounts, the old girl's ready to peg out any day now. But before she shuffles off this mortal coil, the aunt wants to see the girl restored to the bosom of the family, and she's willing to put up a good reward to see this happy event occur."

"And how is it they came to call on you in particular for this job?" asked Adam.

Beachamp seemed to realize something was off with Adam's questions. "Well, it wasn't exactly that way," he said cautiously. "Happens I'm friendly with one of the maids in the house, and she, knowing my business, sent me word."

It was a plausible story. Men such as Beachamp frequently made themselves agreeable to servants in wealthy households so they could pick up gossip, and anything else that might not be nailed down.

It would also explain why none of the Levitton family had told Rosalind they'd hired a thief-taker to try to find Cate.

A very plausible story, Adam thought again. The only problem was, he felt sure it must be a lie from beginning to end.

Which left the question, how did Beachamp come to know so much about Cate Levitton and her disappearance?

"So, you never met this old lady?" Adam pressed. "Who is she again?"

"One Mrs. Marianna Levitton," Beachamp said. "And I have yet to lay eyes on her. Got the whole story from my little maid."

"And what's the maid's name?" asked Tauton.

"Oh, no," said Beachamp. "I'm not having you lot making trouble for her. She'd be out on her ear for having a follower, when all she's doing is trying to help the family."

"And to help you as well," put in Goutier. "How much is the reward, anyway?"

"Ah, I see your game," said Beachamp waggishly. "You're thinking to poach my job, you are."

"Answer him, Jackie," said Tauton.

Again, Beachamp's knowing eyes swept across each of them, weighing, judging. "Fifty pounds," he said. "Which is more than enough for a poor man such as myself." He laid his hand on his breast and dropped his gaze, suddenly assuming an air of modest piety.

Goutier looked at Adam. "I don't believe him. Do you?"

"No," said Adam flatly.

"Well, that's that, then," said Tauton. "You're under arrest, Jackie."

"What!" cried Beachamp. "What for?"

"Attacking an officer," said Adam. Goutier held up his bandaged hand, in case Beachamp had forgotten.

"I thought you were hooligans, after my purse," Beachamp said. "How was I to know you were Bow Street?"

Tauton got ponderously to his feet. "We'll just let the magistrate sort that out."

Goutier stepped forward, just to remind Beachamp that running would do him no good. "Probably you should know

Mr. Birnie takes a dim view of the sort who goes around damaging his officers."

Adam expected Beachamp to protest, but he didn't. He just raised his hands, gesturing that they should all calm down. "All right, all right," he said, looking directly at Adam. "No need to be rude. I'm coming quietly, aren't I?" He held up his hands, and his gaze did not shift at all. "But you might just find out that I'm not the one in trouble here."

CHAPTER 28

A Private Business Matter

". . . that as to anything in the private *conduct of that person . . . Belinda should observe on these dangerous topics a profound silence . . ."*

Edgeworth, Maria, *Belinda*

Fortunately the cab driver was acquainted with the street where Temple & Trigg was located. If he gave Rosalind a measuring glance when she asked to be taken there, he did not inquire as to her business, or refuse to drive her.

Under other circumstances, Rosalind would have waited until one of her male acquaintances could accompany her, perhaps Sanderson Faulks, or George Littlefield. Or Adam. But the matter remained urgent. Therefore, she decided to take the risk and go alone.

Fortunately, the neighborhood had every appearance of at least a middling respectability. The shop itself was freshly painted and looked out onto the busy high street through clean windows. A few select pieces of jewelry and one gold pocket watch were displayed on wooden trays to hopefully catch the eyes of pedestrians. The three golden balls on its shingle overhead were understated and dominated by the gilded lettering that announced the establishment's name.

Rosalind decided to take the shop at face value, paid off her cab, and went inside.

A booming voice greeted her. "Good afternoon, ma'am!"

The man behind the counter was portly and balding. Perspiration gleamed on his mottled brow, despite the fact that the shop was not at all warm. He wore a black coat, a modestly patterned waistcoat, and a simple cravat. A pair of gold pince-nez spectacles hung on a chain around his neck.

"Good afternoon," replied Rosalind. "I wish to speak to Mr. Trigg."

"You are doing so." The man bowed. "I am Adolfus Trigg. Unless you mean my brother, Jeremiah Trigg? He has stepped away for the moment."

"You are the Mr. Trigg I need. I have some receipts with your name on them." Rosalind pulled the tickets from her reticule and laid them on the counter.

Mr. Trigg perused the tickets briefly. "Did you wish to redeem these items?"

"Not immediately. I was hoping to inquire about the person who brought them to pawn."

Clearly affronted, Mr. Trigg drew himself up. "Forgive me, ma'am, but what possible business could that be of yours?"

"The young woman who was holding these tickets has vanished from her home," said Rosalind. "It is also not entirely clear that the jewels were ever hers to pawn."

Pawnbrokers, of course, frequently dealt in suspect goods. But shops such as this tended to be at least somewhat careful about courting notice from Bow Street, or other authorities.

Under Rosalind's steady gaze, Mr. Trigg's heightened dignity bled away and he shrank back down to his previous stance. He also fumbled with his chain and perched his

pince-nez on his high-bridged nose. He picked up the first re-
ceipt and squinted at it for a long moment.

He removed the pince-nez and regarded Rosalind warily.

"I believe I remember the young woman," he said. "Rather
well, in fact."

"Can you tell me about her?"

"What is your interest in the subject?"

"The family wishes her traced. They are very concerned
for her welfare."

He tucked the pince-nez into his waistcoat pocket and regarded Rosalind for an additional moment without speaking.
Rosalind was aware she was being assessed. The man was
judging her clothes, her deportment, her speech.

At last, he heaved a deep sigh. "She said the jewels belonged to her aunt, who was a widow and had suffered a financial reversal. That she was in fact bamboozled by an
unscrupulous stock jobber, and had lost her entire portion.
Her brother had refused to loan her aunt the necessary sum
on any account." He paused. "You should know, ma'am,
that in my profession we hear many such stories. Many of
them are . . . less than strictly accurate, shall we say. Even
when told by ladies of quality. It is supposed that our heart-
strings may be played upon. But I recall that hers had the ring
of truth."

It would, thought Rosalind. Considering that many of the
details had been drawn from Cate's real life.

"Are the jewels still in your keeping?" she asked.

"They are."

"May I see them?"

Again, Mr. Trigg leveled his keen, measuring glance on her.
"Very well," he said at last. "If you will give me a moment,
please."

Mr. Trigg vanished into the back of the shop. Rosalind
waited, and resisted the urge to pace.

Was this possible? Was Mrs. Levitton in financial trouble? Rosalind hesitated. She remembered Mrs. Levitton's flinty bargaining this morning, even after she had just learned how close she'd come to dying. She was an intelligent, experienced woman with a core of iron. It was difficult to believe that she had fallen prey to any stock scheme.

But it was also true that those who were most confident in their own cleverness could sometimes be the easiest to fool.

It certainly would explain why Cate had pawned the jewels rather than selling them outright. Mrs. Levitton might believe that she could restore her own fortunes enough to redeem the pledged items.

No. Rosalind shook her head at these thoughts. It did not make sense. Pawning jewelry was a last resort, not a first. Mrs. Levitton was not an impecunious widow who had played too deeply at cards. She was a woman of business, and property. If she needed money, she could sell one of her businesses, or draw a loan against the shares. She might even sell her house.

And supposing this story was true, why would Cate have pawned the jewels and then immediately run away? Was she callous enough to steal the money her aunt needed to help stave off ruin? Or did she run so that her aunt would not be forced to admit she could not make the dowry settlement she had promised?

Or, had she perhaps found out the trusted Mr. Davenport, who managed the mines, was in some way responsible for her aunt's difficulties?

Rosalind smoothed her hand over the counter. She felt as if time was draining away from her, carried by a flood of unanswered questions.

Rosalind reminded herself to be patient, to trust herself, as she always had. But she could not soothe that last little frightened voice in the back of her mind. *This time is different,* it told her. *This time Alice is at risk. Amelia, who is in your charge, is at risk. This time, you are responsible not for solving a puzzle, but saving a life.*

Fortunately, Mr. Trigg's return shook her out of her spiraling worry. He carried a wooden tray and set it down on the counter. Rosalind felt her eyes widen in surprise.

The receipts had described a topaz and diamond necklace and a matching bracelet. Rosalind had not imagined the stones to be so big. The smallest topaz was the size of her thumbnail, the largest was a full two inches square. She could not count the number of diamonds that framed the amber stones. The gems were set in filigrees and festoons of yellow gold.

Together the bracelet and necklace looked positively garish, but they were also probably worth at least five times what Rosalind could expect to earn in a year.

"Quite something, aren't they?" said Mr. Trigg.

"Indeed they are," agreed Rosalind. "Are they antiques?"

"One would think. This level of baroque magnificence puts one in mind of the Tudors, or the *ancien régime*." A smile flickered across his face. "But no, they are quite new. The maker's mark is that of a well-known Parisian firm."

"Mr. Trigg, can you describe the young woman who brought you these?"

Mr. Trigg considered. "Slim, young, neatly but not expensively dressed. Well-spoken, if a little shy, a pale complexion, but not overly fine. Large dark eyes, and dark hair."

Rosalind nodded. That described Cate perfectly. So, it was not some confederate or some stranger assuming Cate's name who came to this shop. At the same time, she thought of Mrs. Levitton's airy sitting room and its understated elegance and perfect taste. Rosalind found she could not imagine Mrs. Levitton wearing something so garish. As for the rest of the Levitton women, they simply could not have afforded such jewels.

But if Cate had not gotten these jewels from her aunt, where on earth did they come from?

CHAPTER 29

A Quiet Drink with Friends

"A report has just reached me concerning you . . .
which gives me the most heartfelt concern."

Edgeworth, Maria, *Belinda*

The livery in the next street supplied a carriage to take the officers and their prisoner to Bow Street. Beachamp remained positively convivial, for the entire journey. He even kept up a lively conversation with Tauton about pickpockets and petty criminals they'd both known. He was still smiling when Adam and Goutier took him through to the clerks to have his name and the reason for his arrest written into the ledgers. They then ushered him down to the cramped cluster of cells under the station.

Adam handed Beachamp over to Wilder, the turnkey. Beachamp bowed, sweeping off his hat. "Until we meet again, Mr. Harkness."

Disquieted, Adam turned away and started back up the stairs.

"Stand you to a pint?" suggested Goutier as he closed the door behind them.

Adam shook his head. "You go . . ."

"Harkness," said Goutier quietly. "You're thirsty. Let's go over to the Brown Bear and have a drink, all right?"

Adam looked at him. "Do you know, it's been a long day. I think a drop of something would do me good."

The Brown Bear public house stood directly across from the Bow Street station. In addition to serving drinks to the men who worked there, it served as something of an annex to the station. Suspects might be held in the cellar or the rooms upstairs, or even invited across for a quiet drink so that they could be identified by a witness who just happened to be having a drink of their own by the fire.

The fire was banked this afternoon. Despite this, Adam headed to the bench beside the chimney. It allowed him a good view of the rest of the room. Half the customers in the big room were Bow Street men, so it was not that he feared anyone sneaking up behind him. Still, sometimes it was good to be able to see who might be listening.

The look in Goutier's eyes when he'd suggested they get a drink told Adam this was most likely one of those times. Indeed, Adam and Goutier had just settled themselves at the long table when the door opened again, and Sam Tauton sauntered in.

"Thought I'd find you two here." He plunked himself down onto the bench. "Oi! Lizzie!" he shouted to the barmaid. "You've thirsty men here!"

Lizzie was a stout, strong woman with a right arm that could lay a man flat with a single blow. Her first response to Tauton's shout was a crude gesture, but shortly after that, she came round with a tray of pint pots and a pitcher of the pub's bitter ale.

Tauton took a healthy swallow of beer and wiped his mouth. "Ask him yet?" he said to Goutier.

"Just about to."

"What's this?" asked Adam.

"Tauton and me wanted to hear why we really arrested Jack Beachamp," Goutier said. "Not to say we didn't have good cause, what with him stabbing an officer, but somehow I don't think that was uppermost in your mind."

"It's not that it doesn't matter—" Adam began.

"Give over, man." Tauton cut him off. "Something's wrong. What is it?"

Adam drank his beer and tried to decide where to start.

"Miss Thorne is involved in a new business," he said softly. "A wealthy widow is being slowly poisoned."

Goutier made a sound of deep disgust.

"It just so happens," Adam went on, "that the old lady's name is Levitton. And her niece and companion is named Cate Levitton, and this Cate Levitton is currently staying with Rosalind Thorne and Alice Littlefield."

"Well," drawled Goutier. "That is an interesting coincidence."

Tauton nodded in agreement. "I should say. Now, Jackie Beachamp may be a scoundrel, and a thief, and I'm sure he's not above taking his pound of flesh—"

Goutier held up his wounded hand, Tauton gestured toward it with his pint pot. "But slow poison? That's nasty. Can't see Jackie having the stomach for it, or the patience, for that matter."

"But do you know what else is interesting?" said Adam. "How calm that Beachamp was when he found out he was getting arrested."

"Yes. I noticed that, too," said Tauton.

"You think Townsend is keeping an eye on you again?" asked Goutier. "Maybe using Beachamp to do it?"

Adam's relationship with Mr. Townsend was prickly, to say the least. One irritant, unfortunately, was Townsend's mixed view of Rosalind Thorne. Townsend might not know the exact extent of their relationship, but he did know it went beyond the professional or coincidental. Townsend was a blatant social climber, and Rosalind's connections extended to the very upper reaches of society. That meant Townsend's first instinct was to court and flatter her. But Rosalind had also openly inserted herself into several cases that wound up in Bow Street, and that was not something he was ready to tolerate from any civilian, especially a woman.

This, combined with the fact that Adam more than once had exceeded his orders, or simply gone around them, caused Townsend to keep a closer eye on him than he did on the other principal officers. Once, he'd even tried to bribe Goutier to spy for him.

"I wouldn't be surprised if it turned out Townsend set someone on my heels," said Adam. "But it wouldn't explain why Beachamp would know about Cate Levitton. He gave out with far too many details for it to be a coincidence that he dropped that name." He turned to Tauton. "What do you know about the man?"

Tauton took another swallow of beer and rolled it around his mouth while he thought. "He's best described as a slippery character. He's a thief-taker, that you know, and if I hadn't made it clear before, he's the sort that works with the thieves."

Adam and Goutier both nodded. It was an old game. Thief-taker and thief would enter into a private agreement. The thief would rob a house, or a person. The victim would offer a reward for the return of the property. Shortly afterward, a thief-taker would appear on their doorstep, offering their services, and promising that the property would be returned. If the victim agreed to their fee, the thief-taker would go to their partner and collect the stolen items, or most of them. These would be returned to the victim and the thief-taker would claim both fee and reward. All the money would then be split with the thieves. Unless, of course, the thief-taker decided to turn the thieves in and keep the money for himself.

The worst part of it was how difficult it could be to catch such men. Most victims simply wanted their property returned. They were willing to pay what amounted to a ransom, and go about their business. Even if a crooked thief-taker was reported, there was little Bow Street could do unless the man was positively known to have been involved in the burglary.

"What surprises me is that Beachamp's back in town," Tauton was saying. "I thought he'd moved on."

"He get himself into trouble?" asked Goutier.

"More times than I can count," said Tauton. "Man's a gambler. Gets in over his head. Has to leave London every so often until the bully boys in the various dens have forgotten about him. Last I'd heard he'd gone off to Bath to see about the pickings there."

"Bath?" echoed Adam.

"There it is again," said Goutier. "Harkness, you look like your beer's gone off."

"The widow, Mrs. Levitton, she was resident in Bath for quite some time," Adam told them. "She only returned a few months ago."

"Now there is another interesting coincidence," remarked Goutier.

"To be sure," agreed Tauton.

Adam looked into the bottom of his pint pot, trying to sort through his thoughts. "Does Beachamp have anybody he works with regularly? Any fences who take his goods if the owners won't pay up?"

Tauton rubbed his chin. His eyes flickered back and forth as he dug into the depths of his prodigious memory.

"Seems to me I heard once he was working with a woman, a housebreaker. What was her name?" Tauton paused, and then suddenly snapped his fingers. "Finch! That was it. Franny Finch. Ran a gang of lady thieves. Specialized in locked houses and second-story work."

"Could Fran Finch be the maid that Beachamp was talking about?"

"It's possible," said Tauton. "Or one of her girls could."

But Goutier looked frankly skeptical. "I don't like coincidence either, but what are you thinking? That Beachamp and this woman Finch poisoned the aging aunt and kidnapped Cate Levitton?"

"I don't know," Adam admitted. "But why did Beachamp come up with the name Levitton when he needed a covering story? And how did he know she was companion to her aunt, *and* that her aunt was ill and possibly dying *and* that Cate herself had gone missing?"

"And," said Goutier, "if he's really trying to find Miss Cate, why's he following you?"

Adam gestured, indicating his agreement. He and Goutier had gone to the Cocoa Tree before Rosalind called on the Levittons. Even supposing that Beachamp really did have a confederate in the Levittons' house, and supposing that Beachamp already knew about Adam's connection to Rosalind, he still could not have known that Rosalind would become involved with the Levitton family.

Which meant, despite his denials, Beachamp really was following Adam. And the only possible reason for that was Adam's hunt for the elusive Mr. Edwards.

Unless, of course, there was some other connection between Beachamp and Cate Levitton.

Adam froze.

"He's thought of something," said Goutier to Tauton.

"I should say he has," Tauton agreed. He made a gesture with two fingers. "Give over, man, what is it?"

But Adam just stood up. "Make sure Wilder and his men keep a special eye on Mr. Beachamp tonight, will you?"

"You suddenly don't think our cells are safe enough?" asked Tauton.

"Call it a hunch," said Adam. "I don't like even one coincidence on a case. Now, we've got two, at the very least, and I like that even less."

"Anything else you don't like?" inquired Goutier.

"As it happens," said Adam, "I find I really don't like the fact that our Mr. Beachamp was not at all worried about being locked up."

Adam took up his hat and hurried out the door. He had to get to Rosalind. And to Alice.

Because there was another possible connection between Cate Levitton and Beachamp. And that connection happened to also be resident in Rosalind's house.

Amelia McGowan.

CHAPTER 30

The Maid's Point of View

"The curiosity of the servants may have been excited by last night's disturbance. . . ."

Edgeworth, Maria, *Belinda*

"There you are."

Amelia was still helping Rosalind off with her coat and bonnet when Alice emerged from her book room.

"Yes," agreed Rosalind.

Alice, of course, heard the odd, flat tone in Rosalind's voice. "Amelia, I think Rosalind needs some tea," she said. "Can you—"

"Actually, Amelia, there are some things we all need to talk about."

Amelia froze, surprised and, Rosalind was sorry to see, afraid.

"Yes, miss," she said reflexively.

Alice was watching her, trying to guess what was coming. Rosalind moved past them both and went into the parlor. They followed her there. Alice was the one who closed the door. Amelia took her place by the fire, hands folded, ready and waiting for whatever might be coming next. It was only her eyes that betrayed her. Her gaze darted between Rosalind and Alice, trying to read their faces, trying to get ready for what would happen next.

"Did you find out something?" Alice asked.

"Not as much as I hoped," admitted Rosalind. "Truthfully, I wasn't able to do much more than form an impression of the Levittons. They're a troubled family."

"I could have told you that much," said Amelia quietly. "At least, that's how it was when I was in service with them."

Rosalind sat down on the sofa and rubbed her hands together. It was a lovely, warm, spring day outside, and yet she could not shake the chill inside her. "Amelia, I recognize this matter puts you in a very difficult position. It is not right to ask you to talk about your former employers—"

"No, that's all right, miss," said Amelia. "If it'll help Cate, and you." Rosalind did not miss the way her eyes flickered toward Alice. "But, I'm not sure what I could tell you, outside the common way. It was three years ago."

"You can tell me what you saw when you were there. What your impressions of the family were then."

"Come and sit down," suggested Alice.

She gestured to the round-backed chair beside the sofa. Amelia moved forward, but reluctantly. Rosalind could see Alice's disappointment at Amelia's caution. But Alice said nothing, just sat on the sofa beside Rosalind and waited for whatever Amelia chose to tell them.

"You can tell pretty quick whether you're in a good house or not," said Amelia softly. "It was clear from the start the Levittons' was an uneasy place. Lots of sniping and backbiting and everybody out for themselves." She twisted her hands together. "As above, so below," she whispered.

Rosalind nodded.

"They may put the blame on Cate for being the bad girl, but the rest of them made plenty of trouble of their own.

Mrs. Levitton, Mrs. Beatrice Levitton, that is, she was tired all the time. Too tired to keep proper watch over the staff. Left it all to the housekeeper, Mrs. Hatch, and the Hatch, oh, she was a clever one. Her and Cook had a whole set of little ways to make money off everybody's leavings. Never saw so many men coming to the back door. Everything was for sale—candles, flour, oil. They made up the accounts and gave the misses false bills."

"And no one caught them at it?" said Alice.

"No one looked. Mr. Levitton, he left it all to his wife, even though it was plain that she couldn't manage, and his idea of what to do about that was scold her. We all heard him."

Amelia pulled a face. "Mr. Marcus was just the same. His dad scolded him, and he turned around and scolded everybody else, including his mum. Mr. Everett, he was always trying to smooth things over. Tried to make a joke out of everything. Sometimes it worked."

"What about Cate?"

Amelia bit her lip. "See, things was different for Cate. Her mother didn't have the energy for much of anything else, but she doted on Cate."

"Because Cate was her only daughter?" asked Rosalind.

"Because Cate was the one who lived," said Amelia. "At least that's what I'd heard. After she had Everett, Mrs. Beatrice lost four girls, all in a row. So, when Cate came along, she spoiled her her whole life. And didn't that just make the mister go spare." She bit down hard on those last words.

"Did they start blaming Cate for the household problems?"

"They blamed her for being Cate," said Amelia. "Mr. Marcus and their father. She couldn't do nothing right, could she?" Her anger rose, and her speech became less careful. "Too loud, too careless, too sullen, too brazen . . . whatever upset them at the moment."

"How awful," murmured Alice.

"Did the late Mr. Levitton complain of Mrs. Marianna as well?" asked Rosalind.

"Only every other day," said Amelia. "When he got tired of complaining that Mrs. Beatrice was slothful and wasteful, he'd turn around and start complaining Mrs. Marianna was a conniving shrew who led his uncle around by his . . ." She stopped, her cheeks coloring.

"We'll take that as read," said Alice. "Go on."

"I was told that when his brother, Mrs. Marianna's husband, died, there was a rare to-do about the will. She'd been left everything, and the mister, he was going to take her to court over it."

"Did he?" asked Rosalind.

"What they said was that Mrs. Marianna just turned up one day, all in black. Breezed straight into the parlor and called the lot of them to order. She announced she would be giving the mister an allowance, and if Mr. Marcus or Mr. Everett wanted to go to school, or into business, she would set them up. But if the mister said one more thing about courts and his right as her husband's brother, she would drag him and the rest of the family straight through the mud." She paused. "To hear the Hatch tell it, Mrs. Marianna said she was used to scandal and it didn't bother her in the least, but the mister might not fare so well."

"And the mister backed down?" asked Alice.

Amelia nodded. "Didn't stop scolding, didn't stop blaming, but he stopped all the talk about court."

"But he took the allowance?" inquired Rosalind.

Amelia nodded. "Least, that's what the Hatch said. Said the mister and Mr. Marcus had a dreadful shouting match over it, too. Mr. Marcus said he couldn't understand why his father would take money from such a woman."

"But Mr. Marcus takes her money as well, does he not?" put in Alice.

"That, I wouldn't know," Amelia said.

Rosalind considered all that Amelia had just told them. It seemed to fit with her observations of the Levittons. Her heart went out to Amelia, and to Cate. Life in such a house must have been enormously difficult for both of them. Amelia would have had to constantly navigate a household filled with petty corruption and gossip. And Cate . . . she would have to live with the constant contradiction of a mother who cherished her, but a father and brother who always reminded her that her mother did not measure up, and neither did she.

That could breed a tight bond between mother and child. Or, the child could also come to disregard and even loathe her mother, because that's what everyone around her did.

"There's something you should know, Rosalind," said Alice. "Something happened today."

Rosalind waited. Amelia shifted her weight from foot to foot. "Should I leave?"

"No, I think you'd better stay; you may be able to help shed some light on the matter," said Alice. Did she notice the disappointment in Amelia's eyes? If she did, she ignored it.

"Amelia, Cate, and I were going out for a walk this morning," Alice told Rosalind. "But we only made it to the front steps. As soon as we got out of doors, Cate fainted, right there on the steps. She claimed later that she'd overestimated her strength, but I'm sure she saw something that frightened her. Something or somebody."

"Could you tell who? Or what?"

Alice shook her head. "Neither could Amelia."

Rosalind looked to Amelia, who also shook her head. But Rosalind saw the fresh wariness in her eyes. "Do you have any guess as to who it might have been?"

"No, miss," said Amelia. "It could be what she said, she just took a turn. She's been so ill."

It was clear to Rosalind that Amelia wanted this to be

true, but it was equally clear that she didn't believe it. If Rosalind had not been able to read as much in the young woman's face for herself, one glance at Alice would have told her all she needed to know.

Oh, Amelia.

She did not have a chance to say anything more. The urgent rap of the door knocker cut through the room.

"Should I get that?" asked Amelia, who was heading for the parlor door even as she spoke.

Alice had twisted around to peer out the window. "I'd say she'd better. It's Mr. Harkness."

CHAPTER 31

"You will do me justice when you are cool."

Edgeworth, Maria, *Belinda*

Amelia nipped out to answer the door, and Rosalind tried not to see the relief that crossed her face as she did. She turned to Alice.

"I'd better go make sure of Cate," Alice said. "Come find me afterward. And yes, Amelia was lying." Alice's tone was light, and brittle. "I saw it for myself."

Rosalind wanted to say something reassuring, but she had no idea what it might be. Alice left her there. She must have passed Adam in the hallway, because he entered the room only a moment later.

He was worried. She saw it at once. Something had happened that robbed him of his balance. Rosalind rose and went to him. They clasped hands, but only briefly. The house was too busy for any greater display of intimacy.

"What's happened?" she asked.

"I could ask you the same," he said. "Amelia and Alice look like they're both ready to flee the country."

Rosalind found she could not smile at this.

"What is it?" he asked. "Have you learned something?"

"Several things. None of them terribly reassuring." Rosalind sat down. She could not seem to stop rubbing her hands together. Adam sat beside her, and reached for her, but hesitated. Rosalind felt a pinprick of sorrow. This was the first chance they'd had to speak since his proposal to her, and it felt as if her silence on the subject now hung in the air between them.

She closed her hand around his and felt him relax. It did nothing to ease her sorrow.

Rosalind forced herself to muster her thoughts. "Firstly, I think I know where this reward Sir Richard offered you came from, at least in part."

Adam raised his brows.

"I don't know if it makes any difference or not, but it's possible at least some of the reward money was contributed by Mrs. Levitton. Before she fell ill, she was becoming involved with the defense of the Cato Street men."

"Do you think there's a connection between her donating money to their cause, and her poisoning?"

"I had wondered the same thing," said Rosalind. "She says she explicitly returned to London to take up her radical causes again. She is receiving calling cards from prominent hostesses and thinkers, as well as politicians. I even noted one from a highly conservative man, possibly come to persuade her to cease her activities."

"In short, she's a known troublemaker and a person of wide influence," said Adam grimly.

"So it would seem." Rosalind paused. "Or this could all be a case of my seeing a pattern where there is none."

"What do you see closer to home?"

"Money," Rosalind told him. "And family pride. And jealousy."

"Jealousy?"

She nodded. "Marcus Levitton is both proud and insecure.

He has a rigid idea of how the world ought to be. His father raised him to believe Marianna was conniving and vindictive. His income is limited, and he has an uncommonly beautiful wife. Any of these ingredients might be found in a recipe for jealousy."

"I would tend to agree," said Adam.

"And that's not all." Rosalind told him about her visit to Temple & Trigg.

When she finished, Adam stood. Rosalind watched, confused as he walked to the door and opened it. He peered into the hall, and closed the door again.

"What's the matter?" she asked as he came to sit beside her again.

"Rosalind, this is extremely serious. You and Alice may be in danger."

Rosalind's heart thumped hard. "Tell me."

Adam did. He told her about Jack Beachamp, and how he had attempted to divert Adam and the others with a story of a missing girl, who just happened to be named Cate Levitton.

And how he was known to associate with a ring of house-breakers and thieves.

And how he said he had an informant, a maid, in the Levitton house.

Rosalind felt the blood drain from her cheeks. Her knees trembled, a little, but she swallowed her emotion.

"Adam, Alice told me something curious. She said she had planned to take Cate out for a walk this morning, but when they were leaving, Cate fell into a faint."

Adam waited.

"Alice said she was certain Cate saw someone, or something that frightened her. She could not tell what it was, or who, but she is very sure."

"Damn," breathed Adam. "If the house is watched, then they saw me come in. And if whoever this is is a confederate of Beachamp's, they may know I'm with Bow Street."

"I know I should not judge by appearances, but I have difficulty believing a young girl such as Cate . . ." She let the sentence trail away, and a small smile formed. "Of course, the exact person for such an enterprise would be the last person one would suspect."

"Such as a girl of good family, with all the necessary manners and bearing," said Adam solemnly.

"Even if she is not the thief herself, she could be given the jewels to sell or pawn—" Rosalind stopped.

"What is it?"

"Something else Alice told me. Cate has been saying to us that she means to go to Edinburgh to stay with some friends—a Dorothea and Margaret Wallace. She met them while she was in Bath. Their father, Cate said, is a jeweler."

Adam's expression hardened. "Rosalind, I need to speak with her."

"I don't know that that is best."

"Why?"

"If we question her, she may understand that we mean to accuse her of . . . something. Theft. Possibly of attempted murder. She may try to run. Or worse—"

"She may get word to her confederates," Adam finished for her. "And if one of them is responsible for poisoning Mrs. Levitton . . ."

"They may decide they cannot wait any longer for her to die," Rosalind concluded.

Adam swore bitterly.

"I know, I cannot like it either," said Rosalind. "But as matters stand, Cate believes she is safe. She plans to leave in a day or two, at most. These sisters in Edinburgh are expecting her. If we continue to allow her to believe that we know nothing, we buy time to find some better evidence."

"Will it be worth it?"

"It isn't just the magistrates at Bow Street who will need more proof than we have," said Rosalind.

"Alice," said Adam.

"And me," said Rosalind. "Amelia is in my employ. I am responsible for her and to her. I cannot have her accused of taking part in a theft without being certain." She saw the stubborn set of his jaw. "Adam, the situation is delicate."

He looked down at her, and she knew all he wanted to say. The situation was not delicate, it was dangerous. By having Cate, and possibly Amelia, in the house, she put herself and Alice both at risk.

"Very well," he said at last. "On one condition."

Rosalind felt an odd flutter in her throat. "What is it?"

"I am staying here tonight." He held up his hands, forestalling her reflexive protest. "You can lock your bedroom door against me, put me in the scullery or out on the street. I can sneak out at dawn so I can be seen to return at a civilized hour. Whatever strategy you see fit to employ I will join in, but I will not leave you unguarded. Not this time." His hand closed around hers. It was cold. She had never known his hands to be cold. A thrill of fear ran through her.

"Rosalind," breathed Adam. "You know that I would never ask that you stop living your life, just as you will not ask me to stop living mine. But I have come too close to losing you before this. I will not, I *cannot,* trust to luck with danger so close."

She looked into his eyes. She saw the scars on his temple, and the way his ear was creased, and missing the lobe from where a shot had nearly killed him.

"What would you have me do, Adam?"

She had never asked such a question, never put either of them in a position where he would need to answer it. This moment was a test of their trust in one another, their understanding of one another, and they both felt it.

"Write to Sanderson Faulks," said Adam. "When you go out tomorrow, take him as your driver. Have Alice bring George over to stay with her and Cate."

It was in Rosalind's mind to make some comment about feeling faint just at the thought of all this masculine protection for their frail female forms. It was in her mind to take insult at the insinuation she could not defend herself. She could. She had. She might well do so again in the future.

And yet, how many times had she thought to herself that this business was different? And Mr. Faulks had been useful in past instances, not only because he was a man and could move about the world with a freedom that was denied her, but because, like her, his acquaintance was broad and unusual.

And she could not deny that leaving Alice alone with Cate tomorrow was a worry. Cate, after all, was a source of danger to Alice, as well as to Rosalind.

So, it was beginning to seem, was Amelia.

CHAPTER 32

Conversation after Working Hours

"Your reasoning is excellent, if your facts were not taken for granted."

Edgeworth, Maria, *Belinda*

Stafford paused in the doorway to Mr. Townsend's private office, and waited to be noticed. He smiled grimly as he realized it might be some time because Mr. Townsend was busy at his glass. His cravat apparently was in need of urgent attention. Stafford's own cravat was a simple black neck-cloth, unremarkable and unadorned. Mr. Townsend's was a fanciful collection of folds and ruffles that Stafford suspected was meant to imitate the fashionable choices of the new king.

Finally, Mr. Townsend seemed satisfied with his efforts, and he turned.

"Well, Mr. Stafford," he said cheerfully. "You're working late."

"I could say the same for you, Mr. Townsend."

"Just finishing." Townsend closed up several folders on his desk. "We dine with Lord Alcott this evening, and of course cannot be late."

Stafford bowed briefly in acknowledgment of this blatant hint to hurry. "I have no wish to keep you, of course, but there is something important I must bring to your attention."

Townsend hesitated, and Stafford waited for him to ask if the matter could wait. But then, he seemed to think the better of it. "Well, do come in, Mr. Stafford." He settled himself into his desk chair.

Stafford closed the office door and came to stand in front of Townsend's broad desk.

"We have a problem, Mr. Townsend," he said.

Townsend arched his shaggy brows. "I'm sorry to hear it, Mr. Stafford. What is it?"

"Adam Harkness."

"Ah." Townsend shook his head, wagging his ample chin and jowls. "What's he done this time?"

"He's working for the radicals. He's trying to bring them George Edwards, before the Cato Street trial."

Townsend's response to this intelligence was to blink, and then shrug. "The trial's likely to be in a day or two. I've just had word we will have to recruit extra constables to help move the men from the Tower." He folded his hands across his stomach, confident and content. "Whatever Mr. Harkness may think he's doing, he's not going to be able to . . ."

But Stafford's patience was at an end. "Edwards is still in London," he told Townsend. "I ordered him to go to the Channel Islands and join his family there. But he has remained behind."

"Why would he?" Townsend appeared genuinely surprised. "The man can't actually *want* to be exposed."

"He wants more money."

"Ah." Townsend touched the side of his nose. "And you need help persuading the ministers to loosen the purse strings?"

Stafford's temper flared. The idea that he would need this braggart's intercession on any matter under his purview was positively insulting. "Edwards is my business," he snapped.

"I will take care of him. What I require is that you finally deal with Harkness."

Townsend spread his hands on his desk, and Stafford had to suppress a wince. The man was about to begin a speech. *I don't have time for your pontificating.*

Townsend, of course, paid no attention to Stafford's pained expression. "Harkness is an idealist," he began. "And, I admit, he has an idealist's weaknesses. But he's an excellent officer. In all my time with Bow Street, I've seldom seen a mind like his. When I brought his name to His Majesty I said—"

"Yes, yes," Stafford cut him off impatiently. "And every time he's strayed, I've warned you that Harkness's idealism will not be contained, or curtailed, or bought off. And every time you have assured me you have the matter in hand. You have for years, Mr. Townsend, *years* said that you can bring Harkness to a full understanding of the realities of his position, and yours. You have sworn you can instill in him an appreciation of the benefits of yielding to those necessities, and I don't know what all else." Stafford waved his hand with exaggerated carelessness. Townsend's face was darkening now, but Stafford pressed on. "And not once in all those years have I seen a single sign that you've had any effect on the man."

"It is only a matter of time. I—"

"There is no more time," said Stafford, his voice low and dangerous. "We are at a very delicate moment in the history of the kingdom, Mr. Townsend."

"I am fully aware of the times we are in, Mr. Stafford."

"Then you are also fully aware that we cannot permit a rogue officer to disrupt the public order, or endanger our efforts to deter those who might otherwise think that the Peterloo rioters should be imitated."

"Harkness won't—"

"But I say Harkness will, Mr. Townsend," said Stafford flatly. "And I ask what are you going to do about it?"

Townsend narrowed his eyes. Stafford did not permit his

expression, or his attention, to flicker for even an instant. If Townsend did not quite see Harkness as a protégé, he saw him as a useful tool. Townsend did not like having his decisions second-guessed. He also had the ear of the most important of men, and he could make Stafford's life, and his work, very difficult if he chose.

Yes, despite all this, and despite his love of display, Townsend was no fool. He understood that his position was founded on the support he had in Parliament, and in the palace. And there, Stafford could make Townsend's life very difficult.

"Very well, Mr. Stafford," said Townsend at last. "You have made yourself quite clear. I will handle the matter."

Stafford bowed. "Thank you, Mr. Townsend. I trust it will all be taken care of within the week."

"Within the week," Townsend agreed.

Mr. Stafford bowed and left him. That was one matter taken care of. With luck, the other could be dealt with as quickly.

But even before he descended the stairs into the lockup, Stafford knew that was wishful thinking. Peals of laughter rang out of the cellar, and Stafford recognized Beachamp's voice.

". . . and she says well, when it's straight again, you come back and see me!"

Laughter rang against stone and packed dirt as Stafford reached the cells. The doors were all iron-banded wood with barred grills set in each one. The night turnkey, Wilder, lounged on his stool, laughing until his greasy face turned red. Beachamp leaned up against his door, so that his profile showed through the grill. Even so, he saw Stafford before his guard did.

"Well, now, Mr. Stafford," Beachamp greeted him with his usual insolence. "I was beginning to wonder if you'd forgotten about me."

Wilder scrambled to his feet, his ring of keys rattling.

Stafford ignored the guard. "Perhaps I should forget you for a while," he said to Beachamp. "It might teach you to be more careful."

"Faint heart never won fair lady," said Beachamp cheerfully.

Stafford snorted. "The only fair lady of your acquaintance is a thief and a—"

"Have a care now, Mr. Stafford," said Beachamp. "Even I have my limits."

Stafford waved this away. He looked down at Wilder, who stood awkwardly to one side, his dull eyes bulging slightly at this exchange. "Let me in there."

Wilder shrugged, and did as he was told. Once Stafford was inside, Wilder closed the door, and the lock firmly.

Stafford stalked up close to Beachamp. "Do you understand what kind of trouble you have gotten me into?" he demanded.

Beachamp shrugged. "I'm happy to take myself and my business elsewhere. When can you get me out of here?"

"You're arrested for assaulting an officer. It's a breach of the peace. You are going before the magistrate, and likely you'll be committed to Newgate."

"You're going to let that happen?"

"I don't have a choice."

Beachamp's grin grew strained. "I should say you do. You can let me out of here, right now."

"And I've just told you, you're going before the magistrate. You can tell him your tale, and if he lets you out, then you're getting out. You made a mistake, Beachamp. You got careless. I am not in the habit of employing, or saving, careless men."

Beachamp attempted to loom over him. Stafford was aware of what the miscreant saw. He saw a thin, old man, and was wondering why he shouldn't just overpower him and threaten to break his neck so Wilder would open the door. Or at least, that's what he wanted Stafford to believe. But Stafford had already measured the distance between them, and knew exactly how quickly he could reach his penknife, and where to strike if it came to that.

Stafford did not maintain his position by being an easy mark.

In the end, Beachamp just lowered himself onto the torn straw mattress that lay on the floor and folded his arms.

"Well, I suppose that's just too bad for me then," he said.

Stafford watched him for a moment, and then turned to call for Wilder to let him out.

"Too bad for you as well," said Beachamp to Stafford's back.

"What do you mean by that?"

"What's my profession, Mr. Stafford?" Beachamp asked, his tone all lightness and amiability.

Stafford turned. The man was still grinning. But now, Stafford felt a chill run up his spine.

"I don't—"

"What's my profession?" asked Beachamp again.

"You're a thief-taker," said Stafford reluctantly.

"That's right," Beachamp nodded. "I find those who don't want to be found. And do you know how I do that?"

"I presume you look for them," said Stafford blandly.

Beachamp's grin widened. "You might well presume that. But it's a touch more complicated." He leaned forward, rested his elbows on his knees and clasped his hands. "I'm a hunter, Mr. Stafford, and a good hunter makes it his business to know the haunts and habits of his quarries. So, I make it my business to know where the thieves are—their houses, their bolt-holes, their names." He met Stafford's gaze. "That way, when I need to find one of them, I'm already well supplied with the necessary information to find them quickly. Do you see what I'm getting at?"

"I see that you're wasting my time."

"When I found myself in your pay, Mr. Stafford, I made it my business to learn the names of some of the others on your payrolls. Many of the others."

Stafford felt his mouth curl into a sneer. "If you think you can do any damage by letting it be known that Bow Street pays informants, you are sorely mistaken."

"No. Bow Street may not care. The courts, and the newspapers may not care. But your informants are not rich men, Mr. Stafford, and they have associates among the criminal classes. Those associates may have different priorities from the courts." He paused, and added softly, "They may care very much about who is peaching to Bow Street. And they may make their displeasure directly known to your informants in ways that might make a gentleman's skin crawl. This, in turn, may discourage others from continuing to pass on useful information to you, and Bow Street, and the government, and whoever else you might work for."

Stafford wanted to yell at the man, to scream at his effrontery. He wanted to summon Wilder and have Beachamp dragged away to Newgate and thrown in the deepest basement cell. Let a month in the dark teach him to mind his manners and keep his mouth shut.

But Beachamp's threat was real. Stafford did not doubt it.

Stafford hammered on the door. He stepped back, breathing deeply, composing himself, shaking off the anger and the fear.

The door creaked open. Wilder, greasy, flushed with cider, peered around the corner.

"Mr. Beachamp is leaving us," he said. "You did not see how it happened."

Wilder grinned. "As you say, guv'na."

Stafford walked out of the cell. He did not look back.

CHAPTER 33

Unprecedented Acts

"These . . . from a person who wants nothing from you but—your love."

Edgeworth, Maria, *Belinda*

Rosalind could not sleep.

She'd dressed for bed. She'd put out her candle and climbed under the quilts. Now she blinked up at her canopy, listening to the soft sounds of the house, and tried to discern which of them was Adam.

They had decided to conceal his presence from Cate. If they were at all correct in their suspicions, she would be instantly on her guard if she knew a Bow Street man was in the house. So, Adam had left before dinner. Rosalind had observed the usual evening routines of writing letters, sitting up to read, and playing draughts with Alice. Cate even joined them for a while before she pleaded fatigue and took herself upstairs. Alice followed shortly afterward. Then, Rosalind sent Amelia to bed, saying she would be sitting up awhile yet, and would take care of herself when she was finally ready for bed.

Rosalind did have real business. She needed to write her sister, Charlotte. She needed to peruse her books where she copied guest lists and notes of gossip and descriptions of parties from the newspapers. Such notices occasionally contained mentions, about a lady's fan, or a bracelet, or similar article going missing. Usually along with some bit of innuendo about where the lady had last been seen, and what gentlemen had been nearby.

But Rosalind was looking for a different set of connections now.

When she was finished, Rosalind had taken her candle down to the cold and empty kitchen. She'd put the light in the window. A few minutes later, Adam had knocked softly at the door.

What is he doing now? Rosalind wondered toward the ceiling. Was he able to get comfortable on the sofa? Was he asleep? Or was he awake like she was?

Was he thinking of her the way she was thinking of him?

She pictured Adam sitting in the corner of the sofa, his long legs stretched out in front of him and his fair hair silvered by moonlight. In her vision, he waited, still and patient, the way he had learned to on the highway patrol. She pictured his soft smile, his blue eyes, his shadowed profile.

Her heart skipped a beat. And another.

She closed her eyes. She rolled over on her side. It did no good. Her eyes opened again. Her ears strained.

Ridiculous.

And yet she had no idea what to do.

Except that was not true. She did have an idea, and it terrified her. She curled more tightly in on herself, like a child frightened of noises in the dark.

But it wasn't the dark, or the noises that frightened her. It was her own unsteady heart.

A lifetime's training warned her to stay still, to be good, to behave. She had already brought herself to the brink of disaster in giving in to his insistence that he be allowed to stay. What she wanted, or he wanted, did not matter. The rules mattered. The world outside mattered. The world would find out. They always did. Everything else might be forgiven, because she was poor and an old maid and an interesting eccentric. But promiscuity would not be forgiven. Love outside the bounds would not.

Shame burned. Pride rebelled. So did her sense of self.

Rosalind grit her teeth, and kicked back the quilts.

She did not take a candle. She did not want to risk the possibility that Cate was still awake and would see the light flickering underneath her door.

I came to make sure you were all right. That was what she would say when she entered the parlor. It was true, as far as it went. *I came to make sure you had all that you needed.* She would say that, too. It was also the truth.

Rosalind knocked, and pushed open the door, and there was Adam, all silver and shadow and exactly as she had imagined him. Her breath left her, and every thought she had flew out of her mind.

"I came . . ." she stammered. "I came . . ."

Adam was on his feet and across the room. He was in her arms and kissing her in the darkness and she was kissing him back and there was nothing else in the world—only the warmth and strength of him, the desire of him and for him, the need for him. Endless. Bottomless. Ecstatic.

Eventually, the need to breathe also grew urgent, and she had to pull back, just a little.

"I came to make sure you were all right," she told him.

Adam ran his fingers down her cheek, to her throat. "And how do you find me?"

"Astonishing," she answered.

He smiled and her heart swelled.

"Come sit down," he said. "I'll build up the fire."

He'd pulled the sofa closer to the hearth. Rosalind sat and watched him as he uncovered the banked embers and laid on enough coal to produce a small flame. Then he sat and wrapped his arm around her shoulder.

"There," he said. "Now we shall be warmer."

Rosalind tucked her feet up like a little girl and leaned against him. "I think if I were any warmer, I might burst into flame."

He chuckled and stroked her shoulder.

"I didn't answer you," she said. "Before. When you spoke of marriage. I'm sorry, Adam."

"It's all right."

"You've waited so long. . . ."

"You make it sound like nothing's happened," he said. "And yet, here you are in the darkness, in my arms." He pulled her closer. "I trust you, Rosalind, and just now, I am vastly content."

Rosalind cuddled close to his side, and felt the gentle pressure of his arm about her shoulders. She breathed deeply, taking in the scent of the fire, and the scent of him. And she let herself do what was so very difficult. For that moment, she let herself trust and be content.

CHAPTER 34

The Morning After

"I am not base enough to betray her secrets, however I may have been provoked by her treachery."

Edgeworth, Maria, *Belinda*

Rosalind was back at school. She was in the room she shared with Alice hastily trying to stuff a handkerchief full of stolen cake under her mattress. She didn't know why. Just as she didn't know why she was even still at school, or what the strange rumbling sound was, or why her face felt so unaccountably rough or where the pain in her neck was coming from.

All at once, she realized she was at school because under the odd rumbling, she heard the unmistakable sound of girls muffling their laughter. Then, she realized her eyes were closed because she had been asleep just a moment before, and the pain in her neck came from her head lolling at a strange angle, and the weight on her shoulders and roughness of her cheek . . .

Rosalind came fully awake in a single heartbeat and jerked upright. Her sudden motion dislodged Adam's arm from around her shoulders, and brought him suddenly and silently awake as well. Which cut off the rumbling noise, which, it seemed, had been him snoring in her ear, while her cheek rested against his stubbled jaw.

Alice was collapsed against the doorway, both hands pressed over her mouth, and doubled over in laughter.

"I'm sorry," she wheezed. "Oh, I'm sorry. I shouldn't . . . Oh, dear!" She darted out the door and slammed it behind her. Her laughter grew fainter as she, presumably, retreated back upstairs.

Rosalind, her cheeks warm, turned to Adam.

Adam pushed himself off the sofa. His chin was unshaven. Had she ever seen him that way before? She must have. Why did it take her breath away now? It was ridiculous, but the strength of the feeling it aroused in her was not to be denied— especially when combined with the sight of his disordered, curling hair, his rumpled shirt with its open collar, and his stocking feet.

His faint, sweet smile. His laughing eyes.

The way he bowed so solemnly. "Good morning, Miss Thorne."

"Good morning, Mr. Harkness." Rosalind returned her most correct curtsy.

"I'm afraid we may have shocked Miss Littlefield."

"I'm afraid it's more likely we shocked Amelia first. She would have come down to light the fires."

"Ah. Yes, of course. Should I go?"

"No. I'll go see to matters and . . ." She looked down at her wrapper and night dress. "I should dress. I'm sure break- fast will be ready shortly."

She looked up again. Adam reached out and straightened her night cap. Rosalind's feeble attempts at dignity collapsed. A giggle, every bit as absurd as Alice's, escaped her. She slapped her hand over her mouth.

But Adam was only smiling. He took the hand she had over her mouth and planted a kiss against her palm.

Rosalind thought she might melt down like an ice left in the sun.

"Go," he said.

Rosalind went. In fact, she fled.

Alice was, of course, right beside her bedroom door, and she was still laughing.

"Oh, Rosalind. I truly, truly am sorry. I can't help—"

Rosalind opened the door to her room. "Inside," she said in her best headmistress voice.

Alice bobbed an exaggerated curtsy and ducked inside. Rosalind closed the door after them both.

Now that she was in her own room, Rosalind found her knees were shaking. She sank onto the chair in front of her dressing table.

Alice grew suddenly serious. "I really am sorry, Rosalind. I shouldn't have laughed. I know you don't find this situation funny at all."

"No." Rosalind caught sight of herself in the glass. She might not possess a stubbled chin, but she was every bit as rumpled and flushed as Adam had been. She looked entirely unlike herself.

No, she looked exactly like herself. Only it was a self that was never seen except in her mirror first thing in the morning.

Now Adam had seen her disarray. He had seen her cap and her wrapper, her nightdress and slippers. They had done nothing, at least, not anything irrevocable. And yet he had seen her entirely stripped of art, artifice, and manners, and she had seen him the same way. That intimacy opened a new door.

"Are you all right?" asked Alice.

"Yes," said Rosalind, only slightly surprised at how easily the answer came. "A little flustered, I suppose, but yes, I am all right."

Alice hesitated. "Is there anything we should . . . be aware of? That might affect your monthlies, perhaps?"

Rosalind knew exactly what Alice meant, and shook her head. "No. There was nothing of that kind."

"Oh." Alice evidently could not tell whether to be relieved or disappointed. "Well. I'll let you get dressed, and I probably should do the same. And I'll go talk with Mrs. Singh, shall I?"

"I think I'd rather do that myself. Will you check on Cate?"

"Of course," said Alice.

She left then, and Rosalind set about her morning ablutions. The water in the washstand jug was tepid, but she scrubbed her face anyway. Amelia had pressed and hung up her pale green day dress, which also happened to be one she could put on by herself. She unbraided her hair and pinned it up again in a simple twist at the base of her neck. She added a string of jade-green beads.

She looked at herself in the mirror for a long, long time. When she was certain she could meet her own gaze with equanimity and good humor, she got up and left the room.

One of Alice's favorite aspects of her new life as lady novelist was that most days she did not have to care one jot about what she wore. This morning, however, she dressed as carefully as if she was going out to make morning calls. She put on her best blue muslin day dress, and pinned her hair into a neat twist at the nape of her neck. She eschewed her cap, and scrubbed her hands to rid them of extra ink.

Cloaked in the armor of respectability, she left her room. Amelia was nowhere to be seen. She paused for a moment outside Cate's door, and—quite openly and blatantly— listened to see if there was any sound yet from inside.

She heard nothing. Satisfied that she had honored the spirit of her promise to Rosalind, she descended the stairs. There was something important to be done, and she had only a limited time to see to it.

Alice knocked at the parlor door.

"Come in," said Mr. Harkness from the other side.

Alice entered. Adam was standing at the window, but in such a way as he'd be shielded by the partially open drapes. He watched the street outside, giving over his whole attention to that activity, and did not turn at all as she entered the room.

"Mr. Harkness?" Alice said.

Now Adam did turn. He was, of course, still unshaven, but had managed to make himself rather less disheveled than previously. He opened his mouth, probably to say good morning, but she was faster.

"I'm going to ask you a favor," Alice said bluntly. "I've never asked anything of you, not as a Bow Street officer, at any rate, and I never would, but this once."

"What is it?" Mr. Harkness asked. "You know if there's anything I can do, I will."

"Whatever inquiries you're making, with the Levittons . . . with Cate, leave Amelia out of them. For now."

Adam went still. He did not sigh, he did not spread his hands or make any other show. He only said softly, "I don't know if I can do that."

"I know, I know, but the situation is, well, it's complicated. I want some time to ask a few questions of my own."

"Alice, I don't know how much Rosalind's had a chance to tell you, but right now there's a thief-taker sitting in the lockup at Bow Street. He knows your Miss Levitton has run away from home, and he's been following me. That means in all likelihood he's aware of Rosalind, and that I have a relationship with her. He's known to be associated with thieves and housebreakers. Amelia McGowan used to work for the Levittons and now she is here, and Miss Levitton is here, while back with the Levittons a woman is dying slowly of arsenical poisoning."

"I know, I know," said Alice. "None of this looks any good at all." She stopped when she saw the expression on his face. "Yes, all right. None of it *is* any good at all. But you know what will happen if word gets out that Amelia might be involved in any of this. She's a *servant*. Whether she's guilty of, well, anything, or not, she'll be blamed. Not by Rosalind, of course, but by others. And if—whatever this business is—finds its way into the papers, it will be very bad for her."

Adam said nothing. He just looked at her. Alice's cheeks colored and she lifted her chin. "Yes, I care for her, and you know I do, and I'm not going to pretend I don't. And yes, it is because I care for her that I'm asking you to leave her be, just for now."

"I don't know what's happening." Frustration filled Adam's voice. "I've got a mare's nest in my hands and I haven't been able to begin to unsnarl it yet. But it's very possible that by having both these women in your house, you and Rosalind are in danger. Are you asking me not to do everything I can to help?"

"If we're in danger, it's not from Amelia," said Alice. "I'd trust her with my life."

"You are," Adam reminded her. "Yours, and Rosalind's."

"It's not like that."

"How can you be sure? A woman, possibly two women, have been poisoned."

"Amelia hasn't been employed by the family for years!"

"And yet, somehow, Cate Levitton found her, and insinuated herself into *this* house." Adam stabbed a finger at the floor. "And she's stayed here, neatly and comfortably hidden, when—forgive me, Alice—the story she has been telling you about running away from an engagement could easily be a lie."

"Except it isn't. We know that. Rosalind has it from her fiancé."

"Her fiancé knows she left home. He may only assume it was because of the engagement."

Alice bit her lip. She felt her anger burning through her, and she knew her face was flushed red. With every bit of strength she possessed, she forced the feeling down.

"I'm asking for time," said Alice evenly. "That's all. Please, Adam. You know I love Rosalind and would never do anything to hurt her."

"Not knowingly."

"Please," said Alice again. Her heart thudded, this time from fear. He might refuse. He might tell Rosalind, he might insist on speaking with Amelia, with Cate. He might . . .

"All right," said Adam, but the words were slow, and reluctant. Alice felt sure he was already regretting them. "But only because Rosalind promised you would keep George with you today . . ."

"I sent him a note last night," said Alice immediately. "He will be here in time for breakfast."

"And if any of us discover any tie between Amelia and this thief-taker Beachamp, or to Mrs. Levitton's poisoning . . ."

Tears swam in front of Alice's eyes, but when she spoke, her voice was steady as stone. "If that happens, I swear upon my life that I will hand Amelia over to you myself."

Adam took a step toward her. Alice was certain he meant to say something sympathetic, but they were interrupted by the arrival of Mrs. Singh. Rosalind must have spoken to her, because she betrayed no surprise at the sight of Adam, or at the state he was in.

"I beg your pardon," she said. "But a boy is at the kitchen door. He had this for Mr. Harkness." She held out a piece of folded paper to Adam.

Adam thanked her and took the note. He unfolded it and read. When he looked up again, his face creased with a species of anger Alice had never seen in him before.

"What's happened?" she asked.

He did not answer her, not directly at any rate. "Tell Rosalind I had to leave, but I will be back as soon as I can."

He was already moving toward the door, and thrust the paper into her hands as he passed her.

Alice stared at the note. It had been written in a strong, slanting hand, and read:

> *Get back to station. Beachamp's gone.*
> *S.G.*

CHAPTER 35

The Means of Escape

*". . . it is not every man who has clearness of head
sufficient to know his duty to his neighbour."*

Edgeworth, Maria, *Belinda*

"What the devil happened?" demanded Adam as he came into the wardroom where Goutier and Tauton sat, stolid and glum. Adam met Goutier's eyes briefly, but the captain did not make one gesture or any change of expression to hint that he knew where his note had reached Adam so early this morning.

"Wilder says he stepped away to take a piss," said Goutier. "Says he told Cantwell to keep an eye on things. Cantwell fell asleep, he says, and when Wilder came back the door was open and Beachamp was gone."

Adam uttered several oaths. *I should have known. I shouldn't have left it. I should have . . .*

I should have left Rosalind to handle things herself and kept my own eyes on Beachamp.

Except he couldn't have done that. It was beyond him.

"Wilder still down there?" Adam jerked his chin toward the door that led to the stairs, and the cells.

"I asked him to hang about for a bit," said Tauton. "Thought you'd want a word."

"Too right I want a word," muttered Adam.

But he'd have to wait to get it. The door to Townsend's office opened, and Townsend himself stuck his head out. "Ah, Mr. Harkness. Will you step in?"

Adam faced Goutier and Tauton. "A favor?" he breathed. "Take Wilder to the Brown Bear. Buy him a breakfast. I'll be over as soon as I'm done here."

With that, he squared his shoulders and marched into Townsend's office.

Townsend was seated back behind his desk, his hands folded across his paunch, at ease with himself and the world. Adam made himself take a deep, slow breath. It would not do to let Townsend see him angry, or worried. He had to set aside the morning, and the night before, and anything else that might serve to distract him.

So, Adam waited, his shoulders back, his jaw set.

For his part, Townsend contemplated him for a long moment. Then, he did the last thing Adam expected. He laughed.

"You may relax, Mr. Harkness! I've just asked you in to issue an invitation."

"An invitation?" echoed Adam, genuinely surprised.

"Just so." Townsend beamed. "To dine at my house tomorrow evening. I've been promising Mrs. Townsend to bring you, and I've been most neglectful. Unless you're already engaged for the evening?" he added.

Adam found himself caught entirely off-guard. "I am not, sir."

"Very good. It will be potluck, but I do not expect you will care about that?"

"I would be honored to join you," said Adam.

Townsend nodded, seemingly satisfied. "I shall see you tomorrow at seven then, and we will go together."

"Thank you, sir," said Adam. But Townsend was already busy sorting through his papers. The interview was done.

Adam took himself out and closed the door behind himself, quietly. But he could not help but turn and stare. Because for the life of him, he did not understand what had just happened. He knew perfectly well how Townsend worked. For him, social position, and society itself, was all to be used for the furtherance of the career of Mr. John Townsend.

So, there was no question to Adam that this sudden invitation meant Townsend wanted something from him.

But what can that be?

He also had no time to worry about that now. He still needed to sort out why Beachamp was no longer in the cells.

It might be early, but the Brown Bear was already crowded. Men came in for a pint of ale, or for bread and cheese and whatever might be on the fire. Adam spotted Goutier and Tauton seated with Wilder by the windows. Roast fowl, fresh bread, and tankards of warm cider sat on the table between them.

All of Adam's instincts shouted at him to hurry. Beachamp was walking the streets free as a bird, and there was no knowing what might be about. But he forced the urges down. There were things he must make sure of, or he was at grave risk of wasting yet more time.

As Adam slipped into place on the bench, Wilder swallowed uneasily.

"Now then, Mr. Harkness," Wilder said. "Mr. Tauton tells me this is your doing, and I do thank you." He wiped his mouth on his sleeve. "But I can tell you no more than I already said. I didn't see nowt, and I don't know what happened." Wilder stood. "And while I do thank you again for your generosity, I'd best be getting on home."

"Not at all," said Adam easily. "I just knew it'd go hard

with you, losing a prisoner like you did. Stafford and Townsend aren't the charitable sort when it comes to a man's duty. What'll you do now?"

Wilder froze, like a rabbit caught in a hedge, but only for an instant. "Mr. Stafford, he's been very understanding," he mumbled. "Mr. Townsend too."

"Glad to hear it," said Goutier. "Because they aren't always."

"I imagine they took into account your years of loyal service," suggested Tauton.

"That's it," said Wilder, palpably relieved. He took a great swallow of cider as if to clear his throat, and slapped the pot back down. "That's it exactly. My years of service they said." Wilder crammed his round-crowned hat on his head. "Good day to you, gentlemen."

Adam made no gesture to detain the turnkey. He already had what he needed.

"Well, now." Goutier took a swallow of cider and tore a wing off the roast fowl. "That was interesting."

"Do we all assume Jackie Beachamp was let go?" said Tauton over the rim of his cider mug.

"No other reason for Wilder to still have his post," said Goutier. "Question is, where's Beachamp gone?"

Adam considered this. The answer could well depend on who opened the door for Beachamp. Was it Stafford? Or Townsend? Stafford knew Adam was looking into the Cato Street business. Townsend had just invited Adam to dinner, much in the same way Adam had just stood Wilder to breakfast.

But Stafford was the one who maintained Bow Street's network of informants. It occurred to Adam that a seasoned thief-taker might have a great deal of useful information, and be willing to sell it, if he knew he could get a good price.

And Beachamp had been at the Cocoa Tree the night Adam met with Sir Richard.

"I know where he's gone." Adam got to his feet. "He's gone to find Edwards."

"But he can't know where the man is any more than we do," said Tauton.

"Unless you think Stafford told him?" asked Goutier.

"He doesn't need Stafford," said Adam. "Beachamp followed me through the park yesterday. I talked to an old milkman there. The fellow knew Hiden, the one who gave the warning note to the earl. He told me Celia Ings would likely know where Edwards is now. With the fog as bad as it was, Beachamp could have been listening three feet away and I never would have known it."

Tauton whistled low. "It's bad, I admit, but are you sure we should do anything at all? If Beachamp is Stafford's man, on Stafford's business, interfering with him could put all our posts at risk."

Tauton was right, of course, and under other circumstances, Adam might have turned his head away. It would have stung, hard. The Cato Street men were still in prison, facing an evil death they had not earned. He should do whatever he could to bring them some kind of justice. And of course, the reward beckoned. It brought the possibility of a life with Rosalind within reach.

But even that could be set aside to protect his colleagues, if not himself. There was, however, something else that he could not ignore.

"Whatever Beachamp may know, or do about Cato Street, he is also involved in some way with this business around the Levitton family."

"Ah, yes." Tauton refilled his cup from the jug. "This latest business that your Miss Thorne has taken an interest in. Any more about that?"

Goutier was refilling his own mug, and Adam had the feeling the man was deliberately avoiding catching his eye.

"It's more like events have taken an interest in her," said

Adam. "Some of the facts of the case are just as Beachamp told us yesterday. A young woman, Cate Levitton, did run away from her family. She was acting as companion to her aunt, Marianna Levitton."

"Seems to me I know that name," said Tauton.

"She's a political hostess, with a lot of friends among the radicals," said Goutier.

"Oh, aye, that'd be it." Tauton drank his cider.

"She's also been poisoned," said Adam. "Not dead, but dying, and her niece may have been poisoned as well."

" 'S truth," muttered Goutier. "That's a nasty bit of work."

"The niece, before she ran, pawned some jewelry. Miss Thorne found the shop, and the jewels, and it's possible— maybe even likely—those jewels were stolen." Goutier's brows rose. Tauton set his cider down. "Further, when the young woman's companions were taking her out for a walk, she apparently saw something, or someone, that scared the wits out of her, so much so that she fainted and had to be taken back indoors at once."

Adam paused to give all this time to sink in. "So, that's on one side. On the other, we've got Jack Beachamp, who somehow knows enough about the Levitton household to use their troubles as a covering story, and who associates with a ring of female housebreakers. Now, I'll conceed his relationship with Stafford may or may not be our business, but housebreakers definitely are. If Beauchamp is helping a gang of thieves, we need him found."

"All right," agreed Goutier. "Then what do we do now?"

Adam got to his feet. "First, I go point out to our Mr. Stafford that he's been a damned fool. Then, with luck, we'll all be able to make up for lost time."

Adam left them there, and hurried back across the street.

As usual, the lobby at Bow Street was filled to the brim. Angry, urgent voices echoed off the walls as people of all concerns and walks of life crowded toward the clerks. As usual,

Mr. Stafford perched on his stool, attempting to impose some semblance of order on the scene.

Adam pushed his way through the mob, blunt and undignified, and clapped his hand on Stafford's shoulder.

Stafford twisted abruptly around, his face a mask of outraged dignity.

"How dare you, sir!" he bellowed.

"I need to speak to you, Mr. Stafford."

"You will have to wait!"

"I will not wait," replied Adam. "If you will not speak to me, I will go find Mr. Birnie and let them know you may have just destroyed all possibility of convicting the Cato Street men."

For a moment Stafford looked at him as if he'd lost his mind. Adam didn't wait for the man to recover himself. He let go of his shoulder and marched toward the wardroom.

He did not need to turn around to know that Stafford was following.

The door to Townsend's office was closed. Adam knocked once and opened it. Townsend stood behind his desk, admiring his portrait of the Prince of Wales.

"What is this . . . ?" he cried as Adam came inside. Then, he saw the head clerk close behind. "Stafford?"

"Your man is out of control, Townsend," Stafford growled. He also shut the door. "He has taken it into his head to threaten me."

"Mr. Stafford came to the cells last night and set the prisoner Jack Beachamp free," said Harkness. "Beachamp is one of Mr. Stafford's paid informants."

"As that is the case, Mr. Harkness," said Stafford, "I wonder that you find Mr. Beachamp any of your business."

"Beachamp followed me to a meeting at the Cocoa Tree where I met with Sir Richard Phillips."

Townsend raised his brows.

"You admit meeting with radicals then, Mr. Harkness?" said Stafford.

"Sir Richard, who is a member of Parliament, wished to consult with me about finding a certain George Edwards, who he believed had information about the events of the Cato Street conspirators," said Adam. "He is part of a committee being formed for the defense of the men being held, and he offered me the sum of one thousand pounds as a reward for bringing Edwards to him."

"You never told me this, Mr. Harkness," said Townsend.

"No, sir, I did not," agreed Adam. "Neither did I tell you that this man Beachamp overheard this offer and has been following me across London ever since. With the help of Captain Goutier and Mr. Tauton, we finally corralled Beachamp for his assault on Captain Goutier. But Stafford had him released, and I believe that was a colossal blunder."

"I suggest you tread very carefully, Mr. Harkness," grated Stafford.

"Mr. Stafford," said Adam evenly. "I ask you to think about this from Beachamp's point of view. There is a reward out there of one thousand pounds for the location of George Edwards. He now knows how that man may be found. Do you truly believe Beachamp cares that Edwards is in your pay? Or what policy matters rest on keeping him hidden?"

Stafford searched Adam's face. Slowly, Adam could see a sliver of doubt working its way into the clerk's mind.

"Beachamp knows full well that his employment with Bow Street depends on his reliability," said Stafford.

"And exactly how many years will it take Beachamp to earn a thousand pounds in your employ?" inquired Adam. "Beachamp is a gambler. He runs himself to debt and ruin regularly. That is not a man of thought and prudence. He will always play for the biggest pot within reach. Today, that means handing Edwards over to Sir Richard and his radical friends."

"You are very sure of yourself."

"Yes, Mr. Stafford, I am."

Stafford's eyes flickered toward Townsend. Adam pivoted. They all waited while tension filled the air until he felt near suffocated by it. At last, Townsend spoke.

"I would trust Mr. Harkness's judgment in this matter."

"Do you know where this Edwards may be found?" asked Townsend. "It seems to me if you want the fellow to remain anonymous, I'd say you'd better send Mr. Harkness after him."

"And have him claim the radical's reward?" Anger burned bright in Stafford's words.

"I think Mr. Harkness understands his duty to Bow Street, and the Crown, in this matter," said Townsend mildly. "Don't you, Mr. Harkness?"

Harkness bowed. As he did, private hope turned to ash inside him, but he let it go. Other hope, other plans would come. He trusted fate and Rosalind, but now he had work to do.

Stafford's jaw worked itself back and forth several times. "George Edwards is an itinerate plasterer and model maker by trade. But as to where he actually is now, I don't know, and he has taken care that I should not."

Adam regarded Stafford for a long, hard moment, trying to determine if this was the truth. Stafford returned his stare without flinching, or giving any sign he meant to say anything more. At last, Adam turned on his heel and strode out the door.

CHAPTER 36

The Consequences of Eavesdropping

". . . those men of genius are dangerous
husbands . . ."

Edgeworth, Maria, *Belinda*

S anderson Faulks had arrived at Rosalind's door promptly at half past ten, "a torturously early hour for a man of my constitution," he'd said with his habitual air of mock-suffering. He wore a coat of plain burgundy, leather breeches, and plain brown top boots. With his fair hair tied back in a queue, he looked entirely the part of John Coachman, ready to drive her wherever she might choose to go.

There were many reasons for Rosalind to enlist Mr. Faulks for this particular enterprise. Not the least of which happened to be that Rosalind knew he kept his own enclosed carriage and a team of matched chestnuts. She was therefore surprised to see the carriage had been harnessed to a pair of sturdy grays.

"My chestnuts are too well known on the street," Sanderson told her as he helped her into the carriage. "We don't want any ill-mannered fellows hailing me and giving away the game."

Thanks to Sanderson's experience with negotiating London's infamous traffic, it was only a short time before they arrived at Marcus Levitton's residence in Upper Seymore Street.

Rosalind's first impression was that the house was respectable. It was not particularly grand, but neither was anything about it mean or second rate. Rosalind knew from her acquaintances that this neighborhood was rapidly becoming fashionable, so it was a prudent place for a man on the rise to set up his establishment.

The footman who opened the door was dressed in plain forest green and white. He took Rosalind's card and bowed.

"Mrs. Levitton is expecting you," he said. "She is sorry that she was detained by some last minute correspondence, and has asked if you will wait for her in the morning room, where she will join you shortly."

Rosalind, of course, agreed. The footman signaled to the waiting maid to help Rosalind with her things. The foyer was furnished with a heavy, mahogany table for Mrs. Levitton's visiting book and the salver for cards. An elaborate silver vase with two curling handles held a wealth of hothouse roses. Rosalind considered whether she should risk a peek at the visiting book, but she had no time.

"Miss Thorne?"

Rosalind turned to see Everett Levitton descending the stairs.

"How do you do? Come to call on Wilhelmena?"

"Yes. I did not realize you were also in residence here."

"Afraid so." He gave her a sheepish grin. "Can't afford my own rooms and can't ask Marcus to bear that particular expense, so here I am and here I shall remain until . . . well, until further notice I suppose."

"Everett, who . . ." Wilhelmena came down the stairs as well. "Oh, Miss Thorne, I did not realize you had arrived. Everett, what do you mean by keeping Miss Thorne standing in the foyer?"

"My apologies, Miss Thorne." Everett bowed. "I'm afraid my manners are entirely shocking. Ask anyone."

"She can begin with me," said Wilhelmena tartly as she came to stand beside Rosalind. "However, I am glad you are here. If you would care to follow me, I've given instructions for tea to be served in the morning room."

"May I join?" asked Everett. "Or would I be intruding?" Wilhelmena frowned at him. "I'd be intruding," concluded Everett immediately. "Heigh-ho, what's to be done with Everett? I shall take myself up to my lonely apartment and hope I may be summoned later when my face is washed and my hair is neatly combed and I know how to behave myself." He bowed again, and took himself back up the stairs.

Wilhelmena watched him for a moment, and Rosalind was startled to see the anger shining in her dramatic green eyes. But when she turned to face Rosalind, that anger had vanished, and she was entirely the cool, experienced hostess.

"You must not mind my brother-in-law," she said mildly. "When matters become grave he feels it something of a duty to try to play the clown. Shall we?" She gestured down the central hall.

The Levittons' morning room overlooked a narrow strip of garden. The curtains were drawn back, flooding the room with sun. It was a tasteful room, devoid of display. In fact, if anything it was a little spartan. There was only one rug on the floor, and the walls were simply painted. The only decoration was a formal portrait of Marcus and Wilhelmena over the fireplace. The mantel, however, was crowded with invitation cards, many of them gilt-edged. Mr. and Mrs. Levitton were popular guests, it seemed. And these were hardly the mundane round of charity balls and public concerts to which many middle-class hostesses found themselves relegated. Rosalind quickly discerned that several addresses were in Grosvenor Square, the center of the social world, and at least one hostess was known to be an intimate of the new king. Rosa-lind felt her brows inching up.

She also realized she was staring, and edging close to openly snooping.

"That is a lovely array of invitations," said Rosalind con-versationally as Wilhelmena poured their tea and handed her a cup. "You must be anticipating a busy season."

"The season is always such work, do you not find?" replied Wilhelmena, pouring out her own cup of tea and adding a slice of lemon. "I am quite exhausted with going out every night, and planning our own dinner party at the end of the week. Naturally, this is the time when our house-keeper has left us." Rosalind made a sympathetic noise. "She was hired by a hotel," said Wilhelmena confidentially. "A hotel! It is past comprehension, is it not?"

Unless one considered that the position probably came with shorter hours and better wages than she could make in service, it might seem to be. Rosalind did not mention this.

"Have you found a replacement?" she asked.

"Not yet." Wilhelmena sighed. "We dined with Lady Worth yesterday. I had hoped she might be able to recommend someone, but the woman she had in mind has already ac-cepted a place with Mrs. Robbins, and now I don't know what we will do. Our current staff is very capable, as far as it goes. I fear, however, they will not be able to keep things up to Marcus's standards." She noted the inquiring tilt to Rosa-lind's head. "My husband cannot abide any form of chaos in his home, Miss Thorne. An artifact of his childhood, I be-lieve. His mother . . . well, you've seen Beatrice. She is not one to rise gracefully to any sort of challenge."

Rosalind returned a noncommittal murmur.

"We have several important dinners this season," Wilhel-mena went on. "It is imperative everything be perfect."

"I may know of someone looking for a new position," said Rosalind. She had always made it her business to be as aware as she could of experienced persons seeking new situations. There was no better way to earn a hostess's appreciation, and trust, than by being able to help with her "servant problem." "She is quite skilled, but she is also married. I recognize that can be a problem in some houses. . . ."

"Is her husband also in service?" asked Wilhelmena at once. "Would he need a place as well?"

"It would certainly be an inducement, if it could be managed."

"I think it could. Please do write to her," said Wilhelmena. "We have had such troubles of late." She paused, and Rosalind watched her decide not to finish her sentence. "This is extremely helpful, Miss Thorne. But then, that is your reputation, is it not? Being helpful in all circumstances?"

"I recognize it is an unusual mode of living," said Rosalind. "For my personal preference, I believe I would choose quiet retirement." This statement was untrue from beginning to end, but Rosalind had found the sentiment was acceptable to conventionally minded company. "Unfortunately, we cannot always choose our own paths."

"No, that is very true," replied Wilhelmena. Rosalind heard the barely suppressed bitterness under the words. "And you have certainly proven yourself to be most efficient in our present difficulties. I cannot tell you how very glad I was to see those letters arrive from Cate. You have no conception of how distraught Beatrice has been, or what kind of things she has been saying. It is all nonsense, of course, but in Marianna's precarious state of health, I was afraid she might take notice."

"Surely Marianna would make allowances for Beatrice. Her daughter is missing."

"You do not understand the depths of the breach between Marianna and Marcus. She harbors a deep grudge over his unwillingness to accept her as family. He, on the other hand, will not forgive her for favoring Harold Davenport over him.

Then when she took Cate's side against his father . . ." She glanced toward the door. "I have never seen him so angry."

"She took Cate's side? I had understood the family agreed to send her to Marianna's."

"Only after Marianna offered," said Wilhelmena. "Everett tried to make a joke of it, that she was taking in the family strays again."

"Again?"

"Oh, yes. Beatrice is subject to the vapors, and when a particularly bad bout overcomes her, she always goes to stay with Marianna. As far as Marcus is concerned, it is another black mark against his aunt. He says she encourages Beatrice's hysterical tendencies."

"And does she?" asked Rosalind.

Wilhelmena's smile was so thin and so brief, Rosalind almost missed it. "If I was to hazard a guess, I would say Beatrice uses the time as a vacation from her cares at home. She always took Cate with her when she went, you know, and that, I'm sure, was why Marianna was so willing to take Cate in."

"And Beatrice, once her husband died?" suggested Rosalind.

"Actually, I believe that was Everett's doing," said Wilhelmena. "I'm not sure how he managed to impose upon her. Marianna finds Beatrice dull, and somewhat incomprehensible, and yet she has made no move to rescind the invitation."

"Perhaps he persuaded her that Beatrice should be allowed to try to reconcile with Cate."

"Perhaps," said Wilhelmina, but she clearly did not believe it. Rosalind found herself wondering about Everett, the awkward clown and peacemaker. On the face of it, it did not seem likely that he could persuade Marianna of anything she did not already wish to do.

Before Rosalind could form her next remark, the door opened. Startled, she winced, but Wilhelmena just raised her head, her expression at once tired and expecting.

Marcus Levitton stood in the doorway.

"My apologies," he said, although he clearly did not mean it. "Morris told me you had come home."

"He should have perhaps mentioned Miss Thorne had arrived," said Wilhelmena.

"Perhaps he did. Miss Thorne." Marcus bowed, and then turned his attention entirely back to his wife. "Were your errands successful? I believe you were to visit Lady Talbot?"

"Lady Worth," Wilhelmena corrected him.

"Ah, yes, of course, about the pastry cook."

"The housekeeper," said Wilhelmena. "A replacement for Mrs. Deale."

"It must have been a long meeting. You left right after breakfast."

"You know how Lady Worth loves to talk." Wilhelmena smiled, and her expression was as strained as her voice.

"Were you successful then?"

"I'm afraid I was not. However, I mentioned our housekeeping dilemma to Miss Thorne, and she thinks she may know of someone suitable for us."

"Does she? Well, then I suppose we must thank you, Miss Thorne." Marcus made the briefest possible bow toward her.

Rosalind returned a stiff nod. "I'm glad I could be of assistance."

"I hope that you are better at finding new servants than you are missing children."

"Marcus . . ." began Wilhelmena.

But Marcus ignored her. "Because you seem to be spending much more time sitting about gossiping than you do actually looking for Catherine. My aunt may choose to throw her money away on another female oddity, but I do not have to humor her." He paused. "Neither does my wife."

"I apologize for my husband, Miss Thorne. . . ." began Wilhelmena.

"Don't you dare!" thundered Marcus.

Wilhelmena scarcely seemed to notice. "As you can see, he is tired, and not knowing where his sister is has been preying upon his temper. If you had any news at all . . . ?"

"I'm afraid not," said Rosalind. "I apologize for taking up so much of your time, as I know you have a busy morning."

"Not at all. You will write to me about the housekeeper?"

"Certainly, Mrs. Levitton." She rose. "Thank you for the tea. A pleasure to see you again, Mr. Levitton." Rosalind curtsied, and took her leave.

She had just reached the foyer and told the footman she was in need of her things, when she heard footsteps behind her.

"A word, Miss Thorne." Marcus strode up the hall from the morning room. "If you would be so kind?" he added in a sarcastic drawl.

Rosalind took refuge in her coldest dignity. "What can I do for you, Mr. Levitton?"

"You can leave my house and not return."

Rosalind drew herself up, but Marcus took no notice.

"I do not care what oddities my aunt may choose to keep around her. She will have her comeuppance soon enough. But you will all stay away from *my* house and *my* wife, or I will have the law on you."

Rosalind said nothing.

"And you will not insult my intelligence by suggesting your being here has anything to do with my disgrace of a sister. I am fully aware of Marianna's vindictive plans to lure my wife from me, and you are welcome to tell her so." He turned to the footman. "See this woman out, and do not admit her again."

With that, Marcus strode back into the depths of his house.

Rosalind let out a long, slow breath. She also turned. The footman bowed.

"My apologies, miss," he murmured.

With that, the maid was summoned. Rosalind was quickly and efficiently bundled into coat and bonnet and, quite literally, shown the door. Fortunately, Sanderson was at that moment driving the carriage out of the mews and to the front of the house.

"Success?" he inquired as he leapt down from the box and opened the door.

"I don't know," admitted Rosalind.

"How unusual," murmured Sanderson as he lowered the step and extended a hand to help her into the carriage. "Given this state of uncertainty, what is our next port of call?"

Rosalind's mind raced. The night before, she'd spoken of jealousy to Adam. Then, it had merely been a possibility. Now, it had become a certainty. Quite apart from any insult Marcus may have dealt her, it was very plain that Marcus Levitton did not trust his beautiful wife. Even if his probing questions had not made this plain, his shocking accusation that Marianna was attempting to interfere in his marriage would have.

"I think that we need to wait awhile and see who leaves the house next and where they go."

Because while Marcus was jealous and watchful, Wilhelmena was angry, and wary, and Everett . . . Everett was a go-between. But for whom? And how trustworthy was he? It was possible he'd forced Cate into a lie because he believed it would be best.

Then, too, there was the other thing Marcus had said about Marianna, almost in passing—a cold, casual declaration that sent a chill down Rosalind's spine.

She will have her comeuppance soon enough.

CHAPTER 37

The Comfort of Siblings

"Could I borrow a sigh, or a tear, from my tragic sister . . ."

Edgeworth, Maria, *Belinda*

"Oh! Hullo, George. Come in and sit, won't you?" Alice's brother, who was very accustomed to her ways, shoveled the pile of newspapers off the slat-backed chair nearest the hearth, took a cup off the mantel, and filled it from the pot on the hearth.

"Well, the truth of the matter is, you've probably saved me from being thrown out into the street." George sat in the chair he'd just cleared and stretched his long legs out to rest his heels on the hob. Like Alice, George was dark, sharp, and quick. He was, however, a good eight inches taller than his sister.

"You'd really be thrown out by your pregnant wife?" quipped Alice.

"Or someone in her family. Hannah's mother and sisters are all settled in, and they complain I am in the way." He made a face at his coffee. "But when I try to go to work, the

Major says he's tired of my staring out the window like I'm trying to lay eyes on the stork."

"Poor George," said Alice. "I'm sure they all know you mean well."

George drank his coffee, and made another, different face. "How long has this been sitting here?"

"Not that long," said Alice. "I don't think." She poured herself a cup, drank, and pulled her own face. "Perhaps I'm wrong." She set the cup on the mantel. "And how is Hannah? Aside from being surrounded by female relatives?"

"Blooming." George smiled. He also sighed. "Impatient. Her mother is certain it will be any day now. As she's had seven children of her own, I suspect she would know."

"And how are you?"

"I don't know," he admitted. "I want this child. I think I want this more than I have anything in my life. And at the same time, I'm terrified. What if I . . . what if I'm . . ."

Alice took his hand. "You are nothing like our father. You will not desert your child. Children. Because I am quite convinced this is the first of half a dozen."

"I'll have to ask the Major to increase my salary."

"Never fear." Alice raised her cup to him. "When my books are an enormous success, I will make sure they are all provided for. All I ask is you name at least two of them for me."

George grinned. "What if they're all boys?"

"Well, then they'll just go through life profoundly embarrassed, won't they?"

George chuckled and Alice smiled. She started to drink her coffee, remembered it was bad, and set it on the corner of the desk.

"And what about you?" George asked. "How are you doing?"

Alice had not been looking forward to this particular question. If it was anyone else, she might be tempted to put them off, but that would never work with George. She had no choice but to tell him the truth. "I don't know," she said.

"Rosalind says you're in love."

"She may be right."

George leaned forward and rested his elbows on his knees. "Alice, you're my sister. You will always be my sister, no matter what. But . . ."

"But?"

"Are you sure? About Amelia, I mean?"

Alice rolled her eyes toward the ceiling, looking for patience. "Were you sure when you started courting Hannah?"

"When I started, no," George admitted. "But eventually, yes."

"Well, I'm still waiting for eventually."

"And if eventually comes?"

That was, unfortunately, an excellent question. Rosalind had pointed out that it was impractical, not to mention unfair, for her to carry on a romantic liaison with a servant. Rosalind was, as usual, right. Then there was the small matter of not being entirely certain she wanted to continue living with Rosalind if she was also one half of a domesticated couple. Especially if Rosalind's painstakingly slow courtship of Mr. Harkness continued.

"Perhaps we will run off to Wales and set up housekeeping next to the Ladies of Llangollen." The famed Ladies lived in a cottage, wore masculine dress, and regularly hosted parties for the literary lights who came to visit them.

"You would be bored stiff in Wales," said George.

"I don't see why I should be," replied Alice. "I'll have my novels, and I'm told nature is quite lovely, and fresh air is most fashionable nowadays."

"How does Amelia feel about Wales?"

"I haven't had the opportunity to ask her yet. As I said, we are still waiting on *eventually*." Alice paused. "And if you say anything mawkish about not letting her break my heart,

I shall deny you were ever my brother, and your children may whistle for their inheritance."

"You needn't bother. The Major would fire me outright if I dared fall so far into a cliché." Now it was George's turn to pause. "Well, if Wales doesn't answer, we'll find you something."

"We?"

"Hannah was the one who brought it all up. She said you'd probably be wanting your own rooms sooner or later."

"I knew I liked her."

This, of course, made George go all misty-eyed, as he habitually did when thinking of his wife. It didn't last long, however. "All the same, Alice, you will be careful? I don't like this business with what's her name. . . ." He pointed toward the ceiling.

"Cate Levitton," Alice supplied.

"Yes, her. Things are unsettled right now. The king's in a rage, the world's afraid of what's coming next, and . . ."

Alice's brow furrowed. "What has any of that to do with Cate?"

"Her aunt's Marianna Levitton, isn't she? Well, Mrs. Levitton is closely involved with a lot of persons who are making a lot of noise right now, and drawing a lot of attention to themselves."

Alice sighed. "You've been talking with Adam."

"I've been reading the newspapers."

"Trust me, George, this is nothing Rosalind hasn't seen before. I shouldn't be surprised if she didn't have it all sorted out by suppertime."

"I hope you're right, Alice," said George. "I truly do." Before the seriousness could become truly awkward, however, he raised his cup. "And I hope you can convince your cook to brew us some fresh coffee, because, dear sister, this is absolutely undrinkable."

Alice laughed, and reached for the bell. Before she could

ring, however, there was a soft scratching at the door, and a moment later, Amelia leaned in. She was wearing her cloak and bonnet and had her basket slung over her arm.

"If you please, Miss Alice, I'm going to market. Was there anything you needed?"

Alice looked at her and felt her heart begin to melt as it always did, even as fresh frustration built inside her. Because Amelia's voice was too tentative, and her eyes were darting back and forth, and she was twiddling with the end of her bonnet ribbon. Because everything about her said something was wrong.

I want you to tell me the truth! Alice wanted to shout.

Out loud, she said, "Not at present. How is Cate?"

Amelia's fingers knotted around her ribbon. "She said she was going to have a bit of a nap, so I thought it would be all right to go now."

"Very good," said Alice brightly, as if she believed this. "You should check with Mrs. Singh to see if she needs anything—" George raised his cup, and made a pleading face. "Oh, and ask her if she could make some fresh coffee, please."

"Yes, miss," said Amelia, and she ducked out, and Alice tried hard not to hear the word *good-bye* ringing in her mind, because Amelia hadn't actually said that. Had she?

"All right, Alice," said George. "What's the problem?"

"Nothing."

"You're lying."

"I am . . . all right, I am." Alice glared at the closed door. "Something's wrong with Amelia. And I've had enough." She got to her feet.

"What do you want to do?"

"It's not what I want to do." Alice's coat hung over the back of one chair. Her gloves lay on the corner of her desk next to her battered reticule. "It's what I have to."

"Which is?"

"Never you mind." Alice yanked her gloves on. "Your job is to stay here and keep both eyes on Cate Levitton."

"You're not going to talk to her?"

"Ha!" Alice laughed grimly. "That one wouldn't tell me water is wet. I'll tell you what she did say, though. She said she had friends in Edinburgh who would take her in."

"Sorry, missing the significance."

"If she had friends, why bother with this business of running away in the middle of the night? Why not just say, 'Oh, I've gotten a letter, I'm going to visit the Wallaces. Good-bye and I'll write soon!'" Alice felt all her old news instincts rising. "And if she wanted to vanish, she could take the first stage from London, and then get off as soon as they stopped to change horses, and from there, she could go anyplace." Alice swept an arm out, indicating the whole world waiting beyond the windows. "So, either she's lying through her teeth about these Edinburgh friends, or something drove her out of that house, and what's more, she barely escaped with her life! So, what did she discover, hmm? Or what was discovered about her?"

"Alice . . ." began George.

Alice ignored him. She also plucked her bonnet off the corner of the chair where she'd tossed it. "I'll be back in a few hours," she said as she tied her ribbons.

"You aren't going to follow your maid, are you?"

"Don't be ridiculous, George," said Alice. "If I did that, I might get caught."

"Then what are you going to do?"

Alice grabbed her reticule and smiled darkly. "I, dear brother, am going to remember I'm a newspaper woman and follow my nose."

CHAPTER 38

Followers

"Women, you know, as well as men, often speak
with one species of enthusiasm and act with an-
other."

Edgeworth, Maria, *Belinda*

"What shall we do now?" asked Sanderson as he
handed Rosalind into the carriage. "From your expression, your interview with the Levittons did not go as you
hoped."

Rosalind tried to relax her furrowed brow. She met with
limited success. She felt like she had seen and heard a great
deal, if only she could understand it properly.

What was clear was that Marcus Levitton was an intensely
jealous man. Was it possible that jealousy had a foundation?
It was easy to dismiss that possibility. Marcus was the angry
husband of a woman of more than ordinary beauty. His fears
could easily be all in his imagination.

And yet, she had seen how Everett's hand strayed toward
Wilhelmena's when he was frightened. She noted that he
seemed to be in no hurry at all to leave his brother's house,
even though he was a young man of a well-connected family

who could have easily claimed a place at law or in the church, or purchased a commission, or even gone into business.

What then, kept him at home and unmarried? And, if Marcus was afraid that Wilhelmena was unfaithful, why did he permit his unmarried brother to remain in his house?

And could she find out anything about these Levittons when she had been expressly forbidden the house?

"I think," said Rosalind to Sanderson, "that we should keep watch on this house and see who leaves next and where they go."

It might be that the destination would reveal something significant, or, even better to Rosalind's way of thinking, it might provide her with a way to cross paths with either Everett or Wilhelmena in a way that would allow her to open a fresh conversation.

"As my lady requires." Sanderson fastened the carriage door. "I hope you have brought all your patience. This may take a while."

"You sound like you've had experience in such matters."

Sanderson's smile grew mischievous. "Now, Miss Thorne, you must allow me to keep some of my secrets."

With that, he climbed back on the box and touched up the horses, leaving Rosalind little to do except settle back on the bench, watch the house, and think about all she knew, and all she did not.

Sanderson's carriage, although immaculate, was plain black and unmarked. This should have rendered it fairly anonymous, but the street was exceedingly quiet at this time of day. If they simply stood across the street to watch the Levittons' house, they would quickly become conspicuous. Sanderson solved this problem by driving sedately around the block.

After several circuits, Sanderson drew up to the corner and made a pretense of examining one of the horses' hooves. Rosalind climbed out of the carriage to join him. To any passersby it would appear she was consulting with her driver about a horse that was coming up lame. She could rely on the carriage and her plain bonnet to screen her face from anyone who might happen to look casually from the window of the Levittons' house.

Sanderson set the horse's hoof down and patted his neck with the easy assurance of a person who was experienced around horses.

"I had a visit from my younger brother," he said conversationally.

"Did you?" Sanderson had left his family years ago, and for the most part, they had been content to let him go. His elder brother was ambitious, but his ambitions were firmly rooted in the family estate and line, and he had become indispensable to their father. His younger brother, Theodore, was put on the usual course of schools for a young man of a landed family. Sanderson sent him the occasional letter and the occasional gift and everyone seemed to consider themselves satisfied with the arrangement.

"Yes. It seems he's developed a taste for drawing. He'd like to pursue it seriously, see if he has talent, or at least flare."

"What does your father think of that?"

"According to Theo, his exact words were 'not another one.'"

Which sounded very much like Sanderson's father.

"He's asked me to sponsor him. Send him to school in Paris. Let him find out if he's any good."

"What did you say?"

"I said yes," Sanderson told her. "Somewhat to everyone's surprise. Certainly to mine. I warned him I intend to be a harsh taskmaster. I've no objection to him trying out life for himself, but if he's going to school, he must actually go. I believe I was quite firm." He smiled slightly. "I blame your Mr. Harkness for this, you know, and you."

Rosalind arched her brows. "Me? How on earth is you deciding to pay to send your brother to school my fault?"

"Because before I began assisting you and Mr. Harkness in your little endeavors, I was quite content to be the dissolute bachelor. Now, I find I have been drawn into the softly seductive allure of being useful, even in a small way."

"Well, then." Rosalind assumed a prim air. "I hope Theo appreciates all I have done for him."

"I shall see to it the boy writes you a note of thanks," Sanderson returned solemnly. He finished tugging at the harness. "There. I think we have lingered long enough."

Rosalind looked over his shoulder toward the Levittons' house. She was beginning to wonder if this wait was in vain. Perhaps she would need to employ a different stratagem. But what? Her normal way of proceeding took more time than she had. Even without Marianna's restrictions, she did not like to leave Cate in the house. She feared for the friction Cate's presence would cause between Alice and Amelia. More than that, however, she feared the simple fact that Cate could not be trusted.

But even as she considered telling Sanderson they should start around the block just once more, an open landau with a team of sedate bay horses drew up to the front of the Levittons'.

Mr. Faulks turned to see what had caught Rosalind's attention.

"Well, I think we're all right now, miss," he drawled. "Shall we go?"

"Yes, indeed." Shielded by Sanderson's tall frame, Rosalind watched as Wilhelmena, wearing a broad bonnet lined with yellow silk and white lace, came down the steps, with not one, but two maids following behind her. "I believe we shall."

*   *   *

The exercise of following Wilhelmena Levitton was, unfortunately, mostly one of frustration. Enclosed in the carriage, Rosalind was comfortably anonymous, but it also meant she had no way to keep an eye on Wilhelmena's carriage. She trusted Mr. Faulks, of course. But at the same time, she was conscious of an absurd need to see things for herself.

She tried to concentrate on the passing streets and to occupy her mind with considering where Wilhelmena might be going. There was, of course, no guarantee it was any place of significance. She recognized the neighborhood of Bond Street, land of the most fashionable shops. Wilhelmena might well be simply going to purchase some new items needed for her upcoming dinner parties. The presence of the maids might just be to keep her husband's suspicions calm, or it might be she planned to make a number of purchases and expected to require assistance.

It could very well be that whatever lay between Cate and her family, and Marianna and her family, was entirely separate from Wilhelmena and Marcus's marital difficulties, and that Rosalind was wasting what little time she had.

And yet . . . and yet . . . there had been a calculation in Wilhelmena's manner when she spoke to Rosalind about her husband and his family. Perhaps she was just being protective. The family had endured scandal already, and she had a social position to guard, on her own behalf as well as her husband's.

And yet . . .

The carriage stopped. Rosalind risked putting the window down and peering out. They had stopped in front of Rees & Co., a popular draper's shop. Wilhelmena's two maids stood on the walk. From their attentive attitudes, Rosalind guessed they were listening for instructions. She saw Wilhelmena's yellow-gloved hands giving a purse to the older of the pair, who immediately stowed it away inside her cloak. Then, the maids turned away together and hurried into the shop.

"Walk on," said Sanderson from the box. The carriage moved. Up ahead, Wilhelmena's conveyance presumably did the same.

Rosalind dropped back onto the bench. *Well.*

That answered one question. The maids were window dressing to placate and distract Marcus. Possibly Marcus and Everett.

But from what?

Rosalind was still turning both thought and doubt over in her mind, when the carriage began to slow. Rosalind shook herself and looked out the window again, realizing, much to her chagrin, she did not know what street she was on.

The carriage stopped, and rocked gently as Sanderson climbed off the box and came round to her door.

"It would seem that Mrs. Levitton has unconventional ideas of where to go on her afternoons out," he said.

Rosalind peered over his shoulder. They were in a commercial street lined with good shops and several private hotels. She caught a glimpse of Wilhelmena's back as she entered one of those doors. It had a good, redbrick facade and bright windows with freshly painted black trim.

"It may be she goes to meet a friend," said Rosalind. "Perhaps I—"

"She most certainly goes to meet a friend," said Sanderson. "Of a particular sort."

Rosalind raised her brows.

"I blush to disclose this information. That hotel"—he nodded toward the building Wilhelmena had entered—"is operated by a Mrs. Oglethorpe. It is a strictly private establishment that facilitates discreet assignations between men and women who do not happen to be married to each other."

As a gently bred, unmarried woman, Rosalind was not, of course, supposed to have any knowledge of such places or what might go on inside them.

"I see you are not shocked," murmured Sanderson.

"I am sorry if you are disappointed," said Rosalind. "But I have in the past intervened on behalf of an erring personage whose visit to a similar establishment was unfortunately observed."

"Ah, yes. I should have realized." He paused. "Would you like me to go inside and see if I can ascertain whom our Mrs. Levitton is meeting?"

"There is no need," murmured Rosalind.

Because the answer was even now striding easily down the street. He wore a curly brimmed beaver hat and carried a silver-headed walking stick in his gloved hand. His easy stride and lifted chin suggested he was enjoying his walk, and the prospects for his day.

Harold Davenport rested his stick on his shoulder, and disappeared into Mrs. Oglethorpe's hotel.

CHAPTER 39

Reclaiming Personal Property

"Do you imagine that, through this tragical disguise, I have not found you out?"

Edgeworth, Maria, *Belinda*

Fran watched the little chaperone trot down Rosalind Thorne's steps. According to the scullery maid from next door, who'd been out scrubbing steps this morning and was more than willing to take a moment to gossip, that quick, dark woman was a Miss Alice Littlefield, who was a lady writer for the newspapers and might even be writing a whole book!

"Fancy," Fran had murmured.

The pretty maid had left just before Miss Littlefield. She'd come up out of the area stairs, her basket on her arm and looking like she was about to burst into tears. Somebody'd clearly put a flea in that one's ear over something.

By Fran's count, that left the tall gentleman and the cook inside.

And, of course, Cate.

Fran schooled her features into a polite smile and hurried

across the square to knock on the door. She stepped back and waited, her hands neatly and properly folded.

After a few moments, the door opened. It was the gentleman. Fran remembered to look startled.

"Oh! Forgive me, I am calling for Miss Rosalind Thorne. Is this the right house?"

"It is," said the man. "But I'm afraid Miss Thorne is not at home."

"Oh, oh, dear." Fran fiddled with the strings on the reticule hanging from her wrist. "This is awkward. I . . . may I step in a moment, please?" She let her gaze slip toward the street, hinting that she would prefer not to discuss things standing out on the stoop.

The man seemed to understand. He stood back and allowed her to enter.

The little foyer was as Fran expected, with the stairs running up on her left hand as she faced them. A single hallway ran to the right with the first-floor rooms opening from it.

Now for the tricky part. Fran ducked her head as if hiding a blush. "You must forgive me, Mr. . . . ?"

"George Littlefield," he answered, with a slight bow. "My sister, Alice, is also resident here," he added, lest she should be shocked by the unaccountable phenomenon of an unaccompanied gentleman answering Miss Thorne's door.

"Mr. Littlefield." She gave him her best shy smile. "I am Wilhelmena Levitton. Miss Thorne may have mentioned I was going to call?"

"No, I'm afraid she didn't."

"Oh, oh, dear." She tugged at her reticule string again in a further show of uncertainty. "You see, my sister-in-law, Cate, is staying here, and I've come to see her. The family is . . . well, if you're a friend of Miss Thorne's, I'm sure I can tell you." She gave him another tentative smile, indicating that if he was a friend to Miss Thorne's, surely he must be her friend as well. "But there have been difficulties, and we are most anxious to know that she's all right." She blinked rapidly, as if she might cry.

Most gentlemen would have fallen over themselves to escort her inside, and bring Cate to her at once. George Littlefield stayed where he was, and his open, guileless eyes grew just a touch wary.

"I'm surprised Rosalind didn't tell Alice you were coming," he said. "She was planning to be out this morning, and would not have neglected to mention it."

"Oh, perhaps Miss Littlefield simply forgot to pass the message on?"

He was looking at her, far too long and too suspiciously. Who was this man? His clothes said he was of the middling classes, but his air said he was a gentleman. She glanced quickly at his hands. There were ink stains on his fingertips. He had a trade then, perhaps a clerk, or a lawyer, or even a newspaper writer, as his sister was.

"I'm sure Alice would have mentioned it," said Mr. Littlefield. "Or waited for you herself."

Damn. Fran bit her lip, and let her chin quiver. "Please," she whispered. "If I could just see her. Her mother . . ."

She got no further. A harsh pounding rattled the door at her back.

Littlefield frowned. "Excuse me." He stepped around her to open the door.

A girl in plain dress and apron stood on the steps, flushed and panting as if she'd just run all the way across London.

"Bella!" cried Littlefield.

"George!" gasped the girl. "You've got to get home! The baby's coming!"

The color drained from Littlefield's face. He staggered as if the words struck him a blow.

"Yes, yes, of course, yes," he babbled. "I must . . . I . . ." He stared at Fran. "Mrs. Singh . . ."

Who must be the cook. "I can let her know what's happened," said Fran helpfully. "And she can help me leave a note for Miss Thorne."

"Yes, yes, thank you." Littlefield grabbed his hat off the peg by the door. He bolted down the steps, catching the drab girl by the arm as he rushed past. Fran heard him saying something about a cab as she quickly closed the door.

Silence enveloped her. Even in a modest house such as this, the kitchen was down in the cellar, and probably in the back. The cook probably hadn't heard a single sound. And Cate, of course, was in hiding and not likely to come poking about out of idle curiosity.

All the better for me.

Fran hiked up her skirts and ran lightly up the stairs.

The second floor mirrored the first, with the rooms on the right-hand side of the hallway. All the doors were closed. Fran considered her options.

She chose the middle door. She scratched softly, as a properly trained maid would. No answer. She slipped up to the next door, and scratched again.

"*Amy?*" whispered Cate from the other side.

Fran opened the door and ducked inside. Cate was sitting in a chair by the open window. She looked up and then jumped up as Fran shut the door and turned the key. The chair tipped over backward and fell with a thud.

"Hullo, Cate." Fran grinned.

"How . . . !" began Cate, but Fran just shook her head.

"Really, Catie girl, you know my profession. Did you really think I couldn't get in someplace if I wanted?"

Cate looked to the door.

"Now, now, no noise." Fran wagged a finger at her. "It's just you and me here now. Your chaperone's gone out and her brother's gone to see his baby being born. You might see if you can scream for that cook, but that might not end up going so well for anybody concerned. Yourself included."

Fortunately, Cate knew her well enough to understand that she was perfectly ready to back up any threat she made.

"What do you want?" Cate croaked.

"I came to see how you do." Fran stepped lightly across the room, picked up the chair, and promptly sat down in it. "You look to have fallen on your feet among good company. How much have you taken them for?"

"I never . . ." gasped Cate.

"No?" Fran arched her brows. "Ah, but when they find all those jewels you've stolen off me and the girls, are they going to believe that?"

"What jewels? I handed you over everything!"

Fran got slowly to her feet. Cate tried to back away, but Fran was across the room before she could take her first step. She seized Cate's wrist. Not tight enough to bruise, just hard enough to let her know that playtime was over.

"Now, Catie-girl," breathed Fran. "Don't you try to lie to me."

Cate swallowed hard. "Let me go, Fran," she pleaded.

"Just as soon as you tell me where you've put my property."

"Please." Tears shimmered in Cate's eyes. "I don't have anything. I mean it. If something's gone missing . . ."

Fran pressed one finger from her free hand against Cate's lips. "What did I say about lying to me? I'm losing my patience now. Where are my jewels, Catie?"

She opened her mouth to say she didn't know, or maybe she meant to blame Amy. But at the same time, her eyes darted toward the wardrobe.

Fran snorted in disgust, and pushed Cate away. She staggered. Fran stomped to the wardrobe—which was of course unlocked, because this was a quiet, respectable house—and threw open the doors. Inside, along with a pair of neatly pressed dresses, waited a familiar battered brown valise.

"You kept it, I see." Fran helped herself to the bag. "I suppose one never knows when such a thing will come in handy."

"Fran," said Cate behind her. "You've got to understand—"

"No, Catie, I don't think I do." Fran seized the bag and turned to face her. "In fact, you're lucky I'm in a hurry or I'd see to it that *you* understand how much trouble you've caused with this little caper of yours."

Cate blanched and Fran grinned at her, baring all her teeth. "Now, a little bird tells me you're planning on leaving town?" This was a guess, but the signs certainly pointed that way. Cate's nervous swallow told Fran she'd guessed right. "You'd best be getting on then," Fran told her. "And if I was you, I'd not come back."

Fran gave her one more hard shove for good measure, before she barged out the door and down the stairs.

"Here now!" cried a woman's voice behind her. "What's all this!"

Fran didn't permit herself to break stride or waste time looking back. She bolted for the door and left it swinging open in her wake. Fingers brushed her back as she leapt down the stairs, hit the flagstone walk with only the slightest stagger, and sprinted up the street, the heavy bag banging against her thigh and a mad grin spreading across her face as she ran.

Let proper Miss Thorne explain this one to the neighbors!

CHAPTER 40

On the Hunt

". . . but he was so easily led, or rather so easily
excited by his companions, and his companions
were now of such a sort, that it was probable he
would soon become vicious."

Edgeworth, Maria, *Belinda*

London's rookeries were where people wound up when there was simply nowhere else to go. A rookery was not so much a building as a maze of them, connected by rickety stairs and walkways. Walls were put up and taken down at random in the dark, fetid interiors that could stretch on for what might be the length of a whole block in more regulated parts of the city. Most people weren't lucky enough to have a proper room. Hanging blankets divided the living spaces, such as they were. Sometimes there weren't even blankets, just an understanding of whose spot it might be, or the fact that one family could defend its territory against all comers.

It was not safe for anyone with a good pair of shoes to walk here, never mind a man who was known to be an officer of the court.

Adam, Goutier, and Tauton kept close to each other. It was almost noon outside. In here, Adam carried a lantern. Tauton and Goutier had their truncheons out. Even with the other men supporting him, Adam wished for eyes in the back of his head. There was no telling how many people lounged around them in the darkness. If it came to a fight, they stood very little chance of making it out alive.

But for the price of a few pennies given to a grizzled, toothless fellow perched on an empty barrel, they were given directions to the "rooms" Celia Ing had claimed for herself and her children. These rooms were found through a basement that was dark as a mineshaft and up a flight of backstairs that dipped and creaked under their boots. Tauton puffed and swore, as grim as Adam had ever heard him.

A ragged child sat at the top of the stairs, watching their approach with wary fascination.

"Where can we find Celia Ings?" Adam asked.

The child took their time looking them all over, then cried, "Ma! It's some gents!"

A greasy, torn blanket was lifted back. "Whaddayez want wi' me?" a woman demanded.

Celia Ings was a thin, gray woman with a square face and big, rawboned hands and wrists. She held up a single guttering candle stuck to a bit of broken dish.

"My name is Harkness," said Adam. "This is Captain Goutier, and Mr. Tauton."

"Well? What of it?" She folded her arms. "You got news 'bout my man?"

"No change," said Goutier. "I'm sorry."

The woman's face hardened, and she turned away. Adam caught the blanket as it fell. "We've a few questions to ask you, Mrs. Ings."

She shrugged.

There was a packing crate in the corner. Adam reached into his coat pocket, pulled out a few packages and laid them down on it.

"What's that then?" Mrs. Ing asked.

"My mother's baking day," said Adam. "Bread and some cake. A bit of butter and cheese."

Keeping one eye on them, Celia moved to unwrap the paper. Three children appeared, seemingly out of the woodwork. She distributed bread, cheese, honey cake, clouts, and shakes in equal measure to all of them. This rough care completed, she tore off a hunk of the remaining bread for herself and crammed it in her mouth like she thought someone might steal it from her. She may have had reason at that.

"Well?" she said, spewing crumbs. "Speak your piece."

"We're looking for the man George Edwards."

Celia's eyes narrowed.

"Can you tell us anything about him?" asked Adam.

Celia's eyes shifted back and forth. "Luce!" she bellowed.

Another child, a head taller than the others, appeared out of the dark. Celia swiftly bundled the food up in its paper and handed it to her. Luce nodded without a word and vanished. Celia herself shoved her bare feet into a pair of wooden clogs and led Adam and the others out of the warren and into a long, crooked yard. The only way he could tell they were even outside was by the strip of gray sky overhead.

Celia Ings faced them all and folded her arms. "You see what we is," she said. "Ain't got nothing, do we? Ings, he worked the butcher's trade, when he worked at all. Fell to pieces, didn't it? An' wasn't the kids hungry and half dead all winter long? And then this fellow Edwards comes along. He's talking about rising up and killing thems in charge, and Ings, he listens, an' why shouldn't he? What's them toffs mean to us? But Ings knows there's no chance. Who's gonna stand and fight when the militia gets their rifles out, eh?

"But this Edwards, he says if they all get together, there's money to be had, and a thousand Irishmen all ready to fight an' a thousand Scots comin' on down as soon as word's given. Ings didn't believe him at first, but then this Edwards starts buying drink and bread and brings him to hear Thistlewood and I don't know who all else. And what's he got to do all day, 'cept listen? And then, suddenly, he's bringing home money. And bread. Says it was the big shots give it him," she added.

"Did you tell this to Bow Street?" Tauton asked.

"For all the good it did any of us," muttered Celia. "Made my mark on the paper an' all. An' they still took him. An' they say he's in the Tower. Could be in Timbuktu for all I can get to him."

"We want to find Edwards," Adam told her. "What do you know about him?"

She shrugged. "He worked in plaster. Models and figures, ornaments, them things. Would hawk a basketload up and down the streets sometimes."

"Where did he live?" Goutier asked.

"All sorts of places, Ings said."

"Do you know where he might have gone, after Cato Street?" tried Adam.

Celia sneered, and spat. "If I knew that, do you think he'd still be alive? It was him that tipped the nod to the soldiers and all."

"You know that for sure?"

The woman looked at him like he'd lost his mind. "I've said my bit," she snapped. "I've got nothing more for any of you."

"And I understand that. But it's important we know who gave you the money. Which of the big shots was it?"

She shrugged. "What did it matter to me? They paid, that's all I cared about."

Adam wanted to press the point, but it was clear Celia was done talking. It was even more clear from the way that the other people in the yard were beginning to turn their heads that they were close to overstaying what very little welcome they had in this place.

"Thank you," said Adam.

Celia nodded, and spat again. "That way," she said, jerking her chin back behind them. "You'll come up in Present Alley. Head to your left. Yez'll find yer way."

They all thanked her again, and in tight formation they headed up the narrow yard. The buildings leaned close overhead, all but cutting off the strip of sky. Adam tried not to hurry, or to show the unfamiliar knot of fear that was building inside him.

But Celia had not steered them wrong. The yard did spill out into an alley, and to the left, they could make out a proper lane.

"Oi," croaked a tentative voice behind them.

Adam turned. There in the alley shadows stood the girl Mrs. Ings had called "Luce." She emerged into the daylight, careful as a cat, and just as ready to run.

"Can yez get me da' out the Tower?" she asked.

"We can try," said Adam.

Luce rubbed one raw, red foot against the other. "Ma sez not to trust a gent. She sez none o' yez care 'bout the likes of us."

Adam made no answer to this. Celia Ings probably had plenty of reason to deliver this lecture to her children.

"He gone back to the shop," whispered Luce. "Inna cellar, hard by Carlile's shop over in Fleet Street. Bobby Timms sez 'e seen 'im. Sez 'e's lucky it was 'im what saw cuz theys plenty sez it was 'im that peached on da' and all."

"You ever see Edwards yourself?" asked Tauton. "Can you say what he looked like?"

"He had a crooked back," said the child. "An' a long neck. Black hair, all in curls."

"Like mine?" asked Goutier.

Luce shook her head. "Loose and stringy, like. All around his ears. Long ears," she added. "Hands alwuz white, like they'z dipped in flour."

"Thank you," said Adam.

Goutier bent down. "Do you know where Waterby Street is?"

Luce considered him, and then nodded.

"You find Mrs. Goutier's shop there, and you go round to

the back door. Tell her you talked to her man and he says you're a good girl. She may have some work for you."

Luce's wary expression didn't shift. "You be the man then?"

"Sampson," he told her.

Luce nodded. "Fanks."

Goutier nodded back. So did Adam.

They didn't stay. In this place, it would do the child no good to be seen in their company. And there was not a moment to waste. If Luce knew where Edwards had gone to ground, doubtless others did, too.

One of them might have already told Beachamp.

They might not be inside the rookery anymore, but the maze of unnamed alleys and yards was only slightly less confusing. It was Tauton who took the lead. He'd haunted these byways for longer than either Adam or Goutier had been alive. A run-down stable slumped at the edge of a cluster of shops. All of them sold a full range of third- and fourth-hand items, where they were not selling gin. The owner knew the name Carlile, and was able to give the shop's address as number 55.

"Won't find no one there," he added.

"Why not?" asked Tauton.

"Well, they shut it down, didn't they? Ol' Carlile was one of them radicals, hung about with a nasty crowd."

The stableman was also willing to provide horses to the officers, as long as there was ready money, but had no conveyance for hire beyond a market wagon even more battered than the horses.

The problem here being that neither Tauton nor Goutier knew how to ride.

"You go ahead," said Tauton to Adam. "Look the place over for us. We'll catch up as soon as we find a cab."

The nag Adam mounted was old, ugly, and boney, but

mettlesome, and with a mouth like iron. But it was clearly a canny city resident, and when it realized Adam would not be fooled, or brushed off, they proceeded well enough and the animal was even willing to put on a burst of speed when the traffic cleared out. Soon, Adam was trotting toward the Fleet Market and the bridge.

At first glance, it would seem a fool's move for a man being hunted to return to a familiar haunt, but it often worked out better than one might think. A man's home and work would be the first places searched, but then they would be left alone while the search ranged further afield. Also, it was ground the fugitive would know and understand. Most importantly, there would be friends and family willing to help.

Like all of London's oldest thoroughfares, Fleet Street changed character multiple times along its length. This end was broad, winding, and crowded with carts, vans, wagons, and men on horseback like Adam. The buildings were close but not huddled. The world here drove a hard bargain and would take what it could get off the unwary, but there was a rough pride in the work and an eye to better things. Print shops jostled crabbed booksellers, gin shops mixed with coffeehouses.

In the middle of the noise and bustle sat number 55, Carlile's Bookshop—squat, dark, and shuttered, even in the middle of the day. Adam found a porter on the corner willing to hold his horse, and even more willing to tell Adam of the shop's travails.

"Sold banned books they did, got themselves arrested an' all. Filthy French stuff, they said, an' this Yankee fella, Paine, an' all sorts."

"I heard there was a plasterer lived with them," said Adam.

"Was. Maybe is. Dunno. His shop was around back."

"Thanks." Adam added another few pennies to the man's

outstretched hand. "Keep an eye out for two—a tall Black man in a blue coat and tall hat, and a stout, red-faced fellow in green and buff with him. You see them, you tell them what you told me, all right?"

The porter agreed that it was, with a sly smile and a finger laid alongside his nose, to show he looked forward to having a good story to tell when the day was done.

Adam didn't intend to go inside, not until the others arrived. He meant to circle the shop, at what distance he could, looking for signs of recent habitation. When Tauton and Goutier got there to help cover the obvious exits, he'd go in closer.

But when he found the muddy alleyway that led him to the ragged yard and the low door that was 55 1/2, Adam's plan changed in a heartbeat. Because despite the rest of the building being shut up tight, that low door hung wide open.

Adam looked quickly about him and saw no sign of Tauton and Goutier, and no knowing when they'd get there.

It was a lunatic decision, and Adam knew it, but he moved forward anyway, keeping to one side of the tiny yard, trying his best to see in all directions at once. No sound came out of the doorway. No sound came from the yard or the houses on either side that did not belong there.

Adam ducked down and peered into the doorway, and swore, and ducked inside.

A man lay facedown on the floor, a dark stain spreading over the back of his buff coat. A round-crowned hat lay beside him, and a dark, shining pool spread all about him. A wickedly curved knife lay on the packed earth floor, just out of reach.

Adam dropped to his knees and heaved the man onto his back, and swore again. It was a man with a long neck and curling, black hair that hung in strings all around his ears.

George Edwards was dead.

CHAPTER 41

The Peacemaker

*". . . he met her, with the air of a man of gallantry,
who thought that his peace had been cheaply
made."*

Edgeworth, Maria, *Belinda*

And what do I do now?

That question occupied the whole of Rosalind's mind as
Sanderson drove them through the streets to Marianna's house.
It would not be a very long drive. The traffic was clearing as
the shops closed. The fashionable hour was over, and much
of the world had already gone home to prepare for an
evening of parties and routs.

Do I tell Marianna about Harold and Wilhelmena?

It was Marianna whose interest she was engaged to uphold in this business. Marianna had her life threatened. Was
there some connection between the poisoning and Harold
Davenport's affair with Wilhelmena Levitton?

There could very well be. Mr. Davenport had a great deal
to lose if Marianna found out about his affair with Wilhelmena. He might be Marianna's favorite, but he was also her

employee. She could not only refuse to sanction his marriage to Cate, she could dismiss him out of hand at any moment.

Both Harold and Wilhelmena had been at the dinner the night Cate decided to bolt from Marianna's house. Had Cate seen something, or said something?

Or had Wilhelmena?

She knew how Marianna had been poisoned, but when could they have given the poison to Cate? And how? It could not have been at dinner, or even afterward, when Wilhelmena and Cate retired to take tea as custom dictated. Wilhelmena would have presided over the teapot, but she could hardly have poisoned the tea that she herself would have to drink.

Rosalind bowed her head and pinched the bridge of her nose. She did not want these possibilities in her mind. She liked Harold Davenport. She empathized with Wilhelmena's situation, and yet she could not ignore what had been done to Cate and Marianna.

Of course, it was still possible that she was wrong. The affair between Wilhelmena and Harold might have nothing to do with Marianna's poisoning. A family might have many different secrets and many reasons for keeping them.

The carriage turned onto Upper Brook Street. Sanderson brought the horses to a gentle halt and hopped down from the box. In his character of attentive driver, he let down the step and helped Rosalind out.

"Miss Thorne!" called a breathless voice.

Rosalind's bonnet hampered her view and she had to turn herself full around to see Everett Levitton hurrying toward her. He was disheveled and flushed, as if he had run, or ridden, too hard.

Sanderson, still playing the diligent attendant, stepped between her and Mr. Levitton.

"Have a care, fellow," he growled.

Everett pulled up short. "My apologies, but, Miss Thorne, before you go in to my aunt, I beg you, we must speak."

Sanderson glanced back at Rosalind, who nodded. Sanderson stepped aside with a bow. Really, he was taking his part rather too seriously. She would have to speak with him when opportunity arose.

"What is it, Mr. Levitton?" she asked.

Everett drew a deep breath. "I know what you have discovered. Regarding Harold. And Mena."

The words dropped heavily between them. Rosalind barely managed to contain her surprise, or dismay.

"We cannot stand talking in the street," she told him. "We will be noticed and remarked on."

"Yes, of course," agreed Everett. "But, you will let me talk with you first? Before you go upstairs?"

Rosalind nodded her assent.

"Good, excellent. Thank you. Let us go inside. Your man can see to your equipage?"

"Of course. I should only be an hour, Faulks." Sanderson was not the only one who could play a part.

He bowed, his face entirely serious. "Miss Thorne."

Everett showed Rosalind inside. The maid came for her outdoor things. She had just removed her coat when Beatrice came hurrying down the stairs.

"Oh, Miss Thorne," she cried. "My maid said you'd arrived. Have you discovered anything new about Cate?"

"Not yet, Mrs. Levitton," said Rosalind. "Has there been another letter here, perhaps?"

"No, nothing." Beatrice's cheeks were flushed. She carried a crumpled handkerchief and her eyes were bright red.

"Mother." Everett stepped up to her side and put his arm around her shoulders. "Surely you should rest. . . ."

Beatrice shook her head violently. "I cannot. I had thought that if only I could know she was safe, I'd be able to rest, but . . ." She squeezed her handkerchief more tightly, as if she were attempting to wring reassurance straight from the cloth. "With no word, no hint of where she is—but I have thought of something, though I wish to God I had not." She stopped and started again. "The maid, Miss Thorne. The one who corrupted my daughter. What if she discovered that Cate had returned to London? What if she has managed to get her hooks into my daughter again?"

Rosalind bit her tongue.

"I'm sure that's not what's happened, Mother," said Everett. "How would she have heard?"

"These people have their ways," said Beatrice coldly. "You were the one who pointed that out at the beginning."

Rosalind felt her jaw clench. Everett seemed to have said a good deal at the beginning, and all of it at Amelia's expense.

"Cate, she is a good girl, Miss Thorne," Beatrice went on. "But she has a trusting nature, and this McGowan creature, she was so plausible, so insinuating. She induced Cate to steal for her—were you told that? Steal from her own family!"

Rosalind hoped the blank expression on her face would be taken for shock. Everett looked at Rosalind. Rosalind had seldom in her life been in danger of dissolving into true hysterics—but the combination of outrage and maddeningly inappropriate laughter that rose in her throat threatened to push her over that precipice.

"Thank you, Mrs. Levitton." Rosalind was astonished at how steady her voice remained. "What you say is a possibility and you may be sure I have not neglected it."

"There, now, Mother, you see?" said Everett brightly. "Miss Thorne has everything in hand. Will you go rest now?" He took both of his mother's hands and pressed them gently. Rosalind fastened her gaze on the wall and the landscape painting that hung over the umbrella stand.

"Cate will need you more than ever when she's returned to us," Everett was saying softly to his mother. "You won't be able to care for her if you've worried yourself into an illness."

"I know, I know." Beatrice kissed her son's cheek. "What you must think of me."

"I think you love Cate," said Everett. "As we all do."

"Yes, yes, and you are, of course, right." Rosalind could hear from Beatrice's voice she was attempting to compose herself. "I will go up to my room and I think I will be able to rest now. Miss Thorne, you will excuse me?"

"Yes, of course," said Rosalind.

"I'll go up with you," said Everett. "Miss Thorne, have you seen my aunt's picture gallery yet?" He nodded down the hallway. "It's right at the end. She has some very fine works, I believe."

"Thank you, I believe I will take a look," said Rosalind.

While Everett helped his mother solicitously up the stairs, Rosalind retreated down the central hallway to the round gallery. She paced the room slowly, paying little attention to the artwork that hung on the walls. She needed to calm herself, and to focus her mind. She could be angry on Amelia's behalf later.

Right now, I cannot give any hint I know her.

She was repeating this to herself when Everett joined her. He stood beside her, although at a proper distance, and they both made a show of contemplating the landscape in front of them. Doubtlessly, Sanderson could have told her all about the artist, and whether it was any good.

"Tell me more about this maid your mother is so concerned with," she said. "Did she really convince Cate to steal for her? I have never heard of such a thing."

"Yes, well," murmured Everett. "It's easier for Mother to believe that than to believe Cate did what she did of her own volition." He strolled casually to the next painting, a formal portrait of a lady in a lace gown and tall wig. "I must beg you, Miss Thorne, to tread carefully around my mother."

"She loves her daughter," said Rosalind.

"A little too much perhaps," said Everett. When he saw

Rosalind's surprise, he smiled a little. "Does that shock you? It happens sometimes, you know. Cate was always mother's favorite. She could do no wrong. I was jealous, I think." His smile was fleeting. "She'd dreamed of such a perfect future for her perfect girl."

"That must have been a great deal of pressure on Cate."

"Do you know, I believe it was. Regardless, losing Cate once, and then losing her husband, and then losing Cate again like this . . . it's just been too much for her."

"I understand," said Rosalind.

"Do you?" Skepticism filled Everett's words. "Do you understand that my mother can't bring herself to blame Cate for anything? She lost four girls between me and Cate. And for the first couple of years, we weren't sure Cate was going to live. After that, Mother doted on her. Could barely stand to let Cate out of her sight. And whenever Cate got into trouble . . . well, all Cate had to do was say it was someone else's fault, and Mother would believe her."

"Did Cate do this a great deal?"

"Get into trouble? Or tell tales?"

"Both."

Everett sighed. "Yes, I'm afraid she did. It wasn't entirely her fault, of course. I mean, she was a child, and if it was a choice between getting into trouble, especially with Father, or telling a lie—"

"Yes, of course." Rosalind moved to the next painting. This one was a still life of a brass vase full of flowers. Fallen petals lay scattered on a damask cloth.

"You must not think my parents were wicked, or careless. They loved us all, and they did their best, according to their lights. It can be difficult to see such things from outside, but I assure you it was so."

Rosalind nodded. "And did you decide it would be easier for your mother to continue to believe that a servant corrupted her daughter than that Cate chose to leave on her own?"

Everett's brows lowered. "I think that, Miss Thorne, is not your business."

"I apologize," she said immediately.

Everett bowed his head, letting her know he accepted her apology. Rosalind stared hard at the still life, until she was sure of her voice again. "May I ask, Mr. Levitton, how did you know where I had been this afternoon?"

"I saw you," he said. "Because I'd gone to the same place."

"You were following Wilhelmena?"

"Following you, actually," he said, and there was the tiniest trace of smugness in his words. He paused, clearly expecting some display of outrage, or at least surprise. But Rosalind simply regarded him with her usual polite, cool gaze.

"You will have to forgive me, Miss Thorne," said Everett. "But you were engaged by Aunt Marianna, and Mother, to find Cate. I don't understand how this private business between Wilhelmena and Harold can have any bearing on that." He paused. "Unless you're playing a double game?"

Rosalind held her tongue, hoping her silence would be mistaken for surprise at this discovery.

"You are!" Everett exclaimed in a hoarse whisper. "Did Marianna set you on their trail? Or were we all mistaken in how you came to be here? Or was it Cate who engaged you to take Harold's measure while she made herself scarce to throw us off?"

"None of those things, I promise you," replied Rosalind calmly.

"Then how . . . ? It can't have been Marcus who brought you here. Forgive me, but even if he could be so far gone with his desire for revenge that he'd actually gather evidence of crim. con., he'd never hire a woman for the job!" Crim. con. was the popular term for "criminal conversation," what the law called adultery.

"Mr. Levitton," said Rosalind firmly. "I trust you will understand that I cannot betray this particular confidence."

"I beg your pardon. Naturally, you cannot. But . . . you don't intend to *tell* Marcus, do you? I mean, Cate, I suppose, has a right to know what her fiancé is up to. It really is too bad of Harold to be carrying on like this. But, if Marcus finds out . . . I'm not exaggerating, Miss Thorne, not only will he throw Wilhelmena out into the street, but he'll lodge a crim. con. suit against Harold and take him for everything he has."

Criminal conversation was a peculiar and infuriating aspect of English law. The idea being that since a wife's body belonged exclusively to her husband, if another man had intimate relations with her, he was, in effect, robbing her husband, and he, in return, had the right to sue for property damage.

"Is your brother so litigious?" asked Rosalind. Most men would do anything rather than suffer the embarrassment of publicly admitting their wife had been unfaithful.

"Lord, yes! Eight years ago, he had a man thrown into debtor's prison over a sum of fifty pounds. The man's still there, and he might never get out, because Marcus swears he won't forgive the debt." Rosalind suppressed a shudder.

"I'd . . . become aware of Mena keeping company with Harold some months ago. I begged her to break it off. I warned her Marcus was not the most imaginative of men, but he was not a fool. If he discovered them he would not treat her any better than he had treated Cate." His voice shook.

"Does Marianna know?" asked Rosalind.

"Good Lord, no. She'd never have tried to match Cate to Harold if she did. However highly she may regard him, she can't abide a cheat."

Rosalind nodded. "Mr. Davenport indicated that marrying Cate was his own idea and that Marianna's offer of a settlement came afterward. Is that true?"

"I still do not understand what this has to do with finding Cate," Everett said.

Rosalind faced him directly. "Mr. Levitton, before you asked how I am engaged here. I told you I could not betray that confidence. I may, however, tell you that the matter is a complicated and delicate one. I may also say that I am doing all I can to protect both Marianna and Cate. I believe they have both been put at risk of grave harm."

Everett considered her for a long while. Rosalind made no attempt to fill the silence or redirect his regard. He did not entirely trust her, and she did not blame him. She had given him very little reason for trust. For all his foolishness, he was an intelligent man. A wounded one, too. He also had grown up in a harsh household, and had lost his father, struggled against his brother, and loved his sister and his mother, and now he lived through this latest rift and was surrounded by secrets.

"Extraordinary," he murmured. "And yet, I think I believe you." Rosalind hoped he did not hear her long exhalation of breath. "The answer to your question is that the engagement between Harold and Cate was Marianna's idea from the first. I think if Cate had showed aptitude for an independent life, our aunt would have left her to find her own road. But Cate, well, Cate has not got a head for business, or art, or writing, any such thing, so I think Aunt Marianna looked for a way to help her to a future. And what would be better than uniting her two favorites? Especially as neither had a particular emotional entanglement. Or so it seemed," he added ruefully.

Rosalind nodded. On the face of it, it was a perfectly reasonable arrangement. Appearances would be maintained for all concerned. Marianna could make a gift that would do a great deal of good for her favorites, and to the larger world that gift would appear highly laudable. That meant it would be likely to survive should Cate's litigious brother decide to try to find a way to drag the matter into court.

Further, if Cate were married to Harold, Harold had charge of her, and any fortune she might possess. That put her, and her money, entirely out of her brother's reach.

"Does your mother approve of Harold Davenport?" asked Rosalind.

"Oh, yes," said Everett. "Very much. I think she hopes that she'll be able to go live with him and Cate once they're married."

Rosalind imagined the possibility of living with her beloved daughter rather than her cold and jealous son must be an exciting prospect for Beatrice.

She found herself wondering if Beatrice knew about the affair and had, so far, kept it to herself.

"Well," Everett was saying. "You should probably go see Aunt Marianna. From what the nurse says, you may not have many more chances to speak with her," he added. "When Harold comes home, I'll have a word with him."

"Perhaps you should not, just yet, Mr. Levitton. There is a great deal about the present situation we do not know, and tensions are very high."

Everett looked at her steadily and Rosalind thought she saw a spark of anger in the depths of his worried eyes.

"I will think about it," he said. "But Aunt Marianna is waiting for you, Miss Thorne, and you must not disappoint."

"There is one other question I would ask you, Mr. Levitton, if I may?"

A spasm of impatience crossed his features, only to be quickly smoothed away into an attitude of attention.

"I am told you organized a dinner for the family, the night Cate chose to leave her home. Was it your hope to help mend the breach?"

"Well, you are partly right, Miss Thorne," he replied. "I did organize things, or at least I tried to. But as to why it happened . . . frankly, you would have to ask Marcus that. It was his idea."

CHAPTER 42

A Few Pointed Questions

"I know that this must appear to you extravagant; but depend upon it that what I tell you is true."

Edgeworth, Maria, *Belinda*

Alice returned home from her private errands in a foul mood. Nothing was improved by finding the foyer dark and silent.

"George?" she called. "Amelia?"

She barely had time to frown and strip off her gloves when Mrs. Singh appeared at the top of the stairs.

"Miss Alice, if you'd come up, please? I need a word with you."

Alice pulled off coat and bonnet, dropping them both on the seat of the bench beside the door. She grabbed her hems and ran upstairs, not caring that her half boots were shedding mud all the way.

Something's happened to Amelia, something's happened to Rosalind, to George. . . .

When she got to the top of the stairs, she saw Mrs. Singh standing in front of the door to Cate's room with her arms folded. Inside, both Amelia and Cate were sitting beside the bed, as guilty as a pair of schoolgirls caught rifling the head-mistress's desk.

Alice's fear turned abruptly to annoyance. "What is going on?" she demanded.

Mrs. Singh pointed her callused finger at Cate. "This one seems to have been entertaining a thief."

Alice made herself listen to the story of a *person* who came to the door, of George being called away because the baby was on its way, and how that *person* simply walked into the house, and ran out again with a valise belonging to Miss Cate (if she can be called so!), and that was *after* knocking Mrs. Singh to the floor.

Alice knew full well what Rosalind would have done. She would have sat down, possibly called for tea, and calmly sorted through these various occurrences. She might even have gone so far as to call them distressing.

Alice favored a different approach.

"What have you done!" she bellowed at Cate. "We took you in, we sheltered you when someone out there was trying to poison you, and this is what you do . . . !"

"I'm sorry," whispered Cate. "I never meant for her to come here. I was planning to leave. Right away. You can ask Amelia."

Alice glowered at Amelia. "And where were you while we were being robbed? And don't tell me it was the market be-cause I won't believe you!"

Amelia didn't even look up. "She . . . Cate . . . sent me to buy her a ticket for the stage, to Edinburgh."

Alice clenched her fists and gritted her teeth. *Get hold of yourself, Alice!*

She made herself face the cook. "Mrs. Singh, are you all right?" she asked.

Mrs. Singh drew herself up. "I am well enough."

"Good. Do you mind staying with Cate? I need to have a few words with Amelia."

"I should say."

It was the most difficult thing Amelia had ever done, but she followed Miss Alice into her book room, and closed the door behind them. When she turned around, Alice was staring into the fire, her arms crossed tightly in front of her.

"Miss Alice . . ." Amelia began, but Miss Alice turned so abruptly that her words were cut off. Amelia fully expected Alice to begin shouting immediately, but instead she stalked over to the table with the remains of a basket of muffins and a pot of tea. She took up one of the muffins and speared it onto a toasting fork.

"Would you like one?" she held up the fork to demonstrate what she was talking about There's jam and butter." She waved the fork, and the muffin, toward the tray. "I think the nicest thing about living with Rosalind is she never makes a fuss about toasting muffins. My mother used to positively howl if she caught us. And you should have heard the teachers at school." She plumped herself down in her chair and held the muffin over the fire.

"No, thank you, miss," whispered Amelia.

"You've had your tea?" said Miss Alice to the fire.

"Yes, miss."

"Good." Alice pulled the muffin from the fire and dropped it carefully onto a crumb-covered plate. "Then you can tell me exactly what on *earth* you were thinking, lying to me all this time?"

Amelia felt her jaw drop.

"I don't . . . I never . . . not much . . ."

"Not much!" the force of her shout pulled Miss Alice to her feet. "You stole! That's why you got thrown out of your last job! Not because they caught you kissing Cate, because they caught you stealing! And it wasn't the first time!"

"Who told you that!" Amelia demanded, but as soon as the words were out of her mouth, she knew it was the wrong thing to say. Miss Alice's eyes blazed like fury.

Alice took a step forward. Amelia imagined she could feel the heat of her anger burning through the air between them. "I used to be a newspaper woman—do you think I can't find things out?" she demanded. "I went to the registry office and I got the references they have on file for you, and I spoke to the women whose names are on them. Or, I should say I spoke to one, because the other one doesn't exist and neither does the address you gave!"

Amelia felt like there was a hand around her throat. She couldn't breathe. She tried to speak, but all that came out was a small choking noise.

"And you know what the woman I did speak to told me? She said you were dismissed for thieving and she never wrote that reference! Good God, Amelia! How on earth did you find a registry that wouldn't check!"

"Most of 'em don't," she mumbled. "They say they do, but they don't. Too much bother." She felt tears prickle at the back of her eyes. She couldn't cry. Not now. Not when Miss Alice wouldn't believe it was real.

"I trusted you!" Tears streamed down Miss Alice's cheeks. "Rosalind trusted you! We counted ourselves so lucky to have found a girl who wasn't frightened by what she does, and who could fall right in with our household . . . and it was because you were a thief!"

Amelia lifted her eyes, her face flushed, but not with shame, with anger. "Yes, all right, I stole. You don't have any idea what it's like, being an upstairs maid," she croaked. "Oh, yeah, you get a cot in a drafty attic, and you get to eat the family's leavings. But there's the cost of uniforms, and if you've broken anything at all, and money to be sent home to help Mum, and half the times the family in the house don't bother to pay at the end of the year, or invent excuses not to. So you pick up things, sometimes. Here and there." Amelia's words broke off in a sharp, choking sound.

Alice folded her arms and did not let herself move, however much she wanted to.

"She said she loved me," said Amelia. "She told me she wanted to run away. That was all I ever wanted. Run away from home, run away from service, from everything." She wiped at her eyes with the heel of her hand. "But there was no money. I told her I knew what to do, if she'd help, and she said yes, and so we . . ." She turned beet red. "She picked things up, at the parties she went to. Little things. Snuff boxes and ear bobs . . . these people have so much!"

Alice's glare didn't flicker.

"I sold on what she stole. There's plenty of pawnshops that won't ask questions, for just a little extra. Sometimes she came with me, to see. . . . She liked the adventure." She swallowed. "It became, I don't know, fun. I felt like Robin Hood or Dick Turpin or one of them. I guess when she was off in Bath, she kept at it on her own." She bit her lip. "I don't know who that woman was who came here, the one Mrs. Singh talked about. I swear to you I don't. I just wanted to help Cate, because, because . . ." She choked again. "I wanted to help her get away."

When Miss Alice spoke again, her voice was low and cold. "Did you feel anything for me? Or did you just realize you could . . . that I would . . ."

"No!" cried Amelia. "I . . . you're everything to me! When you're in the room sometimes I can't think straight I feel so much!" She pressed her fist against her chest. "I lie awake nights thinking about you. About us. I'd stuff the pillow in my face and cry because I'm so afraid you'll find out what I really am, and now you have and I want to die!"

Alice said nothing. The silence stretched. Amelia's thoughts were pulling in a hundred different directions. She didn't know what to think. She didn't know what to say. All she could do was stand there and wait, and hope, and the hope hurt worse than despair.

"Have you *ever* stolen from Rosalind?" Miss Alice demanded.

Amelia shook her head.

"From me?"

Amelia lifted her eyes, mute.

"What?"

Amelia reached into her apron pocket. She pulled out a handkerchief and held it out.

Miss Alice's beautiful eyes widened.

"It had your scent on it," Amelia told her. "I keep it under my pillow."

Miss Alice stared at the square of linen, and then looked away. But Amelia saw the tears spilling down her cheeks.

"I don't forgive you," she announced.

"No, miss."

"I don't know if I ever shall."

"Yes, miss," said Amelia. Her voice quavered.

"And I want to be perfectly clear, if I *ever* catch you lying to me again I shall be the one to throw you out on your ear. Even if we are in a moving carriage. Do you understand me?"

"Yes, miss." Amelia's voice trembled again. She could not tell if it was because she was about to begin bawling, or laugh out loud because it wasn't over. Not yet. Because Miss Alice believed. She might not understand, not yet, but she believed, and that was what mattered.

"And when Rosalind gets home, you are going to tell her absolutely everything you know about all the Levittons. She probably knows it all anyway, but she'll want to hear it from you."

"Yes, miss."

"And you stop calling me miss!"

"Yes, Alice."

Alice let out a long shuddering breath. Amelia found that her heart seemed to have steadied, which was a promising sign.

"Now, what about this valise?" Miss . . . Alice asked. "The one Mrs. Singh said was stolen? What do you know about that?"

Amelia stared at Alice's handkerchief, and then at Alice herself. She tucked the kerchief into her apron pocket.

"If she took it out of Cate's room, it would be the bag that Cate had asked me to hold on to for her last week, with her clothes and things in it."

"Do you know why anyone would care about that?"

Amelia was aware that Alice was watching her closely. She surely saw the struggle going on in Amelia's heart.

You have to decide. You have to decide right now.

Amelia took a deep breath. "It's got a false bottom," she said. "I found it when . . . well, I found it, and there was a bunch of jewelry hidden inside."

"So, this woman, she broke in to steal the jewels?" cried Alice.

Amelia felt a cheeky grin spread slowly across her face. "Well, if she did, she's in for a bit of a surprise, m . . . Alice."

CHAPTER 43

A Small Matter of Money

*". . . my fortune was the most convenient thing in
the world to a man in his condition."*

Edgeworth, Maria, *Belinda*

As soon as Mrs. Hepplewhite admitted Rosalind, Mrs.
Levitton exclaimed, "Miss Thorne, I beg of you, tell me
you have some news!"

Mrs. Levitton was on the lounge in her private sitting
room. A pile of books and correspondence waited on the
table at her elbow. As Rosalind took the tapestry chair she was
waved toward, Mrs. Levitton tossed down the letter she had
been reading.

"I am about to go mad," Mrs. Levitton declared. "And
poor Hepplewhite cannot endure me much longer. We may
have spoiled one attempt on my life, but I swear she is set to
finish the job."

Mrs. Hepplewhite listened to this declaration with an air
of patient stoicism.

"I confess, Mrs. Levitton, I'm not at all sure what I have to
tell you."

"Come, come, Miss Thorne, that will not do. You cannot

mean to say with all this time you have discovered nothing at all?"

Rosalind thought to point out it had been scarcely a single day since she had last spoken with Marianna, but she decided that would not be productive.

"It is my experience, Mrs. Levitton, that if a person is driven to a drastic action, they must believe both that they have a great deal to gain, and that they have no other choice."

"That would seem sensible."

"What I have not been able to resolve thus far is the question of a gain. Which leads me to a delicate question."

"Are you about to ask me about my last will and testament, Miss Thorne?"

Rosalind nodded.

"I see. So we have abandoned politics for the consideration of simple greed." Marianna folded her hands on her lap. "Well, that is much less interesting, and, may I say, a blow to my sense of self-importance. However, I imagine that despite what the novelists would have us believe, the simplest answer is most often correct."

"That, generally speaking, is the case."

"So, my will. I have made no secret of it. I have left an income to Beatrice, and another to Cate, because I cannot trust Marcus to properly care for either one."

"What about Everett?"

"Everett has the means to make his own way in the world. He has, as of yet, chosen not to do so. I do not feel the need to support this choice with any legacy."

She does not like to be disappointed. Honoria's observation echoed in Rosalind's mind. At the same time, she could not blame Marianna for her choice.

"Beyond that, I have placed everything in a trust and named my attorneys as its executors. The businesses and properties are to be sold. I have given my managers first options to purchase. The monies are then to be used in the support and furtherance of a series of political and charitable organizations."

"And your family knows of your decisions?"

"I have been very frank with all of them. I had hoped candor would prevent any of them borrowing against their expectations, or hanging about waiting for me to close my eyes. I seem to have failed in that end," she added bitterly.

"And you left nothing to Harold Davenport in your will?"

"He will have the option to purchase a controlling share in the mines he manages, but otherwise, no."

"So, he will only have outright ownership if he marries Cate?"

"That is correct, and yes, he knows that."

"And this arrangement is not part of your will?"

Mrs. Levitton's eyes narrowed. "You do not mean to accuse Mr. Davenport of this . . . this outrage?"

"I do not mean to accuse anyone," said Rosalind. "Because I do not yet know enough. I will say that if the motivation for the poisonings is gain, Mr. Davenport seems to be the last person who would take such a step. His clearest route to his fortune rests with you and Cate, but it is you and Cate who were poisoned."

"So, we are back to the beginning."

"It is difficult to know," admitted Rosalind. "It may be the answer has already been presented, but we do not yet understand it."

Mrs. Levitton snorted loudly. "That, Miss Thorne, smells badly of humbug and frustration."

Despite everything, Rosalind felt herself smile. "Perhaps frustration. I hope that I have banished humbug from my daily life."

"There is no shame in a little humbug as a seasoning. It is the duty we must pay to convention."

"It is my understanding that you have never been one to deal in convention," said Rosalind.

Marianna smiled sadly. "I did my best to eschew it when I was younger. Those, however, were different times, Miss Thorne. Better times. A woman could get away with a great deal, if she did it with style, and I had style." Her back straightened at the memories. "We rode and we drove, and drank in the taverns, and made all the gentlemen stare."

"Is that how you met Mr. Levitton?"

"Would it shock you if I said yes? We'd made a wager, Colin and I, over a horse race, and as it happened, I won. He said he'd never met anyone like me, and that I would save his life." Her eyes grew distant. "And I decided to believe him, and I never once regretted it."

Rosalind let the silence sit, so that Marianna could hold her private memory for a moment.

At last she shook herself, coming fully back to present. "But, none of this is to the point, Miss Thorne," she said with an air of mild accusation.

"My apologies," said Rosalind. "I did mean to ask you—I understand there was a family dinner the night Cate disappeared."

"Yes, I heard something of that. I had hoped to attend, but in the end I was too weak."

"Wilhelmena told me Everett arranged it, but Everett told me that it was Marcus's idea."

"What could that possibly have to do with anything?" asked Marianna.

"It is a question of timing," Rosalind told her. "Cate says she was well up until dinner time, and only became ill afterward. It is therefore probable that any poison was administered to her during the dinner."

"How would that even be done without poisoning the whole party?"

"I don't know that yet. But if the dinner was arranged to bring Cate into a situation where the poison could be administered . . ."

"Yes, yes," Mrs. Levitton murmured. Her hands began plucking at her quilts in an agitated rhythm.

"Forgive me, Miss Thorne," she said. "That Marcus would poison me, I can believe. Rather too easily, as it happens. But that he would poison his own sister . . ."

"So, it was Marcus who arranged the dinner?"

"That is what Beatrice said. She believed he was trying to reconcile himself to Harold and Cate's marriage. She, and Everett, had put it to him that not only would the marriage tend to remove any lingering suspicions about Cate's character, but Harold might be more amenable to materially helping with Marcus's various business ventures than I had been, especially if such donations would smooth relations with his bride's family." Mrs. Levitton cocked her head toward Rosalind. "You appear frustrated, Miss Thorne."

"I admit that I am," said Rosalind. "I had believed that money must be at the root of this matter. But I may have been mistaken."

"Well, I cannot blame you," said Marianna. "I would hardly be the first wicked old lady done in for her fortune."

"Which leaves one remaining possibility for someone to wish for your death, or Cate's."

"What is that?"

Rosalind met Mrs. Levitton's inquiring gaze. "Secrets." She drew in a deep breath. "I had hoped I would not have to tell you this. However, one thing I've been able to acertain for certain is that Mr. Davenport is carrying on a romantic affair with Wilhelmena Levitton."

"No," snapped Marianna.

Rosalind said nothing.

"Harold would not be such an inconsiderate idiot. Furthermore, he knows perfectly well that if Marcus ever found out he'd be dragged into court. Not to mention what I would do to him," she added grimly. "I will not bear a cheat or a liar— I do not care who the man is, or how I may have regarded him previously." Outrage shook her voice and lit a dangerous spark in her eyes. "It was Everett who told you this, wasn't it? If you hadn't noticed, Miss Thorne, Everett is not above lying to accomplish his goals."

"What reason would Everett have to lie about a liaison between Harold and Wilhelmena?"

"Who knows!" snapped Marianna. "I certainly do not know! I am imprisoned in here and must pretend to be dying lest I be poisoned at my next meal! I am employing you to find these answers, Miss Thorne, not to subject me to pointless interrogation!"

"Forgive me." Rosalind got to her feet. "And I thank you for your patience. I will return when I have something of substance to tell you."

"See that you do. I warn you, Miss Thorne, this week of yours is strictly on the condition you produce genuine results. I may yet decide to withdraw my support for this deception of yours."

Rosalind curtsied and left her there.

Out in the hallway, she took a moment to catch her breath and compose her features. She was conscious of a sinking disappointment. She had felt it before. It came when an answer she had sought was both certain and unwelcome.

Marianna Levitton had made it very plain that whatever her relationship with Harold Davenport might be, it was not simply that of a trusted employee, or even that of a husband's beloved favorite. It was the secret Marianna kept. Possibly that they both kept.

And that secret might be dangerous enough to Mr. Davenport—or to another member of the family—that they would use any means to keep it from becoming known.

CHAPTER 44

Desperate Measures

"He is one of those men who require great emotions: fine lovers these make for stage effect—but the worst husbands in the world!"

Edgeworth, Maria, *Belinda*

When Fran opened the door to the flat, she felt in fine fettle. Had she been less of a lady, she might have whistled. But the instant she stepped inside, all her good feeling vanished.

Jack was in the chair in front of the fire, doubled over in open and obvious pain.

"My God, Jack!" She dropped the valise and ran to his side. She pushed on his shoulders to sit him up. That was when she saw the blood all over his shirt and waistcoat.

"What . . ." She backed away and looked reflexively at her own hands. There was blood on her palms as well.

"Don't worry, Fran," he said through gritted teeth. "It's not mine. Well, most of it isn't," he added.

"Show me," she demanded.

Jack shifted in his seat to show her his side. Coat, waistcoat, and shirt were all torn, so was the flesh underneath. The long, ragged cut had begun to crust and blacken.

Fran swallowed her gorge and stomped across the flat to get her workbasket and the bottle of brandy they kept in the pantry for both celebrations and emergencies.

The better part of an hour later, Jack was stitched as tight as she could manage, and had drunk the part of the brandy that had not gone to soaking the needle and thread. Fran's mother had always told her that soaking the needle in spirits helped dull the pain and speed healing. Fran didn't know if she believed that, but now was not the time to question such things.

She also helped ease Jack into his other shirt and coat.

"Thanks, Franny," he breathed as he eased himself back in the chair and drank down the last of the brandy.

Fran straightened up, wiped her hands on the ruin of his other shirt, and then clouted him hard on the ear.

"Ahg! Franny!" cried Jack.

"You fool man!" she roared. "What have you been doing?"

Jack actually looked sheepish. "Getting us in trouble, I'm afraid, Franny."

As if that wasn't obvious! "What sort of trouble?"

Jack licked his lips. Fran tried to brace herself. Whatever it was, it was going to be extra bad this time.

"Edwards is dead."

Fran felt her jaw drop. "You're joking."

"I wish I was," he said grimly. "I found him holed up in his old shop. I told him not to fuss, and just come along quiet, that there were men who wanted a word, he'd be paid for his time." Jack lifted his head. "Turns out the bastard was waiting for me. He had a knife ready. It was only luck that he caught my coat on his first pass, instead of a carving a fillet out of my side."

Fran said nothing.

"We fought. I got the knife away from him, and he came at me again and . . ." He winced. "Well, that was that."

"That was that?" she said, her voice perfectly even and deathly cold. "You went and killed the man that was going to bring us a thousand pounds. And now the Redbreasts really will be looking for you. You're going to have to leave the country!"

Jack smiled sadly. "I was thinking Paris this time."

Fran paced across the flat. She should leave him here. Take the goods and just go. Start over with just Jenny Cee and the girls and never mind men and their stupid antics and their stupid promises and stupid, handsome faces. She glowered at Jack, pale as death in his chair by their tiny, smoky hearth. *Serve him right if I did go.*

But then he turned and he looked at her and she saw again the one person, man or woman, who'd never run out on her, never asked more of her than she could give, never once betrayed her secrets by night or day. Stupid, unsteady, sweet-talking, pretty Jack Beachamp was the one thing she could really count on.

"Well, aren't you lucky one of us was thinking ahead." Fran growled and went to pick up the valise from where she'd dropped it.

Jack smiled, a beatific grin that was half delight, and as much brandy.

"I knew you'd see us through," said Jack. "How much did you get?"

"All of it." Fran set the valise down on the rickety table next to Jack's chair and opened the catch. "Very considerate girl, is our Cate. She kept it all packed up and ready to go."

She lifted out one of the lumpy brown paper packages and tugged open the knot in the twine. The paper came open.

Fran Finch screamed at the top of her lungs as lumps of coal tumbled out across the table and onto the floor.

CHAPTER 45

Never Truly Passed

"Scandal, like Death, is common to all."

Edgeworth, Maria, *Belinda*

With some difficulty, Rosalind convinced Sanderson to leave her at her sister's door. She assured him that Charlotte had a carriage and driver of her own, and that she would see Rosalind got safely home. Further, she promised she would write to him immediately so he could come and hear the conclusion of today's inquiries.

"I declare I shall not be able to rest a single minute until you do," he told her.

Now, a footman in plain livery showed her to Charlotte's private sitting room.

"Rosalind!" Charlotte cried as she entered. "I must say, I had quite despaired of you."

"I'm very sorry to be calling so late." Rosalind quickly leaned down and embraced her sister so she did not have to rise from the sofa where she was lounging with her feet up before a good, clear fire. "How are you?"

"Very well, as it happens," Charlotte replied, settling back onto her pile of pillows and resting one protective hand on her swollen belly.

Charlotte's pregnancy was the only reason she remained in town. Her fond husband had planned that they should live in the country, but like many a new father, he found himself anxious for his wife's health and discovered a grave distrust of country doctors. As a result, Charlotte was undergoing her confinement in a London house that was only one street away from Harvey Street, which had recently become a by-word for the most reputable of medical men.

"My dearest hovers over me like an old woman," Charlotte went on as Rosalind settled herself in the overstuffed chair opposite her so they could talk comfortably. "And the doctors are constantly amazed both by my consistent health and his insistent worries."

For some years, Charlotte had been a sought-after courtesan, first in Paris and then in London. But her final protector, who had made his fortune in India, was an older, childless man, and when Charlotte fell pregnant with his child, he determined to marry her and provide the child with a home, and a mother, and legitimacy all in one fell, indulgent swoop.

"That said," Charlotte continued, "I will confess that I am tired, my feet swell, and I'm prone to tears, but I am assured that's all shockingly normal. In a month's time, you should be an aunt."

It was, Rosalind felt, almost too much to contemplate. Yet another new irritating irrationality to deal with.

"Are you afraid?" Rosalind asked.

"Terrified," said Charlotte simply.

"Are you sorry?"

Now her sister looked startled. "About what?"

Rosalind opened her mouth, and closed it again. "What you've lost. What you might lose." *That you might be an invalid if the birth is hard. That you might die. That he might leave you after all.*

"I don't know," said Charlotte quietly. "But I am content. I made my decision for my own reasons. What happens next will happen, and I will meet that as well."

"Yes."

Charlotte frowned, and for a moment she was entirely the older sister Rosalind knew from her childhood with the cutting wit and unforgiving eye. "What's the matter?"

"Nothing, well, no, it's . . ." Rosalind closed her mouth to cut off her stammering. "I am disappointed in myself."

"Why?"

"Because I can't do what you just said. I can't make my own decision for my own reasons. All I can do is cry and be angry and afraid and I can't make myself stop."

Charlotte laughed.

Rosalind drew herself up.

"Oh, dear. I'm sorry. I shouldn't have done that. I apologize, Rosalind, come back down."

"I came here looking for help."

"Which was hard enough, I am well aware. No, Rosalind, don't." She held up her hand. "I am sorry, I shouldn't have laughed. And had I not been so jealous of you, I might not have."

"Jealous?"

"That you have so much in your life to choose from."

"It doesn't feel that way."

"I'm sure it doesn't. But it's the truth. You have made a life that offers you a kind of freedom that leaves much to envy. Independence is not a quality much valued in a woman. As I should know."

Rosalind said nothing. Charlotte's mouth twisted up into a tight smile.

"But the kind of independence I created has a very short span. I knew from the start that I must either quickly make enough money to last me the rest of my days, or I must find a man to keep me permanently. I was not able to do the one, but thankfully, I did do the other."

Rosalind felt distinctly that it would do neither one of them any good if she peered at that statement too closely, so she did not.

"But you do at least care for him, I thought?"

"Oh, yes," said Charlotte comfortably. "He is a good man and faithful to me, but would he be so faithful if I also could not, or would not, give him what he really wants?" She rubbed her hand over the curve of her belly. "Or if something goes wrong and the babe does not thrive?"

"Oh, Charlotte . . ." began Rosalind.

"But nothing will go wrong," said Charlotte quickly. "It will be a few hours of mess and inconvenience and then my child will enter into very comfortable world and both our futures will be entirely secure."

"Yes," agreed Rosalind firmly. "I have every faith in you, Charlotte. And your child." They smiled at each other, and Rosalind decided now was the time to change the subject. "George Littlefield's wife is also expecting any moment now."

"Would a letter of congratulations be welcome, do you think?" Charlotte was not ashamed of the life she had led previously. But she was also keenly aware it created a gulf between her and much of what was termed *polite society*.

"I believe it would."

"Then I shall write one, and you can see it delivered. Now . . ." Charlotte frowned at her again. "You are looking entirely done in, Rosalind. I hope you are planning to stay for supper."

"I did not mean to stay. Only . . ."

Charlotte cut her off with one sharp gesture. "If you wish to talk to me, you will also eat. This child has made me entirely ravenous, and I cannot eat unless you do."

"Well, then I cannot possibly refuse."

"Excellent. Maude"—Charlotte turned to the waiting maid—"you may tell cook it will be two for supper after all."

While Charlotte was not in anything resembling close confinement, she was clearly enjoying this time of informality that her pregnancy had brought her. Instead of the two of them going down to the dining room, a small army of footmen brought a trestle table and cloths up to the sitting room. There followed an array of dishes—sole in cream sauce, stewed capon, asparagus, onion tart, and a compote of preserved fruits served with custard to finish.

"Thankfully," remarked Charlotte, "my doctors do not believe in a reducing diet while pregnant. Indeed, one of them specifically said that in his opinion an expectant mother required more nourishment than usual, not less. I could have kissed him," she added as she helped herself to another slice of tart and more capon.

At last the table was removed and they returned to their places before the fire with cups of tea and sweet cakes to nibble.

"There now," declared Charlotte as the maid finished adjusting her pillows. "You are looking yourself again, Rosalind. So, tell me what's really brought you all the way out here?"

"I really did want to see you," Rosalind told her. "And to know how you were doing."

"Well, I'm sure it's true since you say so, but what else is there?"

What else? Rosalind watched the fire for a moment, attempting to put her thoughts in order. "You used to spend a great deal of time in Bath," she said.

"In my previous life, yes, but I haven't been back since last summer. Thankfully, my husband doesn't care for watering holes."

"I'm wondering if you ever heard anything about Marianna Levitton?"

"Good heavens, Rosalind," Charlotte exclaimed. "Have you become involved with Mrs. Levitton?"

"I take it you've heard of her?" replied Rosalind.

"In a place where half the women were trying to live down some scandal or the other, Marianna Levitton was positively infamous. Drove her own carriage, did her own business, at least as far as the law would allow, was a famous shot. It was even rumored that she rode horseback in *trousers*."

Rosalind arched her brows in mock surprise. Charlotte nodded solemnly.

"This was some years ago, of course, but the stories positively swirled wherever she went."

"Was there ever any talk of her having a natural child?"

Now it was Charlotte's turn to look surprised. "That's what you're here about?"

"I know it sounds like I'm digging for common gossip, but it's important."

"Well, let me think." Charlotte placed her hand on her rounded belly and rubbed it back and forth slowly. Rosalind watched, wondering what it would feel like to have that second life inside, wondering how Charlotte remained calm, how she would face the very real possibility that everything could go wrong. That the child could die. That she could die. That her life, changed forever, might become unbearable in ways that could not be guessed at.

Rosalind knew her fear verged on the hysterical, but such things did happen. Every day.

"Yes," said Charlotte at last. "There was something. A gentleman I was entertaining, we went to a concert. . . . I can't even remember who was singing. He was much older, glad to be seen with a pretty and popular girl. Not too demanding. But at the end, after the applause, the crowds were leaving, Marianna Levitton—well, she was not Levitton then—

but she swept past us on the arm of a fairly good-looking man. The gentleman I was with, he saw her and said, 'Good lord, I wonder if the fellow knows what he's getting?'

"Naturally, I teased him about it, and he demurred, but in the end he told me Marianna—I can't remember what he said her given name was; I am positive this baby has taken up all my wits—but she had run completely wild as a girl, and in the end she had to be sent away. For about nine months."

"Yes," murmured Rosalind. "I thought it might be so."

"Is this one of your particular inquiries?" Charlotte asked.

"I'm afraid so. I . . . do you remember, Charlotte, what Marianna Levitton's given name was?"

She frowned. "I'm sorry, I don't remember. It was something odd, like Messenger. . . ." She wrinkled her brow. "No, Herrald. That was it. Marianna Herrald."

CHAPTER 46

The Cause of Contradictions

*"If a person kills another in a fray, with a
concealed weapon, ma'am, by a sword in a cane,
for instance, 'tis murder by the law."*

Edgeworth, Maria, *Belinda*

It was several hours before George Edwards's body was removed to the cellar of the Brown Bear, and several more
before Sir David Royce, the coroner for Middlesex County,
could be summoned to examine the body.

"Well, there is no mystery as far as what killed this man."
Sir David was a portly, balding man. His eye and mind were
sharp, and unlike many coroners, he had a physician's training. "He was stabbed, and you have the knife there." He indicated the curved blade that Adam had found beside Edwards's
body. "His knuckles are split and his face is bruised, so I'd
say it was a brawl."

Stafford and Townsend stood beside Adam, which allowed Adam to observe Stafford closely. The man's face remained absolutely immobile as his attention shifted from the
corpse to Townsend and Sir David, and to Adam himself.

What are you looking for?

"Thank you, Sir David," said Townsend. "I'm sorry to

have taken you away from your supper." Sir David waved this away, and set about washing his hands in the chipped basin that the landlord had brought down for him.

"Pleased to have the matter be so straightforward," he said.

"If you would be willing to come with me to Bow Street and sign a statement to that effect?" said Stafford.

"Yes, of course." Sir David dried his hands. "Townsend, Harkness. Let me know if there's anything further you require."

Stafford left with Sir David, leaving Townsend and Adam alone with the dead man.

"Well, not the ending I would have seen." Townsend sighed. "Killed in a brawl. But"—he shrugged—"it is the way of things."

Adam was looking toward the stairs.

"What are you thinking?" asked Townsend.

Adam faced him fully. "I am wondering if it is true that Mr. Stafford did not know where his man Edwards was holed up."

Townsend puffed out his cheeks and shook his head. "Well now," he said. "That is hardly something that can be discussed here. I promised you a dinner, and we are past time. Come along."

Adam hesitated. There were questions that needed asking. He wanted to see Tauton and Goutier, and get their opinions on the matter.

"Now, now, no fuss about changing or any such. I promise you Mrs. Townsend is quite used to us rough fellows who come in straight from the street."

Adam wanted to cry off. A dinner at home seemed a waste of time, given what had just happened. He needed to get back to Rosalind to make sure all was well with her. At the same time, he also needed to talk with Townsend, convince the man that there were inquiries that should be made.

"Thank you, sir," said Adam at last, and he followed Townsend up the stairs.

* * *

John Townsend's home was entirely what Adam would have expected—a tall, narrow town house, comfortably furnished on a thoroughly respectable street. Mrs. Townsend was a stout woman whom nature seemed designed as a perfect match for Townsend. She greeted Adam with a comfortable courtesy, brushing off his apologies for his appearance. During the meal, she kept up a steady flow of easy conversation, inquiring after his mother and family, and offering plenty of opportunities for Townsend to regale them both with his own store of anecdotes, some of which Adam had heard three and four times already. The pair made it abundantly clear that news, or work, was to be banished from the table.

Adam ate, and gladly. He'd barely had time for a bite all day. He chatted. He tried not to feel the time crawling past, or to wonder what had happened to Rosalind and Alice, or what Stafford was doing now that Edwards was dead, if he was doing anything at all. He needed to write Sir Richard. He needed . . .

Adam realized that Mrs. Townsend had gotten to her feet. Embarrassed at his own inattentiveness, he struggled to rise himself.

"I'll leave you gentlemen to your port." She smiled at Townsend with fond affection, and at Adam with courtesy.

Townsend brought a decanter of port from the sideboard. A maid servant entered to clear the remains of the meal.

"Never mind that, Deborah," said Townsend. "I'll call you when you're wanted."

Deborah curtsied and left them. Townsend resumed his seat and poured himself a large glass of port. He shoved the decanter to Adam, and leaned back and unbuttoned his waistcoat.

"To the ladies." He raised his glass. "Without whom we would surely perish in darkness."

Adam raised his glass, and drank.

"To the king," said Townsend. "Long may he reign."

Adam, aware that he was being watched, raised his glass. "To the king." Resentment and impatience stirred. He forced them both down. Townsend was clearly leading up to something and he needed to hear what it was before he tried to make his own case.

"Now, I've some news for you, Harkness," said Townsend, confirming Adam's assessment. "You're being sent to Liverpool."

Adam went still. Townsend met his gaze without hesitation, his expression mild, even tranquil.

"When?" asked Adam.

"Immediately," said Townsend. "The lord mayor has written us expressly, asking that I send a man at once."

Adam set his glass down. "With respect, sir, there is this matter of Edwards's murder that—"

"Lavender will deal with it." Townsend reached for the decanter and topped up his own glass. "Or Tauton, if that will ease your mind. I'll have your letters of introduction for you tomorrow." He sipped his wine.

"I would prefer to remain in London. There are several matters requiring my attention here."

"I'm afraid your preferences do not enter into it," said Townsend. "I have been asked to send an officer; you are that officer."

"Sir," said Adam. "It is very clear that Mr. Stafford was the one who let the thief-taker Beachamp out of the cells last night. Beachamp knew Celia Ings was likely to have information about Edwards's location. Beachamp needs to be found and questioned. It is possible he is responsible for the man's death. It is even possible he was sent specifically to get Edwards out of the city so he could not be found by the defense committee for the Cato Street men. Now, it may be—"

"Enough, Mr. Harkness," said Townsend.

"But if that's the case, sir, then—"

"I said enough!" Townsend brought his hand down hard on the table. "Will you listen to me? I'm trying to save you, man!"

Adam stared.

"Good God, Harkness!" Townsend cried. "How can a man as sharp as you be so blasted blind! You're one of the best officers we have and you are hell-bent on destroying yourself!"

Adam paused for a long moment, and then said, "This is about Stafford."

"It is about Stafford and Edwards, and Manchester, and all the rest of it. It is about the fact that you constantly defy orders, you make blatant use of your relationship with the coroner, you involve civilians and women in matters that are strictly Bow Street's provenance. On top of it all, you have everything to lose by your outrageous conduct! I've been trying to tell you this for *years* now."

Adam made no answer.

Townsend leaned forward, his voice growing gentle, even paternal. "You have ambition; I applaud that. You want to make your mark on Bow Street and the world. Excellent! But what you can't see is you are running the risk of destroying yourself. Now, I have given you every chance. I have moved heaven and earth to avoid sacking you. But even with the king's goodwill toward you, I am running out of excuses to keep you around.

"I've tried again and again to guide you," Townsend told him earnestly. "If you want to climb the ladder there are ways. Look at me—" He spread his arms wide. "My father pushed a barrow. I sold carrots and potatoes over a barrel in the market before I joined the runners. Now, I have all that I could have imagined and more. And a family. Mrs. Townsend is worth a small fortune, and I don't mean in money. A man is nothing without a good home, and that means a good wife, who understands the way of the world and can support him on his way. Now, you and this Miss Thorne—"

Adam stiffened.

"I admit, she would not be my first choice for you," Townsend went on. "She's an eccentric—that seldom looks well for an officer. But she's very well placed with some of our most highly regarded families, and there are few doors that do not open to her. So, I can understand why she'd be your choice, but a man cannot count solely on his wife to entirely smooth the way for him. You must make *some* kind of effort to show the right people that they can depend upon you!"

"Have I ever failed to follow the law, sir?" Adam inquired softly.

"Of course not, but there is more to what we do than the law! Think about this practically, Harkness. Suppose you find Beachamp, and prove that he was working on Stafford's orders, and that Edwards was in the government's pay, what then? Suppose you even prove that he went so far as to kill Edwards to silence him. Do you know what you become then?" Townsend did not wait for an answer. "You become the reason that the Cato Street trial fails. If that happens, not only is your career over, but I may not be able to stop you from being taken up for conspiracy and maybe even treason." Townsend sat back.

"That's why I wanted you here tonight. I wanted you to understand what you're throwing away with this mania of yours. You will lose all possibility of a good, solid life." He gestured with his glass, indicating the house, and all it held. "And more. You will lose the respect of your comrades. The regard of your *king*, Harkness. And what do you gain? The possibility of your neck in a noose?"

Townsend drank down his wine and slapped the tumbler back down onto the table. "If you are not willing to save yourself, think about what being associated with a convicted traitor will mean to your family and, Mr. Harkness"— Townsend leaned forward—"to your Miss Thorne."

CHAPTER 47

The Evening's Unwelcome Revelations

*"... the species of alarm which she had felt at this
discovery opened her eyes effectually to the state
of her own heart."*

Edgeworth, Maria, *Belinda*

"Is there anything more you might need, miss?" asked
the footman as he helped Rosalind down from Charlotte's enclosed carriage. "Madame's instructions were that
we should remain at your disposal."

One thing had not changed about Charlotte. She remained
impervious to Rosalind's arguments when they went against
her own inclinations. So, Rosalind was sent home not only
with carriage and driver, but a footman, in case of emergencies.

For a single, intense moment, Rosalind thought to ask the
footman to carry a message to Adam. After today's revelations, Rosalind desperately wanted to feel his arms around
her, and to hear his calm sensible voice as she tried to untangle all that she had learned.

It was disturbing to find she needed him so much. She had
never needed one other person, not since she was a girl.

No, Rosalind corrected herself. She had never permitted herself the luxury of such need. She had deliberately created and maintained her independence as a matter of pride, and self-protection.

But Adam had his own worries, and he would be here soon enough.

She had just opened her mouth to send the carriage away, when it struck her that something was wrong. It was already full dark, but the lamp beside the door was unlit. No light shone upstairs, either. The drapes on the front window were firmly closed, so she could not see for certain whether a light burned there.

Rosalind's mouth went dry.

"Please wait," she said. "There may yet be something more tonight."

The man bowed, and did not straighten until Rosalind had opened her front door.

The foyer was dark. Amelia did not come running. Rosalind's disquiet deepened. The only light she could see was in the parlor. Voices emerged as well, indistinct, but very familiar.

Alice. Amelia. Mrs. Singh.

Uncertain whether she should be worried or irritated, Rosalind pushed open the parlor door.

"Rosalind!" cried Alice. "You're late! I was beginning to worry!"

Rosalind heard her, but the words barely registered. Instead, she stared at the pile of shining color gleaming on the tea table. It was as if someone had shattered a stained-glass window and made a heap of the shards.

Slowly, Rosalind realized that their entirely unremarkable tea table was covered in jewels. She tried to walk forward normally, but she staggered and found her breath quite gone.

"Oh, dear," murmured Alice.

Amelia ran forward to help Rosalind off with her coat, gloves, and bonnet. Rosalind went through the motions mechanically. She could not tear her eyes away from the blazing heap on the table. There was a sapphire and diamond necklace, a pearl bracelet, an emerald brooch, and several rings, all trimmed with diamonds and set in figured gold.

Rosalind could barely begin to guess how many thousands of pounds it all represented. She realized she was oddly dizzy, and sat down abruptly.

"Yes," agreed Alice, coming to sit beside her. "It is a bit of a shock, isn't it?"

"What *is* all this?" Rosalind cried.

"Amelia, it seems, has been busy," said Alice. "So, as I'm sure you will not be surprised to hear, has Cate."

Cate slumped on the stool beside the fireplace. Mrs. Singh hovered over her, her posture making her appear something between a school matron and a turnkey.

Rosalind swallowed, and did her best to collect herself. "Will someone please tell me how all these . . . things . . . have come to be in this house?"

"Cate brought them with her," said Alice succinctly. "They were in the valise that she asked Amelia to keep for her. That valise was stolen today, by a woman named Francesca Finch."

Rosalind felt herself frown.

"Yes, I think I would have trouble if I put that name in a novel. At any rate, Miss Finch is a housebreaker and pickpocket. Cate met her at a party in Bath when Miss Finch tried to steal her ring. It seems Cate had been pilfering from her family for some time before this."

Amelia looked away. Cate stared after her, in mute appeal. The silent exchange told Rosalind volumes about this activity Alice termed *pilfering*, and who had been enlisted to help with it.

Anger and pity both rose up in her. She pushed both away. She could sort through her emotions later.

Alice continued. "Miss Finch, who seems to know a good thing when she finds it, realized that she could make use of our Cate, not only as a hand in picking up trifles at the parties and balls of Bath society, but in helping sell things on to various jewelers and pawnbrokers who could be counted on not to ask too many questions of a gently bred young lady." Alice paused and glared at Cate. "It seems Miss Finch had become rather too well known locally to get the best prices for her merchandise."

Cate was staring into the fire, belligerence warring with resignation in her face.

"It seems that when Cate was getting ready to leave her aunt's house, she decided to fund her travels by not selling on the latest parcel of items Miss Finch had given her. Miss Finch, you may understand, was considerably agitated by this, having creditors of her own. She tracked Cate to our door, and made her way inside. She stole the valise, but reckoned without Amelia's resourcefulness and cunning."

"Alice, you're novelizing," murmured Rosalind.

"Oh, I am, aren't I? Sorry. Well, anyway, it seems Amelia guessed what was in the valise. She took the precaution of removing the jewels, and here we are."

Rosalind picked up the sapphire necklace. Bright, white diamonds surrounded six teardrop-shaped gems that hung from a diamond chain. The sapphires themselves glowed with a blue coloring so deep it was almost black. Rosalind was seized with a girlish impulse to clasp it around her own throat, just to know what it would feel like.

"How did this Miss Finch get inside?" she asked. "Where was George?" She paused. "Where *is* George?"

"That appears to have been very bad timing," said Alice. "Miss Finch and the news that Hannah had gone into labor arrived at the same time."

"Is there—?"

Alice shook her head. "Any word? Not yet. You can imagine I am a bit put out at this turn of events." Her sardonic tone belied the worry in her eyes.

Rosalind laid the necklace down, smoothing her palm across the gemstones as if they were rumpled fabric.

I must think, she instructed herself. *I must deal with what is in front of me at this moment.*

Rosalind straightened her shoulders and turned to her cook. "I am so sorry for what you have been through today, Mrs. Singh. Everything is well in hand here. You may go home. We will talk more in the morning when we've all had a chance to rest."

At this suggestion, Mrs. Singh drew herself up to her full height. "If you please, Miss Thorne, I'd rather not until the officers have been sent for."

"As it happens, there is a carriage outside awaiting orders," Rosalind told her. "You may ask the men there to keep watch until Mr. Harkness arrives. He is expected before too long."

"Very well, miss. If you say so." Mrs. Singh curtsied and took her leave, but not before she gave both Amelia and Cate a long, hard look.

When she was gone, Alice let out a long sigh. "We're going to have to increase her wages."

"At the very least," said Rosalind. She turned to Amelia. "Are you all right?"

Amelia nodded. Her eyes were red, but other than that, she looked no worse for wear.

"Would you like to go to your room?"

"If it's all the same, miss, I'd rather stay." Amelia lifted her chin. Alice nodded her approval. Cate just rubbed her hands together as if she had a chill she could not shake.

Rosalind also nodded. From the way Alice had told her story, it was very clear she believed that Amelia bore little or no blame for the afternoon's unsettling events.

Rosalind turned to Cate.

"Miss Levitton?" she said. "Is there anything you would like to add?"

"So you can pass sentence, do you mean?" Cate grumbled. "What is there to say? Yes, I worked hand in glove with Fran Finch for almost a year. I thought I'd left her behind when we moved from Bath, but she'd followed me to London. Harold had made his intentions known by then, and I tried to break it off. I meant to marry him. I did," she added as she saw the skeptical looks on their faces. "And I didn't want Franny . . . Miss Finch hanging about while I was trying to start over. And she told me she'd go if I sold on one more lot for her." Cate nodded at the shining heap. "So, I said I was. I was waiting for my chance. But then, Aunt Marianna got sick, and Harold was pushing to get a special license so we could get married right away, and I . . . I decided I couldn't go through with it."

"Was that because you found out that Harold was carrying on a liaison with your sister-in-law?" asked Rosalind.

Alice's jaw dropped. So did Cate's, but she recovered more quickly.

"I should have realized you'd find that out," she muttered. "And yes. I mean, I'm not a schoolgirl. I know men keep mistresses, and heaven knows I don't blame Mena for wanting somebody other than Marcus in her life, but—it was just too much," she finished a trifle limply. "It seems I was only ready to live out so many lies at once."

"Did Harold know you'd found out?"

"Perhaps. I don't know."

"Did you tell Marianna?"

"No. I was too busy working out how to leave."

Rosalind watched Cate silently for a long moment. "Did you know that Mr. Davenport is Marianna's son?"

"Good lord!" cried Alice. "Who have you been talking to?"

"Charlotte," said Rosalind. "She remains rather well informed about the gossip around Bath. That's why I was late."

"Ah. Of course." Alice folded her hands on her knees. "Do go on."

Cate got to her feet. "Well, if you do plan to go on, you must excuse me. I am quite tired and I'd like to go back to my rooms."

"Miss Levitton," said Alice with deceptive mildness. "Rosalind won't point this out, so I will. A Bow Street officer will be here shortly. Your future is very much dependent on what Rosalind, and Amelia, have to say about how this mass of jewelry got here."

Cate bit her lower lip.

"Cate," said Rosalind. "I understand that your situation is complicated, and I do not blame you for looking for a means of escape. But there is something you do not yet know."

At least I hope you do not.

"What is it?"

"Your aunt has been poisoned. And so have you."

Cate blinked. Her brow furrowed. "Are you quite mad?"

"I am sorry to say that I am not," Rosalind replied. "Mrs. Levitton's illness was the result of arsenical poison. We are quite certain of this. The symptoms you exhibited when you came to us also point toward poisoning, although much more severe."

"But . . . but who? And for the love of all . . . *why?*"

"That is the question I have been trying to answer since you came to us."

Cate shuddered violently, and shook her head, as if to try to clear it. "I won't . . . I cannot . . . it cannot be true. I will not believe it."

Rosalind did not even attempt to answer this.

A dozen emotions chased each other across Cate's face as memories and possibilities tumbled through her mind. "Why didn't you tell me this before?" she demanded.

"Because the person responsible for Marianna's poisoning could well have been you."

"I . . . you believed this of me!" She stared, and she turned to Amelia. "Did you believe it?"

Amelia said nothing, but her folded hands bunched into fists.

"I believed it was possible," replied Rosalind calmly.

"And what do you believe now?" Cate demanded.

"I believe you have acted foolishly and desperately, but I do not believe you are a poisoner."

"Well, I suppose I must appreciate your confidence in my character," said Cate dryly. "May I ask why not?"

"Because to commit murder one must believe there is no other option. You had already provided yourself with a means of escape." Rosalind gestured at the jewelry. "You had no need, or reason, to poison Marianna, or yourself."

Cate buried her face in her hands and shuddered. "How . . . how has any of this happened?"

Alice rolled her eyes and pulled a handkerchief from her sleeve. She pried Cate's hands from her face and pressed the kerchief against her palms. "Here. Do collect yourself."

"I apologize," murmured Cate. "I cannot, I am not always as stoical as I am meant to be."

"I have only one more question," said Rosalind.

Cate threw up her hands, exasperated, exhausted. "What is it now?"

"What do you want from all this? From all your efforts and this—" She gestured toward the glittering heap of jewels. "What do you truly want?"

Cate held herself still for a moment, but her strength failed her, slowly. Her shoulders slumped, her spine. Her gaze grew distant, seeing what was in her mind rather than the silent room around them. Not once did she even look at the jewels, let alone look at them with desire, or longing.

"My freedom," said Cate. "To go about my days without

reference to anyone else's expectations of who I must be. Without having to use, or deceive, anyone else because it is the only way to live."

Rosalind turned to Amelia. "Do you believe what she says?"

Without hesitation, Amelia nodded. "Yes, Miss Thorne. I do."

"Very well."

Cate's mouth curled into a sneer. "And what, Miss Thorne, does that mean?"

"It means that until we have reason to do otherwise, we will trust you."

"On a . . . Amelia's word?" said Cate incredulously.

"Yes," snapped Alice, obviously at the end of her patience. "Is that so hard to believe?"

Cate met Alice's gaze and it was plain she saw the fire, and the impatience, and yes, the love, all shining there.

"No," Cate said. "No, not at all."

Before anyone had any chance to speak again, the sharp rap of the front door knocker cut through the room. Alice groaned in frustration and peeked through the draperies to see who might be knocking at this time of night.

"Rosalind," she said. "That's Adam."

"I'll go," said Amelia.

"No," said Rosalind. "It's all right, I'll go." She took up a candle and left the room. *Let everyone have a chance to pause and to breathe,* she thought. *Starting with me.*

CHAPTER 48

Declarations

*"Though she strongly felt the pain of this separa-
tion, yet she could not recede from her decision . . ."*

Edgeworth, Maria, *Belinda*

Adam drew back, ever so slightly startled when he saw it
was Rosalind who opened the door.

Something was wrong; she saw it at once. It was in the set
of his jaw as he stepped inside and took off his hat.

Rosalind waited until he had hung hat and coat on the
pegs by the door. "What's happened?" she asked softly.

Adam looked past her toward the closed parlor door. "I
found my man," he told her. "But he was dead."

"I'm sorry." Rosalind took his cold hand and held it.
There was more than that. Even in the candlelight she could
see his eyes were shuttered, and his manner uneasy. Rosalind's heart constricted.

But he did not give her a chance to ask. Instead, he reached
out his free hand and traced the line of her cheekbone. "You
look as if you have had a hard time as well."

She sighed and nodded. Adam raised a questioning brow.
Rosalind hesitated, but only for an instant. Then, softly, she

told him what had happened to Amelia, Alice, Cate, and Mrs. Singh while she was away following Wilhelmena Levitton, and talking with Marianna.

Adam's eyes went wide. "Can you show me?"

Rosalind touched his sleeve. "Adam, will you arrest Cate? Or Amelia?"

"If she has done all you said, she should be arrested," he replied. "And from what you say, Amelia has assisted her more than once."

"They will be hanged or transported," breathed Rosalind. "A theft worth five pounds will send a person to the gallows. These jewels are worth a thousand times that." The more radical papers called it *the bloody code*. The more conventional persons insisted that the laws must be harsh to serve as a deterrent.

"Nonetheless."

"She is guilty, Adam, but mostly she is guilty of not being able to earn her way out of a family that rejected her. And Amelia . . . Amelia only wants to live."

"I know," said Adam. "I do know." He took a deep breath. "Trust me?"

"Always." Rosalind stepped aside and let him precede her into the bright parlor.

"Hullo, Alice. Miss Levitton," he said. "Amelia."

Cate, sitting on her stool by the fire, froze stock still. Amelia's face blazed with anger. Rosalind tried to signal to her that all would be well, but if Amelia saw, she gave no sign.

Adam did not let his attention linger on either of them. Instead, he walked straight to the table and he picked up the necklace Rosalind had laid out earlier and held it to the light.

"Hullo, Adam," Alice said from her spot on the sofa. "What do you think?"

Adam turned toward Amelia. She raised her chin, ready to spit back defiance. Alice's calm faltered, just a little.

"I need to ask you a question," said Adam. "And all I ask you to do is answer me truthfully."

"Amy," breathed Cate. Amelia did not so much as glance toward her. She simply nodded.

"You took these jewels from a woman named Fran Finch?" inquired Adam.

For a moment, Rosalind thought Cate might faint.

Amelia was clearly confused by the question, but realization dawned, slowly. "Yes," she said. "They were hidden in a valise with a false bottom." She added no word about how the valise came into her possession. Tension sang through the room. Adam seemed not to feel it, however. He laid the sapphire necklace back down.

"As it happens, I recognize at least some of these pieces." He picked up the emerald brooch. It was made in the shape of a Brazilian parrot, with a pearl clutched in its beak. "This one is unique, and caused quite a stir when it went missing." He turned. "It is believed this Fran Finch was the thief. Any information about her whereabouts, or her associates, would be very welcome to Bow Street."

Cate winced. Adam waited. Amelia, quickly and sharply, kicked Cate in the ankle.

"I might know something," Cate murmured. "Possibly."

Adam nodded. "Would you know more if it could be promised your name would not be made public?"

"I might," said Cate slowly. Her gaze slid past him to Rosalind. Rosalind had no idea what the girl saw, but it must have satisfied her. "I think so, yes."

"Very well. But that's for later. For now, you should know there's a rather substantial finder's fee on offer for their return." He smiled. "I'm pleased to say that properly belongs to you, Amelia." He laid the brooch back down. "Unless, of course, someone else wants to lay claim to it, and can say how these jewels came to be in a valise that happened to come into your hands?" He folded his hands behind his back, and waited.

"No idea," said Amelia.

Cate hesitated, but only for a heartbeat. Then, she shook her head.

Rosalind was conscious of an odd species of pride. She had seldom seen Adam in his character of an officer of the law. As much as she trusted him, she had not quite known what to expect. Now, she felt it was absurd that she had not trusted him more.

Alice clapped her hands sharply together. "Well, that's all settled then. Amelia, I'm delighted for you, but it is late and I expect we are all going to have a long day tomorrow. Come on, let's get Cate up to bed. She's ready to nod off." She glared at Cate, daring her to disagree.

"Yes, thank you." Cate pushed herself to her feet. "I find I am very tired." She curtsied to Adam, and to Rosalind, and let Alice marshal her out of the room.

Amelia stayed behind. She looked to Adam. She looked to Rosalind. She bowed her head, and dipped her curtsy, and turned at once to follow Alice and Cate.

The parlor door closed and Rosalind expelled a long breath.

"Alice never ceases to amaze," murmured Adam. "How do you suppose she knew I needed to speak privately to you?"

Rosalind smiled. "She can read your face almost as well as I can. She knows something's amiss." She paused. "What is it, Adam? It's more than this man Edwards turning up dead." She did not mention that this meant the promised reward would have vanished with the man's life. She did not ask what the lack of that money would mean for Adam's offer of marriage. All of that could wait. Indeed, she felt sure it must wait.

"I am ordered to Liverpool tomorrow," said Adam.

"What for?" asked Rosalind.

He shook his head. "I am only told that the lord mayor of Liverpool has requested an officer and that I am to be that officer."

"This is, I gather, because of your meeting with Sir Richard? And your involvement with the matter of George Edwards?"

"Among other things," said Adam. "Townsend has made it very clear he is saving me from myself." He paused. "And saving you as well."

"You may thank Mr. Townsend for his concern, but he should not trouble himself on my behalf," said Rosalind pertly. Adam smiled at this, but that smile quickly faded.

"What do you want to do?" she asked.

"I want to do my duty," said Adam. "I want to do right. I want to support my family as a man should. I want . . ." But here words failed him. It was all right. Rosalind understood.

"Have you been home with this news yet?" she asked.

"Not yet."

"You should go. It will give you time to think."

Adam clearly considered this idea absurd. "And leave you and Alice with thousands of pounds worth of jewels in the house? Not to mention Cate Levitton. This Miss Finch may come back for her goods."

"Cate Levitton is not a danger to us."

"But her presence may be."

"My sister's men will stay," said Rosalind. "They are outside even now. I planned to ask them in any case. Alice needs to go to George." She felt a tiny smile form. "It seems the baby has chosen now to make its appearance."

"I understand babies have uncanny timing," Adam said. "But a footman and a coachman . . ."

"These are my sister's men from her previous life as a courtesan. They are specifically employed to prevent her person, or her house, from being disturped. You may rely on them." She hardly liked the idea of asking the men to spend a sleepless night on her behalf, but the fact was the house had already been breached once, in broad daylight. Adam's concern was not out of bounds.

"Very well, I yield the point." Adam placed his hand on his breast and bowed. Rosalind nodded in a show of imperious acceptance. She was glad he was able to joke. It showed that he understood that she was not sending him away because she regretted his presence the other night, or that his trust in her was in any way faltering.

But neither did he move closer to her, even though they were alone. Indeed, she felt how very strongly he was holding himself back. "Rosalind?" he said. "What do you think? Should I go to Liverpool?"

"I don't know if I have an answer to that," she admitted.

"If I go, I am accepting that George Edwards's death will be swept under the carpet. That there will be no inquiry into what role Stafford may have played in the business, and that Jack Beachamp will get off scot-free. Accepting, and agreeing to it," he said bitterly. "If I do not go, I lose my post and my pay, and, if Stafford is frightened enough, I leave myself open to accusations of treason."

"He would do that because he is frightened?"

"He would see it as his duty to the Crown to prevent me from interfering in the work of suppressing dangerous rioters, and Townsend may well stand by and let it happen, because he also believes it to be his duty and because he will not risk his own reputation. And if it happens, my family will all suffer. You will suffer," he added softly.

Rosalind's first instinct was to tell him not to worry about her, but that would be ridiculous. Of course he must worry. If what he said was so, if he really was risking a treason charge . . . she must worry for him, and for herself. Society might excuse her the infraction of asking for money for her services, but if it became known she had a close association with a man charged with treason?

No reputation, no matter how strong or well-established, could survive that.

And yet, she herself could not, would not, say so much in this moment. There was another, deeper, more important truth to be spoken.

Rosalind laced her fingers through his.

"You must do what you know to be right," she told him. "And when you are done, I promise you, Adam, that I will be here for you."

CHAPTER 49

A Sleepless Night

". . . treat me with sincerity, and suffer me to be
your friend."

Edgeworth, Maria, *Belinda*

That night, when Rosalind carried her candle down to the parlor, she found she was not the only one left sleepless. Cate Levitton had drawn the round-backed chair up close to the hearth. She sat there with the poker in hand. As Rosalind watched, Cate viciously smacked one of the glowing coals to release a fresh burst of spark and flame.

"I couldn't sleep," Cate said, without looking away from the fire.

"Neither could I." Rosalind set the candle down on the tea table and pulled her shawl more closely about herself. She also lifted the edge of the drapes and peered outside. Charlotte's footman lounged beside the stoop, arms folded, but his head alert.

"Are we safe?" asked Cate bitterly.

"It would seem." Rosalind let the drape fall and instead settled onto her usual place on the sofa.

Alice had provided a bandbox to transport the jewelry to

Bow Street. Rosalind had watched regret bleeding into Cate's expression as Amelia, with Alice's help, rewrapped her trove and stowed it away. Alice had expressed her intention of using all the items as buried treasure in her next book. Amelia had laughed and the two proceeded to trade increasingly elaborate descriptions for Alice to use.

Cate had watched, and held her tongue, and, Rosalind noted, swallowed her tears.

"I thought I was so clever," said Cate to the tiny fire in front of her. "I thought I would simply slip away, and none would be the wiser." She waved the ashy poker at the empty air. "I would set myself up as a fine, independent lady, just like Aunt Marianna, and drive my own carriage and ride horses and drink in the taverns and shock the world." She stabbed the poker deep into the fireplace ashes. "I can't ride," she said. "And I can't drive, and I hate beer."

Despite everything, Rosalind felt herself smile. "Not everyone is suited to life as a *belle esprit*." She hesitated. "Cate?"

"Yes?" Cate smacked another coal. Fresh sparks scattered. Rosalind resisted the urge to remind her if the house caught fire, Cate would go up in the conflagration with the rest of them. "Did you know about Mr. Davenport's parentage?"

Cate carefully put the poker back into the rack with the rest of the fire irons. "Yes," she said simply. "Aunt Marianna told me."

"Does Mr. Davenport know?"

She nodded. "It seems that when Uncle Colin died, Harold went and asked Marianna if he was Uncle's by-blow."

It was a reasonable assumption. It was quite common for a man to take an "orphaned" child as a ward or apprentice. That way the man could provide for the child without having to acknowledge the blood relationship.

"It seems Aunt Marianna had talked Uncle Colin into being something of a blind for her," said Cate. "If uncle was the one who took up Harold to mentor and educate, everyone would assume Harold was his. No one would stop to think that he might actually be hers." She rubbed her hands together. "Aunt Marianna is very good at that sort of maneuver."

"Is that why she wanted you to marry him?"

"She said the marriage would be good for us both. We would have plenty of money, we could live as we pleased, and we'd be safe."

"From what?"

"From Marcus, for one. He would have no way to gain control of me or any money she might give me, not even if he lodged one of his lawsuits. And possibly safe from my poor decisions," she added ruefully. "By the law, it's easier for a husband to protect a wife than for a woman alone to protect herself."

Rosalind was silent a moment, acknowledging this truth. "Do you think she knows about your thefts?"

"It's possible." Cate sighed. "Obviously, I never thought to ask her. But it would not surprise me to learn that's why we left Bath. I doubt she thought Fran would follow me. I certainly didn't," she added ruefully.

"She cares for you," said Rosalind.

"Yes," agreed Cate. "Rather a lot, I think. After everything, she still wanted me found." She looked at her hands again.

"Why didn't you ask her to help you?"

"Because I wanted to prove I could do it myself. Because I didn't want to depend on anybody. Even Aunt Marianna." Her voice dropped to a whisper. "Especially Aunt Marianna. Marcus and my father were always whining about what she owed the family, meaning what she owed them, of course, and when she wouldn't give over voluntarily, they tried to find ways to force her. I didn't want her to think I was like that."

"What of these friends in Edinburgh?"

"The Wallaces."

"Do they exist?" asked Rosalind.

If this question surprised Cate, she gave no sign. "They do, as it happens. But I very much doubt they will be glad to see me if my hands are empty." She stretched those hands out toward the fire and watched the play of light through her fingers. "As has been pointed out to me, even in Edinburgh one is expected to pay for board and lodging. So, I expect I will not be going to them."

"Then, what do you wish to do?"

"I don't know," answered Cate. "But it seems I will have to go home and face my aunt. Assuming we are able to discover which of my family tried to murder us both." She stopped. "You do think it was someone in my family? Aunt does have other enemies." She spoke almost wistfully.

"I am afraid it must be family," said Rosalind. "The timing of your illness makes it difficult for it to have been someone else. Unless you met with someone that last day you have not told me about?"

Cate shook her head. "I was at home all day until dinner. I was putting on a show of being on my best behavior."

"What happened at dinner?"

Cate lowered her hands. "The dinner was a disaster. Marcus was full of himself. All insinuations and blame. He kept hinting how much I owed him, how I would ultimately need his permission to marry, whether I was of age or not. There was also a great deal about how carefully Harold should step, lest he trip and fall."

The candle flickered. Rosalind drew her shawl a little closer.

"Why did you leave in the middle of the night?" she said. "If you had planned to go anyway?"

"Oh, that was because of Everett," said Cate. "As Wilhelmena and I were getting up to go to the drawing room for tea, he caught up with me. He told me that Marcus was planning to . . ." She swallowed. "He said Marcus had bribed one of Aunt Marianna's maids. He said she'd told him about me and my . . . associates. That if Aunt Marianna did not give him what he wanted, he was planning to turn me over to the magistrates."

"And you believed this?"

Her smile was sharp. "Oh, yes. It is exactly the sort of thing Marcus would do."

"No, I meant, you believed Everett was telling the truth?"

"It should be obvious that I did. I left the house that night." Cate narrowed her eyes at the fire. "Do you think Everett was lying? About Marcus knowing something?"

"It is possible," Rosalind said. "He may have had his own reasons for wanting you out of the house." Everett was a peacemaker, but Everett was also a manipulator. Society was filled with such persons. The ones who presented the face of reconciliation and friendship, and quietly, and sometimes underhandedly, worked to arrange things in their own favor.

Cate fell silent, and Rosalind did not move to ask her any more questions. Cate had done a great deal of harm. She had endangered Amelia and Alice with her schemes. But Rosalind was conscious of a sympathy for the young woman. Rosalind's own family had been broken and her father outrageously selfish. Cate's family, however, was proving to be actively malicious. It was a deeply painful thing to have to come to grips with, no matter who one was, or what one might have done.

Into this silence trickled the sound of male voices from outside. Rosalind lifted the drapes again. In the lamplight, she saw Charlotte's man was arguing with another. Both were gesticulating broadly. The new man pointed at a piece of paper in his hand.

Rosalind's heart thumped. She snatched up the candle and hurried into the foyer. Cate followed close behind and hovered at her shoulder as Rosalind undid the bolt.

Both men outside stopped their squabbling immediately. The new man snatched his cap off his head.

"What is it, Parsons?" Rosalind asked the footman.

"This fellow says he has a message for you, miss," Parsons replied.

"Yes, I'll take it." She held out her hand. Parsons's expression remained dubious, but he passed her the folded note.

There was no seal, and no direction. Rosalind opened the paper and read. And her heart stopped.

"What is it?" Cate leaned in close.

"I'm so sorry," breathed Rosalind as Cate read, and gasped.

The note was from Mrs. Hepplewhite, and very obviously written in haste.

Miss Thorne:
You are needed here. Word has come that Mr. Everett Levitton has fallen down the stairs and is dead.

CHAPTER 50

Home Truths

"She suddenly left the dangerous shades, and went to her mother, to seek protection against herself."

Edgeworth, Maria, *Belinda*

Dawn came slowly to London.

Adam sat in front of his mother's hearth. The coals were banked. The air was chill. If he listened, he could hear the early morning sounds—the crow of a distant city rooster, the creak and slam of a nearby door. A voice shouting. Another answering. The bells would soon toll the hour, yet again.

He'd made no move to go to bed, much less pack his bag to prepare for his journey to Liverpool. He'd just sat on the bench and watched the shifting glow of the coals beneath their blanket of ash.

Footsteps came down the stairs, followed by an exasperated snort.

Meg.

"Well, Mother, here he is," his sister called up the stairs.

"And where else would he be?" Their mother stumped down the stairs and bustled into the kitchen. "With a face long as a winter's night, just like when he came in."

As Mrs. Harkness delivered this blunt assessment of her oldest son, she also took up the poker. Deftly, she began uncovering the coals and adding more fuel from the scuttle so that the fresh flames leapt up and spread.

"Come on." She slapped Adam's shoulder as she passed him. "As you're up, you may as well make yourself useful. Bring the buckets."

Adam didn't even think to protest. He just grabbed the two big wooden buckets that waited by the side door. His mother tucked the basket of crumbs and vegetable peelings under her arm and strode out into the yard.

While Adam plied the pump, his mother scattered the feed for the chickens and geese.

"Now," she said as she watched the quarrelsome fowls gathering for their meal. "What's the matter?"

"Nothing's the matter." Adam traded the full bucket for the empty one.

"Oh, yes?" Mother drawled. "You just sat up all night because you'd nothing better to do. Try again, sir," she added sharply. All at once, Adam felt he was seven years old again and trying to hide an apple behind his back.

Adam worked the pump handle a few more times. "I've been ordered to Liverpool."

"Well, isn't it just as well I washed your good shirt."

"I've been ordered away to keep me out of trouble, and to give me time to think about how much I need my post."

His mother sighed. "What have you been doing to pull Mr. Townsend's nose this time?"

"Ma!" cried Adam, genuinely surprised. "I don't pull his nose."

"Oh, no, of course not." Sarcasm filled each word. "You pull his nose *and* kick his shins, and do whatever else you can to make a nuisance of yourself where he's concerned."

"You make me sound like a boy acting out of spite."

"I never said so," she shot back. "You just don't care for

the way he does his job, and you want to do better. So, you get in his way as often as you can."

Adam meant to protest, but his mother turned her sidelong glance on him, all but daring him to interrupt. Adam closed his mouth.

"And all your certainty and troublemaking has left him with no choice but to get you *out* of his way," she concluded.

Adam stilled the pump handle, but he found he couldn't quite let go. "You agree with him?"

"I didn't say that either," Mother answered. "But since you two are at such loggerheads, he has no more choice than you do. If you weren't as good at your trade as you are, my boy, you might have left him another way. But you're that good, and you're that stubborn, and so there you both are." She shoved the empty feed pan into his hands. "What does your Miss Thorne think of it?"

"She leaves it up to me." All through the long night, the memory of her calm, trusting expression had stayed in front of him. The way she held his hand. The way she declared her acceptance of whatever choice he made.

Mother waded through the milling birds to the nesting boxes. "She would. When are you going to get off your heels and speak to her properly?"

Adam said nothing. Mother eyed him, even as she began carefully rifling the straw for eggs. "Unless you've already spoken to her?"

"I've spoken. She hasn't answered. At least—"

"She's not said yes?" Mother concluded.

"No, she's not."

"Will she?"

"I don't know."

Mother shook her head. "I swear sometimes I don't know which one of you I should rap on the knuckles first. Well, as I'm sure she asked you, what do you want to do?"

"If I go to Liverpool, I'm going against my conscience,

against the law, against . . . against what ought to be right," he said. "If I stay, it could well be a bridge too far for Townsend, and Stafford, not to mention Magistrate Birnie and all their important friends. I could get the sack, and worse, and then what?"

His mother laid another brown egg into her apron and shrugged. "Then you shake the dust off your heels and go on."

"But what about you?"

"And now, at last, we come to it." She turned and her expression softened. "You've looked after all of us for a long time now, Adam," she said. "I've a bit put by. Tom's in work, Davey's sure to be advanced at his firm, and Neddy's about to take up his position. We're fine, my son. If you need us to hold you up for a bit, then so be it. We're well able to take you on for a while. And, while you're thinking on what I've just said, you might also think about putting your pride in your pocket and realizing it's not only Mr. Townsend who knows you're worth having about the shop."

Adam bent and kissed her forehead. "I love you, Ma."

"Get along with you." She patted his cheek. "Do what you need to. And talk to your Miss Thorne. I've seen the two of you together. You'll bring things round."

That was when Meg leaned out the side door. "Adam! Visitor for you!"

His mother patted his cheek again. Adam ducked back into the house with mother and her apron full of eggs right behind him.

There in the kitchen, with his hat under his arm, stood Sir David Royce.

"Sir David!" Adam exclaimed.

"Mr. Harkness. Mrs. Harkness." Sir David bowed to Adam's mother. "Please excuse this early visit, ma'am. I've come for a word with your son."

"Well then, I shall leave you two to your business," Mother said genially. "Come inside when you're done for a cup of tea."

Sir David bowed as Adam's mother passed. Adam gestured that the coroner should join him in the yard. Once they were outside, and Sir David had replaced his hat on his head, Adam asked, "What can I do for you, Sir David?"

"You can tell me what was behind the business with the dead man I examined yesterday," said Sir David bluntly. "I don't know that I've ever seen Stafford so tense. I thought he might break in two. Come to that, I don't know that I've ever seen him come down to have a look at a corpse before."

Adam said nothing, at first. He trusted Sir David, and had worked with him often. But this matter was different. This was not a matter of facts, or even of theories. This was politics and duty and the future of more people than himself, the love he felt for his office and his work.

And so much more.

And yet, Adam had seldom been so aware that he had no idea which direction to turn.

"The dead man is George Edwards," Adam said. "He was a part of the Cato Street conspiracy. Probably as a spy in the pay of the government."

Standing in the yard of his mother's house, with the chickens and the geese squabbling noisily with each other, Adam told Sir David the whole of his involvement with the questions of Cato Street, high treason, Sir Richard, George Edwards, Jack Beachamp, and John Stafford.

Then, he told the coroner how he had dined with Townsend the night before and been summarily ordered to Liverpool for his own good.

Sir David gave out a long, low whistle.

"I wish there was something I could do to help you there, Harkness. Do you want me to speak to Mr. Birnie? He might listen."

"And what then?" Adam asked. "I may keep my posting, but I'd have won nothing but Stafford's suspicions, and Townsend's. I'd spend the rest of my days wondering what way they'd find to finally do me in." He shook his head. "I won't stay under those conditions."

"Well, then, if you're in want of work, I'll do what I can." Adam frowned. "I wouldn't . . ."

Sir David laughed. "Of course you wouldn't, that's why I'm offering. I've got discretion in the men I hire on to help with my inquiries. You'll not get as much respect as being with Bow Street, and I'd only be able to pay you when there was actual work, but it would help tide you over until you found something steady."

Adam found himself looking to the side door.

"What is it?" asked Sir David.

"Just something my mother said."

"A man should always listen to his mother."

Adam laughed. "She'd be the first to agree with you. Will you take that cup of tea?"

"Gladly," said Sir David. "Much to Lady David's dismay, I left the house without mine this morning."

But as Adam turned, he found himself face to face with Meg. "Adam! Was just coming to fetch you. Captain Goutier's inside, and he says he's got a message from Miss Thorne. There's trouble with a family called Levitton."

CHAPTER 51

The Effects of Desperation

". . . but you see that this is an affair of life and death."

Edgeworth, Maria, *Belinda*

The first light of London's faint, tardy dawn had barely begun to outline the rooftops when Rosalind and Cate arrived at Upper Brook Street.

Rosalind had not intended to take Cate with her. Cate, however, firmly represented that she had no intention of staying behind. Rather than waste time arguing the matter, Rosalind hurried to rouse Amelia from her bed. Cate must be gotten dressed. Alice must also be woken and told all that had happened.

"Don't worry, Rosalind. I'll take care of everything here. Unless I hear something from George about Hannah and the baby, of course—" Which was the best that could be done.

Parsons, the footman, protested at being left behind, but Rosalind pointed out, politely but firmly, that he was needed to keep watch on the house, and Alice, and there might be additional errands to be run, or messages carried.

Blessing Charlotte a hundred times in her heart, Rosalind

had climbed into the carriage with Cate while the coachman had touched up the horses.

Now, Marianna's footman, Kinnesly, hollow-eyed and half dressed, opened the door and stood back to let both Rosalind and Cate inside.

"Where is my mother?" demanded Cate. But she did not have to wait for an answer. The door to the front parlor was open, and through it, they could see Beatrice slumped on the sofa.

And Beatrice could see them.

Beatrice rose, trembling so badly Rosalind feared she might fall. Cate's mother lurched forward, hands outstretched. Cate ran to Beatrice, and caught her. The pair of them stood together, arms around each other with Beatrice weeping inconsolably on Cate's shoulder.

Rosalind quickly dragged the door shut and faced Kinnesly.

"Where is Mrs. Marianna?"

"Upstairs, miss."

Rosalind raced up the winding stairs and arrived breathless on the second floor. To her relief, Mrs. Hepplewhite was standing outside the door to Marianna's apartments.

"I heard you arrive, miss," the nurse said as Rosalind reached her. "Mrs. Marianna wants you to go in to her at once."

"I will," said Rosalind. "I need your help, however. What I am about to ask is outrageous, but we have no time for convention."

"What can I do, miss?"

"Go to Mr. Levitton's house. Say that Mrs. Levitton sent you personally. Offer to assist with laying out the body, and look at his injuries."

"I beg your pardon?" cried the nurse.

"Please," said Rosalind urgently. "I know this is entirely outside all propriety, but I also do not know when, or if, the coroner can be summoned, and it is very possible that Everett Levitton has been murdered."

The desire to protest the request, and the assertion, flickered behind Mrs. Hepplewhite's eyes, but only for a moment. In plain truth, they both knew that if she had not already been suspicious, she would not have sent for Rosalind.

"I'll go fetch my cloak," she said.

"There is a carriage outside," Rosalind told her. "You may tell the driver you are acting on my instructions." She would have to apologize to Charlotte for making blatant and extended use of what was supposed to be a much shorter loan.

Rosalind did not waste time knocking on Marianna's door, or even attempting to compose herself. She strode directly into Marianna's apartment and found the older woman sitting up in front of her fire.

"Miss Thorne!" Marianna cried. "Thank goodness!"

"Can you tell me what happened?" Rosalind asked.

"Little enough," answered Marianna. "We were awakened with a message from Wilhelmena. Everett had been found by the servants when they woke to start work this morning. He had fallen down the stairs and his head was broken open."

"Marianna, I must beg your pardon for being so blunt," said Rosalind. "But we have no time. Everett may well have been murdered."

"You can't be serious." Marianna blurted the words out and then shook herself. "But of course you are. Good God! Has the world gone mad!"

"I cannot answer that," said Rosalind. "Please, I need to make use of your writing desk, and I will need to send a servant to take a message."

"You may have all you need." Marianna waved her toward the desk by the window. "But why would Everett be killed? The boy was feckless!"

"Everett gathered and kept other people's secrets," said

Rosalind. "And they knew it. I may be wrong, but given all that has happened thus far, I think we must act as if it was murder before the perpetrator has time to cover over their traces." *As the poisoner had done so well.*

Marianna heaved herself to her feet and grabbed for her stick.

"Mrs. Levitton . . ."

Marianna waved her off. "Miss Thorne, you cannot expect me to sit quietly in this room when my nephew may have been done to death."

No, she could not, especially when it was beginning to appear that she had already made a colossal error in keeping so much to herself. Secrets were always the danger. Even when she was the one who held them.

"Help me downstairs, Talmidge," Mrs. Levitton snapped at her maid. "Then you will come back up here. Miss Thorne is to have whatever she needs, and if anyone has a quarrel with this, you may send them to me."

Rosalind heard the door shut but did not look back. She found pen, ink, and paper waiting on Mrs. Levitton's desk. She took a deep breath to bring some composure to her galloping thoughts and began to write.

She addressed her first letter to the coroner, Sir David Royce. Rosalind had been of assistance to him in several cases of violent death. She had confidence he would listen to her when she said there was a matter he needed to attend to as soon as possible.

Marcus Levitton would not be willing to answer her questions, or let anyone in his household answer them. He saw her as nothing but an oddity and a harpy in league with Marianna, whom he actively hated. He had already forbidden her the house and she was not sure even this tragedy would provide her a way to regain entry. The coroner, however, had the authority of law to make an inquiry in all cases of sudden or unnatural death.

Next, Rosalind wrote a letter for Adam. He would not have left town yet. The stage for Liverpool would not depart until noon. His word could bring a trustworthy man from Bow Street—Captain Goutier, perhaps, or Mr. Tauton. Someone who would listen to her, and believe what she told them.

Rosalind left her letters and her instructions with the maid and hurried downstairs to the front parlor.

Marianna stood beside the mantel, facing Beatrice and Cate, who sat on the sofa and held each other's hands. To Rosalind's surprise, they were not alone.

"Miss Thorne." Mr. Davenport swept off his high-crowned hat and bowed hastily. "Wilhelmena sent me word at my club that I should come at once." He swallowed, more uncertain and pale than Rosalind had seen him before. "I was delighted to find Mrs. Levitton so improved."

From his face, he was also more than a little surprised.

"And now that you are here, you may accompany myself and Beatrice to Marcus's house," said Marianna. "Miss Thorne—"

Cate cut Marianna off. "I want to go, too. I want to see him."

Marianna leveled a hard, skeptical glower toward her, but Cate did not shrink away.

"Very well." Marianna gave a one-shouldered shrug. "We will all go. Marcus will already be out of his wits, so I don't see how the whole party can make things worse. The carriage is being brought. Kinnesly!" she barked. "We will all need our coats!"

The footman bowed and hurried away.

Mr. Davenport turned to Cate. "I'm glad you're safe," he said.

"Thank you," she replied, without getting up from her mother's side.

"I hope one day you'll decide to tell me the whole of what happened."

Cate's gaze shifted from Mr. Davenport, to Marianna, to

Rosalind. "That will depend on what we find has happened to Everett."

"What do you mean, Cate?" demanded Beatrice. "He has had a fall. Wilhelmena's letter said there had been a fall."

"Yes, of course," said Cate soothingly. But Rosalind knew Mr. Davenport did not miss the way her attention stayed focused on Rosalind.

It was a slow drive to Marcus Levitton's house. Marianna kept an old-fashioned coach-and-four, which had the advantage of allowing the entire party to ride together. But even with four sturdy horses and a pair of link boys with torches, the driver was impeded both by the creeping morning fog and the market traffic filling the streets.

The five of them sat in silence, doing little more than avoiding each other's eyes. Even Rosalind did her best to keep her attention pointed out the window.

At last they reached the Levittons' house. Mr. Davenport assisted Marianna to the door, while Cate took charge of her mother. Rosalind plied the knocker. The footman, Morris, answered by the third knock.

"Mrs. Levitton." He bowed as they stepped inside. "May I say how very sorry we all are."

"Thank you, Morris," said Marianna.

Beatrice sagged against Cate.

Footsteps sounded on the stairs overhead.

"Get them out of here!" bellowed Marcus as he hurried down to the foyer. "They have no business being here!"

"Marcus . . ." began Mr. Davenport.

"You as well, you parasitic bastard!" Marcus barged past Mr. Davenport to his footman. "I gave direct orders they were not to be admitted!"

At the sound of her husband's shout, Wilhelmena emerged into the hallway. Her carriage was straight, although her face was unusually pale.

"Marcus, please!" Wilhelmena admonished as she hurried into the foyer. "You must calm yourself."

"Calm myself!" Marcus barked out a cold laugh. "With this . . . this collection on my doorstep! With my brother dead in my house! With my wife . . . my wife turning against me!"

"You do not know what you are saying," breathed Wilhelmena.

"Don't I, madam?" he replied icily. "How did Davenport even know to be here, hmmm? Answer me that."

"Marcus, stop this," gasped Beatrice. "He is here because Marianna asked for him."

"I will not stop!" Marcus roared. "I am master in this house and for once in my life, I will be listened to!"

"Didn't Everett listen?" inquired Cate. "Is that what happened?"

Marcus went dead white and then flushed scarlet. "You little . . . !"

"*Enough!*" Marianna slammed her walking stick against the floor. "We will *not* quarrel in the hall like a group of schoolchildren! Everett is dead, Beatrice is fainting, and the rest of you . . . I don't even know where to begin. Wilhelmena, is there a fire in the morning room yet?" Wilhelmena nodded. "Excellent. We will go there. Marcus, help me." She held out her arm for him to take.

Marcus wavered, caught between anger and expectations. Rosalind remembered how Cate had spoken of Marcus's ingrained sense of honor, and that, it seemed, was what won over now. His expression was one of wordless fury, but despite that, he took Marianna's arm and led her down the hallway toward the morning room.

Cate supported her mother, with Mr. Davenport close behind them. He looked over his shoulder at Rosalind. Rosalind nodded acknowledgment, but did not move to follow. Her absence would be noticed shortly and she would be sent for, but for the moment, she had been mostly forgotten.

*   *   *

As soon as the family had vanished into the morning room, Rosalind turned to find a small, elderly man in a black coat and trousers standing deferentially by the stairs.

"Are you the butler here?" Rosalind asked him.

"Yes, miss. Dalton." He bowed. "I've gotten the household together belowstairs to await instructions and prevent idle chatter. I hope that will be satisfactory?"

"Very. Thank you. I will go upstairs and see to matters there. Sir David Royce, who is the coroner, may be arriving, or send a message shortly. If I am not down before then, please send for me."

"Yes, miss. And the family . . . ?"

"Mrs. Marianna Levitton is taking matters in hand with the family. They are in the morning room. I'm sure there will be other orders soon."

"Just so, miss," agreed Dalton. "I will see to them."

"If I may," asked Rosalind. "Were you aware, did Mr. Everett have any visitors yesterday?"

Dalton considered this question for a moment. "No, miss," he said, with a bland, professional politeness. "Mr. Everett was home all day, yesterday. I am not aware of any late visitors."

"Thank you," said Rosalind.

Dalton bowed. Rosalind gathered up her hems and hurried up the stairs.

All the way, she considered how a servant with a jealous and exacting master might be reluctant to speak with a stranger about the family's business, all the more so under such circumstances.

She was also conscious of the fact that she had asked if Everett had had any visitors yesterday. Dalton, however, had taken time before he spoke, and then said there had been no late visitors.

It occurred to her that these were not at all the same thing.

CHAPTER 52

Causes, and Repercussions, of Death

*"The unlawfulness arises from the killing without
warrant or excuse . . . it may be by poisoning,
striking, starving, or drowning, and a thousand
other forms . . ."*

Impey, John, *The Office and Duty of Coroners*

The hallway on the second floor was dark and still, but one door had been left open. Rosalind crossed through into a private sitting room, paneled in dark wood and furnished with club chairs and a leather sofa. A few books and a number of journals and ledgers had been left scattered about. Rosalind felt a tightness in her throat, walking through this remainder of Everett Levitton's life.

The door to the boudoir was also opened. Through it, Rosalind saw Mrs. Hepplewhite moving about an old-fashioned bed hung with heavy velvet curtains. She saw the outlines of the corpse laid out straight on the white bedclothes.

She must have made some noise because Mrs. Hepplewhite glanced back and saw her. She grabbed up a ragged strip of towel to wipe her hands, and came out into the sitting room, closing the door behind herself.

"What can you tell me?" asked Rosalind.

Mrs. Hepplewhite was plainly angry, and it was not at Rosalind's question.

"The poor young man's skull was broken," she said. "In all my years, I'd only ever seen such a thing once before, and that person had been kicked by a cart horse." She paused, visibly attempting to retain control of her emotions. "Miss Thorne, I do not want to say this, but I was told he was found at the bottom of the stairs."

Rosalind nodded.

"Those stairs"—Mrs. Hepplewhite gestured toward the door—"they're steep, but not overly so. I would not have thought a simple fall would cause a man's skull to be damaged that way. I would have thought there would have to be . . . help."

"Such as if he'd been pushed?" said Rosalind evenly.

"Even then," said Mrs. Hepplewhite. "My guess, if I may, would be that something struck his head. Something heavy and quite solid."

"Thank you, Mrs. Hepplewhite," said Rosalind. "I am sorry to have drawn you into this."

Mrs. Hepplewhite shook her head. "Such things should not be permitted," she said firmly. "Not in any household."

"No," agreed Rosalind. "No, they should not."

Mrs. Hepplewhite agreed to remain with Everett's body until the coroner could arrive. Rosalind, lost in her own chaotic thoughts, descended the stairs. Her skin crawled as she rested her hand on the railing, and try as she might, she could not bring the sensation under control.

What do I say? What do I do? she asked herself the whole, long way down. She reached the foyer, and stopped. She blinked. Something was missing.

The table with its visiting book, and silver vase of hothouse flowers. The patterned rug under foot.

The rug would have been moved as soon as Everett was taken away. It would have to be scrubbed before the blood could set and stain. But what of the table and the vase?

Rosalind had not thought it possible for disquiet to settle more deeply inside her.

While she stared at the blank space where the table had been and willed some plan to form in her mind, a sharp rapping sounded on the front door. Rosalind looked about herself and realized there was no servant to be seen. Neither were they likely to have heard the knocker, if, as Dalton told her, they were all gathered belowstairs.

Rosalind smoothed her skirt and went to open the door. Two men stood on the steps, and she knew them both.

"Sir David. Mr. Harkness." Rosalind strove to conceal her surprise.

Why are you here! she cried silently toward Adam as he stepped inside. *You were meant to be gone already.*

"Thank you for coming so quickly," she said. She could not seem to shift her gaze from Adam's face. He looked half determined, half apologetic. She did not understand what had happened, but she did know she was glad to see him.

"As it happens, your note found us together," Sir David was saying. "What happened here?"

Rosalind wrenched her attention back to the coroner. "One of the family members, Everett Levitton, was found by the servants early this morning. It appeared he had fallen down the stairs and died of it."

"Appeared?" Sir David's shaggy brows arched.

Rosalind nodded. "He is upstairs now. You should find a Mrs. Hepplewhite in attendance. She is an experienced nurse and has what I believe to be some significant observations about the man's injuries."

"I see." Understanding sparked deep in Sir David's eyes. "Well, it would seem you have, as usual, put all things in good order, Miss Thorne. I should properly speak to the master of the house first, but I believe in this case, I will go see your experienced nurse. Will you tell the family that I have arrived and will attend them shortly?"

"Certainly."

Sir David nodded his thanks and started up the stairs, leaving Rosalind alone, for this moment, with Adam.

"I'm glad to see you," she told him, softly. It was maddening that she could not risk reaching out to take his hand, or even so much as touch his sleeve. "But you should go, now. Sir David will make sure all is in hand, and the stage for Liverpool leaves—"

Adam's answering smile was grim. "I am not going anywhere. Sir David has asked that I attend him as needed today. May I take it this matter is related to the poisoning?"

A thousand questions blossomed inside Rosalind, but she set them all aside. "The truth is I don't know. It may be entirely separate."

"That is a great deal of tragedy for one family," Adam remarked. "Where is Miss Catherine?"

"With her mother and the rest of the family in the morning room."

"All right. I'll go see about the servants. If you can deal with the family as you think best until Sir David can speak with them?"

Rosalind nodded. "You should ask about a table, and a heavy silver vase that used to be in the hallway. It may have been removed in order to be cleaned." She hesitated. "I asked the butler if Everett had any visitors yesterday. He told me only that there had been no late visitors. I am not certain this was the truth."

The corner of Adam's mouth twitched. "I will make particular note of that."

"Thank you, Mr. Harkness," said Rosalind.

Adam bowed. "You are welcome, Miss Thorne."

A green baize door waited on the right-hand side of the

foyer. Adam ducked through it. Rosalind, unobserved for this one moment, closed her eyes and pressed her hand against her stomach. She stood this way until her breathing steadied. Then, she opened her eyes and walked down the hallway.

Inside the morning room, Rosalind found the Levittons and Mr. Davenport arranged in an awkward live tableau. Marianna was seated alone with her back to the windows. With her imperious air and ebony walking stick, she looked like a queen before her court. Marcus had his back to the rest of the gathering. He stared out those same windows at the narrow, spring garden with its burgeoning flowers and greening shrubs—a view entirely at odds with the winter chill that filled the room.

"Miss Thorne," said Wilhelmena as soon as Rosalind entered. "What . . . what can you tell us?"

"Wilhelmena!" snapped Marcus. "You are not to speak with that creature!"

"Then I'll do it," said Marianna. "What can you tell us? Was that someone at the door?"

"It was the coroner," said Rosalind. "Sir David Royce."

"How did he get here?" asked Mr. Davenport. "Marcus?"

Marcus's face twisted in an attitude of disgust. "Don't be ridiculous."

"I sent for him," Rosalind told them.

"You dare . . . !" thundered Marcus. "This is *my* house."

"And it is possible that murder has been done," replied Rosalind.

"Slander!" bellowed Marcus.

"Why?" inquired Cate. "She didn't say you did it."

For a moment, Rosalind thought Marcus was going to strike his sister. Mr. Davenport evidently thought so, too, because he stepped between them. "Marcus, you have to collect yourself."

Rosalind watched Marcus measure himself against the

broader man, and remember that Mr. Davenport had doubtlessly led a rougher life than Marcus himself ever had.

Marcus took one step backward. "I will see you in court,
sir," he said, and his smile held an even sharper edge than his
words. "You and these harpies, and anyone who dares side
with you. You will all be held liable for your trespass and
your slander, and that will be just the beginning."

"Are you including me in that threat?" inquired Marianna.

Marcus's eyes shifted. "Oh, yes, Aunt. I have had enough
of your manipulations and predations on my family."

While this threat still hung in the air, a knock sounded on
the door and it opened. Sir David stepped into the room.

"Mr. Levitton?" he said uncertainly.

Marcus turned. After a moment's struggle, he managed to
recover his gentleman's dignity. His expression smoothed and
his shoulders straightened.

"I am Levitton," he said.

The coroner bowed. "Sir David Royce, at your service. I do
apologize for the intrusion. If I might have a word with you?"

Marcus bowed and moved to precede the coroner out the
door.

"Wait!" Beatrice tore her hands out of Cate's and struggled to her feet. "Wait, please, Sir David. I . . . I haven't seen
him yet. Please, may I see my son?"

"I am so sorry, madam," said Sir David gravely. "You certainly may, but I would not recommend you go alone."

"I'll go with her." Cate spoke stoutly, but her cheeks remained pale.

"We will go together." Marianna pushed herself to her
feet. "Come along, Beatrice, Cate. Mr. Davenport, you as
well. You might be needed."

The women and Mr. Davenport left together, with Cate
once again holding tightly to her mother's hand. Rosalind
watched them, and then turned to see Wilhelmena. She held

herself straight as a willow wand, and her eyes glittered. But it was not with grief or fear.

Wilhelmena watched the Levittons leaving together, and she was jealous.

"Sir David, we may speak in my book room," Marcus was saying. Then, turning to his wife, he added, "You had better see to the staff, had you not, Wilhelmena?"

She rose calmly. "Yes, of course."

Marcus opened the door, and waited while Wilhelmena preceded the men from the room. As he did, he shot Rosalind a triumphant glance.

Checkmate, it said, and, *You'll have nothing from my wife.*

The door closed, and Rosalind was alone. She was tired, and thirsty, and despite the fire and the thin shreds of sunshine that filtered through the fog, she was quite cold. She sat down on the tapestry sofa, and prepared to wait.

As she anticipated, she did not have to wait long. Barely five minutes by the mantel clock had passed before the door opened yet again, and Wilhelmena slipped inside.

"Miss Thorne," she said. "I am sorry for my husband, I am sorry—" Her breath hitched, a distressed, hiccuping noise.

"How can I help you?" Rosalind asked.

"I barely know." Wilhelmena wrung her hands. Her pale cheeks flushed and she glanced over her shoulder. "I don't even know how to speak of this."

Rosalind waited.

"Last night, I heard shouting outside my rooms," she said. "I thought it must be Marcus. I almost did not go out—"

Rosalind imagined Wilhelmena lying in her bed, staring up at the canopy in worry and frustration, trying to decide what she should do.

"But in the end, I did go into the corridor, and I saw . . ." She stopped again. Rosalind kept her silence.

"I saw Marcus," she said. "I saw him on the stairs with Everett. Marcus pushed him, Miss Thorne." Her voice faltered. "Marcus pushed him and he tumbled down, into the foyer. He, Everett, moved to stand, but Marcus had grabbed the vase from the table and, and—" She shuddered again, and pressed her hands against her face. "You have helped other women in such difficulties, Miss Thorne. I beg you help me now." She raised her face. Tears sparkled in her emerald eyes. "I cannot. If I am not believed, and even if I am, I . . . what he might do to me . . ." She swallowed. "I'm afraid for my life."

Rosalind reached out and took Wilhelmena's slender hand and felt how cold it was.

"I will do all that I can," promised Rosalind. "But I have a question, and I must beg you to tell me the truth."

Wilhelmena glanced over her shoulder at the door. It remained closed. She nodded.

"Did someone visit Everett late last night?"

She shuddered, and she dropped her gaze. Her face was so tightly drawn, she looked like some elfin creature rather than a human being. Her hand tightened around Rosalind's.

"Yes," she said. "It was Mr. Davenport."

Chapter 53

Difficult Conclusions

". . . without that wrestling match of theirs, the
truth might never have been dragged to the light."
Edgeworth, Maria, *Belinda*

The carriage ride back to Marianna's home was tense and silent. Rosalind found herself helping Cate support Beatrice, who seemed unable to rally from her grief. Cate, pale and hesitating, held her mother's shoulders and tried to give what awkward comfort she could. Mr. Davenport sat beside Marianna. But where the others were sunken into their individual grief and worry, Mr. Davenport remained alert, watching all the women, trying to guess their secret thoughts.

His round, clear eyes, Rosalind noted, turned most frequently to her.

When they arrived at the Upper Brook Street house, Cate was able to give Beatrice over to the care of the maids to take upstairs, and her relief was palpable.

Marianna faced her niece and Rosalind, leaning heavily on her stick, and plainly exhausted.

"Well, let's not stand here in the hall." She turned and limped through the nearest door.

The formal parlor was filled with stiff, old-fashioned furniture. Neither fire nor candle had been lit. Mr. Davenport hurried to Marianna's side so he could take her arm as she lowered herself into a mahogany and damask chair. Marianna did not protest this attention, which surprised Rosalind a little.

Cate closed the door. Mr. Davenport went to the drapes and pulled them back to allow what light and warmth the day had to offer.

Cate rubbed at her face, and her throat.

"Are you all right, Cate?" asked Mr. Davenport.

"I don't know. I . . ." She swallowed. "I don't know," she repeated. "I think it hadn't sunk in before. Everett . . ." She breathed her brother's name. "He tried so hard. To make everything all right. I used to get angry at him. All I wanted was to escape. But he wanted to find some way to keep the family together. Not like Marcus. He just cares about appearances, about everything happening the way it was supposed to. Everett wanted there to be something real, a home, something. He was no good at it. He could be wrongheaded, but . . . he tried, and I never did." She twisted her hands. Mr. Davenport started toward her, possibly to try to offer some comfort, but she turned away from him, just slightly, and he stopped where he was.

Marianna tried to straighten her slumping shoulders, and failed. "Well, Miss Thorne, what do you recommend we do now?"

Rosalind considered. "There is something else I believe you should know."

"Naturally," said Marianna blandly.

"Wait," said Mr. Davenport quickly. "I think I may know what it is. You found out that I went to see Everett last night, did you not?"

Cate and Marianna turned to him, both startled, both accusing.

"What business did you have with Everett?" demanded Marianna.

"He sent for me. He wanted to give me a warning," Mr. Davenport answered. "He said he believed that Marcus was getting ready to file suit against me."

"For what?" asked Marianna. Cate, Rosalind noticed, kept very quiet.

"Fraud," answered Mr. Davenport, and Cate started. So did Rosalind.

"Marcus apparently has bought some shares in the mines," Mr. Davenport went on. "He believes he has evidence of improper speculation with corporate funds, and embezzlement and a few other things."

Mr. Davenport said all this very smoothly. He must have been readying the story for quite some time, Rosalind realized. Either that, or Mr. Davenport was a very good liar. At least as good as Wilhelmena.

"That's all nonsense!" said Marianna. "We'll have it dismissed in ten minutes."

"Of course," replied Mr. Davenport. "But Everett felt I should know. I left around midnight, and, so you are aware, Miss Thorne," he added with studied blandness, "Everett was very much alive at the time."

"I hope you told the coroner this," said Marianna.

"I did," said Mr. Davenport. "Him and that fellow he had with him." He shrugged. "Another man might have tried to hide his visit, I suppose, but that's not my way."

"No, indeed," murmured Rosalind. "You should also know that before we left, Wilhelmena came to speak with me."

Now, it was Mr. Davenport's turn to be startled. But he quickly recovered his composure.

"Good heavens," he murmured. "That took some nerve. Marcus does not like to be crossed."

"She told me two things," Rosalind went on. "She said

that you, Mr. Davenport, had come to visit Everett yesterday. She also said that she heard quarreling in the middle of the night and that she witnessed her husband push Everett down the stairs."

"Marcus!" cried Cate. "She says Marcus killed Everett!"

Marianna narrowed her eyes at Rosalind. "Do you believe her?"

"She spoke very positively," Rosalind said. "I do not know what Sir David will conclude about the injuries, or what Mr. Harkness has heard from the servants, but Wilhelmena begged me to help her, and said that what she saw has put her in fear of her life."

"Marcus would never hurt her," said Cate. "He's jealous, but he loves her. In his way," she added, but there was doubt in her voice. "But . . . Marcus killing Everett? Marcus . . ." She let the sentence die, but Rosalind heard what she did not say.

Marcus poison me?

"In a fit of temper he might do anything," muttered Marianna. Her hand trembled where it clutched her walking stick. "I never believed I would say such a thing—but this is too much for me. I cannot think." She rubbed her brow. "I am too old for this nonsense."

"You should rest," said Mr. Davenport. "Let me take you upstairs. Cate, you can help us."

"If I may," interrupted Rosalind. "Miss Levitton should come back to my house so she can pack her things and return here."

Cate stared at her like Rosalind had suggested she fly to the moon. "Are you serious?"

"I am," Rosalind told her. "I believe it will be of help to your mother, and your aunt." Rosalind met her gaze, and willed her to see there were still things that must be said between them, but that they could not speak openly here.

It was Marianna who settled the issue. "Go with Miss Thorne, Cate," she said. "Get your things. I will have your room put to rights. And no arguments," she added as she got to her feet. "I am done with arguments for today."

Marianna loaned them her carriage for the drive back to Rosalind's house. Rosalind did not press Cate to talk with her along the way. Cate deserved some time to collect herself after all the shocks and grief of the morning, and Rosalind needed to recover her composure, and to understand her own thoughts.

And to decide what was true. *How am I to decide what is true?*

Mr. Davenport was lying about his conversation with Everett. Wilhelmena was lying about what she had seen last night. Marcus was lying about his ability to harm those he felt had wronged him.

One of them had tried to poison Marianna and Cate. One of them had murdered Everett. Was it the same person? Or had there been two persons acting for two separate reasons?

Rosalind found she did not know, and could see no path toward an answer.

At last, they arrived at home. Amelia was there to open the door and help Rosalind and Cate off with their things.

"Is Alice here?" asked Rosalind.

"She's gone to her brother's." Amelia grinned broadly. "The baby's come. A big, strong girl, they're saying, with a healthy pair of lungs. Mother and babe are both very hardy," she added before Rosalind could ask.

Relief, gratitude, and delight rushed through Rosalind with a strength that came near to making her stagger. She suddenly remembered she'd had nothing to eat all day. "That's wonderful, Amelia, thank you." She paused. "How are you doing?"

"I'll be all right, miss," she said, and her voice was steady. "We talked, Miss Alice and I, and we've sorted things out."

Cate's cheeks paled a little, but to her credit, she appeared able to set her feelings aside. "Well, I had best go upstairs and get my things. I'm going home, Amy," she said.

"We'll be sorry to see you go," replied Amelia.

Cate's mouth twitched. "I doubt it, but thank you. Will you help me pack?"

"Yes, miss," said Amelia.

Rosalind watched the two of them start upstairs. Amelia, it seemed, had made her choice, and Cate appeared ready to accept it. Another wave of relief washed over Rosalind. Tired beyond measure, she took herself into the parlor and dropped gracelessly onto the sofa.

What do I do now? She rubbed her hands together. *Where do I even begin?*

She must have been sitting like that for some time, utterly lost in her tangled thoughts, because she was badly startled when Mrs. Singh pushed the door open. The cook came in carrying a heavily laden tea tray.

"Oh, but I didn't . . ." began Rosalind.

"But you should." Mrs. Singh set the tray down in front of her. "Miss Levitton tells me you've had nothing all day. You cannot continue without something to eat."

Rosalind felt herself smile. "You are quite right, of course. Thank you."

Mrs. Singh nodded and left Rosalind there. Almost of their own accord, Rosalind's hands began to move—to pour the tea, to use the tongs to lay her preferred slice of lemon into the cup, to select a sandwich of fresh farm cheese and cress and lay it onto a plate.

But instead of eating and drinking, she simply sat and stared at the tray.

She wished Alice was here, or Adam. She wanted to talk to someone, to settle and sort her mad whirl of thoughts.

Someone had poisoned Marianna and Cate. Someone had thrown Everett down the stairs.

Wilhelmena said it was Marcus. Cate, by her actions and her intense surprise, said it could not be. Marianna wouldn't put it past him. Beatrice was insensible in her grief. Harold was concocting stories to cover up his true movements, and behaviors.

Mr. Davenport and Wilhelmena were engaged in a romantic affair, and Everett had known.

Had Everett summoned Mr. Davenport to the house to threaten him—threaten them—with that knowledge? Or could he have simply let it slip within Mr. Davenport's hearing? Or Wilhelmena's?

It was known that Everett made use of secrets in his keeping. Fear might have proved motivation enough for either Mr. Davenport or Wilhelmena to cause his death.

But what of Marianna's? And Cate's?

How do I discover who tried to poison them when I cannot even say how one of the attempts was made? Rosalind fell back and squeezed her eyes shut. She wanted to sweep the tea things to the floor. She wanted to cry and scream and do any of a dozen things.

She did not. She straightened herself, so she would not be seen looking ridiculous if anyone came in. She addressed herself to her tray again. She took a bite of sandwich. She took a sip of lemon tea.

She set her cup down.

Mrs. Singh, well aware that someone, or indeed several someones, might join Rosalind, had provided additional cups and saucers. She had also included a jug of milk, and the sugar bowl.

Rosalind took up the bowl and cradled it in both hands. Memory assailed her, first of Wilhelmena sitting in her beautifully appointed morning room, sipping her tea and answering her husband as he rapped out his suspicious, intruding questions. Then, of Cate at breakfast, dropping lump after lump of sugar into her tea.

The door opened. Rosalind's head shot up, and she nearly dropped the bowl. Cate walked hesitantly into the room, followed closely by Amelia.

"I'm sorry, am I intruding?" asked Cate.

"Not at all." Rosalind set the sugar bowl down hastily. "Sit down. Will you have some tea?"

"Thank you." Cate sat in the round-backed chair. Rosalind poured out the tea and gave the cup to Cate. She took up the tongs and dropped a sugar lump into her cup, and another, and a third.

Amelia cleared her throat. For a moment, Rosalind thought she'd been caught staring at Cate's tea like a starving woman staring at a bread loaf. But as Cate blushed, it became clear that this signal was for her.

"Miss Thorne," Cate said. "The first time Amelia said I should ask you for help, I did not. And I regret that." She took a swallow of her sweetened tea. "I have been . . . I don't know what I have been. A fool. Selfish beyond words. Thoughtless beyond measure. All of that. More than that." Her eyes were dry as she spoke. There was no sign of the weighing and judging that Rosalind had seen before when she was trying to see which lie was most likely to be believed. "I know you have no reason to believe me." She stopped and swallowed. "But I need you to try. I don't know what Wilhelmena said she saw, or thinks she saw—but whoever might have pushed Everett, it isn't Marcus."

Rosalind waited.

Cate put her cup down. "I can't believe I'm saying this." She was speaking to the walls, the fire, the chair, anywhere but Rosalind. It was as if she thought that by looking at another person, she would lose courage. "Marcus is cold, unimaginative, and a fool. But he's a coward. That's what our father did to him, and to Everett—" Her voice wavered. "And me. But he's honorable as well. He *believes* all that nonsense about how a gentleman is supposed to conduct

396 Darcie Wilde

himself. If he pushed Everett, if Everett fell, Marcus would be the first to confess. I don't know who tried to kill Marianna, or me, or who did kill Everett, but it was not him." She stuck her chin out. "I know what I am, Miss Thorne, and I know what I've done. But I will not have my small-minded, stubborn, selfish, older brother hang for something he didn't do."

Rosalind looked past her to Amelia, waiting, as ever, beside the fireplace. "Do you believe her?"

Cate bit her lip. Amelia walked forward, one step, two steps. Cate raised her eyes, and met the challenge in Amelia's hard, canny gaze. They stayed like that, immobile, silent, with the anger and tension of years of love and betrayal singing between them.

At last Amelia nodded. "Yes, miss."

Rosalind nodded as well. "As a matter of fact, I also believe you, Cate, and I agree with you."

Cate started. "You do?"

"Yes. There was no way in which Marianna's death would, or could, benefit Marcus. Your death would only ensure that the affair between Mr. Davenport and Wilhelmena would continue unimpeded. That is assuming, of course, Marcus knew for certain about the affair. Even then, he might have viewed your marriage as a benefit to him."

"Because Harold would stop pursuing Mena?" put in Cate incredulously. "As if anyone would choose my looks over hers—"

"But once you two were married, Harold would have control of a substantial fortune. Marcus could then sue for criminal conversation and demand large damages. If he won, he would have revenge on Wilhelmena and Harold for embarrassing him, as well as on Marianna by gaining the fortune she had denied him."

Cate stared blankly at her for a moment, and then pressed her hand against her mouth. "Oh, good Lord. That's exactly what he would do, too."

Rosalind nodded. "So, even if Everett did tell him about the affair, or Harold's parentage, or any other secret, nothing would change from Marcus's point of view. Indeed, he would have every reason to keep Everett alive."

"As a witness at trial," said Cate.

"Yes," agreed Rosalind. "He could demand a damage so large it would land Mr. Davenport in debtor's prison from his inability to pay. And we know that Marianna would well refuse to rescue Mr. Davenport, because she abhors an unfaithful man."

"But Harold can't be the poisoner either," said Cate. "Without our marriage, he'd get nothing from Marianna. And he'd have no cover to continue meeting Wilhelmena. So that leaves . . ." Cate swallowed. "Good God."

Rosalind nodded.

"How would we ever prove such a thing?" cried Cate. "There's not a man living who will look at her and believe she would harm a fly."

"That is not strictly speaking true," said Rosalind. "But you are right, we need proof, and that proof does not exist. Yet." She set her own cup down and folded her hands. "Tell me, Miss Levitton," she said conversationally, "exactly how good of a liar are you?"

CHAPTER 54

Polite Fictions

". . . nor can it be my wish to extort from you any mortifying confessions."

Edgeworth, Maria, *Belinda*

"Hullo, Wilhemena," said Cate as she breezed into the morning room.

It was early morning, just on the cusp of the time for visiting hours. Rosalind and Cate had talked for several hours the day before, and eaten the entire contents of Mrs. Singh's tray. Rosalind had written several urgent letters. She'd even managed to get a night's sleep, although a fitful one. She kept waking to wonder if she should have put her plan into place immediately. So many things could go wrong in the darkness.

Adam sent no word. Neither did Sir David. The only note Rosalind got was from Alice saying she would stay another night, although the flat was so full of Hannah's female family she was fairly sure she'd have to sling a hammock to have a place to sleep.

"Cate? Miss Thorne?" Wilhelmena stared at them both from her place on the sofa. Then she saw Amelia follow them into the room, and genuine shock overtook her. She pressed her hand against her stomach.

Amelia made no sign that she had been noticed, or that she even recognized Wilhelmena. She just took her place beside the hearth, the picture of the perfect anonymous house maid—silent and attentive, with lowered eyes.

Rosalind pretended to ignore her movements, as was expected with regard to servants. "I apologize for calling so early. We do not mean to stay long," she told Wilhelmena.

Wilhelmena looked from Rosalind to Cate and back again. She clearly wanted to point out she'd given orders that she was not at home. She wanted to ask how they had been admitted at all to the house, when Marcus had forbidden them absolutely.

But Marcus had left, presumably for the day. Rosalind had watched him go before she and Cate had knocked on the door. She also knew that the footman had been given instructions to admit them, despite what had been said previously.

"You must forgive me," said Wilhelmena. "It's only that I am very tired, after everything that has happened. And there is so much to do, and Marcus has gone to speak to his solicitor and left it all to me." She made a show of taking a deep breath and gathering her tattered nerves. "What is it I can do for you?"

"Oh, we're just here to congratulate you," said Cate brightly.

This also startled Wilhelmena, almost as badly as Amelia's presence. "I beg your pardon?"

"On your scheme," Cate went on. "It really is quite remarkable. I thought I'd learned a thing or two about such tricks." She plopped down into the nearest armchair. The movement was bold, and rude, as they had not been invited to sit. "But yours, Mena, is positively exquisite."

Wilhelmena frowned. Somewhere, she'd learned to add a

layer of dignity to her bright beauty, and the effect was imposing. "Cate, I don't know what you're going on about, but really, I have a terrible headache and since Beatrice is not here, nor, I expect even capable of rising from her bed, I am left . . ."

"You have so much to do, yes." Cate winked at Rosalind. Rosalind allowed her eyes to narrow, ever so slightly. "So you said. Does that include telling the coroner what you told Miss Thorne? About Marcus murdering Everett? Do you intend to plead for Marcus's life? It would be a nice touch, considering you're the one sending him to the gallows."

For one heartbeat, anger blazed in Wilhelmena's eyes. But it was quickly swallowed by shock, and outrage.

"I spoke in confidence, Miss Thorne!" she cried. "I begged for your help!"

"You did," said Rosalind. "And it was possible I might have believed you, but I had a piece of information that did not figure into your calculations."

"I don't understand!" Wilhelmena pulled a handkerchief from her sleeve and pressed it to her eyes.

"I already knew you had poisoned Cate, and Marianna."

Wilhelmena froze stone still. Her hand shook as she lowered it. *"What?"*

"You tried to poison Marianna," said Cate. "And me. With arsenic."

"You're wrong," breathed Wilhelmena. "Or you're lying." Her hand trembled again. "Or you're stark, raving mad. I don't know which. But I think you had better leave."

But Cate just continued to smile. "Do you know, Wilhelmena, staying with Miss Thorne had been a marvelous education?" Her sideways glance turned positively admiring. Rosalind herself was tempted to believe the emotion was real.

"I'm a thief," Cate went on. "Marcus will have told you

all about that. But Miss Thorne has taught me how much better it is to have information rather than jewels. There's so many ways gossip can be turned into money, you see." She clasped her hands. "You do see, don't you, Wilhelmena?"

"How could I possibly?" answered Wilhelmena coldly.

"Oh, dear." Cate sighed to Rosalind. "You did say she would not be inclined to drop her pose quickly."

"What pose?" demanded Wilhelmena coldly. "Cate, truly, you have to leave. I have too much to do to deal with your nonsense. Miss Thorne, please, you are a rational woman. . . ."

"And she knows a remarkable amount about all sorts of things," put in Cate cheerfully. "Including the fact that when there's a murder in the family, you only need to look for who had the most to gain."

Wilhelmena's jaw tightened.

"At first I thought that in our *particular* case it must mean Harold. I mean, if he and I had gotten married and I died afterward, he'd be both rich, and free. You two could have run off together." Cate grinned saucily as Wilhelmena drew herself up. "But, then I thought how much better it would be if he was rich and free, and you were a blubbering widow. Then no one would have to run anywhere. You could just get married. So, obviously, the thing to do would be for Harold to marry me, and then cause me, and Marianna, to die in short order, and you could both blame Marcus for it." She spread her hands triumphantly. "Very tidy. Very efficient. Very Harold. He's not, as you know, like other men." She shook her head. "Except there was one thing. Well, two things, really."

Cate waited. Wilhelmena clearly knew she was expected to ask what this one thing might be, but she seemed determined to express her strong disapproval by maintaining her silence. Cate rolled her eyes at Rosalind and then leaned forward. "Miss Thorne worked it out. You see, while Marianna was clearly meant to die slowly, I was meant to die quickly, and Harold and I weren't even married yet. And then, well—" She shrugged. "I know Harold rather well, and he would never kill his own mother."

Wilhelmena's hands clenched into fists, but instead of speaking, she reached for the bell.

"I would not recommend it," said Rosalind. "There is more to be said."

"There is nothing more I wish to hear!"

"Not even if it will save your life?" inquired Cate. "The courts take a very dim view of lady poisoners, however pretty. And I expect even Marcus will be somewhat non-plussed when he hears all this. He may even forget to defend you as his property."

Wilhelmena lowered her slender hand. "Do you honestly believe my husband would believe a single word from either one of you?"

"Oh, I'm sorry. You misunderstand," said Rosalind. "We do not mean to tell Marcus."

Cate's grin turned positively feral. "We're going to tell Marianna."

Wilhelmena's face went dead white.

"Marianna employed me to find her poisoner," said Rosa-lind. "Finding Miss Levitton was something of a ruse so I could continue that inquiry. A, what do you call it, Miss Levitton?"

"A cover," supplied Cate cheerfully. "And while I'm not at all trustworthy, Miss Thorne is the soul of honesty, and dis-cretion, and everybody knows it. She will be extremely sorry and reluctant to have to give your name to Aunt Marianna."

"It is all a lie," spat Wilhelmena.

"Whether it is or is not doesn't matter," said Rosalind. "Because when I tell Marianna, and Cate confirms it, she will believe. And you will find yourself in a great deal of diffi-culty."

Wilhelmena drew herself up straight. Her green eyes flashed

in anger, but that anger was caged. Rosalind read her frustration in her clenched fists and the pallor of her cheeks.

"What do you want?" she asked quietly.

Cate nodded in approval. "You were right, Miss Thorne,
she did come around to our way of seeing things."

Rosalind smiled, and dropped her gaze in a show of mod-
esty.

"Before we get into the question of price, we need to know
how much you've told Harold," said Cate. "He'll have to be
dealt with as well."

"I did not tell him anything," said Wilhelmena. "He
would never have agreed to it. He would have us all continue
as we are, with me having to endure Marcus and all his suspicions, living in constant fear of him throwing me into the
street." Her lovely smile turned into a sneer. "I would spend
my life dependent on *his* generosity—cowed and looking
over my shoulder, living for the love of him and trusting he
would continue to care for me. Oh, yes," she said, and each
word dripped with disdain. "Such a fine life that would be."
She leaned forward. "Cate, you understand what it is to have
to take your own freedom. You cannot blame me. I only did
what I had to."

"But you also killed Everett," said Rosalind quietly. "You
pushed him, and you used the vase to break open his skull."

"Yes," agreed Wilhelmena evenly. "I still need Harold.
You see, they might not convict Marcus."

"And if they don't, you mean to try to give them Mr. Davenport?"

"It is not what I want," said Wilhelmena. "None of it. But
it was that or live trapped. You understand, Miss Thorne.
You understand, Cate. I only—"

The door opened.

Wilhelmena's chin jerked up. She had not seen Amelia
move, because one did not pay attention to the movements of
servants. She had not seen Amelia's hand turn the door's knob.

But now Wilhelmena saw Marianna standing at the threshold, leaning heavily on Mrs. Hepplewhite's arm.

She saw Adam Harkness right behind them.

Marianna shook her nurse off and shuffled into the room until she stood face to face with her daughter-in-law.

"Why didn't you tell me how it was?" she asked. "Why didn't you say you could not live in this house anymore?"

Wilhelmena laughed once, a sharp, harsh sound. "And what would you have done?"

Tears shone in Marianna's eyes. "Whatever I could."

EPILOGUE

Futures, Imperfect

*"But the danger is over; you need not look so ter-
rified."*

Edgeworth, Maria, *Belinda*

On April 14 and 15 of the year 1820, eleven men were
tried and convicted of high treason in the Cato Street
conspiracy. During the trial, a hastily printed, entirely anonymous pamphlet was distributed, accusing the ministers of
having hired a spy to incite the men to violence. Sir Richard
Phillips waved the pamphlet about during in a fiery speech in
Parliament, and demanded the trial be halted and a new investigation carried out.

Some suspected the gossip writer and novelist A.E. Littlefield of being behind the subversive writing, but nothing was
ever proved. Nor was there any consensus on where Littlefield could have gotten such accurate details about how the
men came to be captured.

Two days after this, Wilhelmena Levitton was tried and
convicted for the murder of her brother-in-law, and the attempted murder of her sister-in-law, and her husband's aunt.

After this verdict was rendered, her husband, Marcus

Levitton, shut up his house and departed London, without leaving any forwarding address.

Harold Davenport also left town, quietly, and without any fanfare. He returned to Cornwall with the stated intent of putting the business of the Levitton Mines into good order, after which he planned to depart for Canada to seek new opportunities there.

Also quietly, and without any fuss, Catherine Levitton returned to her aunt's house, to help care for her mother, and to try to sort out what she meant to do with the rest of her life.

While Cate unpacked her bag and resettled herself into her room, Marianna invited Rosalind to take tea in her private sitting room.

"Well, Miss Thorne, I believe I owe you a great deal," said Marianna as she poured the tea with a steady hand, and added the slice of lemon that Rosalind preferred. "And more than just the amount your man arranged."

"I am glad I was able to be of use."

Marianna leaned back in her tall chair, and cocked her head in an attitude Rosalind had come to understand meant she was keenly examining the situation in front of her.

"I have a mind to invest in you," she said.

"I beg your pardon?"

Marianna smiled. "While I was cooped up in here waiting to see if you would discover who wanted me dead, I had to do something to keep occupied. So, I spent some of that time writing letters to people who know you personally. Including Honoria Aimesworth."

Rosalind found her tongue had frozen to the roof of her mouth.

"Everything I have heard is that you are honest, diligent, and very, very successful at this innovative profession of yours, and that you are increasingly busy," she added. "I must say, I entirely approve of the existence of someone willing to help the women of London with their private difficulties."

Rosalind drew herself up. She readied herself to thank Marianna for the compliment, but Marianna was far from done.

"But it occurred to me that there are those who might need your assistance who are not necessarily able to afford the fees that you must charge. Women such as Amelia McGowan, for instance. Or Cate."

Rosalind found she did not know what to say to this.

Mrs. Levitton nodded, as if she had been fully answered. "Therefore, I propose that I, and a few friends I know of, should invest in your business. Such investment will provide you with the means to hire what assistance you may from time to time require, and to meet such other expenses as your business may incur. We will expect reports, of course, but that is a matter we can go over as discussions progress. The contract will also stipulate that you, at least occasionally, help those who face difficulties, but are unable to pay."

"An investment contract between a group of women?" Rosalind murmured. "Is such a thing even allowed?"

Marianna's smile turned sour. "I'm sure if men in power are allowed to learn of its existence, they will object most strenuously. Questions may be raised in Parliament." She shrugged. "Therefore, we will regard it as matter of private correspondence, and I will have to rely on you to keep your word. Will you keep your word, Miss Thorne?"

Rosalind met her twinkling gaze. "I have never yet broken my word once I have given it."

"Very good," said Marianna. "We shall drink to it. Your health, Miss Thorne." She raised her cup.

"Your health, Mrs. Levitton," replied Rosalind solemnly.

They drank and they laughed, and talked of the future for quite some time.

After that, there was only one thing left to do.

*   *   *

"Where's Amelia?" asked Adam as Rosalind let him into the house.

It was evening. Rosalind had sent a message from Marianna's to Mrs. Harkness, asking for Adam to call. He had responded promptly, as she had known he would.

"Amelia's gone to look at rooms with Alice. She's given me her notice, you know." Rosalind led Adam into the parlor. The drapes were closed against the encroaching evening, and the lamps and the fire lit. The room was warm and filled with a comfortable glow.

"I take it, then, she received the bank draft for her finder's fee?" Adam asked.

Rosalind nodded. "I was afraid she was going to faint when she saw it. We knew it would be substantial, but none of us expected three hundred pounds."

"Has she said what she might do with the money?"

"She's thinking of opening a school for women and girls who want to leave service, to teach them reading and figuring and how to present themselves and so forth."

"I imagine Alice will be a great help with that."

"I imagine so," agreed Rosalind.

Adam looked about mildly. "What of Mrs. Singh?" he asked.

"I've already sent her home for the day," Rosalind told him.

Which meant the house was empty, save for the two of them. Adam's brows rose.

"So, here we are."

"So it would seem," she agreed. "And you have left Bow Street."

"I have. I could no longer do what was required of me."

"What does your mother say to that?"

Adam sighed. "My mother says she wishes she could get hold of Mr. Stafford and Mr. Townsend and give them a piece of her mind to feast upon. She further suggests they would have indigestion for a month."

"I'm sure she's right," said Rosalind. "What will you do now?"

"I don't know," he admitted. "Sir David says he can make use of me as one of his men, but that will only be occasional work."

"What do you want to do?"

He sighed. "I want to be the man my family needs. That *you* need. I want you and I to be able to choose what we will be to each other, without being forced into one role or another by the rest of the world."

"And for yourself?"

"I expect I want much the same as you. I want to be useful." He stepped closer to her. "And I want to ask you . . . what of us, Rosalind?"

Slowly, she took his hand, marveling, as always, at the contained strength of it. Daring, and lost in her own impulse, she kissed the back, and pressed it against her cheek. Adam reached out with his other hand and ran his fingers down her temple. She shivered at the warmth of his touch, and the casual ease with which she accepted that he should touch her, and that she should invite it.

"We cannot continue as we are," she said.

He did not answer her. It was not a question.

"If we marry . . . if we marry, I cease to exist," she said. "Everything I have built, everything I have become . . . it is gone, because by the law, only one of us exists, and that's you. I trust you," she added.

"I know."

"But I do not know how to trust this world of ours."

He turned his hand to cup her jaw. Rosalind found herself closing her eyes to better savor the sweetness of his touch. "Then we must trust each other."

"I have . . . a proposal," she said.

"A proposal?" murmured Adam, caressing her chin ever so slightly.

She nodded. Her mouth had gone very dry. "How . . . how would you feel about working for me?"

Adam's hand stilled. "For you?"

Rosalind nodded again. She took his hand from her jaw and held it. "With me, perhaps would be the better phrasing. You said Sir David will continue to have need of your expertise, and Mrs. Levitton suggested I take on some help for the work that I do. I cannot think of anyone better than you."

Adam stared, and Rosalind felt a knot of fear forming under her heart. But slowly, his surprise melted, and she saw the light of possibility in the depths of his eyes.

"We would stand a very good chance of rubbing roughly up against each other." Adam stopped. "Perhaps I should find another way to put that."

"Perhaps you should," said Rosalind, her voice dry. "But I find I do not mind the idea so very much."

He took a step closer. "You do not?"

"No." She tilted her face toward his. "Not in the least."